THE
POISONS
WE
DRINK

THE POISONS WE DRINK

BETHANY BAPTISTE

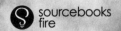

sourcebooks
fire

Copyright © 2024 by Bethany Baptiste
Cover and internal design © 2024 by Sourcebooks
Cover design by Liz Dresner/Erin Fitzsimmons/Sourcebooks
Jacket art © Michael Machira Mwangi
Internal design by Laura Boren/Sourcebooks
Internal images by Laura Boren/Sourcebooks, © vectortatu via Gettyimages

Sourcebooks and the colophon are registered trademarks of Sourcebooks.

Published by Sourcebooks Fire, an imprint of Sourcebooks
P.O. Box 4410, Naperville, Illinois 60567–4410
(630) 961-3900
sourcebooks.com

Cataloging-in-Publication Data is on file with the Library of Congress.

Printed and bound in the United States of America.
LSC 10 9 8 7 6 5 4 3 2 1

I dedicate this book to all my haters.
I only got this far outta spite.

Resentment is like drinking poison and then hoping it will kill your enemies.

—commonly attributed to Nelson Mandela and others

CONTENT WARNING

Please beware that this book contains morally gray characters, complicated parent-child relationships, police brutality, fantasy violence, fantastical racism, magical coercion, gun violence, politics, parental death, child death, and dying/death. In addition, there are depictions of post-traumatic stress disorder, anxiety, and depression. Other content warnings include self-harm (such as needles for finger pricking and daggers for palm slitting to perform spells), blood and gore, sexual situations, real and fantasy drugs, underage drinking, and profanity.

Please be mindful of these topics and triggers.

Self-care is essential if you're sensitive to any of the above.

A LETTER FROM
THE AUTHOR

On November 9, 2016, I woke up in grief. Racism and hatred won on a political stage and killed my hope as a woman, a Black woman, and a Black American woman. The first stage of my grief was denial. I graduated to anger. That feeling sunk its teeth into me and wouldn't let go for months.

One day, I popped in a DVD of *Practical Magic* for comfort and fell asleep on the couch, dreaming of a pink-haired witch. She wouldn't get out of my head until I wrote her down. My pain became her story of potions, protests, and politics. Her undying devotion to her younger sister, family, and friends symbolized my loyalty to the Black community. Her sentient magic represented my anger.

At first, this book was my grief journal, but over two years, it became a tribute to Black sisterhood, the struggles and strides of Black people, and the strength it takes to wake up each day in a country that doesn't love you. In the world I imagined, love potions could be weaponized against hate and prejudice. Creating characters that would be understood rather than loved or hated was a priority.

I made *The Poisons We Drink* with two cups of *Practical Magic*, a gallon of Black girls, a sprinkle of bad witches, and a pinch of unbreakable bonds. But when everything's all boiled down, this story is my heart.

CHAPTER
ZERO

An internal gift exists within all breathing things to recognize where one stands in the food chain. Witchers are what humans could've been, but according to scientists, a missing link in the evolutionary chain sent the two species in separate directions. However, magic doesn't make witchers superior to humans. For what humans lack in magic, they make up for it with something even more dangerous. Power.

—Candis Joyner, a witcher journalist for *The Societal Mirror*

JUNE 4, 2023

HE SHOULDN'T HAVE COME HERE. HE STOPPED JUST PAST THE doorway's mouth, squinting his aging eyes behind his thick spectacles. Even in the dark, he sensed them all weighing his worth.

Witchers.

The old man gulped, his heart doubling in pace.

A row of thirteen light bulbs dangled above the bar and aimed a spotlight on a dark-skinned Black man enjoying a wood-tip cigarillo. He had fine dreadlocks woven into two thick braids. A white bar towel swirled across the counter's marred surface without a single hand to aid it.

"Uh, good evening, sir," the old man stammered.

The bartender's closed eyelids didn't twitch or peel up at the pathetic greeting.

"I have an appointment with," the old man swept his eyes for eavesdroppers, lowering his voice to a whisper, "Prospero."

The bartender brought the cigarillo to his lips for another draw. Two puffs of wispy gray rushed out his nostrils and muddled together in a cloud. His eyelids opened to unveil cold dark irises.

The old man shrank back as the bartender planted his hands on the counter and leaned in.

"Does it look like I'm a fuckin' receptionist?" His teeth clenched the polished wood tip. The dull golden light revealed his muscular arms and the inked rattlesnake on his right forearm.

The old man shook his head quickly.

Not at the question but in disbelief as the snake moved.

Before his brain could properly process the sight, the tattoo snapped forward as if to strike. He stumbled backward, earning the bartender's deep-chested chuckle.

"Don't be so mean, Bram," an Indian American woman said, feigning disappointment as she sat on a nearby barstool.

The lime-green parakeet perched on her shoulder so still that he might have mistaken it for a toy. Until it turned its head to stare him down. Its eyes glowed and flickered like embers as it scrutinized him before the incandescence petered out.

A familiar.

Taking flight, it glided across the bar area, disappearing through the mouth of a corridor.

The woman shot him a charming smile as she lifted her whiskey glass to her lips, ice clanking inside the confined sea of dark liquor.

"You weren't—you weren't there a moment ago," he said, his tone full of self-doubt.

A sudden ache of confusion pulsed in his head.

The woman winked as she placed her tumbler down, tracing stiletto-nailed fingertips around the rim.

"I'm a bit of an opportunist for making fashionable entrances," she said. "I'm sure a gentleman such as yourself understands that."

The old man stuttered, "I'm not one for fashionable entrances."

And though he was more than eager to make an unfashionable retreat, he understood it was too late for that now.

He was too deep in a lion's den to scurry away like a mouse.

She giggled at his expense.

"No need to be ashamed," she assured. "We won't judge."

Bram snorted his disagreement. "I judge."

The woman ignored the bartender's comment. "Our mutual friend sent me here to collect you, Mr. Mou—"

"Mouse," the old man sputtered.

A human's true name had more worth than money in dealings such as these.

"Mr. Mouse it is, then," she said, nodding once.

"And what might I call you?" he asked, hesitant.

She downed the rest of her drink in one go and uncrossed her legs. Her silk-ruched gown the color of plums rippled as she slid off the barstool.

"Nisha," she replied, her finger beckoning him. "Now, please follow me."

Mr. Mouse trailed behind her and kept his attention on her head of loose inky-black curls curtaining down her back, too afraid to lock eyes with other witchers not as kind as the one in front of him. He didn't consider them animals, but they scrutinized his movements like predators.

"Good luck," Bram said. "You'll need it."

Nisha guided him down a hallway, leading him past an odd fixture.

A wooden phone booth.

The sight made his eyebrows scrunch together.

In a thriving age of wild youth and technology, that phone booth didn't belong.

It was a relic of another time—like him.

An old testament to a world that died when the new millennium took its first breaths and witchers willingly made themselves known to humans. *The Great Discovery.* That's what historians coined that period when the truth split society at the seams.

The metallic creak of rusted hinges reeled him back to the present, the door yawning to reveal the manager's office filled with a mighty mahogany desk, quilted leather chairs, and an imposing bookshelf brimmed with dangerous knowledge.

His escort rounded the desk and leaned down to whisper in the ear of their *mutual friend.* A slow turn revealed a man in his late twenties with green hair parted and slicked back. His sepia eyes had a weary wisdom to them as if he were the oldest thing here.

Prospero's lip quirked up at the old man's arrival.

"Please, come in and join us, Mr. *Mouse,*" Prospero said, gesturing to an empty seat before his grand desk. "I won't eat you."

"He already ate," Nisha quipped, remaining at her employer's side.

Mr. Mouse peered from beyond the doorway before he complied. He jerked his head around, startled as the door creaked shut on its own. Timid steps led him to a quilted leather seat—his spine as straight and rigid as a steel rod.

"Very few humans have the nerve to walk into the Golden Coin and utter aloud a name many fear. I commend you for your bravery," Prospero said.

"I'm not brave," Mr. Mouse said urgently. "I'm desperate."

A dreadful cough crawled up his lungs and throat. He emptied it into his arm's crook. When the fit passed, he swallowed bloody spit like a bitter, coppery pill.

"It's not impossible to be both," Prospero returned as Mr. Mouse caught his breath, "but I understand that time is of the essence for you and your delicate situation. However, I assume you have my fee before we begin this consultation."

"Yes," Mr. Mouse wheezed out. His shaky hand yanked the meaty envelope from his jacket's pocket, dropping it onto the desk.

Nisha's sharp nail opened it with a surgical slice.

A melody of rustling paper filled the office as the crisp hundred-dollar bills traveled through a counting machine. A pleased smile etched her mouth.

Prospero snapped his fingers, and a crude gold coin materialized in his hand. The coin swayed as it rose and rolled across his palm.

"There are many options to choose from, but all come at a cost—"

"Money isn't an issue," Mr. Mouse said, his unexpected boldness surprising himself. He softened his tone, his stiff backbone relaxing as if he were indeed among friends—and not natural enemies. "I have enough of it. Had had enough of it. It won't help. I've accepted that."

The coin stilled on Prospero's pale knuckles. "Then what is it you desire?"

"I want—" Mr. Mouse hesitated as his old sins surfaced like faded scars and peeled open to bleed out guilt and regret. "I want love from someone that no longer wants anything to do with me."

Prospero chuckled.

Softly at first, then louder until the sound melted away and the only evidence of his amusement was the widening ancient smile of a trickster.

"You passed a phone booth in the hallway. It's home to the Black Book, a phonebook for every need and greed you desire. Step inside and search for the Love Witcher," he instructed, flicking the coin.

Mr. Mouse's fumbling hands reached out to catch it, but it halted midair directly in front of his face. His cheeks burned with embarrassment as he grabbed it.

Tiny vibrations of magic soaked into his fingertips, bloodstream, and bones.

He felt light-headed and liberated all at once as he grasped the key to his problems.

"Thank you, Prospero." He bowed his head as he got up, feeding off the sudden energy surging through his veins. Was this what hope felt like?

The door immediately opened for him.

Prepared to leave, he froze at Nisha's voice.

"Be careful, Mr. Mouse," Nisha said. "The love you seek will glitter like gold to draw you in, but it's nothing more than a mirage, and mirages *always* fade. If love is what you desire, a familiar's love and loyalty are unconditional." She folded her arms on the chair's crest. "I can summon the perfect one for you."

In search of hers, he glanced around the office. "If they're so loyal, where's yours?"

A soft smirk of mischief curved her lips. "Oh, he's around."

Briefly, Mr. Mouse considered the offer of a magical companion, but his heart refused to budge. He wagged his head, turning to leave. "When you've done the things I've done and seen the things I've seen, a mirage is a welcome change. Pretending gives a comfort I don't deserve."

As he exited the office and the door began to shut behind him, Prospero said, "As long as you know it for what it is."

Mr. Mouse did, and he always would.

He entered the phone booth. A fat leather-bound telephone book waited for him. Peeling back the cover, he dove into a world of advertisements and lofty-priced promises glowing like stars against the black pages.

His eyes combed hungrily, searching for any mention of a Love Witcher in a bewildering sea of witchery trades he didn't understand.

He huddled over the monstrous book, sweat glistening on his brow.

His heartbeat throbbed in his achy tight throat.

"There," Mr. Mouse blurted, jabbing a fingertip at the full-page ad with a border of pulsing hearts.

He found it.

A trembling hand brought a phone to his ear as he jammed a coin into a slot and dialed.

"How did you get this number?" The answerer's sharp words possessed a heavy accusatory air, inducing his guilt before he even dared to open his mouth.

"From the Black Book. I need your expertise."

"And what *expertise* do you think it is?"

This call was dangerous. They both knew it.

"Love," he uttered.

He suffered a long, painful pause.

Finally, she spoke.

"I'm listening."

CHAPTER
ONE

A negative empath can detect, feel, and sometimes even feed on others' negative moods, emotions, and temperaments. However, this ability can be unpredictable: both strong and subtle emotions might occasionally go undetected. Despite its inconsistencies, the negativity from others can cause the negative empath either pain or pleasure, and for magical adepts, it can even amplify their power temporarily.

—Witcherpedia, an online witchery encyclopedia

JUNE 5, 2023

VENUS STONEHEART DIDN'T NEED TO READ MR. LIONEL'S MIND TO know he couldn't stand her ass. All the things he wanted to do and say to her broadcasted loudly in his glare as they stood on their respective sides of the street. His hatred for her swept across her skin like a tide of pinpricks.

"Good morning, Mr. Lionel."

He wrinkled his nose in disgust, hawking a wad of spit in her direction.

The glob splattered onto the street, glistening like a hideous jewel. He greeted her with this when he moved in three weeks ago. His first attempt promptly dribbled down his chin. The sight made her bite her inner cheek until she tasted blood to hold in all her laughter.

Every morning since, they bound themselves in this odd morning ritual.

Venus believed it was rewarding to help him get better at something. She also had a running bet with her uncle and little sister that she could get the old man to spit in the shallow pothole two feet and seven inches from his curb.

Today, he was about a foot off.

She refrained from congratulating him on his new improvement as he straightened the skewed Iron Watch signage on his front yard.

An emblem of witcher hatred.

Deanwood, a witcher enclave in northeast DC, had its fair share of vacant houses. Several were abandoned by witchers who fled to California or Canada for safety.

Some families got forced out by banks or landlords. That was the case for the family that once lived in the house Mr. Lionel now owned. Like most gentrifiers, he probably thought being here would help *clean up* the neighborhood.

But Deanwood didn't need cleaning.

It wasn't dirty.

When she blew him a kiss, his hatred sharpened against her skin, pinpricks intensifying to jabs as punishment.

In her robe's pocket, she clenched a fist at the pain.

Some empaths could feel everyone's everything. Others could only sense shades of happiness or the depths of confusion. As for Venus, the universe played in her face by making her a magnet for negative emotions.

A beacon for anger, fear, hate, and worse to find their way out of the dark.

Having had enough, Mr. Lionel shuffled back to the porch with his newspaper and slammed his iron-barred door shut.

Iron, a witcher's natural enemy, kept him safe.

She relaxed as the link between them severed.

"Good morning to you, too," Venus muttered, swirling on her bunny slippers to go back inside. Her cousin Tyrell snored loudly on the living room couch, belly-up and head dangling off the cushion edge.

She strolled into the kitchen, claiming her usual spot at the table.

Her half-awake uncle entered right after her, wearing his ribbed tank top, basketball shorts, and a satin robe. His slippers slapped the tile floor with every step. Occasionally, he'd crash here after all-night shifts, using exhaustion as an excuse not to drive five miles south to Anacostia.

Though he wouldn't admit it, his real reason was loneliness.

"Hey, Uncle Bram," she greeted, slipping the newspaper out of its thin plastic sleeve.

He shot her a tired grin. "Morning, Pinkie."

She rolled her eyes at the nickname, alluding to her cotton-candy-pink dye job.

A fresh batch of morning joe waited in the coffee maker. At Uncle Bram's doing, invisible hands prepared two mugs and carried them toward the table. He trailed right behind the cups, spiking his coffee with a splash from his trusty flask.

She combed through shiny sheets of grocery coupons and sales, always searching for things she needed for her main hustle. All the while, her pastel-purple mug found its way to her.

Uncle Bram nodded his gratitude as she offered up the newspaper she had no use for.

A comfortable silence fell between them until one of Tyrell's gurgling snores reached the kitchen.

Uncle Bram brought his mug to his lips but paused at the sound.

He arched a thick eyebrow at her. "Again?"

Again, as in after another fight with his mom, Tyrell decided to claim their couch as his for a few days.

"Yup," she answered, shrugging.

Uncle Bram took his first sip, his eyes bulging as he rattled out a cough.

Acute concern edged her voice. "Um, you okay?"

He blinked away tears as he let out a wheezy chuckle. "Yeah, this is good stuff. It's waking my ass up."

"Naw, sounds like it's beating your ass." Venus drew in her brows, unconvinced.

Janus, her younger sister, dragged herself through the back door, looking like a cross between roadkill and a hangover personified. Her mane of ombre gray curls was a frizzy mess. Smudged mascara adorned her eyes. The loose blue crop top she wore had questionable stains.

Venus closed her eyes briefly, relief whispering through her. Then she went for a sip. "Good to know you didn't *die* last night."

Translation: *Thanks for not returning any of my texts, you bitch.*

"It's not my time to go yet," Janus croaked. She stole the mug from Venus's hands and gulped from it boldly.

"Oh, thanks for the coffee, Vee. No problem at all, Jay," Venus said, feigning annoyance to disguise her amusement.

"I'll say thank you for the coffee after I drink it all," Janus replied matter-of-factly as she plopped into her designated spot and propped up her glittery Converse sneakers.

Uncle Bram brushed her feet off the table, and she whimpered in protest.

Another loud snore from the living room garnered Janus's attention. She blinked. "Again?"

"Again," Venus and Uncle Bram chorused.

Then their uncle eyed Janus over the edge of his newspaper. "Since you made it back in one piece, I suppose it's safe to assume the SWIGs didn't raid your little party?"

SWIGs, an acronym for Security for Witchers-in-Gathering, was the name of an iron-armed police tactical response unit. The law prohibited witchers from holding social assemblies or occupying public establishments in gatherings of thirteen or more. And to enforce said law, the SWIGs used brutal tactics to bring witchers in or take them down.

Venus no longer had an appetite for parties. Parties, no matter the size, seemed too intimate for her now. Too many bodies and emotions in one confined place made her claustrophobic. Aside from dodging iron bullets and avoiding arrest, a raid was the worst place for somebody like her. A breeding ground for negative emotions as witchers ran for their lives and SWIGs took lives.

Only adding more oxygen to a fire bottled up inside her.

A fire that ached to be an inferno.

If it broke free, *everyone* was fucked.

"Yup, different party." Janus hid her smug smile as she drank more coffee. "Not that it matters anyway. I'm pretty sure I'd get away without breaking a sweat."

Three years ago, she could barely open a portal to go two streets over. Now, she could go to familiar places within a city radius and open a doorway as quickly as twisting a doorknob.

Uncle Bram frowned, lowering his newspaper. "Don't get cocky, Jay. All it takes is a split second for a Swigger to pull a trigger while you're trying to summon a doorway. Callings aren't bulletproof."

All witchers possessed two things: a birthright and a calling.

A birthright was innate magic typical to all witchers, but callings were unique abilities awoken on thirteenth birthdays. No one truly knew how many callings were out there, though. Some were common or hereditary, and others were rare. Each had its struggles and limitations that only time or luck could sort out. Uncle Bram could crush bones and lift cars with his superior strength. So, he kept his touch gentle, used his magic to handle things his hands couldn't, and avoided giving hugs. Sometimes, he even enchanted fragile possessions he found joy in, so they wouldn't break. Like his coffee mug and flask. Tyrell inherited shapeshifting from his mom. For him, change brought nothing but pain. So, he preferred to be himself even if bodily urges wanted the opposite for him.

As for Venus, sensing emotions was only the iceberg tip of her calling.

Janus pursed her lips. "I'm better than you think, Uncle Bee."

"I ain't doubting that, but someone out there will always be better than you at something," Uncle Bram said. "For us, it's humans that like aiming guns loaded with iron bullets."

Janus darted her eyes over to Venus as a silent petition for support.

"Uncle Bee's right. The SWIGs are busting too many parties. I don't think it'll kill you to be a homebody until everything cools down." After saying her piece, Venus noticed the subtle wince of betrayal glitch across Janus's face.

Guilt sat heavy in her stomach, forcing her to revert her attention to the coupon pages.

Janus snorted a bitter laugh as she stood. "I'm sorry if I'm not scared shitless by humans."

Venus cast her gaze to the kitchen ceiling, her lips crimping in slight irritation. Not enough caffeine was in her system to deal with this back-and-forth, but she set the record straight anyway.

"I'm *not* scared of them either, Jay. I just know what they're capable of."

"If humans do terrible things, then why do you work for them and take their money, Venus?" Though delivered as a question, Janus's words felt like an answer and opinion all rolled into one.

"To pay the bills. Electricity, food, and clothes aren't free. Without money, *you* wouldn't have a home to stumble into hungover and looking like a hot mess." Venus levied a *play-with-it-if-you-want-to* glare at her sister.

Uncle Bram mouthed the word *damn*.

Then their mom, Clarissa, entered the kitchen. Long, brown micro-locs spilled from her high ponytail, framing her oval face. She wore a red T-shirt and mom jeans ironed to perfection. Her seven-year-old white sneakers looked brand new.

Already ready for the day.

"Janus, shouldn't you be trying to recover properly from your nightly escapades?" she asked coolly.

"Ma'am, yes, ma'am." Janus gave a two-finger salute and departed, taking along the stolen coffee.

Venus felt a foreign annoyance flare up in her rib cage.

Janus's annoyance.

Her sister invaded the living room and sat crisscross before the flat-screen, hiking up the volume obnoxiously loud. A tiny act of rebellion everyone else ignored.

"A potential client called last night," Clarissa said, fixing herself a cup.

"How did he get our number?" Venus asked.

"Prospero," Uncle Bram answered, his magic turning a page.

Clarissa claimed her seat at the head of the table.

"I'm assuming you've met him," she asked her older brother, mild intrigue tingeing her tone.

"He came into the bar last night looking for Prospero. Nisha had a bit of fun beforehand," Uncle Bram said, shaking his head. "He insisted on being called Mr. Mouse."

Venus restrained her snicker.

With an alias like that, the dude was *asking* to be played with.

She cleared her throat. "And how did that work out for him, Uncle Bee?"

He whistled, hiking his eyebrows. "I'm surprised he didn't faint. I'm sure Prospero didn't mind one bit. That finder's fee of ten grand'll prob-ably go toward his expensive-ass wardrobe."

"I don't mind, either," Clarissa said. "Clients like him are the best. They'll pay just about anything to get what they want." She smirked, resting her elbows on the table.

Venus didn't blame her mother for searching for silver linings. Money made shit a little easier to swallow, but running an illegal operation was tricky.

And deadly.

Once, Clarissa was the Love Witcher, but her greed backfired and sent her to early retirement. For a long time, their family struggled until Venus was old enough to help.

After all, bills didn't pay themselves.

Venus hustled as a brewer, a maker of potions. Brewing possessed more risks than rewards, resulting in a near-dead trade. Human fairy tales and movies always depicted misconceptions about brewing. Tossing a few oddly named ingredients into a bubbling cauldron and chanting a spell didn't equal a voilà.

Brewing required a price.

Brewing demanded a pain so excruciating that if you lived, you'd wish you died. The culprit was called the degree of recoil, a potion's chemical blowback.

Brewing was a fatal art, but doing what she did helped keep her calling at bay.

"Are you thinking about me, sweet girl?" A croaky voice breezed into her mind's depths.

Go away, she whispered into the dark of her mind, sounding so meek and unsure she immediately hated herself for it.

"Venus Genevieve, are you listening?" Her mother's words sliced through her thoughts.

Venus blinked, startled for a moment. She made a quick recovery but steeled herself far too late. Though Uncle Bram gave her a concerned look, she dreaded her mother's critical regard, always trying to find a crack in her foundation. Always in search of a glimmer of weakness, no matter how minuscule.

Clarissa cradled her WORLD'S BEST MOM mug, clicking a manicured fingernail on the porcelain. "Did you take your reinforcement potion this morning?"

The question hung in the air like a rancid odor, and Venus wrinkled her nose accordingly.

"*Venus*," Clarissa drawled out the syllables in the way only disappointed mothers could. "You promised to be more consistent."

"I'm sorry if it wasn't on my mind before my first cup of coffee." Venus massaged her temple as a headache wafted in.

"It should be. We can't leave anything to chance." Her mother's anger crept in slow, snaking around Venus's limbs and tightening ever so slightly.

"I don't think the world will end if I don't take it right now."

"Would it be so bad if it did?" The voice whispered to her and only her.

Shut the hell up, Venus ordered within herself, adding more boom and authority to the command, which pleased her.

"I guess we'll never know because that's exactly what you're about to do." Clarissa marched to the fridge and slung open the door, retrieving a polished oak box with a golden buckle lock. She withdrew a corked glass vial brimmed with fluid the color of crushed mulberries, muttering about low supply.

As Clarissa's hand delivered it, resentment burned in Venus's chest.

"How does it feel to know your own mother doesn't trust us?" The voice taunted.

"Do you even trust...me?" The word *us* singed her tongue's tip, and she bit down hard as a tiny punishment to herself.

"I don't trust *It*," Clarissa replied, holding out the vial.

Such a simplistic, deceiving name for her deviation.

Sentient parasitic magic that imposed will as *It* sought fit. And as *Its* host, she was a deviant, merely a vessel to administer and infect. Most witchers could not bend another's will without the help of a potion, but for the rare unfortunate few like Venus, swaying, bending, and breaking a prey's volition was as easy as breathing.

To be a deviant meant she and *It* were dangerous and unpredictable.

Especially when *It* made others want to hurt each other and worse.

Much, much worse.

Her mother and Uncle Bram peered at her intently as she took the vial, watching her as if she were an animal expected to do a trick.

"So pathetic. Go on. Show both of them how you're such a good girl," It taunted.

Venus uncorked the vial, guzzling swiftly. The reinforcement potion slithered down her throat like curdled milk, tainting her taste buds with an awful combo of citrus and copper.

She coughed violently, tears swelling in her eyes. Her stomach lurched with a wave of nausea. Hugging her belly, she hunched forward. Her body trembled as the potion seeped into the fabric of her being to reinforce a cage for *It*.

It quieted down, but she still sensed *It* like a secondary heartbeat.

Steady and unwavering.

A constant reminder *It* would die when she did.

"As I was saying, Mr. Mouse will schedule a pickup at the usual spot. Techie'll meet him beforehand as your buffer," Clarissa resumed. "Are you listening?"

A terrible ringing echoed in Venus's ears. She barely heard her mother underneath it, muffled but understandable, as if her head were underwater.

"Yes," Venus rasped out.

"Oh, and we're out of—"

A fed-up Uncle Bram growled, "Rissa, shut the hell up for a minute. Give the girl some time to recover."

Clarissa exhaled sharply. "She'll be fine. The effects will wear off in two minutes."

"That ain't the point." He rose to offer Venus his coffee as a chaser. An ineffective method for washing away the harsh residue of magic that coated her throat, but she appreciated the gesture.

"Thanks, Uncle Bee," Venus croaked, gathering her strength to take a great gulp.

His eyes cut over to his younger sister, and he requested tightly, "I wanna talk to you for a sec."

Clarissa's narrowed eyes locked with his, her thinning patience matching his, but she stood nonetheless. They both exited through the back door.

Venus didn't need to be a fly on the wall to know the topic of discussion unfolding outside. Clarissa's love was odd and jagged. It never quite fit as it should, but there was no other place for it to go. Uncle Bram argued with her about it, hoping his words would sand down hers, but it never worked. Her mother's love was here to stay.

Too embedded in her chromosomes to evolve.

After the potion's side effects subsided, Venus tested the strength of her legs and wobbled toward the living room as Janus flipped through the channels while Tyrell snored.

A beautiful older Afro-Latina anchor stared dead straight at them.

"...believed to be the latest victim in a string of murders plaguing DC. Bringing the body toll to ten witchers. During a press conference, the chief of police asked for patience from the witcher community during this ongoing investigation. This prompted a response from the Witchers Against Species Persecution cofounder Malik Jenkins."

Janus's slumped spine perked up at the mention of her dad. She untangled her crossed legs and crawled a little closer to the screen, engrossed as the segment played snippets of his response video.

"...*we will continue to fight for equality for witchers and h—*"

Humans. Malik was going to say "humans," but the video switched seamlessly to another incomplete statement that fit just as well.

Venus rolled her eyes at that, gripping the couch's cushioned arm for support.

"...*hold law enforcement responsible for their poor efforts in this investigation while a ruthless killer targets innocent witchers. Justice will be swift, kindred and allies. We'll fight to ensure it.*"

Janus appeared so childlike and eager at that promise.

Then the TV switched off.

Behind them, their mom stood there with the spare remote in her hand. "What have I told you about watching that nonsense?"

Clarissa often used the word *nonsense* and her ex-husband's name interchangeably, which always, always, always set Janus off.

Venus bit her bottom lip hard, bracing herself for the explosion.

"It's *not* nonsense!" Janus said, jumping to her feet. "There's a killer out there hunting down witchers, and the police don't care at all! WASP wants to change how humans treat us. Why is that such a bad thing? How can you shoot down something *you* helped—"

Two bolts of ire lit up Venus's insides, clashing together.

The battle made her body a battlefield.

Her heart punched and her blood incensed.

"That's enough, Janus!" Clarissa snapped, her tone vicious and eyes bright with authority. "Fighting against the system is like going against a house of cards. The deck will *always* be stacked against you!"

Tyrell jerked awake, his brow wrinkling deep in confusion.

Instinct pushed Venus to stagger before her sister to act as a shield.

Janus flinched, her boldness shrinking back. Her anger gave way to a spike of fear. A point that drove itself into Venus, making her grimace.

Uncle Bram threw his hands up defeatedly, casting his sister a disappointed glance before he walked away.

Clarissa composed herself, pointing to the hallway. "I think it's time for you to rest in your room. You've had quite a long night. Your sister and I need to handle business."

"Even if the deck's stacked against me, I refuse to fold," Janus retorted, storming out of the room.

"As I was saying earlier, we're out of burner phones. You need to make a store run," Clarissa informed coolly, peeping at her wristwatch purchased with blood money. "You have little time, so I suggest you hurry."

Venus clenched her jaw, watching her mom return to the kitchen.

"What the hell's going on?" Tyrell asked, rubbing the sleep from his eyes.

"Doesn't matter," Venus said. "It's over with now."

CHAPTER
TWO

Brystle isn't just a witcher-friendly rideshare app. Its existence is an ongoing protest against the Limit-12 Law. We offer a safe, affordable alternative to public transportation. As the country's largest witcher-owned employer, we pay our drivers fair wages and are 100 percent committed to their safety. Movement is progress. That's our motto. Join us for the ride.

—Khalil Robinson, CEO of Brystle
Audio excerpt of a 2019 commercial

TO SURVIVE THE OUTSIDE WORLD, VENUS NEEDED TO BLEND IN.

To be forgettable.

She gazed into her vanity's mirror, fixing her chestnut wig's blunt bangs. Always striving for perfection, she hoped no one noticed because getting caught meant ending up like her father.

Dead.

Childhood photos outlined her mirror frame. She stared at the one of her dad and a one-year-old her sitting on his shoulders. He grinned with all his teeth while she giggled with all of hers. Venus didn't inherit his deep dimples, but she had his amber eyes. In the picture, her pair and his radiated with warmth. A warmth that petered out as she lived on.

Her mom took the photo mere days before her dad got killed for breaking the law.

The Limit-12 Law.

To witchers, Darius Knox was a legend, but to Venus, he was nothing more than a cautionary tale of what happens when you give too much of a fuck.

Her sister meandered in and flopped down on the unicorn-themed bed with outstretched arms.

Janus took in a deep breath and then sighed it all out. "I'm sorry for being a bitch earlier. I know you do what you do for us. For the family."

Venus reached for a comb to tame any unruly strands. "It's cool. You had a long night. I didn't have enough coffee. Shit happens."

It was only a matter of time before someone offered an olive branch.

Neither could ever stay mad at the other for long.

"Now that *all's forgiven*," Janus began in a singsong voice, "you need to come with me to this auroras party on Friday."

Venus stiffened, then unscrewed a tube of magenta lipstick. "I think I'll pass."

"Come on, Vee. It'll be so much fun. Ty's coming too," Janus whined, clasping her hands together in a plea.

Only born a few days apart, Venus and Tyrell were inseparable growing up, causing a lot of hell, headaches, and, eventually, hangovers. As soon as Janus could, she followed behind them like a little duckling. Once, their mom never cared if they went to parties as long as they never went alone. But these days, she didn't care if they left solo, in a pair, or a trio, as long as they made it back home by morning, half-dead or alive.

While her sister felt at home at parties, Venus had good reason to be a homebody. She always needed her wits about her, which meant no more alcohol to forget or trysts to remember. Though she hadn't lost her taste for boys and girls, she wasn't about that life anymore.

For everyone's sake, she couldn't be.

Home was her fortress and her bomb shelter.

She'd never forgive herself if something happened to her little sister or big cousin.

She'd never forgive *It*.

Then again, *It* didn't starve for her forgiveness or approval.

It hungered for something much worse.

Venus squeezed her eyes shut, clenching the silvery tube.

Don't think about that, she inwardly urged herself.

"Just say you'll think about it. Five days is plenty of time to change your mind." Janus's words reeled her out of her own head, her distressed reflection greeting her.

A trail of magenta clumsily veered off the road map of her lips, smearing over her silver septum ring.

She erased the mistake with a tissue.

"I'll think about it," Venus promised, "but don't get your hopes up."

Janus squealed giddily, flailing her limbs all over the place.

A fine example of getting one's hopes up.

"I didn't say yes." Venus crumpled up the tissue. She threw it at a bejeweled wastebasket at her feet and missed. She resisted the urge to solve the matter with a tiny pinch of magic.

Instead, she kicked the stained wad underneath her vanity.

Out of sight, out of mind.

As a brewer, she lived by a code. One rule required her to swear a vow of abnegation to conserve her well of magic. A timeworn tradition to increase a brewer's odds of surviving a potion's degree of recoil. It stoppered most magic not used for brewing, but it wasn't leakproof or without its cracks. The vow couldn't stop something like a premonitory dream or prevent her from being stalked by negative moods.

Magic sometimes seeped in or bled out. While Venus tried to seal up the cracks with reinforcement potions so her deviation wouldn't escape, the negative emotions of others pursued her.

As magic gave and took, the scales were often lopsided. There is no such thing as a win-win solution with magic. A little win, then a lot of lose.

"You didn't say *yes* now, but you will." Janus said it so matter-of-factly that Venus wondered if her sister dreamed a glimpse of the future.

She reapplied the rich hue and smoothed her lips. "If you know I'll go, why even bother asking?"

"I was trying to be polite."

"You're doing a marvelously shitty job at it," Venus teased, rolling her eyes.

"That should still count for something, though. Plus," Janus propped up on her elbows, batting her eyelashes dramatically, "how can you say no to a face like this?"

Venus snorted a laugh. "It's easier than you think."

"But you won't because you *love* me." The word *love* rolled off her sister's tongue like a sweet song.

"Depends on the day."

A flying pink pillow smacked Venus's back.

They both broke into a fit of loud laughs, which eventually died down to closemouthed giggles.

Moments like these operated on borrowed time.

In the Stoneheart household, time was money, and their mom was the timekeeper.

"Remember when we were little and pretended to live in a cottage in the woods?" Janus asked softly, situating herself against the mountain of pastel pillows.

"Of course," Venus said.

She thought about their childhoods often, an era where *It* didn't exist yet.

In their tiny-ass backyard, a dirty yellow playhouse stood—a historic monument of their youth. Uncle Bram built it himself as a housewarming gift. Back then, they pretended to be enchantress sisters living contently in a magical cottage to feel alive.

Nowadays, feeling alive meant doing illegal shit that could potentially kill them.

"I want that, Vee." Janus snuggled her cheek against a penguin plushie. "I want to run away and live in a cottage deep in the woods. Just you and me. We'll be wild."

Venus plucked a pair of dark shades from her vanity, slipping them on. Her mind swelled with daydreams of them dancing madly with wild animals around blazing campfires, picking juicy berries, and swan-diving from waterfalls.

"We'll be wild," she agreed, liking how the promise tasted on her tongue.

Like a coin, DC had two sides: an illusion and the truth. The illusion was what the world knew best. The crisp white monuments of supposed heroes and hope stood tall. The museums worshipped human victories and mistakes. A downtown brimmed with grand hotels, high-end stores, and trendy joints where the wealthy reigned, the tourist roamed, and the poor never rested.

On the battlefield of Capitol Hill, lies and promises were cherished weapons.

And the White House was nothing more than a poisonous time capsule of good old American dreams.

Then there was the truth: neighborhoods living in the shadow of illusion. There lived dreamers and those who didn't even bother anymore. A haven for no-gooders, unconventional achievers, the forgotten, and the downtrodden.

These streets were her home.

Venus drove a few blocks over, parking at the corner pharmacy where her aunt worked as a cashier. Faded ad posters of liquor brands, cigarettes, and candy blanketed the dirty windows like a paper quilt.

Black bars protected the pharmacy, but the metal wasn't iron.

A silvery bell above the door jingled as she entered. No one occupied the front checkout counter or the pharmacist's window. She got two pre-paid cells from between displays of baby medicine and condoms.

Mr. Davids, the resident pharmacist, reclaimed his post.

Aunt Keisha invaded the aisle she was in.

"Already getting into trouble, I see." She tsked at Venus. Her emerald nose piercing and the gold cuffs in her box braids glinted. A playful light touched her amber eyes too, twinning a spark always found in every photo of her twin brother, Darius.

It became apparent that her aunt was stressed when Venus smelled cigarette smoke.

She trailed behind. "I *am* trouble."

"Definitely a familial trait," Aunt Keisha replied, her smile sad and her dimples shallow as she rang up the items, putting them in a crappy plastic bag. Sometimes, Venus liked to take inventory of her aunt's face, itemizing features her dad had, too.

As if it'd help her understand him better.

"How's my troublemaker of a son?"

The question caught Venus off guard, bringing her back to reality.

"Getting plenty of beauty rest on our couch," she answered, paying in cash.

Aunt Keisha relaxed at the news. "Tell 'im just 'cause he's eighteen now doesn't mean he's too grown to return his mom's calls. He listens to you."

Because I don't yell at him, Venus wanted to say.

Instead, she said, "Must be my charming personality."

"Say you will." Aunt Keisha held out the bag of goods. "I know shifting is painful for him, but if he refuses to practice, it'll backfire on him."

"I'll talk to him," Venus promised.

She opened the stubborn plastic packaging in the car and programmed each cell's number into the other's contact list.

Being a Brystle driver was the perfect cover for handling business.

No open invitations for witnesses or trouble.

She drove to Columbia Heights, a neighborhood in the city's northwest quadrant. Once a thriving witcher homestead, gentrification pushed everyone out. All that was *witcher-owned* became *witcher-friendly*. It sent a very clear message to witchers that they could visit but could not stay.

Venus parked outside the Hideout, a hidden gem in this tiny part of the world.

The WITCHERS WELCOME sign dangled proudly on the door.

A digital counter hung from a window, keeping a tally of the witchers inside. To the naked eye, humans and witchers were indistinguishable, but a witcher's blood naturally ran hot at 108.6 degrees Fahrenheit. A biological fact humans exploited when they developed government-mandated heat sensors.

Venus used the café as a neutral location to pick up prospective clients.

Her mom had formed a partnership with Techie, a human ex-bouncer-now-barista putting himself through college as a tech major. For a cut of the profits, he did pat-downs and confiscated cells to use as a bargaining chip.

The Witcher Crime Task Force, the mother department of SWIG, had become increasingly clever in busting illegal witcher operations through hacked phones on undercover agents.

"Right on time," Venus said as a purple tack popped up on her Brystle app's map.

The Brystle dashboard light turned on as she accepted the gig.

A bespectacled old man barged out of the café. He piled inside her car with a reddened face, hacking into a handkerchief. Techie watched from inside the café with a smirk.

"Your friend has a rude attitude and very rough hands," Mr. Mouse huffed breathlessly, shoving the cloth into his pocket. "He also took my phone!"

"I'll remind him to use moisturizer next time," Venus said, regarding the man in the rearview mirror.

His face soured at her humor.

Then he, too, looked at her.

His anger crumbled away, disbelief widening his eyes. "You're just a child."

"I'm old enough to vote and drive a car," she said.

And enlist in the military if she were human.

She turned eighteen four days ago and graduated from high school shortly before that.

Mr. Mouse frowned, adjusting his glasses. "You're still a child. Is this how the Love Witcher conducts her business? Heavy-handed cavity searches in café bathrooms and teenaged drivers to chauffeur her clients?"

Venus eased the car back into the flow of traffic. "I *am* the Love Witcher, Mr. Mouse."

"You're not the woman I spoke to on the phone last night." His mistrust grew with every word that fell from his lips.

"Did the woman you spoke with last night call herself the Love Witcher?"

An unspoken thought flickered across his face, and he calmed himself, casting his eyes down in defeat. "No, she didn't."

"I apologize for the misunderstanding, Mr. Mouse," Venus said. "She's my secretary of sorts. She takes all my calls and arranges all my meetings."

The truth felt like a lie.

Clarissa Stoneheart was nobody's secretary.

She was the boss.

"That doesn't negate the fact you're a child." He shook his head.

"Don't mistake my age for inexperience, Mr. Mouse. Only a handful of brewers live in DC. Yes, they're older and more experienced, but they have dedicated themselves to other disciplines."

Mr. Mouse voiced impatiently, "What's the difference? A brewer should be able to brew any potion if given the right recipe and ingredients."

A brewer could never be a master of all potions, only a *single* discipline. Health, trickery, powers, and luck were the known few in an endless list of disciplines a brewer could pledge to. But dabbling in another discipline meant breaking a pledge, and breaking a pledge meant forfeiting all magic.

A choice her mom made, but sometimes, Venus wondered what life would've been like if her mom *hadn't* broken her pledge for a bag.

A brewer's discipline was a calculated decision often based on tradition.

Venus came from a bloodline of love-brewers. Her mom, a stringent instructor, taught her the lessons Stonehearts before her once learned themselves.

"A pediatrician and a brain surgeon start out in medical school before they pick their respective fields, but you wouldn't ask a pediatrician to perform a brain surgery, would you?" she asked, used to this lack of faith in her talent. "I was taught by one of the best master brewers in the world." It wasn't a lie to give the man some comfort.

Mr. Mouse scoffed. "Then why can't she do it?"

Her lips pursed in annoyance, her grip tightening on the steering wheel.

"Do you know the punishment for possessing a potion with the *intent* to give, Mr. Mouse? It's five years. And do you know the punishment for *giving* a potion to someone, regardless of said person's knowledge? Ten years. Brewers get fifteen to life for brewing and selling."

She flipped the wig's tresses over her shoulder to flash him a bitter smile. "It doesn't matter who brews your potions, Mr. Mouse. If we're both caught, we both go to prison."

No, if she thought he'd jeopardize her anonymity and freedom for a single moment, his prison would be a cold slab at the morgue—his sentence courtesy of a bullet.

The old man paled, his jaw quivering.

She enjoyed how small and powerless he looked in her backseat.

"Do you understand that, Mr. Mouse?" she asked, driving into a car wash.

He nodded nervously, then stuttered, "Why are we here?"

She selected the Ultra-Supreme Squeaky-Clean option, feeding the menu machine a ten-dollar bill.

"This car wash is seven and a half minutes. That's plenty of time for you to tell me what you need so I can tell you what I need. No more, no less. Afterward, I'll take you back to the Hideout," she explained, readying the car.

As the session began in the dark tunnel, she said, "State your case, Mr. Mouse."

"I need a love potion," he answered, his voice jittery and rushed as if he heard the ticking sound of a countdown clock.

"For?"

"Someone who no longer wants anything to do with me."

"You need to be more specific, Mr. Mouse." Venus examined her tangerine-orange nails, pondering which color to paint them next.

He blurted out, "My son. He despises me for the things I've done. Hell, I hate myself for the things I've done. I was an accountant with a gambling problem. Debt piled up, and the loan sharks wanted their money, but I lost everything. So, I left.

"I abandoned my wife and nine-year-old son like a coward. It took years to build a life elsewhere, but I made money the honest way and made wiser decisions. Over the years, I've tried to reconnect with him, but he refuses. I want his forgiveness. I want to be the father I should've been for him while I still can."

Venus sieved through his sob story, pulling out the only valuable nugget of information she needed. "You want *storge*."

Mr. Mouse blinked, his brow wrinkling. "What?"

"Love operates on a spectrum of eight kinds. *Storge* means familial love, and I can brew you a potion for that," she guaranteed.

An *eros* potion induced lust. A *ludus* potion encouraged uncommitted love which was perfect for no-strings affairs and one-night stands. *Agape* potions were a popular choice for spouses in crumbling marriages. *Mania* potions drove a drinker to make the culprit their object of obsession. A *philia* potion restored friendships. Sometimes, she got clients who wanted *philautia* potions to learn how to love themselves again. But her most demanded product was her *peitho* potions to incite a drinker's love for an idea.

Though Venus had the knowledge and skill to brew every type of love, her mom taught her which might bring her trouble and which wouldn't.

Too eagerly, Mr. Mouse asked, "How much would it cost for this storge potion?"

"It depends on how strong you want the potion to be," she responded. "The number of notes a potion has determines the strength and expiration date. The more notes, the longer it lasts, but very few potions last for life, and none are in the discipline of love."

The more notes, the more devastating the degree of recoil, she refrained from saying.

Most clients didn't give a fuck about a brewer's suffering.

"Singular-note potions are ten thousand, binary-note potions are twenty thousand, and trinary-note potions are fifty thousand," she informed.

Mr. Mouse gawked. "Fifty thousand dollars for one potion?"

"Fifty is a fair price," Venus said, shrugging.

He threw his hands up. "How generous!"

"Time is running out, Mr. Mouse," she said as the car progressed through the hectic tunnel, nearing the light at the end.

"Fine, I'll buy the binary-note potions," he said hurriedly.

A rush of satisfaction flooded her veins, but she remained stoic. "Do you have twenty grand?"

"Do I have a choice?" Mr. Mouse bit out.

Her lips quirked up at his attitude.

What a feisty mouse.

She handed over the burner phone and its charger.

As the car wash session drew to a close, she instructed, "You have five days to bring me the money. I was kind enough to set the alarm for you. There's one on my burner, too. If you haven't contacted me back before the alarms go off, everything we've spoken about in this car becomes null and void. I'll dispose of my phone, so you'll have no way of contacting me. Don't bother crawling back to Prospero, either. He won't help you.

"However, if you get the money, text me the word 'done' and nothing more. I'll text you the next steps. Is that understood?"

As the car wash's fan roared to life, Mr. Mouse shouted, "Yes, I understand!"

The ride back to the Hideout was silent, but his palpable anxiety buzzed in the air, vibrating against Venus's skin.

Eager to escape, Mr. Mouse reached for the door handle.

"Oh, and Mr. Mouse," she spoke up, prompting him to halt nervously. "I won't fault you if you can't come up with the cash or decide not to go through with this," she said, eyeing him over her shoulder. "However, I've got some trust issues. So, to ensure you don't try anything silly like… scurry off to the WCTF, my barista friend has a knack for hacking into phones and finding all sorts of yummy data. Just keep that in mind, okay?"

His entire body stilled, his face draining of color.

He gazed at her wide-eyed and terrified as if he were truly seeing her for the first time.

"Your cell is waiting for you at the cash register." She flashed him a sweet smile. Mr. Mouse gulped hard and exited the car, scampering inside the Hideout.

The corner of her lips curled up as she drove away.

CHAPTER
THREE

Iron is a witcher's mortal enemy. A whiff leads to respiratory ill-ness. Witcher skin burns when touched. A taste is fatal. Ironskin, also known as Liquid Gold, is a trinary-note potion that gives the drinker immunity. Iron as an ingredient further decreases a brew-er's low survival rate. As a highly desirable Class X–prohibited magical concoction, its black market price is seven figures.

—Witcherpedia, an online witchery encyclopedia

JUNE 6, 2023

AS VENUS SUNBATHED ON A FLAMINGO-PINK TOWEL, SHE RESTED her cheek on her crossed arms. She relished summer days like this when the sun hung high and her fucks to give were low.

Behind closed eyelids, she enjoyed a rare sense of peace. The rein-forcement potion she had downed three hours prior brought her a quiet mind. The brew's potency was robust enough to gag *It*, but that perk only lasted a couple of hours.

Beyond that, *Its* silence was *Its* choice.

Psychological warfare *It* used to keep her on edge.

But her magic wasn't the only thing capable of spoiling a moment like this.

Venus kept the burner phone in the back pocket of her shorts as the harbinger of bad news. Silence meant peace. An incoming text message meant sometime soon, she'd bleed and more.

But even that wasn't the worst thing that could happen.

"How many more minutes until *she* comes and fucks up the vibe?" Janus drawled, occupying the beach towel to the right.

She, as in their mom, Clarissa.

"I'll give it five," Venus mumbled.

"Four," Tyrell yawned as he lounged in a lawn chair to the left, draping a forearm across his brow.

"I say three tops," Janus wagered. "Y'all two wanna bet?"

Tyrell patted his pocket for good measure. "I'm broke."

"Nope," Venus said.

"You're always broke," Janus grumbled at him before she addressed Venus, an audible pout staining her voice. "Aw, why not?"

A lazy Venus dredged up the effort to pin her little sister with a knowing gaze over the rim of her sunglasses. "Because you'll bet if I'm right, you won't go to the auroras party, and if you're right, then I'd have to go."

"How could you've possibly known that, Vee? Did you break your vow of abnegation to read my thoughts?" Janus asked teasingly, hiking an eyebrow.

Venus snorted at the absurdity. "No, I'd never break my vow. You're just predictable as fuck."

Janus gasped in offense, clasping a hand to her chest. "I'm not predictable."

"Fine," she sighed, rolling onto her back to bake evenly. "You're consistent."

"That's much bet—Hey! That's the same thing!" Janus elbowed her in the ribs, knocking free a bright laugh.

Tyrell lifted his sunglasses, regarding his cousins sleepily. "And what if I'm right? What do I get?"

"You get to say I told you so," Janus growled through her teeth as she entered a playful slap battle with Venus, whose belly ached from laughing harder.

A grin split across his lips and he put his sunglasses back in place. "Aight, bet."

"Venus." The brisk utterance of her name gutted her happiness, bleeding out every ounce of playfulness she gave into.

Clarissa had arrived within three minutes as Janus had speculated.

Venus propped onto her forearms and twisted halfway to acknowledge their mother stationed at the back door. "Yes, ma'am?"

"Inside now," Clarissa ordered, waiting expectantly for immediate compliance.

Venus rose and wiggled the waistline of her frayed denim shorts up over her hips to buy herself some time. Tyrell thumped a fist to his chest twice in solidarity.

Sympathy softened Janus's face, but her cocky voice strutted into Venus's head: "*I win.*"

I didn't bet, she mouthed, smirking. Janus's pity wilted like a sun-overdosed flower, a bratty glare blooming in its place.

Venus flicked her tongue out before she crossed the backyard, retreating into the house. She knew she was walking into a trap but was uncertain of what kind until she clocked the medical box on the table.

"We're low on reinforcement potions." Clarissa sat and unclasped the box, extracting a blood-drawing kit. "Sit."

Venus claimed a seat and laid her arm on the table, accepting her fate. She kept her expression blank as a needle punctured her flesh. Crimson emptied into a bag while hate poured into her. She didn't hate needles. Needles were child's play compared to the suffering of a potion's recoil inflicted.

She hated these moments where she felt more like another chore on Clarissa's to-do list than Clarissa's child. A single drop of the intended drinker's blood was all a brewer needed, but it was as if her mother didn't trust her blood enough to behave as an ingredient. Much like her mother didn't trust her. Much like she couldn't trust herself.

Once done, Clarissa offered her a cotton ball and a roll of self-adhering elastic bandage.

As Venus patched up the puncture, she studied the fattened bag. "I can take that to Elder Glenn's."

As a master brewer of health, Elder Glenn made all the reinforcement potions Venus drank daily and the mending potions she needed when brewing broke her. He sold them dirt cheap to her mom due to a debt. A debt that was classified as *grown folk's business.*

"I'll do it myself like always," Clarissa stated.

Venus curled her bare toes, frustration sifting through her. "If I'm capable of having clients, I think I'm capable of handling my own bl—"

"If you think I'll go back and forth with you, you thought wrong," Clarissa asserted. "I will deliver this to Elder Glenn, and you will go get the supplies for Mr. Mouse's order. Take your sister to help. Is that understood?"

Her mother's irritation washed over her like boiling water.

"Yes, ma'am," Venus pronounced, a soft bitterness slinking into her tone.

The Stoneheart sisters strolled along a route of cracked, uneven sidewalks as the sun beamed down on them, their brown skin glistening with a light coat of sweat. They were heading to Carter's Pantry, one of the few witcher-friendly grocery stores in the city.

Her foul mood stuck like gum to her shoe after what had happened in the kitchen. And her nerves grated at Janus smacking loudly on gum that should've tasted like rubber by now.

"You know, talking and walking makes walking less boring." Janus grinned, playfully nudging her shoulder into Venus. "And I have the perfect conversation starter—"

"No," Venus said swiftly.

Janus ignored the rejection, tossing her arms up and singing, "Friday's auroras party!"

Venus groaned at the mention, her eyeballs rolling skyward. Janus bumped her shoulder again, causing her to veer off the sidewalk this time.

"Come on, Vee. It'll be fun, just like old times. You, me, and Ty getting lit." She batted her eyelashes, lacing her fingers and plopping her chin atop. "Knocking back pixie juice, getting high, and throwing it back until dawn. That's what summer is all about."

"Like I told you before, I'll think about it."

Now, it was Janus's turn to roll her eyes. "You think way too much. You rarely go out unless it's something to do with your hustle. It makes no sense how you pay so many racks for those reinforcement potions and you don't trust them enough to go live your life."

Venus shook her head slowly at her sister's persistence. "I didn't sign up for a lecture, professor."

Their stroll slowed to a halt in the grocery store's parking lot. Ahead, a pack of Iron Watchers gathered at the curb outside the main entry doors. Their hate barged into Venus, making her feel tight in her own skin.

Twenty-three years ago, a group of violent vigilantes founded the Iron Watch, an anti-witcher organization, with the mission of "arming the masses with knowledge and iron to protect their God-given *human* rights." At first, no one paid them any mind as they went door-to-door and occupied street corners and sidewalks, passing out printed propaganda.

But inked words had meaning if one believed in them, and as the humans attempted to coexist with witchers as equals, an exploding population didn't want peace.

"Naw, we'll come back another time." She wagged her head, turning on her heel.

Janus sucked her teeth, walking on. "If you're too afraid to go in, I'll go myself. Just text me what you need. The Iron Watch don't scare me."

"Why are you so damn hardheaded?" Venus blew out her cheeks as she swirled back around.

Her reluctant strides caught up to Janus, who beelined toward the main doors blocked by the Iron Watchers. She intervened quickly by grabbing her sister's forearm and dragging her toward the side entrance.

Venus divided Iron Watchers into whiners, barkers, and biters.

Whiners kept their hate secret, hiding behind the safety of their phones and computers. Barkers acted upon the hate, taking to the streets in gas masks and with flyers to let the world know witchers were poison.

Then there were the biters. Biters touched witchers with their iron jewelry to relish the sound of sizzling flesh and screams. They enjoyed the torment and suffering of witchers. Some even resorted to quicker solutions like guns stocked with iron bullets.

Venus had no desire to learn if the Iron Watchers, only feet away, were all bark or bite.

Janus wanted all of the smoke though, that was certain.

A human woman attempted to enter the store, but the Iron Watchers crowded around her, offering flyers and trying to pitch different causes. The word *bill* and the phrase *ironing up* hit Venus's ears as she took Janus into Carter's Pantry.

They passed through the heat sensors, two chimes filling the air.

Red digits on the digital counters throughout the grocery store ticked to the numbers eleven and then twelve. If any other witcher dared to enter after them, an alarm would trigger and alert the SWIGs to pay a visit.

A nasty sort of visit.

Venus released her sister's arm to grab a squeaky-wheeled shopping cart.

"Did you hear those bastards?" A sour-faced Janus planted her feet on the cart's lower tray, holding on as Venus steered to the seasonings and spices aisle. "I think they want Mr. Carter to iron up the store."

For a business to iron up meant barring their windows and doors with iron. It meant switching automatic doors for ordinary doors with iron doorknobs. It meant iron decorations and furniture everywhere.

Ironing up meant no witchers were welcomed.

Jerome Carter had always been a human ally to witchers. Everyone regarded him as an oldhead who doubled as a national treasure and the kind of baby boomer with a heart so big and warm it eclipsed the sun. His wife of forty-six years, Florence, was the High Witcher of the neighborhood's coven. Their deceased eldest, Owen, had inherited her witcher genes. Their youngest, Lamonte, was born human, though.

To iron up his grocery store went against everything he stood for.

Everything he was.

Venus tossed cinnamon sticks, nutmeg, and cloves into the cart.

"It wouldn't surprise me if he did," she said, throwing in vanilla beans and damiana next.

Janus arched an eyebrow, leaning over the basket. "Why do you say that?"

"Because humans are predictable, Jay." She plucked a bottle of basil leaves off the shelf. The human woman the Iron Witchers cornered earlier overheard the statement, gawking at them, insulted.

Venus and her sister shot identical smiles, giving wiggly-fingered *toodle-y* waves.

The woman scoffed, marching around the corner.

Once alone again, Janus grazed her fingertips across the shelved products. "So, you've always felt Mr. Carter would iron up this place?"

"No, I meant the humans who make all the rules will force him to eventually," Venus clarified. "*They're* the predictable ones, but who exactly will tell them it's wrong?"

"They know it's wrong, but they don't care who it hurts."

Venus shrugged. "Sounds about right."

Janus frowned, cocking her head. "Do you even care about any of this?"

"I try not to," she admitted.

"Why? Why don't you care that humans hate us for existing?"

Quite simply, Venus didn't want to end up like her father. She didn't want to be a face on a mural like the one of Owen outside. She didn't want to be a hashtag, a news segment, or a statistic.

She wanted to live in peace, not rest in peace.

What was so wrong with that?

"What do you want me to do, Jay? Go to one of those WASP protests where I'd get beat with iron batons and cuffed with iron shackles? Oh, that's only if the Swiggers aren't trigger-happy that day. Is that what you want?"

"No," Janus said firmly, hopping off the shopping cart. "I want you to act like this world is worth saving."

Venus stopped pushing. "And what if I don't think it's worth saving? What if all I want to do is watch this bitch burn down because there's no good left in it?"

"If that's what you think," Janus began angrily, then composed herself, squeezing her fists as she continued in a softer concise tone. "If that's what you want, then you'd be no different from *that thing* inside of you."

Their eyes latched onto each other, intense and unwavering. A woman eased her cart beside theirs, uttering a quick *excuse me*, and reached past Janus to get a seasoning bottle.

Her sister's words and anger stabbed her chest deep.

A tightening, burning pain sparked and grew and grew and grew, but that didn't deter a wintry smile from dominating her lips. "Well, thank goodness you have a caring heart that's big enough for the *three* of us."

"You know what? I think I'll go get some soda." Janus swirled on her heel, putting distance between them.

"Good idea. That'll help wash all that bitterness coming out your mouth," Venus retorted.

"At least I can get rid of my bitterness. Yours, however, is a personality trait." Janus tossed the insult over her shoulder as she stalked away.

CHAPTER
FOUR

All beings emit invisible energy called auras. It is part of the witchers' birthright to gain insight into a being's species type or magick strength. Human auras are muted in color, quiet, and obedient. The auras of most witchers and familiars are polychromatic swirls, while the auras of deviants are black. Due to their similar auras, humanoid familiars, known as agathions, are commonly mistaken for witchers.

—Witcherpedia, an online witchery encyclopedia

"DAMN, SHE DIDN'T HAVE TO DRAG YOU LIKE THAT," IT SAID.

"I'm not really in the mood right now," Venus hissed, trucking across the store to get to the produce section.

Her skin crawled from *Its* scratchy laugh. *"You're never in the mood."*

"I wish you'd get a full-time job instead of renting space in my head for free," she said, snatching up a package of fresh strawberries.

"If you don't want me to rent space in your head, then let me out to stretch my legs."

"That's a good one." Venus snorted, yanking off a produce bag from a holder stand.

"I'm not playing games with you. I mean what I say."

She stopped in front of a display of Granny Smith apples. "All you ever do is play games. Mind games."

"Only when I have patience."

"Is that what this is? This is you being patient with me? How kind of you."

"*I don't have to be. Being in captivity hasn't changed my nature.*"

"So, you think you're an animal?" The apple Venus picked up had a deep brown bruise on it. Her head shook at the coincidence, because, in a way, her magic was like a bruise that would never heal.

It severed its tone to a taunting whisper. "*No, but I know you're a monster. Let's not forget I'm here because of you. You have no one to blame but yourself.*"

Humor bled out of her at *Its* words—at *Its* reminder.

Venus stood there frozen, unsure of what to say or do. Suddenly in her back pocket, the burner phone vibrated, nearly making her jump out of her skin. She put the apple down and pulled out the device to stare at Mr. Mouse's one-word text:

DONE

If only she could apply that word to the parasitic relationship between her and *It*.

If only.

She grabbed a bouquet of white tulips from an open-face refrigerator in the floral department.

Flowers had an unspoken language, and each had something to say. White tulips represented a plea for forgiveness and a wish for a new start. Red roses were a symbol of passionate love. Sunflowers meant adoration. Receiving yellow hyacinths was a sign of jealousy, and geraniums insulted your intelligence.

Potions had their own language, too, which made flowers the perfect ingredients.

If Mr. Mouse wished for his son's forgiveness and to mend their torn relationship, white tulip petals would help.

At checkout, Venus typed out a text asking Janus where she was.

As she went to hit SEND, the Iron Watchers entered the store.

Their iron jewelry's pungent odor assaulted Venus, a hideous burn coating her nostrils and crawling down her throat. Her watering eyes stung, tears teetering at the edge.

The walls caged in the scent.

Nearby, an employee hunched over and wheezed as he escaped through the STAFF ONLY door. Other witchers made similar escapes to the back of the store or out the side entrance.

She felt the hot teeth of their fear sinking into her.

It released a mocking sigh. *"This will be very interesting. It's a shame I have to sit this one out because of that silly little reinforcement potion."*

The last thing I needed was your help anyway, she said inwardly.

"Do you think Janus would appreciate my help?" It purred.

Dread socked her in the stomach at the mention of her little sister.

A trembly thumb mashed the SEND button to that *where are you* text. Seconds later, dancing dots in a text bubble popped up.

Janus: i was in the restroom when folks ran in. i made a portal to the parking lot. blood-tether is going buck. i'm coming to get you.

Blood-tethers bound two folks together so they could always find each other when trouble found them. When they were younger, Clarissa made them forge one.

Venus texted a NO as a blond Iron Watcher approached her and the human cashier. Blondie wore an iron bracelet and an assortment of iron rings.

Their proximity worsened her symptoms, leaching her strength. She worried her trembling legs would give out if she tried to run. Her heart lost rhythm, pounding hard against her rib cage.

Blondie sized her up, his chin tilting down when his gaze reached her shoes. He knew *exactly* what she was. Venus couldn't hide the quivers running down her frame, the tears staining her cheeks, or her labored breath. However, when he offered the cashier a stack of scarlet flyers, Venus also knew what he was.

A barker.

Blondie's voice streamed out the gas mask's mouthpiece. "We'd like to leave some of these with the store for human customers to—"

A sudden swing of the STAFF ONLY door revealed Mr. Carter.

He marched their way, clapping his hands together once. "Unless y'all wanna add handcuffs to your jewelry collection, the Gas Mask squad needs to vacate the premises. Immediately."

Protectively, he stood in front of Venus.

"But, sir—" Blondie began.

"I said what I said. End of discussion."

Like a live wire, Blondie's anger crackled up her spine, each painful jolt echoing in her bones.

"Witchers don't care about you or any of us humans," Blondie growled, standing firm. "They could burn this place to ash once they've used you."

His buddies closed in.

The scent of iron coiled its fingers around Venus's throat and squeezed, her eyes bulging behind her sunglasses. Black spots danced along the edges of her vision. She sucked in a tiny desperate breath.

"How much longer before you break?" It asked, amused.

Not much.

Mr. Carter propped his fists on his hips. "I'll give y'all until the count of three to leave before I have you and your little friends arrested for trespassing, *Zachary*."

Zachary reared his head back in shock. "How did you—"

"I've seen you here with your grandmama Betty, and if I'm not mistaken, that's her 1988 Pontiac Bonneville parked out front. Ain't it, son?"

"Come on, Zach. Let's go," a brunette chick sneered. His friends grabbed his shoulders, pushing him toward the exit.

Venus exhaled shakily as the iron's grip on her loosened.

"Much appreciated. Have a lovely day," Mr. Carter said.

Relief jolted Venus as the last Iron Watcher left.

Though the iron's pollution waned, mild tremors raked her hand. She curled her fingers into a fist.

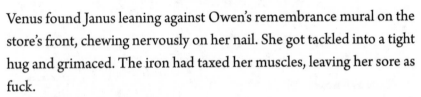

Venus found Janus leaning against Owen's remembrance mural on the store's front, chewing nervously on her nail. She got tackled into a tight hug and grimaced. The iron had taxed her muscles, leaving her sore as fuck.

"I'm so glad you're okay." Janus pulled back just enough to trace the outline of her inky-black aura. "*Are* you okay?"

Sometimes, trauma snapped magic like a bone, and it healed all wrong, twisted and infected, making it hard to read a deviant's aura.

Venus nodded, her smile weak. "I will be."

All she wanted was a bubble bath and to sleep for a week straight.

Janus gave her one last squeeze before she stepped back, taking half the grocery bags to lighten some of Venus's burden.

As they quietly strolled across the parking lot, Janus stepped on a discarded Iron Watch flyer. Blood-spatter font read:

REGISTRATION ACT IS A MATTER OF LIFE OR DEATH!

Another anti-witcher bill to add to the never-ending political buffet.

Venus never kept track, because Janus always did. The thought of asking what the bill was about made her feel uncomfortable. It meant a subject she disliked piqued her curiosity. A topic her sister could ramble on about for hours.

She decided not to chance it.

Venus pulled out one white tulip with a free hand and offered it to her sister.

Janus accepted it, tucking it behind her ear. "I'm sorry for dragging you earlier. I just get so worked up about all the bad things witchers have to deal with, ya know?"

"Your dad is the same way," Venus noted.

Maybe, Janus was wired the same way as him.

Much to their mother's dismay.

"I guess the apple doesn't fall far from the tree." Janus paused, hesitating to say what she wanted to say next. "Darius was like that, too."

Darius Knox.

A name all witchers knew.

He was one of the three founders of Witchers Against Species Persecution.

After the Great Discovery brought the existence of witchers to light, the world spiraled into panic and many coped with change by committing terrible acts. Witcher hunts became a thing on college campuses. At Georgetown, a fellow witcher was beaten nearly to death with an iron poker during a hazing ritual gone wrong. The frat boys claimed self-defense, and the public believed them.

Enraged by the ordeal, Darius and his two college buddies, Malik Jenkins and Owen Carter, founded WASP and organized the first campus protest. Their expulsion from the college was swift. Word of their protest and expulsion became national news, causing the WASP movement to spark and ignite across the country.

Three idealistic friends turned into revolutionaries, then legends overnight.

It was almost like they were invincible.

Almost.

An Iron Watch nail bomb killed Owen in 2007, making his only child an orphan.

A bullet to the head put Malik in a coma in 2013, making Janus something like an orphan but not quite.

As for Darius, he became the movement's first martyr in 2006.

"Yeah, he was," Venus concurred casually, "and he got gunned down for it at a street protest after our government passed the Limit-12 Law. A law that is still in place to this day. So, in the end, was his death worth it?"

"He died doing what he thought was right. That makes his death worth it and he's a hero for that."

Venus didn't understand why Janus spoke of Darius so tentatively. She couldn't mourn a man who died when she was one year old. No cherished memories of him teaching her how to ride a bike or inspecting her closet for monsters. But it would've been a lie if she had said his murder didn't impact her. His cautionary tale made her unwilling to repeat his mistakes.

Venus squeezed her eyes shut momentarily, irritation settling in her veins. "Well, not everyone wants to be a hero, Jay."

With a past like hers, she knew she could never be one.

"You don't have to be a hero to do what's right, Vee."

Venus eased out a tired breath. "Let's just stop talking about this, alright?"

"Fine," Janus said, but they both knew the conversation was far from over.

As a summer day was long, Janus was stubborn as hell. Her wokeness included the self-appointed responsibility of waking everyone else up.

But being woke didn't mean the rest of the world was asleep.

Sometimes, people were tired of waiting.

CHAPTER
FIVE

Mediums use a summoning spell to slit through the veil between the living world and the spirit one. Familiar-forging happens when a Spirit pledges servitude to a bloodline, earning the physical form of an animal or, in rarer cases, an agathion. Very few can switch between the two. A familiar's assigned appearance and speaking ability are contingent upon a medium's mastery and magic strength. Years of servitude fortify magic strength. Anima does not exist in familiars because they are extraplanar spirits, not living beings. Their essence is loyalty.

—Witcherpedia, an online witchery encyclopedia

JUNE 9, 2023

MUSTARD PAPER BANDS BLINDFOLDED BENJAMIN FRANKLIN'S face on two crisp stacks of hundreds. Venus thumbed through each as a precaution.

"I hope you don't intend to count that here," Mr. Mouse said in the backseat, his voice jittery. "I can assure you it's all there."

She looked up from the brown paper bag to watch him in the rearview mirror. Ever since she picked him up, an invisible motor kept his knee bouncing, thumbs twiddling, and shifty eyes darting around.

Rain pitter-pattered. Windshield wipers squeaked and swished.

"I believe you," she admitted, "but I don't trust you."

He jerked his head back, his eyes blinking rapidly. "Believing and trusting go hand in hand."

"Believing the money is all there and trusting there isn't a GPS tracker hiding in it are two different things, Mr. Mouse," she said.

"I underestimated your thoroughness." He paused, clearing his throat. "Regardless of your unorthodox methods."

A slight smile curled her lips at the compliment. "I'd rather be underestimated."

"And why is that?"

"I enjoy proving people wrong more than letting them be right."

Mr. Mouse parted his lips to speak, but he gave a razor-sharp gasp before he succumbed to a coughing fit. His handkerchief muffled the severity, but his pained pale face was proof enough. It was the second time he'd nearly coughed up a lung in her car, but it was the first time Venus realized how frail and meek he was.

As he struggled to recover, a truth smacked into her:

Mr. Mouse was *dying*.

Her incognito uniform's dark shades impeded her ability to read human auras. She peeked over the rims to stare in the rearview mirror.

An ultrathin gray-green aura clung to his skin.

"How much longer do you have?" she asked.

He sagged against the seat, exhausted, his breaths shallow. "Long enough to see my son not despise me." A pause. "If I die before this potion wears off, will he still love me?"

Venus nodded.

"So, he'll come to my funeral." Mr. Mouse breathed, his face full of relief.

A decent person would've said something comforting, but that required sympathy. It didn't matter if Mr. Mouse was dying or not. He wanted to poison his estranged son, out of desperation.

The only thing that mattered to Venus was money.

After storing the bag away, she merged into a rain-slicked river of white headlights and red taillights.

"Underneath the front passenger seat, you'll find a bag with two vials inside. You've got two tasks, and one depends solely on the other. The first is the hardest for some."

Mr. Mouse nudged his glasses back up the slope of his nose. "That being?"

"You must fill the first vial with drops of your son's blood."

His gravelly laugh unraveled into another cough.

"That won't be possible," he panted, shaking his head.

Venus shrugged. "Alright, then a lock of hair will do."

"That's absurd! And how am I to do that?" His face soured.

His bitterness congested her lungs, which made her want to cough.

Despite the urge, she cleared her throat. "How you'll do it isn't my problem, but if you can get his blood in the first vial, then fill the other with yours. If you can only get his hair, then I'll need your hair. Like I said before, one task depends on the other."

A drinker's blood or hair as an ingredient bound the potion to them. In most disciplines, only the drinker's offering mattered, but love was different. Other than self-love ones, most love potions complicated the hell out of things. Both the patron and the drinker had to provide equal offerings to forge a fake-ass bond between them.

A law that didn't need to be penned in every recipe through the disciplines.

But at least, patrons had choices.

Brewers had no choice but to bleed and more.

No brewer blood, no brewer suffering, no brewed potion.

It was as simple as that.

As Mr. Mouse folded his arms over his chest, he scoffed. "For twenty grand, it seems like I'm doing most of the work."

"I doubt that."

Venus came home to disappointment and rejection. That's what yellow carnations stood for, and one lay on the welcome mat, waiting for her. She picked it up, giving the stem a slow turn. She turned halfway to see Mr. Lionel's silhouette in a lit window. Then the curtains fell back into place.

She snapped off part of the stem and tucked the bloom behind her ear as a badge of honor.

Venus twisted the house key into the front door's lock. Soft fur brushed against her ankle, making her squeak. Her eyes jumped to their family's familiar, a black cat with a heart-shaped white patch on his chest. He helped in the kitchen on brewing days; on all other days, he was at her mom's beck and call.

Clarissa inherited him after Granny Davina died twenty years ago.

As with many familiars, Patches was a family heirloom. And in his case, a hundred-and-fifty-year-old one. An old photo album in the attic contained yellowed black-and-white Stoneheart family photos. Janus's favorite photo was taken in 1908. In it, Patches sat on their great-great-grandmother Hattie Stoneheart's lap.

"What the fuck, Patches? You scared the shit out of me," she said, opening the door.

Patches strolled in.

Once inside, a calmness whispered through her.

She pressed her back against the front door as if to keep the outside world at bay.

Although she was home, there was still work to do.

She still had to report to the boss.

Apparently, Patches did, too.

Venus knocked on her mother's bedroom door, and a *come in* seeped through the wood. She obeyed, lingering in the doorway.

Clarissa sat on the floor, in her pajamas, a photo album blanketing her lap. Her brown microlocs were twisted into a high bun and protected by a lemon-yellow headwrap.

Patches padded into the room, taking his place at her side.

She arched an eyebrow, turning a page. "Well?"

"All the money's accounted for," Venus said, tossing the cash-filled paper bag onto the bed.

"Good." Clarissa picked up a bottled beer to sip on, her attention glued to old family photos.

Venus tilted her head, her tongue prodding her inner cheek.

Clarissa Stoneheart didn't drink. Nor was she sentimental.

Yet here she was doing and being both.

Having seen enough, Venus jabbed a thumb over her shoulder. "Well, good n—"

"Tomorrow's the anniversary of your father's death," Clarissa informed her. She never spoke of him. Darius. At the Limit-12 protest, he died in her arms, earning her the right not to talk about him.

Clarissa rarely talked to anyone, though.

She only spoke at them with all her commands and demands.

No room for compromises or arguments.

All business, all the time.

Family was no exception.

Sometimes late at night, Janus would crawl into Venus's bed, and they'd whisper conspiracies about why Clarissa Stoneheart was the way she was.

A couple of weeks ago, her sister asked, "I get why she's angry at the world, but why is she always angry with us, too?"

The question stumped Venus. Even now.

Caught off guard by the announcement, a soft *oh* was all she could muster.

"This was his favorite beer." Clarissa scrunched up her face after another taste. "It still tastes like crap, though."

Venus raked her teeth across her bottom lip. "How many have you had?"

"Too many. Or we wouldn't even be having this conversation," Clarissa admitted, the bud of a rare smile on her lips. "Every year, I drink one for him and I regret it. But this time, I think I went overboard."

What was Uncle Bram's favorite old saying?

What soberness conceals, drunkenness reveals.

Curious, Venus crossed her arms, leaning against the doorframe. "What makes this year so different than the others?"

"You made it to eighteen."

As in, her mom didn't expect her to live this long.

The statement should've upset her, but to be honest, she hadn't expected it, either. Brewing warped her perspective on life and death. While other eighteen-year-olds thought about how they'd live, she pondered how much longer before a potion's recoil led to her tragic demise.

Clarissa opened the metal box and reached within, pulling out an old envelope. "Darius instructed me to give you this after you turned eighteen."

Surprise snaked around Venus's lungs and squeezed, forcing a tiny breath to rush out of her. Her eyes fixed on the five-lettered name scrawled across the bubblegum-pink square.

Her name.

Hesitantly, she took it, afraid of its physical lightness and the gravity of her dead father's words within.

Up until that moment, Venus was an heir with no inheritance.

Now, she held his heart in her hands.

A loving letter addressed to her.

The word *loving* was like a thorn in her brain. An adjective she couldn't apply to her mother, who had yet to look at her since she got here.

Boldness swelled in her chest. "Why am I such a disappointment to you?"

Clarissa looked up at her, wide eyes blinking in surprise at the question.

A pause stretched between them.

"You're not, Venus." Clarissa set aside the beer and closed the album. "I didn't—"

She stopped herself, sharpness flashing through her eyes.

Her suspicion knifelike against Venus's throat.

"Where did you get that flower?" she asked, an accusation coloring her voice.

The abrupt shift of topic whiplashed Venus. Suddenly, she felt like a little kid caught with something she had no business being caught with.

"I found it on the welcome mat. I think it's a gift from Mr. Lionel."

"Give it to me," her mom ordered, palm out. "Now."

Venus surrendered it, confusion tightening her brow.

"Go," Clarissa ordered, scrutinizing the flower as if she wanted it to wither on command. "Don't let the door hit you on the way out."

Her mom's thorny order should've stung her, but instead, a fucked-up sort of amusement bloomed inside her at how a flower summed up the nature of their relationship so perfectly.

Rejection.

After closing the door, she heard her mom address Patches. "Show me everything you saw."

Venus dragged herself into her bedroom and eased down on the cushioned seat at her vanity. She turned the wrinkled envelope over, her fingertips grazing the lip sealed by a red heart sticker dulled by time.

Years of being locked away should have preserved it more, but its creases told Venus another story. One where Clarissa held her dead husband's letter and drank his favorite beer that tasted like ass in remembrance for the last sixteen years. Not that she'd ever admit it.

She already showed Venus too much tonight, like an influencer with no filter.

Bare skin, flaws, vulnerable.

Feeling those things too felt like a threat.

Venus spared another look at the letter before she dumped it in her vanity's drawer. Plucking off her sunglasses, she removed her wig and the constricting wig cap.

Her dark-skinned mannequin head stared blankly at her as she placed the tresses on it.

Unmoved, unfazed.

Everything she aspired to be.

Snatching a tissue, she wiped away her magenta lipstick. With her face naked, she was free to be herself again and take her ass to bed. Wrapping her hair in a scarf, she stripped down to her underwear, climbed under the covers, and snuggled in.

"Nope, nope, nope," Janus chanted disapprovingly, bursting through the door and flipping the lights on. "Wake your behind up!"

Screwing her eyelids tighter, Venus growled, "Go away, Janus, before you catch these hands."

Janus snorted a laugh as she marched to the closet doors and launched them open. "I'd like to see you try. Now, get up. We've got an auroras party to go to."

Plastic hangers clicked against each other as she scoured through outfits.

Venus grabbed a pillow and used it to block out the noise. But the peace was short-lived as Janus ripped it away, tossing clothes onto her face.

"Get dressed, Vee. We've got to go!"

Venus rolled onto her back, shooting her sister a death glare. Her stubbornness anchored her to the bed.

To motivate her, Janus repeatedly smacked her head with the stolen pillow.

Venus snarled, flinging back the covers. "Alright, damn it!"

Knowing her job was done, Janus skipped happily to the door.

"Thank you for your cooperation. You got ten minutes to get cute!"

CHAPTER
SIX

As a species, witchers are very social creatures. Their innate tendency to gather makes them dangerous to humans. Their magic and sense of belonging strengthen as they increase in numbers. They will always protect each other when threatened.

—*Witcher Hierarchy: An Introduction to Witcher Society*

A RAIN PUDDLE WAS EITHER A NUISANCE TO STEP AROUND OR A delight to jump in, but it was much rarer to step in one and come out elsewhere. If not for violet energy radiating around the puddle's edges, Venus would've thought it all to be a joke.

Yeah, it'd been over a year since she crashed an auroras party, but was this really what it had come to now? Sneaking portals into muddy puddles at a Deanwood playground?

This was dumb as fuck, but Venus had little choice in the matter.

She glared her little sister down.

To which Janus had the audacity to say: "You should've stayed your ass home if you're gonna act like a sourpuss."

Venus scoffed, crossing her arms. "And who came into my room and pillow-attacked me until I had no choice but to agree to this foolery?" She grimaced, adding, "And who the hell says 'sourpuss' anymore?"

"I've only been gone a day and y'all already fighting?" A boy their age strolled into their argument. He had deep waves and a tight lineup. A diamond stud glinted in his ear. He adjusted his shades with a little wiggle, exuding an air of cool.

Up until he slipped on a patch of damp grass.

Which only proved that their cousin Tyrell was underneath the stranger's smooth exterior. From the top of his head to the soles of his feet, he could change everything about himself. Skin tone, height, and even clothes.

Tyrell was a chameleon, but the one thing he could never shapeshift was his lovable goofball self.

Venus grabbed on to him before he pregamed with some 100 percent organic mudslide.

Janus chewed her lips, struggling to hold in a laugh.

He gathered himself up, wearing his signature dimpled grin. Dimples he inherited from Aunt Keisha. Dimples that always reminded Venus of her dad.

It took Venus a lot of elbow grease to convince him to go back home and make amends with his mom.

You good? her eyes asked him.

We good, his eyes answered back.

From a moving car's window, Aunt Keisha shouted, "Y'all three watch out for each other! Love y'all!"

"Love you, too!" Janus yelled back.

Tyrell shook his head, glancing at the red taillights speeding away. "Moms wouldn't let me come unless I shifted, then she insisted on dropping me off."

"We're really proud of you, Ty," Venus said, propping her cheek on his shoulder.

Janus nodded. "Yeah, we know how hard it must've been for you."

Tyrell raised his eyebrows. "We'll see how proud y'all will be of me when I lose shape on the dance floor."

Summer warmth blanketed the night.

Fresh rain, soaked grass, and mud invaded Venus's senses.

For some odd reason, she liked where they were.

A comforting slice of peace before all the madness.

"Now that everyone's accounted for. Let's get this over with," she urged, winding her wrist as a *hurry-this-up* gesture.

"Don't be such a sourpuss." Tyrell jumped into the puddle portal without a second thought, falling out of sight.

Not a ripple to disrupt their reflections as she and her sister gazed down at the unconventional doorway.

Venus vowed to jab Tyrell's ribs.

Janus hopped in next, abandoning her.

With a deep breath, she leaped into the puddle, free-falling through bone-rattling bass thumps and neon strobe lights. She landed in a crouch, rising in a stumble.

Venus glanced around the auroras party she had dropped in on.

Overhead, the purplish portal swirled like a storm's eye.

A window to the night sky above the playground.

According to Janus, the organizers picked an abandoned warehouse in Alexandria, a twenty-minute drive from Deanwood. With the fear of a SWIG raid, witchers never partied in the same place twice.

All over the place, there were portals for entry and escape.

Party organizers always tried to keep the portals well hidden, but an occasional human would stumble onto one and report it to the Suspicious Witcher Activity hotline.

Even if a raid could snuff out an aurora party, others would always spark to life somewhere else. Because when witchers gathered in numbers, something special happened.

A heady dose of euphoria.

An addictive sense of home.

A mounting swell of empowerment.

A connection no human could ever understand.

"Plot twist. You didn't run off." Janus's voice breezed into her mind.

Sensing her sister's presence, Venus swirled around to face her.

At parties, witchers tended to speak telepathically to save their vocal cords some punishment, but Venus herself didn't have that luxury. Her vow of abnegation prevented that, making the form of communication one-sided.

So, she texted: you woulda hunted me down if i had.

Janus read the message, her smile smug. *"Damn right. Let's go!"*

She tugged Venus through the crowds.

Magic slithered all around them, imposing and near-tangible like an October fog. Invisible to human eyes and witchers caught up in the music and drug-like high of freedom.

Visible to those with clearer heads.

Venus always had a clear head.

For her, it was dangerous not to.

She winced as a sharp pulse pooled at the base of her skull.

A door knock from something that wanted out.

"Come get y'all's poisons." Tyrell's voice entered their heads as he rolled up with red plastic cups filled with pixie juice, a glowing spiked punch the color of aquamarine.

Janus grabbed hers and didn't hesitate to down it all.

Venus declined.

While potions were a precise science, pixie juice was a mixture of guesstimating, mystery, and pure vibes.

Tyrell shrugged and chugged hers, then his own, walking away.

Disappointment rolled off Janus in waves, lapping at Venus's skin.

At that moment, her sister's soured face was a near-spitting image of their mom's.

Venus frowned, texting: i can have fun without drinking.

A human then swaggered over, his attention solely on Janus. Venus thought about stepping in to tell him his efforts wouldn't work, but she knew her little sister could handle herself. Janus proved her right, looking up from the text message just as he flashed a grin. She crinkled her nose, narrowing her eyes at him. Instantly, his confidence dissolved as she sent a rejection right into his mind.

It could have been a stern warning, a firm hell naw, I'm aroace declaration, or a mix of the two. Either way, his resignation felt like a thorn in Venus's side, but his embarrassment stung worse.

Janus flung her cup to the side and dragged a grateful Venus deep into the party's heart, away from his dejected little ass. His dismal mood lost its grip on her with each step they took.

Fueled by pixie juice, her sister danced, riding the beat.

All dialed in on a frequency Venus was too sober to intercept.

Janus planted hands on Venus's hips, guiding them in a carefree sway.

It didn't take long for Venus to lose herself in the music, getting drunk on the shimmery currents of magic that surrounded and slithered around her.

Too drunk.

Auroras parties got their name because auras pour from bodies, mingling merrily like an aurora. Witchers fed off the collective energy.

If you partied enough, you built a certain tolerance.

Venus hadn't been to an auroras party in over a year.

Back then, she had a reputation.

She gave hungry kisses, stole hearts, guzzled down pixie juice, and danced until the SWIGs or the morning sun came. All to lose herself, but losing herself was like offering herself on a platter to *It*.

So, she stopped going.

It had won enough.

She hadn't expected to get messed up so badly by coming here tonight.

Venus pried open her eyelids and found herself drowning alone in a sea of dancing bodies. There was no sign of Janus. She stood in a swirling kaleidoscope of glistening skin and sensations.

Through her mind's fog, someone stood out in crystal-clear clarity, their stormy aura a twin to her own.

A gaze the color of jade green snared her.

She *knew* those eyes, but her brain felt fuzzy like old TV static.

A muzzled *It* hammered a pang inside her skull again, the pain driving a nail of realization into her crown. She shook her groggy head to erase the illusion, but it didn't waver.

Venus stumbled through the crowd, desperate to get to the fringes. Swimming out of the colorful madness was like fighting against a powerful undercurrent. When a dark, deep electronic beat gave way to an energized trap song, she got tossed around as partyers got hyped.

Nearly to the dance floor's rim, she smacked hard into somebody.

The collision made her stagger backward.

A pair of deep brown hands steadied her. Her chin cocked up as her regard settled on the green eyes she had mistaken for a hallucination moments ago. She took stock of high cheekbones, an angular jawline, snowy eyebrows, and bone-white hair with shaved sides.

Now, she was face-to-face with Owen Carter's only child, Jerome Carter's grandchild, and once upon a time, her best friend.

The name *Presley* rested heavily on her tongue, but she couldn't get it out as a lightness tunneled through her.

Her knees buckled.

Presley circled an arm around her waist to keep her from falling.

Their words stepped into her head, delivered in a deep, mellow, textured tone: *"I got you."*

They led her away to the restrooms.

A free-for-all utopia.

Folks relieved themselves at the urinals. A few perfected their makeup and fixed their hair at the sinks and mirrors. Others strolled out of stalls as a party of one, a pair of two, or a company of three.

As two girls jointly left a stall, Presley eased Venus onto a toilet seat. They shut the creaky door and slid a lock into place. The cramped space made their tall, swimmer-like stature appear giant.

They lowered into a crouch between her legs. "You good now?"

Venus chewed her bottom lip, nodding.

The cloudiness within her cleared up bit by bit, but not fast enough for her liking.

"You must be surprised to see me." Presley tucked a pink strand behind her ear, their palm's diagonal scar grazing her cheek. Their arms donned full-sleeve tattoos of bare ebony branches moving as if trapped in a soft breeze.

Venus's lashes fluttered at the comforting gesture.

She forgot how much she missed the kind of touches friendship brought. Forgot how much she missed the hand-holding, arm-linking, piggyback rides, clapping games, thumb wars, and unwavering hugs.

"That's an understatement," Venus muttered, letting her curiosity overtake her as she weakly curled her fingers around their wrist. She squinted as she turned their hand over, her fingertips grazing their scar.

Only two things would warrant a scar like this: blood-tethers and blood oaths.

Love and the need to protect forged one.

Fear and the need to control shaped the other.

"How'd you get this?" Her forehead puckered in thought, gears inside her head turning more slowly than usual.

Withdrawing their hand, Presley shook their head, amused. "When'd you get to be so nosy?"

"I'm only nosy when I'm not sober." Venus rested her temple against the stall wall, pouting for not getting an answer. She didn't push it any further, because scars had memories and some memories had sharp edges.

She had *more* than plenty.

"When did you get back in town?"

"Two days ago," they said, shrugging. "Got homesick."

"For three years you've been in the witcher utopia of Toronto, and you missed living in this fucked-up country?"

"I missed my grandparents," they said, then asked: "You here by yourself?"

She wagged her chin. "Jay and Ty are around here somewhere."

Their white eyebrow quirked up. "And left you alone?"

"I'm *not* alone, though. Whether I like it or not, my deviation keeps me company." She flinched as regret ate at her, hitting bone.

A distant expression clouded Presley's face. "We both played with fire and got burned."

"Yeah, badly," Venus agreed.

"We don't play with fire, you fool. We are fire. We burn, burn, burn," Its voice rasped out through the cracks of the reinforcement potion. The husky words felt like jagged yellowing nails of bony fingers biting deep to leave a mark.

To make a statement.

Venus dampened her lips, preparing herself to ask the thing she'd kept in her pocket for three years. "That's why you left, right? Because of what happened?"

Presley nodded. "I needed time. I stayed with some kinfolk on Mama Renny's side."

Three years ago, they texted her everything would be okay.

Venus's belly was full of sleeping pills, so she didn't hear the notification chime and slept through the night instead of crying through it. In the morning, she tried to reply but received a message error.

The number you have reached is not in service.

That message error told her the truth Presley couldn't admit.

Nothing would be okay.

Wanting to play catch-up, Venus asked, "What's your deviation, Pres?"

"Magic augmentation. I can—"

"Amp up others' magic," she finished. "Nifty."

Presley pushed long fingers through their hair, their sigh regretful. "Not quite. Some folks can't handle the overflow, and they drown in their own magic."

For some fucked-up reason, Venus found comfort in knowing she wasn't the only one with a body count above one.

"My deviation is a big fan of murder," Venus said.

"Well, that's *terrifying.*" A hint of humor danced in their tone.

A tiny, tired laugh bubbled in her throat. "I'm terrified outta my fucking mind, Pres."

"You need to go home and sober up."

Earlier, the last place she wanted to be was at this damn party, but now she didn't want to go home, either. Disappointment and rejection waited for her there.

"That's not gonna go over well with my kinfolk," she said. "We're not leaving until the sun comes up or the SW—"

Somebody burst into the busy restroom, yelling, "SWIGS!"

A tsunami of everyone's fear flooded her veins.

She hunched over at the intrusion, panting to keep her head above the overwhelming sensation.

Panic ensued as everyone made a mad dash out the door.

"Aw, shit," Venus cursed as she stumbled to her feet, cradling her head.

Presley snatched up her hand, towing her out of the stall and into utter chaos. "Keep up."

SWIGs in tactical gear marched in from a northwest portal with aimed guns. Partyers stampeded toward the other doorways. Venus winced at the *clap-clap-clap* of gunfire and piercing screams. The chorus of fear grew louder inside her, seeping into the marrow of her bones.

"*Venus.*" Janus's panicky voice barreled into her mind. "*Where the hell are you?*"

She whipped her head around, frantically searching for her little sister. The blood-tether lurched her in a direction opposite from where Presley was shepherding her.

"I need to find my family!" Venus shouted, wrenching her hand from Presley's grasp.

They nodded. "Lead the way!"

Together, they raced through the unrest to get to her sister and cousin.

Some witchers stood their ground, staying behind to fight.

To hold a united front so others could flee.

Anger braided together with all the fear and coiled down her spine.

Magic ripped Swiggers off the ground and sent them soaring into the walls, leaving deep, crumpled dents. Others caught fire, the flames growing wild and greedy.

"Janus!" she screamed, following the blood-tether's intensifying hurtful yanks as she neared wherever her sister was.

"Venus!" Janus shouted back as they rushed to each other.

Adrenaline sobered her up as she cradled Janus's face, her gaze hunting for injuries. A bloody cut glistened in a slant across her left temple, and a dark plump bruise stained her cheek.

Her sister's mouth fell open at the sight of Presley, but she shook her head as if to expel a question.

"The hosts are closing up the portals!" Janus said. "If we want to make it out of here alive, I've got to make a doorway! Stand back now!"

Presley grabbed a reluctant Venus's arm, tugging her back.

Janus rubbed her palms together in a circular motion before she jerked them apart, a black slice filling up the space between her hands. Their only escape route widened and yawned.

A parking lot awaited them.

Tyrell sprinted to them. "Aye, y'all! Wait for me!"

"Like we'd leave your ass!" Janus tossed back as they all rushed through the conjured portal.

Others followed suit, escaping into the empty lot.

A chick yelped as an iron bullet struck her shoulder, the impact making her fall forward. Her human boyfriend dropped to his knees and crawled to her, gathering her into his arms.

"Jay, close the doorway! Now!" Tyrell ordered, pointing to the horde of cops rushing toward the portal. She clapped her hands. A colorful wave of magic reverberated, the doorway shrinking as an assault of iron bullets came.

Venus tackled her.

Presley dodged out of the way, too.

A Swigger charged toward them, leading his tactical troop. He rushed to break through before the portal sealed, but only an outstretched arm made it, plopping to the ground.

The injured woman's continued shrieks echoed across the parking lot. She contorted in her boyfriend's hold as the iron bullet punished her witcher blood. Smoke rose and flesh sizzled. Her gunshot wound grew and grew as the metal ate away at her.

Venus's muscles burned from the woman's sheer terror.

She gritted her teeth, embracing herself.

Janus got off the ground and conjured another doorway to Alexandria's only witcher-friendly hospital.

"Go get her help," she ordered the boyfriend.

He stood up, struggling to hold the writhing woman as he hurried through the doorway.

Venus sprawled out on the warm concrete, relieved. Presley offered her their hand and she grunted as they helped her up. The word *thanks* queued up in her throat, but Tyrell's sudden roar of pain cut her off. He hunched over as his clothes morphed, his skin color changed, and his bones broke and shifted. Sweat and tears dripped off him as he rebecame himself.

Discontentment flared across his face, and he kicked the severed arm.

"Dammit!" he snarled.

Her sister concurred, drawling out an *oh fuck*.

"How are we going to get rid of this thing?" Janus asked, fear creeping in her tone as she stared at the damage her doorway caused.

"*Burn, burn, burn,*" It cooed.

"We'll burn the thing," Venus stated, despising how easily the words rolled off her tongue.

She resented how she agreed with *It*.

Presley's voice came into her head. "*Wouldn't be the first time.*"

Venus stiffened, those five words triggering her memory of that night three years ago when they both set what they'd done ablaze.

The night they both became deviants.

CHAPTER
SEVEN

A familiar's essence is loyalty. In the past, brewers harvested
and ate their familiar's loyalty to fortify vows and replenish
wells of magic. This is called a fealty feast. In today's world, this
isn't illegal. However, it is widely frowned upon. This delicacy
sells on the black market for six figures.

—*The Familiar Manual*, 2009 Edition

JUNE 16, 2023

A WEEK HAD PASSED SINCE THE AURORAS PARTY. THE NEWS NET-
works gobbled up the story and spat out segments daily. Nine casualties.
Seven witchers and two humans. Twenty-six injured. A total of eighteen
were arrested, probably wishing they were dead. The nastiest raid yet.

When a news anchor reported that a Black witcher with gray-and-
black ombre hair aided fugitives and gravely injured a SWIG officer, Janus
turned into a paranoid hermit with a hefty hundred grand bounty on her
head. She used an alert ward spell around their property and peeked out
the curtains.

If Clarissa had been an avid news watcher or newspaper reader, the
WCTF would've been the least of Janus's worries. Luckily, their mom
believed the news was made for and by humans.

Not meant for witcher consumption.

Meanwhile, Venus didn't have the luxury to stew in a soup of worry and fear.

She had an operation to run.

Mr. Mouse completed his tasks. Unable to get ahold of his son's blood, he bribed a barbershop apprentice to snag some hairs during a routine appointment.

There were many ways to brew love, and each had the potential to kill you.

Venus sprinkled the hairs from the two vials into a boiling pot of withered white tulip petals. Three sprigs of velvety mint followed two cups of red wine. After that, she added cinnamon sticks, nutmeg, cloves, vanilla beans, damiana, basil leaves, thyme, and rosemary.

Venus unscrewed a jar of raw honey and lovebug corpses, drizzling a half cup into the bubbling brew.

A binary-note potion contained two keynotes: a base liquid and a notion.

A notion defined the potion's purpose.

She cupped her hands together and whispered into them:

Leach strong hate from a son's heart
For new beginnings with Father to start

Warm breath from her words manifested into a fidgety ball of green vapor. When she dropped it into the brew, it popped and fizzled. A glowy green froth came forth suddenly but expectedly, rising to the pot's brim but never daring to spill over.

The easy part was finally over.

Now, it was time for the part brewers hated most.

She might lose a finger or two or three. An eyeball could dangle by a veiny thread from her skull, or her brown flesh could blister off.

Venus prickled her index finger with her needle charm necklace. A ruby droplet eased out of her fingertip, too small for her liking. She pressed her thumb in, forcing out a fatter, more pleasant offering.

She called Patches into the kitchen.

He leaped onto her shoulder, all his teeth and claws radiating magic.

A familiar could absorb some of a potion's recoil and care for the brewer afterward. Even though familiars were not invincible, they were too sturdy and otherworldly to feel pain.

She hoisted her finger high over the cauldron, hot steam licking meanly at her.

A miserable Janus shuffled into the kitchen in rumpled pajamas and panda-bear slippers.

"Get the hell out, Jay!" Venus snapped.

Her little sister backed out of the room quickly, squeaking, "My bad!"

As her blood fell in, she braced herself for the recoil, grimacing as a white light blinded her vision. Rosy smoke billowed from the cauldron, shrouding the kitchen and clogging her lungs.

Wind whipped violently at her.

A boom rattled her bones.

Then came the terrible heat, lashing its flailing, desperate limbs.

The brew was a living monstrosity without loyalty to Venus, its creator.

Patches growled as he lunged toward the pot, striking with all his teeth, claws, magic, and might. The attack weakened the recoil, but it still knocked the cat aside.

It seized Venus's arms by digging its nails into her, tugging at her to fall in. A raw scream tore out of her throat as it dug deeper and deeper until it hit bone, swiveling her arm at an unnatural angle.

Then it released her.

Venus collapsed to the tiled floor. Right arm mangled, sharp bones protruding.

"I could've helped you, but you won't let me out," It sighed.

Venus heard *Its* mocking pout. *It* always did this, dangling a remedy in her face like a forbidden fruit. Her blood breathed life into every potion she brewed, which made her its mother and the fucked-up magic within her a sibling.

And what did siblings do best? Fight.

But if she let *It* out to defend her at the stove, there would be nothing to protect her against *It*.

Venus hoped there'd never come a time when she had to use *It* as a last resort to save her skin. And blood. And bones. She'd rather die first than give over the freedom *It* thought *It* deserved.

"No. Never," Venus gritted out.

"Never say never."

"Are you alive in there?" Janus called into the hazy pink smoke.

"Barely," she croaked, agony raking through her. "Open the window."

Janus commanded the window to sweep up and summoned a gush to help thin out the smoke. Then rushed over to Venus, wrinkling her nose as she assessed the damage.

Patches joined her side, anchoring his eerie gaze on her arm.

"Well," Janus said, attempting optimism, "you didn't lose any fingers this time."

"Lucky me," Venus groaned, tears prickling her eyes. "Patches, could you—"

He snapped the protruding bone back into place with a twist of magic, wrenching a guttural scream from her.

She bowed her back, sobbing, "No, Patches! I was going to say get *the mending potion*."

He bowed his head in apology.

"I'll get it." Janus rushed to a cabinet to fetch one brewed by Elder Glenn. She squatted and uncorked the vial, pouring the syrupy stuff into Venus's mouth.

The potion came alive on her tongue, worming down her throat.

Biting her bottom lip, she kept her cries muffled as bones snapped into place, severed muscle strands and tissues weaved back together, and bloody lesions wrenched shut, sealing themselves into thin scars.

A glaze of sweat broke out all over her skin, her charred and blodied clothes clinging to the dampness.

After a beat, Janus asked, "You good, Vee?"

Venus nodded, sitting upright. Janus helped her up and she stumbled to the kitchen table for a rest. As her eyelids drooped shut, tires screeched, jolting her senses.

Janus hugged herself and shuddered as the arrival triggered the alert ward.

The front door let out a high-pitched whine, then a slam vibrated the air.

Upon entering the kitchen, Clarissa's expression was unreadable. Her arrival added a thick tension to the atmosphere, raising tiny hairs on Venus's nape.

Their mother went to the tamed brew, stirring it. "Damage report?"

"Broken bone," Janus answered for Venus.

"Good," Clarissa noted. "Send a text to Mr. Mouse to let him know the drop-off will happen tonight."

Shock kicked Venus's mind into a scramble. "But why?"

Janus clenched her teeth in a classic *oh-shit* kinda way.

But it was too late to fall back, so Venus steeled her nerves and doubled down. "Why can't I just do it tomorrow?" Her unwillingness anchored her to her seat. The mending potion stitched her back together but didn't strip away the fatigue deep in her marrow.

Her body had broken once tonight.

If she pushed herself any further, she feared it'd break again.

Clarissa narrowed her eyes. "You'll need a clear schedule for tomorrow, Venus. Now do as I say."

Janus watched on helplessly, chewing her thumbnail as a nervous tic.

A silent war of dominance unfolded. Both too stubborn to lose.

A ringtone punctured the intensity.

The sound cracked their mother's glacial front, a flicker of nervousness peeking through before she iced it over again.

She pulled out her phone but didn't accept the incoming call yet.

"The drop-off is *tonight*," Clarissa asserted. Her command felt like a dagger to the gut, killing their conflict for good.

When she marched out of the kitchen with Patches at her heels, she left behind one casualty.

Venus's wounded pride.

Frustration fueled the anger inside her, a bolt of fire giving her weary bones the necessary push to obey like the good little worker bee she was. She stood on unstable knees, planting her palms on the table for support.

The only kind she'd get from here on out tonight.

Venus mustered up enough strength to spoon the potion into the bottle. The glimmery green liquid folded into itself to make room for more.

Meanwhile, Janus tiptoed to the kitchen's arched ingress, poking her head out.

"What are you doing?"

Her sister craned her neck, trying to improve her range of eavesdropping. "She's pissed. Something's happened."

"She's always pissed at someone about something," Venus said as she corked the potion, lifting it to the sunset's dying amber light. A delicate web of vines with flower buds crept across the glass, a tendril choking the bottle's neck. As the concoction cooled, its toxic green hue changed to a deceptively soft fairy-tale pink.

A spectrum of colors splashed onto her face.

How could something so beautiful nearly cost her life?

"Yeah, but this feels different. If I could get a *little* closer." Janus slunk out the kitchen doorway's mouth as their mother's voice went up an octave, but distance and a door muffled the words.

Confusion edged into Janus's tone as she analyzed. "Did she...say *I-don't-care-if-she-knows* or was it *I-don't-care-if-he-knows*? No, I think Mom said *she*. Or maybe, it was *he*." Seconds later, she sucked in a breath. "Oh, here she comes. Here she comes."

She hurried across the kitchen and plucked a box of cookies from a cabinet, shoving two into her mouth to appear inconspicuous.

Venus rolled her eyes at the lousy attempt.

"I'm leaving," Clarissa announced.

Janus spoke around her cookies. "But you just got back."

"A matter needs my attention. Janus, you're responsible for dinner," she stated coolly. "And as for you, Venus—"

Venus's curt response was, "I know. Do the drop-off."

Clarissa ignored the interjection. "After the drop-off, I need you to go to Elder Glenn's. Your reinforcement potions are ready."

Venus had little strength to resist the urge to gawk. "But *you* always go."

"I know. Now, I need *you* to." Clarissa then paused, her gaze sliding between Venus and Janus. "Try not to set things on fire or get anyone killed."

In between her munching, Janus asked, "So, is that a no to sacrificial bonfire parties, then?"

With the little time Mr. Mouse had left, his eagerness to get his hands on his order didn't surprise Venus. He wanted to be back in his son's good graces, even if that meant using a storge potion to carve himself a spot.

After she dropped off the commission, she drove toward Elder Glenn's. Her mind stirred up a fantasy where she poured that brew down Clarissa's throat. But Venus was unsure if it would've been enough to soften her mom's heart or if that version of motherly love was the only type her mom's heart could afford to give.

She parked her car a block away from Elder Glenn's and journeyed the rest of the way on foot. A black curtain peeled away after she knocked on his windowed back door. A corner of an older man's face peeked out.

The door creaked open to reveal the bald, dark-skinned man. A Merlin-like beard framed the immortal frown engraved on his lips, deepening the facial landscape of wrinkles.

"Where's Clarissa?" His suspicious glare pinned her.

"She's busy, so you'll have to deal with me," Venus stated tiredly, every inch of her screaming for rest.

He widened the door's berth, a reluctant invitation. "You're late. Clarissa's never late."

She entered the master brewer's cozy kitchen. Pewter cauldrons and pots hung from a vast ceiling rack above. A kettle hummed a bubbly note on his stovetop.

Shelves and open-faced cupboards teemed with a catalog of ingredients, canned and corked. Brewers were natural hoarders possessed by an innate desire to gather all of nature's riches, for one could never be too prepared.

A curved alcove lingered near the stove, grimoires lining its shelves. Cherished leather-bound heirlooms passed down from generation to generation, from mentor to pupil.

A thick garnet-hued cookbook rested with a split belly on a book stand, its secrets exposed to her eyes if she dared.

"Don't be a coward. Just a tiny peek," It whispered. The encouragement

grew on her like weeds as the reinforcement potion's effects waned. Curiosity beckoned her to oblige—to break a cardinal brewer rule.

Healthy Glow (Trinary-Note)

This potion's purpose is to ensure or maintain a healthy aura. A well-balanced aura generates the reliability of a Drinker's magick if witcher or enhances the overall condition of physical, emotional, and willpower, thereby heightening aura intensity if human. The potion's effects wear off in extreme stress situations. Caution the Patron for—

An aged hand flipped the handwritten book shut.

Venus stepped back, startled.

"You know better than to eye the grimoire of another discipline," Elder Glenn said gruffly.

It barked out a laugh, *its* amusement bursting within her like fireworks. She bit the inside of her cheek to taste blood as punishment for being weak enough to listen to *It*. She needed the obnoxious laughter polluting her head to stop, but she didn't want an audience to see her desperation.

Least of all, a fellow brewer.

It loved to feast on her embarrassment and humiliation.

Guilt averted her gaze. "I've never seen a recipe for a healing potion before."

"As it should be, you brew love. Unless you want to end up magic-less like your mother. Is that what you want to be? Helpless and unremarkable like a human?" Elder Glenn grilled.

Venus looked at the grimoire again, eyeing it in a different light.

No more magic if she broke her pledge by brewing a healing potion.

No more *It*.

"*I'd like to see you try,*" *It* taunted.

Elder Glenn shook his head, as if she bubbled in the wrong answer on a multiple-choice test. "You are your mother's child."

"What's that supposed to mean?" she snapped.

"It means sixteen years ago, she brewed a potion from this very book very well knowing the consequences," he said, slipping it back on the shelf, "and now you want to as well."

Venus blinked, her face scrunching up. "You let her brew one of your potions?"

"They were very persuasive," he admitted tiredly, his fingers lingering on the grimoire's weathered spine. A thoughtful expression softened his face.

"They? Who's they?"

His frown sprung back in place at her questions.

Questions he had no interest in answering.

Or maybe, he deemed her unworthy of answers.

He handed over a fresh batch of reinforcement potions and showed her to the door.

CHAPTER
EIGHT

To a witcher, a coven is like a pack to a wolf. Covens are a crucial part of a witcher's identity and nature. An elected High
Witcher leads covens. An elected Grand Witcher controls a
dominion, a network of local covens. A Grand Witcher is the
highest rank in a witchery hierarchy.

— *Witchery Hierarchy: An Introduction to Witcher Society*

JUNE 17, 2023

VENUS'S BUNNY SLIPPERS SHUFFLED DOWN THE CONCRETE PATH
as she went to retrieve her morning paper. She paused halfway as a low
reverberating hum drifted into her ears, which only meant one thing.

Another witcher had mailed her something of importance.

She went to the mailbox and withdrew a black envelope.

She broke the wax seal of a bubbling cauldron and pushed back the
lip to pull out the invitation.

Witchery had many trades. Smiths forged enchanted metal into
magical items. Scavengers could track any person or thing. An invitation
penned by a Calligrapher opened doors to a destination of the sender's
choosing.

Pen script glistened in morning light with flecks of a Calligrapher's
magic as Venus read.

Brewer Stoneheart,
A joyous occasion is upon us.
As tradition stands, your attendance is a must.
Be patient for this invitation's glow,
For then, a key shall be bestowed.
A ruby drop is the price to pay
To witness this pledging day.

"You idiot," Venus whispered, her voice full of pity.

Pledging ceremonies were rare, because most witchers valued their lives enough not to be brewers. The time had come for a pledgling to devote themselves entirely to this trade and a discipline.

Memories of her pledging day were tearstained.

The screech of rusted hinges and the slam of the screen door jolted her from her thoughts. Mr. Lionel marched down his porch steps and to his morning newspaper.

"Good morning, Mr. Lionel," she called out, adding: "Thank you for the lovely flower you left."

He paused, staring at her as if she had lost her damn mind.

Then like always, he grabbed his morning paper, spat on the asphalt, and continued with his day.

While she craned her neck to see how close he was to the pothole, a sleek black WCTF patrol car turned onto their street.

Venus stiffened, hoping it would continue on its way.

She walked back toward the house at a measured pace, not wanting to draw any attention. She felt a flicker of relief when she was only a wrist's twist away from sanctuary. But the sensation dulled to nothing as brakes whined, a purring engine died, and car doors closed.

A deep imposing voice gave an order. "Hold it right there."

Her heart clobbered her rib cage, hungry to feed off her fear.

Did the WCTF finally catch up to Janus?

Venus closed her eyes and exhaled deeply before facing a salt-and-pepper-haired man in his fifties. A brunet man with a buzzcut and a short beard stood beside him.

They weren't Swiggers.

Swiggers didn't wear suits, neckties, and spit-shined shoes.

Detectives did.

Before her, the detectives had the same anti-witcher guns as Swiggers, which made them untrustworthy. It meant that she and her sister were not safe until these men were far away.

Her nostrils burned and her throat tightened as she breathed in the scent of iron bullets from their holstered guns.

Salt-and-Pepper asked, "Is this the residence of Clarissa Stoneheart?"

Her brow bunched up. "Yes, sir."

She instinctively stepped back when Salt-and-Pepper tugged at his lapel to reach inside his jacket. She should have felt foolish when he pulled out a notepad, but things could still go wrong.

There was still time for her assumptions to be proven right.

He flipped it open, plucking a pen from his breast pocket. "What's your relationship to her?"

"I'm her daughter," she answered.

"And did she give you a name?" he sighed. "Or did she leave that part of the birth certificate blank?"

Buzzcut smirked.

Anger burned in her belly at the mockery.

Don't react.

DON'T react.

DON'T. REACT.

"Venus Stoneheart," she replied, keeping her tone calm. "Did something happen to my mom, detectives?"

"I'll get to that in a minute," Salt-and-Pepper replied dismissively, jotting on his pad. "When was the last time you saw her?"

A sense of dread crept over her like a vine. "Last night."

Buzzcut asked, "Where did she go?"

"I don't know," she admitted.

"Who did she meet with?"

She parted her lips to speak, but Buzzcut held up a hand.

"Let me guess," he said. "You don't know."

The duo exchanged amused glances.

Once more, she asked, "Did something happen to my mom?"

As Salt-and-Pepper kept writing, he gave his partner a permissive nod.

Buzzcut replied flatly, "We regret to inform you the body of Clarissa Stoneheart was found at Meridian Hill Park earlier this morning. We need a blood relative to identify—"

Venus watched as soundless talking lips moved.

An endless sharp ringing clouded her ears, pulverizing her thoughts to dust. She nodded as if she understood everything being said to her, biting her lower lip hard until she tasted blood.

Time slowed down to an unforgiving crawl, warping her perception of reality.

Warping her sense of self.

As Venus tried not to come apart all at once, she did not even realize their departure or that her trembling hand had a note with the city morgue's address.

Her mom's body was on a cold slab, awaiting identification.

Venus clasped a hand over her mouth, wheezed gusts rushing out her nostrils. As her knees buckled, she fell against the front door, sliding downward until her bottom hit the welcome mat.

JUNE 21, 2023

A small gathering crowded an open grave with a coffin suspended over its mouth. An overcast blocked the summer sunlight, bathing this tiny corner of the world in dreary gray. Miss Florence, Coven #1570's High Witcher, recited a passage from an old leather book with yellowed pages, Mr. Jerome at her side.

Janus buried her teary face into Venus's black lace dress. After four days, Venus had cried all she could cry. Now, her sister wept enough for them both.

Uncle Bram gently rubbed their backs as a gesture of quiet solidarity. They had lost a mom. He had lost his baby sister. Aunt Keisha, Tyrell, and her youngest son, eleven-year-old Hakeem, stood beside them, mourning in their own ways.

Throughout Venus's veins, everyone's sorrows ran like a river of ice. The impending rain thickened the air with warmth and humidity, but she was chilled to the bone. Goosebumps covered her skin.

Patches was closest to the coffin. The familiar sat like a statue, his gaze unwavering.

Off to the side, a dour-faced graveyard worker stood watching, arms crossed. As per Limit-12 Law, he had to supervise the event.

Tiny hairs rose on Venus's nape as she sensed *something*. Janus must've felt it too, because she lifted her head, searching for what brought it. Their eyes panned the witcher cemetery and found Malik Jenkins in the distance. Cloaked in a tree's shade, he watched the service.

An observance he wasn't invited to because inviting Clarissa Stoneheart's estranged ex-husband to her funeral would've been fucked up. Still, Malik sent a heart-shaped wreath of white lilies and roses to the grave site. White lilies said *sympathy*. White roses whispered *reverence for the dead*.

At Venus's side, Janus stiffened at the sight of him.

Malik acknowledged them with a somber nod, then vanished into thin air.

Janus clasped her hand over her mouth to muffle her loud sobs as he left.

A limo tailed by an SUV came to a stop. A brawny olive-skinned man in dark shades and a crisp suit exited the limo's front passenger side, opening the next door down. He offered a leather-gloved hand, and an Indian American woman in a black pencil dress and cat-eye sunglasses emerged. Another bodyguard used an umbrella to protect her from the onset of a drizzle.

The Grand Witcher.

A soft grimace of confusion overtook Venus's face.

Why was Madame Sharma here?

Venus felt a dart of hatred hit square in the chest, its needle sinking deep. Her pained eyes swiveled toward the source.

Miss Florence.

Miss Florence shot the Grand Witcher a glare packed with enough hatred to set half of DC on fire. She continued to quote a poetic verse about peace in the afterlife, her commitment unwavering.

Nearly everyone was too lost in their grief to notice.

Except for the Grand Witcher.

Venus caught a glimpse of an emotionless Madame Sharma nodding once at Miss Florence.

The exchange felt like a face-off.

No, like a quiet war.

Whatever the fuck it was, Venus didn't care. It didn't belong at her mom's funeral. She cleared her throat. The noise recalibrated Miss Florence's focus, her gaze returning to her rituals book.

At the funeral's conclusion, the Grand Witcher and her brigade drove off.

Janus crumpled into Uncle Bram's and Aunt Keisha's arms as they led her away. Her painful sobs grew louder the farther they took her from the grave site.

Tyrell hung back, claiming a spot beside Venus as she stared sightlessly at her mom's coffin, an ache nibbling at the rim of the black hole inside her. He slipped his hands into the pockets of his dress pants, keeping silent.

"Don't," she said, her voice soft with exhaustion.

"I ain't said nothing, Vee," he sighed.

"Ty, you've said a lot without saying anything at all." She paused. "Go with them. Janus needs you."

He peered over his shoulder as their family comforted each other by a trio of cars parked along the cemetery's grassy rim. "But what do you need?"

"To be alone," she admitted.

Tyrell heaved a defeated sigh, rubbing his nape. She stole a sideways glance as an uncertain frown curled at his lips.

"Aight," he finally said. "See you at the repast?"

"Yeah, I RSVP'd. It'd be rude if I didn't," Venus said.

Tyrell snorted a laugh, shaking his head. After he left, she edged forward. Her fingertips traced a curved grain on the varnished wood damp with raindrops.

Tears stung the backs of her tired eyes. Morbid thoughts plagued her as she recollected all the moments that led up to this moment.

As per witcher tradition, whoever was closest of kin had to prepare the deceased's body by bathing and dressing it.

Janus didn't have the stomach for it.

So, the responsibility fell to Venus.

From her peripheral, she spotted Mr. Jerome and Miss Florence. She squared her shoulders and straightened up, swirling on her kitten heels to face them.

"Oh, sweetheart," Miss Florence cooed, cupping Venus's cheek. "I'm so sorry this happened."

Did you know it would happen? Venus's tongue burned to fire off that loaded question, but she held back.

Miss Florence's calling was textual precognition, the ability to foresee the future through writing. By touching another, she could glimpse into their *immediate* future, penning an event or a dilemma she called plot points in riddles. Often, she had writer's block, though, unable to find any single plotline simply because the future was fickle as it was selfish, wanting to keep plot twists and endings to itself.

But even then, not all premonitions could be trusted.

Some plots shifted, twisted, and veered off course, except for her own. Her future always stayed on one path. Steadfast and true. Lucky fucking her.

Clarissa had been a loyal client of the old woman's fortune-writing sessions.

Did you know this would fucking happen?

"Thank you, Miss Florence," Venus replied.

Miss Florence glanced at her husband, trying to nudge a word out of him. Jerome had taken her mom's death very hard. He had been in her life since before she even took her first breath. He watched her grow up, then watched Venus and Janus grow.

Mr. Jerome cleared his throat, dabbing his reddened eyes with a handkerchief. "You know we're here for you and your sister, Venus."

Miss Florence smoothed an affectionate thumb over the apple of Venus's cheek. "Yes, come by the house anytime. When tragedies like this happen, the future can seem uncertain. I've got a blank journal with your name on it. A writing session won't cure how lost you feel, but it might give you a hint of what lies ahead."

Why would she want to know her future if she could barely look her past in the face?

As the old couple turned away, Venus glanced at where she had last seen their Grand Witcher. A question she was willing to ask bubbled up within her.

"Actually," she uttered, garnering their attention. "There's something I'd like to know."

"Speak your mind, chile," Miss Florence encouraged, her smile grandmotherly.

"I know High Witchers have to report all coven deaths to the Grand Witcher's office, but that doesn't explain why Madame Sharma came today." Venus paused. "Don't you think it's odd she did?"

Miss Florence's smile thinned into a straight line. "I don't think it's odd at all. Sometimes, old friends like to pay their respects, too."

Venus threw up behind the Golden Coin, her sorrow manifesting as bile. She braced her hand against the brick wall, gulping deep breaths to bury her sobs. High heels clicked on asphalt. A manicured hand ushered a plain bar napkin into her sight. Venus accepted the gesture and dabbed her mouth dry.

Clearing her throat, she croaked, "Thanks."

"Always doing everything on your own." Sadness dyed Aunt Keisha's one-note laugh. "Even mourning."

Venus straightened her backbone, still facing the wall. "How did you know I was here?" She hadn't gone inside to join the repast yet and be the grieving daughter for a live audience.

"A hunch," Aunt Keisha sighed. "The day we buried your daddy, I found Rissa in this spot doing exactly what you're doing. So close yet so far away."

The two regarded each other for a heavy moment.

Venus swept her stinging eyes over Aunt Keisha.

She didn't want a heartfelt conversation or a back-alley therapist.

She needed to survive any way she could now.

"I'll be there in a minute," Venus promised, her smile weak and fake as fuck. Aunt Keisha seemed equally conflicted by and resigned to by the reassurance.

Then she stepped into Venus's personal space and kissed her forehead. "I got you, baby girl. You know that, right?"

The tender act stirred nothing in her.

No sense of comfort or warmth or love.

She felt like the Tin Man.

Hollow with no heart.

Venus didn't answer. She closed her eyes and waited in the dark of her mind to be left alone again.

Once her aunt returned inside, she sat on a stack of crates.

"Poor, poor little Venus," It cooed mockingly. *"No mommy or daddy anymore."*

Underneath the nothingness, a tiny ember of anger flickered to life in her chest.

"Fuck you, *It*," she said dully.

It tsked. *"Oh, you can do better than that."*

The bar's creaky back door opened again.

Footsteps grew closer.

"Please," Venus snapped, burying her face into her hands, "gimme a minute."

"Take all the time you need."

The voice froze her blood. Her gaze slowly traveled upward and settled on a familiar face.

"Presley." She swallowed at the thick lump in her dry throat. "You came."

They squatted down to her level. "Of course."

Her finger twisted around a loose black thread hanging from her dress's hem, blood swelling in her fingertip. "Why aren't you inside with everyone else?"

"First off, it's a full house in there. Second, *you're* not in there."

Witchers couldn't even gather in numbers to mourn at funerals. So, secret repasts were like a middle finger to the Limit-12 Law. Uncle Bram invited all of Coven #1570's members, hoping a packed bar would smother the grief.

Or at least, help pretend it wasn't there.

Presley opted not to attend the funeral with their grandparents to keep attendance at the grave site low. Since Bram chose the Golden Coin as the repast's venue, the old couple stayed home. The bar's reputation as a hellmouth to an underworld of witcher crime never sat well with the community's oldheads.

An enchantment of invisibility hid it well, but as a one-stop shop for all needs and greed, it attracted desperate humans to a neighborhood desperate for peace.

She released a tiny breath as a sharp knife sunk into her achy chest. "It's easier to just...exist out here."

Presley nodded their chin toward the back door. "Bram's about to make a toast."

"So, you're here to fetch me?"

Presley's lip corner quirked up, then fell back into line. "Naw, I'm just here for you."

Venus nodded, coiling the thread tighter until it finally snapped. Presley gathered up her hand, gently unraveling the string. Her lashes swept shut as she felt something she didn't think possible on a day like this.

A twinge of relief.

Presley massaged her fingertip, smoothing the blood back into place.

Between them, silence thickened the air until it became unbearable for her.

"A few weeks before Mom—" Venus broke off, unable to bring herself to say the word *died*. "Janus asked me why Mom was the way she was with us. I had no answer. Still don't. Yesterday, I *washed* and *dressed* the body of the woman who raised me, Pres, and I *barely* knew her. Isn't that fucked up?"

Tears pushed against her eyes, but she crammed her lids tighter to keep them at bay.

"Very, but she raised—"

She interjected, "A criminal. A murderer."

"—a devoted daughter who'd do *anything* for her family," Presley finished, their eyes softening. "You took up brewing to help out."

Venus snatched away her hand. "What did that get us, Pres? Because my family needed money, I took a client behind Mom's back. Then everything went sideways, you got caught up in it, and now we're both deviants. All because of me."

"It wasn't your fault. You didn't know—"

She leaned in, anger mottling her face. "If it wasn't my fault, *why* did you leave, Presley? *Why* did you cut me out of your life for three damn years?"

Silence. The kind of silence that spoke volumes.

"I'm not mad you left, Pres," Venus said. "I would've done the same thing. I'm mad you'd rather lie than tell a truth we *both* know."

A conflicted look outfitted Presley's face, their eyebrows folding down.

"It's been more than a minute, baby girl." Aunt Keisha came back outside, intruding on the reunion. "Oh, am I interrupting something?"

"No," they both lied smoothly.

"I'm just saying my goodbyes." Presley gave her forehead a soft peck, then stood. "I'm sorry I can't stay."

It whispered, *"They can't stay because you drove them away."*

As Venus watched Presley go, her aunt watched her watch them go.

Aunt Keisha then escorted her inside, boldly linking arms with her. They passed the Black Book's phone booth, making her realize she didn't just lose a mom.

She lost a boss.

"You can't be empty-handed," Aunt Keisha reasoned, towing her toward the bar counter.

Nisha Sharma carried Kiwi, her parakeet familiar, on her shoulder while she served as bartender for the night. The sight surprised Venus as she only saw the woman use her hands to hold a drink, count money, and draw blood.

Earlier that day, her younger sister, the Grand Witcher, had attended the funeral unannounced with an entourage of guards. Now, as a courtesy to Uncle Bram, Nisha acted as the repast's barkeep. Despite their reputation as cutthroats, both Sharma sisters displayed compassion in their own way today.

"Two whiskeys, please."

"Two whiskeys coming right up."

As soon as Aunt Keisha got what she asked for, she assessed Venus, looking for chinks in her armor like her mom did.

Past tense, as in never again.

The thought drove a blade of sorrow straight into her heart, but she bottled the sob in her throat like a potion.

Not here.

Not in front of her aunt.

Not in front of the others.

Adjusting her black headband, Venus sighed wearily. "I'll be fine, Aunt Key."

They both knew it was a lie, but it was enough to evict her aunt from her personal space.

Nisha fixed her another option, pouring from a brass pitcher.

With a barstool's help, Venus claimed a seat on the countertop, accepting her new drink. "What's this?"

"It looks like vodka, but it tastes like water." Nisha smirked, adding, "I know you're not a drinker anymore, little Stoneheart."

Venus shot her a glance of gratitude as Uncle Bram lifted a shot glass high, demanding the attention of all.

His voice seemed to fill up every crook and cranny of the Golden Coin. "I'd like to pose a toast to my sister."

As if he had cast a spell of submission, all in attendance raised their glasses high.

"Every struggle and tragedy Clarissa Abigail Stoneheart faced strengthened the wall she built to protect herself and her daughters," he said. "Her daughters were her whole damn world. She showed her love her way, but she would've killed for them. She would've died for them without hesitation."

Uncle Bram locked eyes with Venus. "Everything she did, she did for you and your sister."

"To Auntie Rissa," Tyrell shouted.

"To Clarissa!" The room chorused.

Venus spiraled with no relief to soften the fall. A remedy wouldn't help her forget how broken she'd be upon impact. She was now an orphan of a dead father she didn't remember and a dead mom she had known all her life but never understood.

Venus gazed into her water as everyone else downed their choice of booze.

For a moment, liquor dangled the promise of numbness in her face.

Although Venus wanted not to feel for just a little while, she recognized it was pointless.

Some folks were destined to feel everything.

So, she sipped her water and felt.

"Has pitying oneself ever helped anyone?" Nisha pondered. Her curiosity caused her feathered familiar to cock its head at Venus.

"Neither has listening to advice in dark, dingy bars," Venus replied, the sorrow loosening her tongue. A soft pink muscle Nisha could've easily cut out of her mouth for such disrespect.

Instead, Nisha hid her smile as she tasted her poison.

"And what advice would you like to give me? This, too, shall pass? When life gives you lemons, make lemonade?" Venus asked, grappling to subdue her bitterness.

"Oh, heavens no," Nisha giggled, stealing another taste. "Death changes something in you. You die in a way. It sours any of your sweetness. It paints your heart black."

Shivers crawled down Venus's spine as Nisha's words swept over her.

"Accept that you're not the same person you were, but don't pity yourself. Self-pity doesn't turn back time. That's like being trapped in a cage while life goes on," Nisha said. "So, what will it be, Venus Stoneheart? Will you embrace what you've become?"

"I guess only time will tell," she muttered, peering at her distorted reflection trapped in the water. Nisha's questions seeped into her psyche like a perennial stain.

Tyrell came over, his face taut with worry.

He rubbed the back of his neck. "Uh, Janus locked herself in the restroom."

CHAPTER
NINE

A deviation is a contaminated volatile form of a witcher's calling due to severe trauma. In some cases, this mutated magic can temporarily infect and manipulate witchers and humans alike.

—*Witchery Hierarchy: An Introduction to Witcher Society*

IN A DIMLY LIT CORRIDOR, TYRELL GUIDED HER TO THE RESTROOMS.

Venus knocked on the restroom door, her voice gentle and tired. "It's me, Jay. Open up."

As moments bled by, she pressed her forehead against the wood. Her sister's grief soaked through, spilling over her skin.

"Janus, you gotta let me in. It's just you and me against the world now." An old memory became fresh again as she closed her eyes. "The day Mom bonded us with a blood-tether, do you remember what she made us promise each other?"

One day, Clarissa kept them home from school. She welcomed them underneath her blankets. Showing them a knife, she said, *"The world will turn against you for being what you are and when that day comes, the two of you'll need each other to make it through. I won't always be here to protect you. Bram and Keisha won't always be here to protect you."*

Then, she sliced their young palms, instructing them to hold hands and utter the blood-tether's spell.

Faced with silence, Venus continued, "My blood is your blood and your blood is mine—"

The lock clicked undone and the door creaked open.

Holding Patches close to her chest, a teary-eyed Janus choked out, "Let our fates intertwine as a part of a greater design. Unbreakable this bond through rain, hail, and shine."

She squatted to put the familiar on the floor, giving his ear a loving scratch.

Venus helped her sister stand up, then engulfed her in a hug. "Not even death can break us apart."

"I miss her so damn much, Vee," Janus cried, burying her wet face into Venus's neck.

"I know. Me too," she whispered.

"Why would someone do this to her? Why would they take her away from us?"

Iron bullets took their mom's life. A fate identical to a string of other witcher victims. But there was no eagerness from the detectives assigned to the case to determine who was responsible.

Dead witchers didn't get justice.

"They'll get what's coming to them, Janus," Venus promised.

"I just want to talk to her one more time," her sister whimpered.

Tyrell replied hesitantly, "Uh, I might be able to help with that. I've got a Ouija board back at the house."

Venus squinted at him warningly, freeing a hand to smack him upside the head. "Now's not a good time to be a jackass, Ty."

He winced, massaging the sore spot. "I'm not joking. Y'all know great-Auntie Georgette was a medium. She taught me a thing or two when I was little. We don't need a Ouija board, but Spirits like to communicate by possessing an inanimate object or a person. So, which one of y'all wants to volunteer?"

Silence.

Tyrell shook his head. "Mm-hm, thought so. Ouija board it is. Y'all down for it or naw?"

Janus broke away from her, sniffling. "I'm in."

Then the duo turned their attention onto Venus, and she hated how they stared at her so expectantly, waiting for her to agree without a second thought.

To go along with this meant she'd have to break her vow of abnegation, which came with its own set of consequences.

"Looking at me like that isn't going to make me say yes any quicker. This is an all-around bad idea. None of us have a calling in mediumship. All kinds of foolery could go wrong. There's not even a guarantee that Mom'll even respond."

"But what if she does, Venus? What if we asked her what happened? Who took her away from us? Are you telling me you wouldn't jump at the opportunity?" Janus said, her tone brimming with impatient anger. "Yes, it's us against the world, but the world took our mom away from us. I can't sit around and do nothing."

"*You can almost see her heart turning black in her chest,*" It chuckled. "*Yours was black long before then, though. Remember what you and Presley did?*"

Venus ignored It, focusing on the pain that glistened in her little sister's eyes.

"Alright. I'm down."

The trio gathered around a Ouija board on the living room floor, while lit white candles were situated in a circle around them. Tyrell flipped through the pages of great-aunt Georgette's leather-bound journal as the host sat at the table.

Hakeem happened by on his way to the kitchen and snorted. "Mom's gonna freak if she knows you're playing around with that thing. You remember what happened last time?"

Venus blinked, a sharp frown carving into her face. "Last time? What happened last time?"

"Not enough practice," he answered.

"That's not very reassuring." Venus leered at him.

As his annoyance sifted through her, he said, "Communicating with the dead never is."

Hakeem added from the kitchen, "You're not gonna be able to hold shape if you keep wearing out your magic."

"Can you worry about you, please?" Tyrell snapped.

Her cousins' sidebar argument inspired a headache to barge into Venus's head. "Are we doing this or naw?"

"We're doing this." Janus kept her tears at bay, her tone determined. "There's no turning back now."

He settled on a specific page and ran his finger along the spell scribed before he glanced around the group. "Hold hands and close your eyes."

The trio acted out the command. Magic hummed as sacred as breath, but if concentration was Tyrell's aim, hearing the microwave's digital beeps in the background as Hakeem prepared to heat a nighttime snack wasn't helping.

Tyrell growled, "Keem!"

"My bad, my bad," Hakeem squeaked.

When Patches laid across the lid of the Knox family's terrarium, Leap, a brown tree frog familiar, began barking.

Over the dull hum of the microwave at work and Leap's racket, Tyrell cleared his throat and commanded, "Repeat after me."

Restlessness grew underneath Venus's flesh like a fungus as she expected a severe penalty for the infidelity she intended to commit.

Spirits, spirits, hear our cry.
We come before you but an ally.

As she uttered the first words, her vow of abnegation snapped like a bone, agony exploding within her like a bomb. Blood gushed out her nostril and crawled down her face, dribbling onto her chest. Tears rivered her cheeks. She quivered and gripped their hands tighter, climbing over the dire urgency to topple and suffer.

We're grateful for all that you do
And your generosity is what we need of you.
There is a soul that we seek,
Let her come forth.
Let her speak.

As they concluded the spell, her pain died down to a soft whimper, petering out. A visible shudder rushed through their bodies, and an airy sigh breezed across the room, coaxing goosebumps onto their collective flesh.

Their eyelids snapped open in unison, the candles' flames stretching wildly.

Croaky whispers of too many voices caressed the crevices of their minds, chanting eagerly, "*Her name, children. Her name.*"

"Clarissa Abigail Stoneheart," they chorused.

Like repelling magnets, their joined hands broke apart, but the separation was short-lived as their fingertips gathered on the heart-shaped planchette lying on the board. Their faces reflected the terror congregating inside Venus. Their bodies were no longer theirs.

Hakeem strolled by with his hot pocket on a plate, tsking. "You should've learned from last time."

"Not right now, Keem," Tyrell ground out, exercising the only function the Spirits allotted him.

Venus narrowed her eyes toward her sister. "Is this the part where I say I told you so?"

Ignoring the question, Janus chose to bicker instead. "Tyrell, I thought you said the Spirits *only* possessed people if there wasn't an inanimate object around?"

With a suck of his teeth, Tyrell said, "I ain't say that. I said Spirits could possess an inanimate object *or* a person. The operative word is *or*. Spirits like having options, and these Spirits have the option to do both."

Janus huffed, "Wonderful! We're all going to d—"

The planchette twitched underneath their fingertips.

They glanced at each other uneasily.

A smothering silence hung in the air, pressing in and holding tight.

Janus gulped, then whispered, "Mom? Is that you?"

Their fingertips guided the planchette slowly across the polished wood board, landing on a YES, which lingered by a smiling sun near the board's left corner.

Venus let out a shaky breath at the revelation, and Janus blubbered. Her dead mom's voice at her fingertips pushed her over the edge.

Tears bubbled up hot and stinging as she demanded, "Who did this to you? Tell us!"

The planchette slid toward the black letters branded on the board and picked out each letter.

L-E-A-V-E

I-T

B-E

With the message spelled out, the candles' flames winked out one by one.

The group regained control of their bodies limb by limb.

"Leave it be?" Venus repeated in disbelief, her eyes growing wild. "Leave it be!" She screamed and shot to her feet. "Even in death she's so goddamn controlling!"

Janus choked on a sob as she raced out of the living room, locking herself into another bathroom.

"Even in death, she doesn't trust you to bring those who killed her to justice. Avenge her, Venus. Start a war until you find peace," It cooed.

The mention of war had appealed to her, if but for a moment.

Her stomach twisted and churned in disgust—in regret.

"Let me out, Venus. Let me help," It pleaded sweetly.

"Stop it, stop it, stop it," she yelled, stumbling across the room. She repeatedly banged her head against the wall, punishing herself for even daring to consider *Its* offer.

"Venus, stop it!" Tyrell demanded.

A curious Hakeem stepped foot into the room. "What's going on?"

"Let me out, let me out, let me out," It bit out. *"Yes, fuck, yes!"*

Venus shook her head frantically, chanting *no* in a surging panic.

Why wasn't the reinforcement potion working?

"Hakeem, go back into your room!" Tyrell shouted a millisecond too late.

She broke like a dam. Raven-black stems of magic flooded out of her in search of prey.

Tyrell leaped over a couch to reach his brother, but *It* was faster, stabbing him in the back. Then *It* took shelter in Venus again, rich laughter bathing her insides.

He froze and his jaw slackened, a dark stain glossing over his unfocused eyes. Venus cupped her hands over her mouth, her chest heaving from ragged breath.

Hakeem's meek, uncertain voice whispered, "Ty?"

Tyrell snapped out of his trance, his sheer rage slamming into her chest. A crude growl escaped him as he lunged at his brother, his hands swiftly coiling around Hakeem's neck. They fell to the floor in a heap, Ty's arms trembling as he choked the boy with all his might.

Hakeem forced out a struggling gasp, too young and powerless to fight. His potent fear squirmed inside her, desperate for air.

Venus scrambled around the living room, whipping her attention in all directions as she searched for anything to stop all this madness. She grabbed a lamp as Patches vaulted off the terrarium, his lips curling in a snarl. Leap left his tank, following suit.

Patches rammed into Tyrell's head to stop the attack. Tyrell rolled off Hakeem from the blunt force, his unconscious body sprawling across the floor.

Hakeem coughed violently, rubbing his throat. As Leap came between Venus and them, his barks grew desperate. She was a Knox by blood, so he couldn't stop her as Patches did to Tyrell.

Loyalty to Stonehearts made the cat powerless against her, too.

Which meant no one could stop her.

No one could save her or them from *It*.

She dropped the improvised weapon, hot-white shame ripping her in two.

"Venus." A pointed intake of breath yanked her gaze to a horrified Janus.

"I...Janus, I don't know what happened. I didn't mean to—" The words shriveled in her throat as she took a cautious step forward, and Janus flinched accordingly. No words could erase the horror stenciled on her sister's face or the trust fractured.

Not even her dead mom trusted her.

So, she did what cowards did best and ran.

How could she expect anyone to trust her when she couldn't even trust herself?

A jittery Venus stalked up to the windowed back door, knocking desperately.

"No appointment," a cranky gruff voice bled through the door, "no time of day."

Venus leaned in and whispered, "It's me, Elder Glenn."

He glowered as he let her in. Adrenaline and guilt siphoned through her, tangling together meanly.

"Is there a reason you're bothering me at this hour?" He cocked a gray bushy eyebrow. "Without an appointment, no less? As a brewer, you should know the importance of wasting valuable time."

"Our family's familiar had to knock my cousin out to stop him from choking his little brother because It broke free," Venus said.

He scoffed as he shuffled to his whistling kettle to tend to the matter.

As he busied himself with fixing a mug of hot tea, he said, "As a brewer, you know a trinary-note potion's effects can last months. You've consumed one every day for the last three years. Clarissa and I knew reinforcement potions were a temporary solution to your problem. She also knew that your dependency on them would be detrimental. I told her as such. In giving you one, Clarissa encouraged you to avoid your deviation, not to master It. Instead of facing your problems, your mother taught you how to bury them."

A prescription of reinforcement potions and the practice of abnegation was supposed to keep It in check and stifle Its influence over her. A persuasive motive to soften the harsh reality of becoming the next Stoneheart brewer.

"There has to be another way to keep It at bay," she urged, desperation burrowing into every syllable.

"Let's be honest with ourselves, Stoneheart. You don't want to keep your deviation bottled up forever. You want total eradication."

Her hands curled tightly at her sides as she heard his unadulterated pity.

A subliminal plea for her to give up and go home.

"That's exactly what I want!" she snapped, marching over to his alcove bookcase. "We both know there's only one way to do that."

Venus rose to the tips of her toes and grabbed the wine-red grimoire her mom used to break her brewer's pledge and forfeit every drop of her magic. She slammed it onto the counter, flipping frantically through the pages.

Tears rivered down her cheeks and dripped onto penned recipes lifetimes older than her. "Which recipe did she use, Elder Glenn? I want to continue the family tradition!"

"I forbid this!" When his hands grabbed her shoulders, she jerked away from him, throwing back an elbow that hit him square in the face. The impact knocked his head back and a colorful curse word flew out of him. He wrapped his arms around her waist, dragging her away from the grimoire.

Venus flailed and thrashed in his hold, reaching a desperate hand out for an anchor. She grabbed a fistful of a page yellowed by time, ripping it out.

"Think, Stoneheart, think! If you break your pledge, how will you take care of your sister?"

The question knifed through her, bleeding out all her defiance as a reminder seeped in.

She wasn't just a destroyer.

She was a big sister, too.

Venus squeezed her teary eyes shut and went still.

Elder Glenn's words washed over her. "No magic, no potions. No potions, no money."

He let her go.

Reality strapped weights of responsibility on her, forcing her to sink to her knees.

Towering over her, he panted. "You've prolonged the inevitable long enough, Stoneheart. Sister Nature and Sister Magick are ancient and relentless forces. They never do as told. They rebel, never fitting the cage in which we attempt to contain Them. I know this better than most."

A thoughtful expression settled on his face as he gazed at a framed photo of a woman on a shelf lined with purple succulents.

Succulents symbolized undying love.

Venus knew precisely what he meant.

As a brewer disciplined in health, Elder Glenn could not treat his sister Yolanda's aggressive breast cancer by her own wish. He continuously put himself within inches of death, bearing through high degrees of recoil until she could no longer stomach his suffering.

"You must learn to live with your deviation or be consumed by *It*," he said, extending a wrinkly hand. "Now, give me the recipe."

Venus handed him the crinkled paper. "You want me to accept a death sentence."

"It's not always a death sentence, Stoneheart. Live with *It*."

"I tried to"—her voice cracked—"but *It* hurts people."

Horrific memories flushed through her system. The overwhelming scent of blood, the loud claps of four gunshots, and *Its* pleased laughter saturated her senses.

"I'm familiar with your past, Stoneheart," Elder Glenn said, opening the torn paper. "I sympathize with your plight. However, you aren't the only one here cursed with the misfortune of watching others die around them."

"Then you know there's no learning how to coexist with *It*. So, if you can't help me, then I respect that," Venus said, using her laced sleeve to wipe away her tears, "but don't tell me to let The Sisters have Their way with me."

As he eyed the recipe, Elder Glenn let out an uncharacteristic low chuckle. "Sister Nature allows you to find chaos in order and order in chaos. There are 544 recipes in that grimoire. In a moment of chaos, *you* tore out the exact recipe your mother used to break her pledge."

Shock rippled through her and pooled into her trembling hands.

Leave it be.

He returned to the grimoire, laying the paper where it belonged. "Sister Nature will do whatever She likes with you, Stoneheart."

Venus felt *It* in her bones, asleep and sated, while she suffered.

She swallowed at the thickening lump in her throat to smooth away the quivers in her voice. "I refuse to wait around to see what Sister Nature has next for me."

Rising to her feet, she made her way to the back door. "I'll figure this out on my own."

"Let's hope whatever you come up with won't get you killed."

Venus looked over her shoulder, pinning him with her reddened eyes. "Maybe, that's what She has planned for me next."

Then she left, somehow feeling heavy and hollow.

CHAPTER
TEN

Maintenance of magic requires two practices: purification and restoration. A purification bath rids a witcher's body of impurities caused by exposure to iron and other repellents. A restoration potion or tea replenishes magic depleted by illness or overexertion. A witcher's magic may turn against them if neither is done regularly.

—Witcherpedia, an online witchery encyclopedia

JUNE 24, 2023

TO PURIFY MEANT TO SWEAT SO THE IMPURITIES COULD FIND A NEW host. Milk and scalding water acted as a singular conduit, a channel of ease for contaminants to travel through. Fresh flowers were used as a sacrificial host, withering up as the impurities took hold.

Most witchers partook in Purification like clockwork monthly.

Brewers, however, did it more frequently to maintain their vow of abnegation's integrity. Though Venus had renewed hers three days ago, only time and fidelity could fortify it. Could make her worthy of it.

I denounce my magick for this pledge of import
Never to be broken as a final resort
To the life of a brewer, I'm eternally pledged

Though rewards and consequences are wicked and edged
To breathe life into this inanimate brew
May The Sisters show mercy for what I must do
Beyond a cauldron, this vow I will keep
If betrayed, the price paid shall cut and be steep

Since the séance three days ago, regret haunted Venus.

Neither she nor her sister had the bravery to mention what went down.

After Aunt Keisha returned from the repast, Tyrell and Janus confessed to the incident. Not the séance. Hakeem backed them up. Venus called to apologize the next morning. Too ashamed to do it in person. Too scared of what her fucked-up magic might do next.

Tyrell assured her that everything was fine between them.

Hakeem forgave her.

Aunt Keisha pitied her.

Despite all that, Venus hated herself for being irresponsible. She should have refused the séance, but she didn't. When she broke her vow of abnegation, the consequences helped *It* escape.

Her misfortune was entirely *her* own fault.

"Stop hogging all the room." Janus splashed milky bathwater on her for encouragement.

Unbothered by her sister's disdain, she snuggled the back of her neck against the tub's curved rim, her fingers toying with a silky petal floating by. The ocean of lit wax candles tinted them in a lazy amber glow.

Janus's brow creased, her troubles darkening her face. "I think we're terrible daughters. Vee, I think we should do more than this. Someone killed our mother and they're still out there."

"You know what she said." A speckle of irritation swelled within her, their mother's postmortem command steeping within her mind.

Leave it be.

The words felt like twisting stabs to whatever remained of her heart. She wished her sorrows were an impurity, but no flower-laced milk bath could wash that away.

Sorrow couldn't spiral down the drain.

"Well, she's not here to call the shots anymore, Vee," Janus growled. "We get to make the decisions now. I don't care what it takes or how many doors I've got to knock down to get some answers."

Venus exhaled sharply, narrowing her eyes. "And if you knock on the wrong door, trouble will answer, Jay. Have you already forgotten that the WCTF has a bounty on your head?"

Janus slinked her shoulders. A flicker of worry rippled across her face, but she recovered. "I'm not afraid of the WCTF anymore."

"Well, I am," Venus snapped, rawness oozing in her words. "I've already had to bury a mom, but I refuse to let you die before me, Janus. I forbid you from doing whatever foolery you've got planned."

A shocked laugh erupted from the other end of the tub. "You forbid me? You can't tell me what to do!"

Authority lit up in Venus's eyes. "Mom gave Uncle Bram guardianship over you, and Uncle Bram left me in charge of you. So yes, I can tell you exactly what you'll do."

Janus crossed her arms stubbornly, like a defiant child. "And if I don't?"

"Then I'll pour a peitho potion down your throat," Venus assured venomously. "Don't try me, Jay."

She didn't want to force-feed her sister an idea, but needs always outweighed wants.

She had already lost *too* much.

Any more, she'd lose her damn mind.

Lose herself.

Lose to *It*.

Janus gaped. "You're a fucking monster."

"And water's wet," she tossed back, sharpening her tongue.

Janus jerked to her feet, milky water sloshing. She snatched a towel off a wall rack and stormed out of the bathroom, screaming her frustration. As Janus moved farther away, her frustration loosened its painful grip on Venus's insides.

She dunked herself underneath the water, a self-prescribed baptism to wash away all her wrongdoings, but instead, she watered her internal hate and it bloomed twofold.

"You're becoming more and more like your mother each day," It whispered affectionately. *"All the worst parts of her."*

Venus ripped herself upright, gasping violently for air. As her magic oozed from cracks in her flimsy vow of abnegation, she hunched as pain festered inside her bones. The flowers floating around her withered an unnatural black. Tentacles of darkness emanated from her, slithering hungrily around the waters. She scrambled out of the bathtub, her dripping body clambering over the edge.

She grunted as she hit the floor.

"It was foolish as fuck of me to think you'd leave me the fuck alone for a while," Venus hissed, crawling back.

It hadn't so much as said a peep in the days since the incident at Aunt Keisha's. Venus wasn't sure if the stunt at the séance weakened *It* or if doubling up on reinforcement potions actually worked.

"Consider my silence a token of gratitude for letting me out to play for a little while."

"You aren't supposed to come out and play at all!"

It chuckled, *"My time is coming, Venus. You'll see."*

On slippery feet, Venus hurried out of the bathroom. She slammed the door shut as if trying to cage in the culprit. But it was free to roam inside her. *It* was an impurity within her body she couldn't rid herself of, poisoning her mind and will for as long as she took a breath.

In this war of theirs, one of them had to surrender.

JUNE 25, 2023

An eerie sense of overwrought dread had made a home within Venus Stoneheart. A desirable neighbor for another dreadful thing her body housed. As expected, the potency of her reinforcement potions dulled. Drinking them, however, gave her a sense of normalcy, which she desperately wanted to cling to.

With time running out, Venus took an uncharacteristic novel approach to find a silver lining: at least she still had time on the clock.

Neither Janus nor Bram had an inkling they were eating breakfast alongside a girl tangled in a vicious battle for dominance. Her body, the prize. Around her, a conversation unfolded. While physically present, her mind wandered elsewhere, stuck waist-deep in thought.

Uncle Bram posed, "What we gonna do this year for that old cat's hundred-and-fifty-first anniversary?"

"I don't care," Janus said, her tone full-on grump, "as long as we don't have to wear those cheesy mouse-ear party hats like we do *every* year."

He sucked his teeth at that. "Aye, I pay good money for those hats."

"You already ordered them, didn't you?" Janus sighed heavily.

A pause. "They'll be here next week."

Venus awoke from her daze after being kicked under the table. She hummed a quizzical *hm*.

"Pass the coffee," Janus huffed impatiently, pointing a forkful of syrupy pancakes at the glass pot slightly out of reach as if a soft push of magic was too illogical a choice.

Venus saw through her sister's games. Janus, the WCTF fugitive at large, was still furious about being denied a chance to play a vengeful vigilante. The threat of being potioned into submission infiltrated her so much, she committed to punishing Venus in tiny ways. However, the rush she felt from the minor acts were mostly fleeting as Venus pretended to be unfazed.

Remorse flooded her heart for being at odds with her little sister when they needed each other the most.

"Here you go." She smiled unwaveringly, complying with Janus's request. "Anything else?"

Janus's fork clinked as she dropped it onto her plate. "You know what? I lost my appetite."

Then she stomped out.

Venus didn't mind being the villain in Janus's eyes if it meant keeping her safe.

"Like to give me a heads-up on what the hell was that all about?" Bram queried over the rim of his newspaper.

Venus sipped her coffee, accepting the intense interaction as the new norm. "She wants to avenge Mom's death like a superhero. I told her no because Mom told us no."

Bram blinked his eyes in utter surprise, trapped in gaps he needed her to fill in for him.

"We may have taken part in a séance after Mom's repast," Venus admitted, wincing in anticipation of Bram's reaction.

Séances performed by young inexperienced witchers often ended badly. The Spirits were easy to offend as being dead often made them cranky for apparent reasons. An angry Spirit might slip itself into a new body for a taste of life, or worse, you yourself might become a Spirit leaving behind your mangled corpse.

They all made it out alive but not unscathed.

Uncle Bram frowned deeply, curved wrinkles carving his cheeks. "Y'all been keeping this from me the whole time?"

He didn't point two fingers of blame.

Just the one aimed at her, the responsible older sister.

"I didn't want you to worry." Venus dragged her teeth along her bottom lip. "But I promise everything's under control."

The lie rolled off her tongue so easily she almost believed it herself, but it was a futile effort as Uncle Bram stared at her, unconvinced. Then his broad shoulders shook as he let out an exasperated laugh, his magic folding the newspaper and dropping it aside.

"If everything were under control, y'all wouldn't be keeping secrets from me. You know, like the fact Janus amputated a Swigger's arm and now she's wanted by the WCTF."

Venus gaped at him, a defensive panic tensing her up. "Uncle—"

He held up a hand, forcing her words down her throat.

"Don't, Vee. It's much too late for that now. Good thing I read the newspaper every day, or I'd be in the goddamn dark. I've just been waiting for somebody to fess up, but *a séance*? Y'all done lost y'all's damn minds," he said, his tattooed snake shaking its rattle.

A sign Venus needed to tread lightly. Her shoulders slumped as if she were a disobedient child at the other end of a well-deserved stern talking. But the fact he didn't know what happened *after* the séance gave her some ease.

The only one who could've ratted them out about the incident was Aunt Key. As co-siblings-in-law, she and Uncle Bram had a tight-knit bond. Though they regarded each other as brother and sister, what she'd never be for him was his snitch.

It just wasn't in her DNA.

"With Rissa gone and me in charge, I wanted to give y'all time before

I moved in here on the first of August." Uncle Bram tapped his fingertip on the kitchen table, his strength making it shudder and groan. "Every few days, I come to check in, but y'all have the house to y'allselves for the rest of the summer. To cope and grieve. Not play in Death's face."

"I know I fucked up. Everything's just..." Venus whispered, searching for the right words, but the ones that came didn't do her justice, "...too much."

As his stern expression softened to one of pity, Venus bit her tongue to hold back six words.

Don't look at me like that.

People only pitied her when her misfortunes outweighed theirs. She expected it from the coven or some neighbors, but not Uncle Bram.

Why would he do that to her?

Venus wished he had kept that disappointed look in his eyes. It's what she was used to—not meeting expectations.

"I'm here to help, Venus," Uncle Bram said. "Just tell me what you need."

"I need time to sort through things," she said.

She would do what she did best for her sister's sake. Brewing kept the bills paid and food in the fridge, but only time could fortify her renewed vow of abnegation. She needed every ounce of her power to face a bubbly cauldron.

"That's a tall order to ask for, with all things considered."

Yes, the WCTF threatened Janus's freedom, but only if the anti-witcher law enforcement agency had a lead on her sister's whereabouts. And they didn't, or an army of Swiggers would've swarmed the Stoneheart residence days ago.

Venus rose from her seat, planting her palms on the table as she leaned in. "You best believe I will do everything in my power to protect my sister."

For as long as I can, she added within the depths of her mind.

"Now, you're thinking more realistically," It taunted.

She added, "I want your trust, Uncle Bram, but I don't need it to do what I have to do."

Bram eased back in his chair, eyeing her vigilantly. A sad sort of smile twitched at his lips. Venus should've celebrated the symptoms of his acceptance, but it made her wary of what he could be thinking.

"What?" she probed.

He wagged his head. "You sound like Clarissa."

Shock seized Venus's throat, caging her gasp.

The statement didn't sound like a compliment or an insult. More like an assessment he was conflicted about.

"I had so many conversations like this one with Clarissa about you," he admitted gingerly. "It's funny how things come full circle, but I'll tell you exactly what I told her. When you hold someone tight to protect them, you might be the very force hurting them."

His magic opened his newspaper once more, flipping through the pages. He hummed a *mm-hm* when he found what he had been looking for and offered it to her.

Hesitantly, Venus read the article:

REGISTRATION ACT CASTS
A CONVINCING SPELL

Among this year's parade of legislative offerings, one bill stands out. Senators Roland Fells, Diana Jacklyn, and Gregory Cole have drafted anti-witcher legislation called Bill S.31669. It proposes a registration system accessible to law enforcement agencies and the public, citing public safety.

This extensive bill contains some notable details, such as fields for species type and a witcher's calling for all government-issued licenses. Registration will consist of an investigative process during which witchers fitting the description of fugitives wanted by the WCTF will be cleared or arrested. Witchers who are uncooperative will be charged with obstructing justice.

Senators on both sides face a difficult situation as petitions grow and office lines flood. The Iron Watch and Witchers Against Species Persecution will hold protests in the coming weeks.

On voting day, a handful of senators could tip the scales. The most intriguing wildcard is none other than Senator Winston Mounsey, the young politician who unexpectedly snagged a seat in midterm elections one year ago by beating incumbent—

The newspaper fluttered out of her grasp. She couldn't stomach reading another inked word. Her mind flashed back to the flyers that the Iron Watchers tried to pass out at Carter's Pantry.

She had only glimpsed the blood-splattered header: *Registration Act is a matter of LIFE OR DEATH!* Now, she understood why the Iron Watch sent out their troop of messengers armed with those flyers and a ravenous eagerness to bring the bill to fruition.

The bill's intent was disgustingly ruthless.

Register witchers?

Humans never ceased to amaze her.

First came the Limit-12 Law. Then, humans segregated schools by ironing them up or transferring their children from witcher-tolerant schools to anti-witcher private schools. The humans forced kindhearted business owners like Mr. Jerome to iron up their businesses or risk paying hiked-up insurance costs.

Now, the humans wanted witchers to register, listing their names, addresses, and callings in the name of "public safety," but a witcher's privacy being public knowledge would make them a defenseless public enemy.

Not only that, witchers fitting the description of WCTF-issued fugitives, regardless of guilt or innocence, would endure interrogation and be held in custody until deemed innocent.

Venus tried not to envision Janus being interrogated and tortured in the WCTF's custody until she admitted the truth. She'd spend the rest of her days as an Ironside inmate.

"So, what's the plan, Pinkie?"

"If that bill passes—"

"When," he corrected.

"If," she reiterated precisely, "that bill passes, we'll send Janus to a witcher-friendly boarding school out of the country."

Bram tilted his head. "That kinda tuition is pricey."

Venus thought for a long moment, her mind racing.

"I'll hustle harder," she said. "As long as someone wants a love they can't get on their own, money is easy to come by."

Uncle Bram arched an eyebrow. "Yeah, but Janus in a boarding school?"

"Better a boarding school abroad than an Ironside prison."

The rotary phone's metallic ringing jerked Venus awake, her heart pumping with ragged breaths.

The sound came from her dead mom's room.

A threshold neither Venus nor her sister dared to cross.

Hesitantly, she entered the time capsule, every aspect untouched. A magnificent canopy bed stood as the bedroom's focal point, but the desk tucked away in the far corner drew her attention. The pink rotary phone poured out another bell-like shrill into the night among a wooden holder filled with fountain pens, an opened scheduling book littered with missed appointments, and a framed photo of Clarissa Stoneheart's daughters as young girls with brilliant smiles and wonder-filled eyes.

She picked up the phone. "How did you get this number?"

"From the Black Book," said the caller at the other end, a woman's quavering British voice teetering on the edge of a full-out sob.

"Hello? Hello? Are you there?" the woman cried in a near panic.

Venus cleared her throat and assured, "Yes, I'm listening."

The woman pleaded, "I need your help, Love Witcher. I need it now."

She almost felt guilty for plucking a fountain pen from its wooden home as if she had disturbed a sacred ground. Sandwiching the curly-corded pastel phone between her ear and shoulder to free up a hand, she uncapped the pen and rested its sharp tip on a lined block in the appointment book.

"I can fit you in tomorrow at—"

"No," the caller snapped. "No, I need to see you tonight. I'll even pay you up front. I know your fee for what I want, Love Witcher. I know of your work."

Venus stood irresolute in front of the work desk, feeling like a little girl playing dress-up in her mother's clothes. As if this role she had stepped into was much too big to fill. Answering calls and scheduling clients had always been her mother's duties.

All Venus could think about was, what would Clarissa Stoneheart do? Would she stay firm and risk shooing away a client? Or would she give in to the client's demands?

It chaffed, *"Don't you need money for your little boarding school plan to work? You'll also need extra dough for Janus to survive when you aren't there to take care of her anymore."*

She clenched her jaw tightly at *Its* words, despising herself for seeing small but glittering nuggets of truth in them. She needed money for the final two years of Janus's schooling and life beyond that.

"I normally don't do this," she said, "but I'll make an exception just this once."

The woman chanted her gratitude. "Thank you, thank you, thank you!"

After giving the woman a specific time and a designated location, she hung up the phone and closed her eyes, sorting through the pros and cons of what she had just signed up for.

At this time of night, with such brief notice, there were no routine safeguards to conduct this initial meeting with a potential client. The coffee shop and the car wash were closed. Techie was counting sheep somewhere in the city.

This meeting was risky, but with the threat of Bill S.31669 looming over her head, it was a risk Venus was willing to take.

She quietly exited her mother's room and inched open the next door down, peeking in at her eye-mask-wearing sister, snug as a bug in her bed.

Yes, it was all worth the risk.

Rain slickened the downtown streets, storm clouds blotting out a waning moon. Venus drove toward a bus stop along Pennsylvania Avenue's 30S-line route. If she went farther south, she would pass the pristine white Capitol Hill, where every witcher's fate hung in the balance weeks from now.

After switching between radio stations, she paused on one as its late-night host bickered at his audience: *"Here's a lesson in Punnett squares, you dumbasses. A witcher and a human can have witcher and human offspring. Two witchers can have only witcher offspring. Two humans can only have human offspring. Stop chasing witcher tail if you want to keep your family tree magic-free."*

Venus rolled her eyes, switching off the radio.

The text notification bell made her check her cell phone at a stoplight.

Her body tensed as she recognized who had messaged her.

Pres: i don't like what went down between us.

Four days ago, she demanded Presley admit that she destroyed everything, but it did nothing but drive them away from her. Neither of them had tried to talk things out since then. Every night, she typed out I'm sorry, but she could never bring herself to hit SEND. Instead, she'd tap-tap-tapped her thumb on the BACKSPACE key, caught between shame and cowardice.

The text Presley sent tonight was like the opening of a door she had been too afraid to knock on.

Venus chewed her lip hard as she sent a reply.

Venus: me neither.
Pres: we need to talk tonight. face2face. you home?
Venus: no, but i'll stop by your crib when i'm done.

She nearly jumped out of her skin as a honk brought her back to the road and a green light.

It wasn't long before Venus had the prospective client in her backseat. The woman wore a loose trench coat with an oversized hood to hide her face. It was clear from her aura that she was a witcher.

British-accented words flew out breathlessly. "Thank you for coming on short notice."

Venus ignored the woman's gratitude and merged back into the weak traffic stream. An uneasy silence wafted within the car as she drove toward Columbia Heights, which was only two miles away.

As distrust nibbled at her, she considered dumping the woman on a random curb, but a reminder struck her.

You need this money.

She parked in front of a Greek restaurant.

"The money," she demanded.

"Oh, right. Of course," the woman stuttered and fished through her big purse to recover a brown paper bag, handing it over.

Venus opened the bag and thumbed each stack of money, searching for anything suspicious like a dye pack or a GPS device but found zilch.

"I'm listening," she said.

"My business partner has asked something of me."

"So, you need a potion convincing him otherwise?"

"Not he, dear. *She*. And not quite," the woman admitted, the accent melting away like ice. "I've already done what she's asked."

Venus stilled when she recognized the voice, shock stalling her mind.

Getting rid of her hood, the woman bared her face. "It's good to see you again, little Stoneheart."

"Nisha," Venus whispered, shaking her head slowly in disbelief. "I don't understand."

Nisha smiled. "You will. Soon enough."

CHAPTER
ELEVEN

A trinary-note potion contains three keynotes: a base liquid, a notion, and a drop of anima. While its effect typically lasts ten months to a year, certain trinary-note health potions do possess a lifetime duration. The degree of recoil is severe and often fatal.

—Witcherpedia, an online witchery encyclopedia

VENUS RECEIVED INSTRUCTIONS TO DRIVE TO SWADESH, A DOWNtown Indian restaurant.

When she eased the car to a stop in front of it, a blond-haired man in dark shades and a crisp black suit opened her door. She suspected he'd been assigned as a chaperone. After helping her out of the car, he shadowed her steps to the restaurant entrance.

To keep her on course, fingers of his magic grasped her shoulders.

Under a deep-red awning, two more guards flanked the door in identical uniforms.

More guards lurked inside the dim restaurant. Women and men wore blank-slate faces, their cold eyes observing her every move. A chill rattled down her spine, goosebumps sparking across her flesh.

Venus passed a dining area with long polished tables, glittering red chandeliers, and elaborate arrangements of fresh tuberoses, marigolds, and sunflowers. As she advanced into the establishment, she became increasingly uncertain about what the hell she had gotten herself into.

In the car, Nisha said her business partner was a *she*, ruling out Prospero. But he was the only one Venus could think of who had enough bank to own a place like this and have so many guards.

The chaperone's magic led her down a narrow corridor to an ornate set of arched doors. The doors parted to reveal an intimate banquet room. A spread of tempting cuisine covered a fine dining table. An all-too-familiar face resided at the end of it, dressed in a tailored burnt-orange suit and adorned with an oval locket necklace with black-painted swirls and a long fishtail braid draped over one shoulder.

Venus had never once considered the possibility that Nisha's business partner was her younger sister, Matrika Sharma.

The Grand Witcher.

In the doorway, Venus lingered in awe at her superior's tempestuous aura, which denoted unmatched magic. An unseen force shoved her shoulder and she stumbled into the room.

The doors closed at her back.

A chair slid out, waiting for her.

"Please join me, Venus Stoneheart," the Grand Witcher said.

Walking across the dark wood floors, she lowered her bottom into the seat offered.

"How was the trip?" Madame Sharma asked, cocking her head.

"Lovely," she lied, her backbone stiff as a rod.

Madame Sharma spun a finger slowly aimed at Venus's head. "You've got questions running wild inside there. I'll answer them soon enough."

Venus parted her lips to beg for answers, but the Grand Witcher clucked her tongue.

"As the saying goes, patience is a virtue. It's a good thing you've got a lot, because I don't have much for those who don't keep their tongues to themselves and know their place."

Fear tied Venus's stomach up in knots. She screwed her lips shut, keeping her tongue in check.

"You're such a quick learner," Madame Sharma chuckled softly, crooking a finger at a silent protector tucked away in a shadowy corner. "I would not be a good host if I did not invite you to partake of any of this delicious fare."

An olive-skinned bodyguard with dark hair and a square jaw came to Venus's side. While he draped a red cloth napkin across her lap, his towering stature cast a shadow over her. Then he returned to his designated post.

Venus plucked the fabric off her thighs and dropped it onto the empty plate. "I'll pass."

Madame Sharma inclined her head but did not seem offended by the rejection. The twinkle of interest in the woman's eyes did not go unnoticed by Venus.

And seeing it terrified the hell out of her.

"Very well, then. Let's talk business." Madame Sharma nodded before she sampled from her plate. "I'm in dire need of your services tonight."

Venus blinked in surprise. "And what exactly are you in need of?"

"A trinary-note peitho potion. I hope you're up to the task."

Neither she nor her magic was up for anything.

Her luck fared far better if she skipped into oncoming traffic.

"I'm sorry to disappoint, Your Grandness," Venus stated delicately. "I cannot perform such a request."

Madame Sharma spoke in between her chewing. "Is that so? Pray tell, why?"

"Recently, I broke my vow of abnegation. My magic has yet to replenish fully," she admitted tentatively. "Without enough magic or even my familiar, brewing a trinary-note potion *will* kill me."

The Grand Witcher hummed, nodding her head as she listened.

"Would you like us to fetch your familiar? As old as he is, I'm sure his loyalty is ripe and tasty. That should fortify your vow, correct?"

Venus shifted in her seat, knots coiling in her belly. "I have no appetite for a fealty feast."

Madame Sharma exhaled a mocking sigh, feigning pity. "I suppose by the night's end we'll see if your prediction was accurate, Miss Stoneheart."

"Your Grandn—"

A desperate gasp replaced Venus's words midway.

Her fingers went to her throat as an unseen rope tightened around her neck, choking off her air supply. She let out a gagged scream, and her feet kicked wildly, her eyes bulging. Darkness nibbled at the edges of her sight.

Like a dog on a leash, it jolted her back into the chair.

She let out an ugly desperate gasp after being set free.

Tears swelled in her eyes. Shock tremored through her body.

Madame Sharma tsked at the culprit that put Venus back in her place. "Shame on you, Ilyas. It isn't polite to cut others off when they're talking."

Ilyas stepped into the light once more, bowing his head. "Forgive me, Your Grandness."

"It's not my forgiveness you should ask for," Madame Sharma replied.

"Please forgive me, Miss Stoneheart," Ilyas said, his need for exoneration never reaching his icy gaze. His words meant nothing to either of them, but his eyes told the truth.

He wanted to punish her for disrespecting the Grand Witcher.

I say return the same courtesy. Let him know what it feels like to choke, It rasped.

Rubbing her throat, Venus croaked reluctantly, "I forgive you."

"Now that we've made nice. What were you saying before? Were you expressing your gratitude for being chosen to serve your Grand Witcher?" Madame Sharma wondered, feigning innocence.

The word *no* wouldn't be taken for an answer.

Venus understood that now.

Ilyas handed the Grand Witcher a ringing phone. She answered it by saying nothing. The smile on her lips was a canary-eating one that sparked fear in Venus's heart.

"The other special guests have arrived, which means it is nearly time for you to brew." Madame Sharma returned the phone to her guard, a sense of finality snaking through her voice. "All the ingredients you need are in the kitchen. Ilyas, if you will."

"It would be an *absolute* honor, Your Grandness," Ilyas voiced.

How could they possibly know what ingredients she needed?

None of them were brewers. Furthermore, none of them had ever brewed love.

Venus felt more powerless with each passing second. As per the Witcher's Codex, she had a duty to obey the Grand Witcher or face the consequences. Although bound by the ancient laws inside that sacred book, she knew this meeting was *off the books.*

Unofficial. On the low. *No one* could know.

In witcher society, the Grand Witcher's station was highly respected. A surefire way for that title and all its privileges to be taken away was by hiring a brewer to make an illegal love potion.

Which made this meeting even more dangerous.

Therefore, Matrika Sharma had just as much at stake.

So, Venus's best chance of survival was to brew a potion that could kill her. If choking was the punishment for not knowing one's place, she wasn't eager to know what would happen if she outright rejected the highest-ranking witcher in her dominion.

"Though ingredients are essential, Your Grandness, I need to know what idea the drinker needs to love," Venus said.

"The drinker has to love the idea of punishment and death for his crime," Madame Sharma revealed. "I want him to laugh at his own undoing."

"Consider me intrigued. I knew this would pay off," It purred.

Venus ignored *It*, too appalled by the Grand Witcher's admission to scold *Its* blatant thirst for violence. A peitho potion that made the drinker beg for death?

The thought sent her stomach into another fit of knots.

"And what is the drinker's crime?"

"Killing your mother."

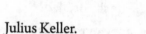

Julius Keller.

Numbness slithered underneath her flesh, claiming her as its prey. She struggled to understand the gravity of what occurred in the private dining room. The Grand Witcher had found the human who had killed her mother, his last victim in a murder spree of eleven.

She offered Venus the bastard who killed her mother.

In an instant, her reluctance to brew turned into ash.

Julius Keller was *hers*.

Her palms drove into the swing doors. Melodious aromas greeted her as she stalked into the empty kitchen. The scent of smoke, burning flesh, and spilled blood would arrive in minutes.

But for as long as her mother's murderer begged for his own demise, it'd be worth it.

Canned ingredients, vials, and a worn but opened leather-bound journal awaited her on the stainless-steel counter.

A Love for Sweet Death:
A Trinary-Note Peitho Potion

This potion is intended for Patrons seeking justice or

revenge for loved ones harmed or taken away by tragic means. Drinkers will fall for the idea of a sweet death at the Patron's command or hands as a punishment for their crimes. Caution the Patron for absolute certainty. Ingredients are as follows in this exact order:

1 cup of graveyard dirt
3 tablespoons of ground dark cocoa
a sliced half of blood orange
4 teaspoons of turmeric
1 cup of orange lily petals
¼ cup of saffron
1 pig heart
6 sprigs of dill
2 cups of salt

Beyond her vision bathed in red, she stared at the potion recipe and its sharp cursive sprawled across the aged pages. A flash of recognition ignited within her. She snapped the journal shut to check the front cover for its owner's name:

Not for the Faint of Heart:
Love Potions for the Heartless

Owned by Davina Stoneheart

Her eyes grew wide and her grip loosened, a thunk filling the room as the journal fell back onto the counter. Shock pierced through her rage. How did the Grand Witcher get ahold of her grandmother's grimoire?

Her home kitchen contained an inheritance of grimoires she had studied from cover to cover during her apprenticeship. She had committed each recipe to memory.

Venus thought she'd inherited *all* the Stoneheart grimoires. Until now. She wanted to know how the Grand Witcher got hold of this, but her need to avenge her mom won out.

She flipped back to the specific recipe and went to work.

"Graveyard dirt, ground dark cocoa, half a blood orange, turmeric, orange lilies, saffron…" she muttered to herself, emptying calculated amounts into the pot of gurgling water atop a stove next to her. Her nose wrinkled as she dropped in a bloody pig heart next, her triple-spiked septum ring poking at her Cupid's bow. After sprinkling in the dill sprigs, she poured in the salt and dripped blood from two corked vials.

The potion's base liquid—the first keynote—was finished.

A fierce wrath flared within her as she cupped her hands over her mouth and ground out the following words:

A life is what you stole,
Be certain of that.
Your death is the toll,
Consider it tit for tat.
Beg for your death,
It's what you deserve.
Laugh 'til your last breath
Whilst others observe.

Her curse floated out as a shimmery green breath, forming into a jittery ball. Water bubbled and frothed at the pot's edge as the materialized notion splashed into it.

The third and final keynote was vital, and retrieving it alone was dangerous. All living things possess it as their very essence. Some humans labeled it as a *soul*, but witchers called it *anima*.

Venus only needed a snippet of hers.

Anger clouded her mind, making it difficult for her to focus. She wagged her head to dispel her vengeful thoughts and bridged her fingertips, pressing her thumbs into her sternum.

As she inhaled, her entire being drew a deep breath of concentration.

Then she emptied her lungs, slow and steady.

Jerking her thumbs outward, she winced as a glowing thread unraveled from her chest and entangled itself in her fingers. Like a game of cat's cradle, her fingers wove the anima with intricate gestures.

She literally held her life in her hands.

One false move and that'd be the end of her.

No potion, no retribution.

Sweat beaded her forehead, her hair sticking to her skin. Faster and faster she went until it fractured at long last. The web of starry string melted through her fingers and pooled into the hollow space between her palms, forming a perfect droplet.

Her anima hovered like a suspended jewel, and she gently seized it, dropping it into the brew. A crackle hit her ears, and flashes illuminated the unruly froth like trapped lightning inside thunderclouds.

Venus wondered if she was living her last moments.

She wondered if she'd see Julius Keller's rightful execution.

Her mind wandered to the last words she ever said to Janus and Bram, wishing she could take some back. She thought about all the awful things she'd done, too. She promised herself that if she made it through this, she'd be a better sister, niece, cousin, and...whatever she was to Presley.

Venus promised herself a thousand different things, hoping to make good on them.

"*I can help you,*" It offered.

"No, your help comes with a price," Venus hissed as she pricked her finger, allowing her blood to free-fall into the brew.

An explosion rattled the kitchen. Pots and pans toppled over. A tragic force of fury, fire, and smoke collided into her, holding tight and yanking her up. Its embrace snapped her bones like twigs and twisted her limbs to its liking. Then, like an uninterested child, the potion released her. She crashed to the floor like a discarded rag doll.

Her burned body lay on the tiled floor, twitching in agony.

Excessive ringing echoed in Venus's ears.

There was a peculiar twist in her elbow and forearm. Raspy wheezes tumbled from her bloodied lips as she struggled for breath, broken ribs having punctured a lung. Jagged points of femurs perforated her shins. Moments before, her fingers had held her life in their grasp, but now they held on by a thread. Tears streamed from the corners of her eyes, the saltiness stinging the exposed tissue.

Primitive fear crushed against Venus's chest, wringing out her last breaths. Panic thrashed her heart as her will—her life—slipped away. Her only chance at giving her mom justice bled away, too.

Venus didn't want to die.

Not yet.

She needed to *look* her mother's killer in the face.

She wanted to *see* him burn.

With each dazed, teary blink, the shape of a figure standing over her came into focus. With a nose wrinkled in disgust, Nisha gazed down at Venus alongside her familiar. Uncorking a glass bottle, she said, "You look absolutely terrible, but we can't have you dying now, can we? There's so much to do."

Nisha drained the syrupy liquid into Venus's mouth. It came to life on her tongue, slithering down her throat, putting her body back together again. Yanking rude bones into their proper spots. Sealing up gaping gashes. Pasting sheets of hanging flesh back onto her face, arms, belly, and legs. Reattaching an unhinged nose. Bursting from her gums, new teeth replaced the broken ones. Against the dyed pink hair, her natural honey-brown hair sprouted from the singed splotches on her scalp.

She was being remade.

She was being reborn.

The excruciating pain was twofold from what the trinary-note potion's degree of recoil made her suffer through. Venus writhed at Nisha's feet, violent wails tearing from her lungs.

She cried for help.

She cried for mercy.

She cried for her mom.

Her torment deteriorated into crumbs, aches afflicting her mended being. She grimaced as she lifted her hand, flexing her healed fingers. A current of relief coursed through her veins.

This was the life of a brewer.

To be broken and put back together again.

Her tattered garments dangled from her as she rose to her unsteady feet.

"Well, we can't have you walking around looking like that for your big moment." Nisha propped her fists on her hips. "The kitchen staff restroom is behind you. You'll find an outfit and toiletries to clean yourself up with. Though the healing potion does wonders with broken bones and bloody wounds, it does nothing for the horrid scent of burned flesh."

Weak knees and unconfident legs carried Venus to the restroom.

After stripping herself bare, she cleaned off her crusted blood with an entire package of baby wipes. To get rid of the sharp coppery taste in her mouth, she brushed her new teeth and picked out sharp fragments of her old broken ones. As she combed out her unruly nest of hair, tangled clunks fell out.

A strapless fishtail gown the color of rose gold hung off a hanger. Chocolate and cream metallic threadwork adorned the sweetheart neckline and the bodice, which tapered into layers of soft tulle ruffles. She knew the outfit wasn't suitable for the execution of a killer, but she had no choice.

As a final step, Venus doused herself in liberal spritzes of cotton candy perfume.

Bracing the sink's counter, she regarded the weary pink-haired girl trapped in the mirror, anger hardening her tired eyes.

With the potion completed, *nothing* could keep her from Julius Keller now.

After retrieving her phone from the pocket of her damaged jeans, she stared at its shattered face. Part of her wanted to tell Janus that their mother's killer would die tonight, but now she couldn't.

"*Only a tiny part wanted to,*" It whispered. "*You want this kill all to yourself.*"

She didn't argue because she knew *It* was right.

Deep down, she wanted Julius Keller for herself.

The less her sister knew, the better.

Venus drifted back into this never-ending night's madness.

The trinary-note potion was a slimy eager creature, hungry to escape the crucible it was born in. A droplet of her anima planted a seed of life inside the brew. Its oozy tentacles crept sneakily over the pot's rim to assess its creator's tolerance, but Venus snatched up a ladle and swatted its limbs.

It retreated briskly into the bubbling goop.

A storm of annoyance brewed in her chest.

Trinary-note potions were pests if you lived long enough to deal with them. She spooned the four gallons' worth of slimy neon-green concoction into a compact frosted bottle.

Thorny tendrils and bloodred buds grew from nothing, swaddling the glass. Green liquid gave way to a berry red hue. Nisha presented a palm for Venus to relinquish the bottle, but she gripped it, narrowing her eyes.

"Where is he?" she demanded croakily, her voice regaining vigor.

"So eager you are, little brewer." Nisha smirked. "You needn't worry. I must escort you to the grand finale, but the responsibility of delivering that potion also falls to me. The sooner you give it to me, the sooner the fun will begin."

Every fiber of her being screamed as she handed over the potion. "Making a murderer pay for his crimes isn't fun. It's justice."

"You never know. There might be something inside you that enjoys what's to come." Striding to the manager's office, Nisha hoisted the bottle up to the bleached light, cocking her head as if she were inspecting a diamond's clarity.

Venus clenched her jaw to lock away her objections.

Using her fingernail, Nisha drew a circle on the ordinary door, activating a portal spell made up of intersecting lines and hexagons. She sank her fingers into the hexagonal ports, rotating the innards of the magic circle like a combination dial.

Much like Janus's calling, there were limitations to range-bound portal magic, but a spell of this complexity had the power to cast a wider radius. Twenty, fifty, or a hundred miles, Venus wasn't sure, but wherever she'd go, her feet would step onto American soil.

The door yawned wide, revealing a contentious man tied to a massive wooden stake in the middle of a glade. A circle of unlit wood torches floated around him. Black tape over his mouth muffled his protests.

The moon's glow bled a soft light, washing the stage of an impending execution in dreamy shades of blue.

The audience gathered around the pyre, dressed in their finest attire. Moonlight glistened on the flamboyant fabrics of silk tuxes and shimmery cocktail dresses, skewing silhouettes on the grassy ground.

The Grand Witcher sat on a throne of twisted wood like an empress. Nisha beckoned a finger at Venus.

She fixed her glower on Julius Keller as she walked through the egress stitching two opposing worlds together. The doorway crumbled away, abandoning the magic circle still suspended in midair.

"The brewer prevailed," Nisha announced triumphantly, holding up the bottle as proof.

Madame Sharma applauded softly, which prompted her congregation to follow suit.

"Very good, Miss Stoneheart," she said.

Venus glared at the killer as she spoke. "Thank you, Your Grandness, for providing me with this opportunity."

Madame Sharma laid a cheek onto her propped fist, a pleased smile etching her lips. "Yes, it is quite an opportunity. It's that murderer's judgment day, and we're all eager to know if the great Clarissa Stoneheart's pupil is worthy of such a legacy."

Her mom taught her the irrefutable pleasures of defying doubtful others' expectations.

"Prove them wrong," her mom would say. "Make them eat their words."

"I look forward to it," Venus said.

To proving you wrong, she added to herself. It would be a better tribute to Clarissa Stoneheart to do that than fresh flowers on her fresh grave.

The Grand Witcher shifted her attention to the star of tonight's main spectacle.

He yelped as magic ripped off the duct tape. A chorus of laughter broke out from his spectators as he spat profanities and slurs.

Demons, jinxmongers, abominations, plagues.

"You'll all regret this," he growled. "If you kill me, you'll start a war."

Venus's veins blazed with his hatred, anger, and disgust.

The Grand Witcher's even voice pervaded the clearing, hammering down like a gavel. "The war has already begun, Julius Keller. It began long before you shot your victims with iron bullets. It began long before you joined SWIG and made an ironclad pledge to the Iron Watch. For years bastards you like have destroyed lives, uncaring about the destruction and innocents left in the rubble. All the countless dead and those wishing for your death."

An inmost air lurked underneath the speech.

Venus strained her ears, discerning a thin trace of survivor's guilt or a swathed testimony.

Or maybe, it was mere empathy.

If you sat on a high throne, you had a prime spot to see the suffering of others.

A Swigger, devoted to toxic rhetoric, hunted her mom and others like mere prey because he knew the law was on his side. The ironclad brotherhood tainted every rank of SWIG. Hiding behind their badges, they achieved monstrous unmatched authority.

Julius snorted. "No witcher is ever unarmed. Your mere existence is a weapon against humans. Those are the words I live by."

"And they'll be the words you will die by," Madame Sharma replied mockingly.

Nisha ascended veiled stairs, towering over Julius. She dug her fingernails into his chin, jerking his head back. Free from its bottle, the potion crawled inside Julius's sneering mouth in the shape of a spider.

For as long as Venus had been a brewer, she'd never seen the fruits of her labor take root in others. Under her mom's tutelage, she learned and lived the three B's: *brew*, get your *bag*, and *bounce*. But for tonight, she didn't want to *bounce*.

Venus wanted to stay and watch Julius Keller *choke* on her potion.

Her imagination ran wild as she envisioned her creation forcing its way down his throat, burrowing a home within his volition.

Gnawing away at his resolve.

His eyelids twitched madly, glassy black paving over his eyes.

A dark glee engulfed her as he succumbed to a violent seizure.

Nisha floated to the ground, joining the private assembly.

Suddenly, his body stilled and his gaze turned to the Grand Witcher.

"What do you wish me to do?" he questioned pliantly.

"To die laughing at the hands of your victim's daughter." The flames burst to life upon each torch one by one.

All eyes turned to Venus as a torch floated to her. Without hesitation, she took it, relishing the weight of the wood and its powerful bright fire. As she walked toward her mother's killer, spectators parted a pathway for her. She threw it on the gathered wood Julius stood on, her anger clawing at her vow of abnegation.

She trembled to call forth her own fire, not borrowed ones.

"I'm sure you can do better than that," Julius encouraged, chuckling heartily. "If I'm to be burned to death by you, little girl, then I want it to be grand from start to finish."

"You heard the human, little Stoneheart," Nisha said nearby, smirking.

Venus marched from one torch to the next, snatching and flinging each into the logs until none remained. Soon a vigorous blaze reached up to devour Julius.

He tossed his head, howling a manic laugh as he burned and burned and burned.

She witnessed every moment, but her sorrow and rage didn't burn away like ash. Her mom's message from beyond the grave haunted her, dampening her red-hot fury.

Leave it be.

Leave it be.

Leave it be.

Guilt squirmed in her belly at disobeying the command, even

though her hands had delivered retribution. As her gaze fled Julius's trial of fire, it caught in Madame Sharma's optical web. While the others watched the roasting, the Grand Witcher seemed more interested in her.

The piercing regard broadcasted to Venus a declaration:

This night wasn't over until Matrika Sharma commanded it as so.

CHAPTER
TWELVE

Sister Nature gifts the wonders one can see and
Sister Magick bestows wonders one cannot believe with
one's eyes.

—A witcher proverb

JUNE 26, 2023

HORS D'OEUVRES AND CHAMPAGNE FLUTES FLOATED AROUND THE
room on sterling trays. Burning a murderer at the stake was enough to
shoo away any remnants of hunger and thirst for Venus. The ghostly
stench of roasted human flesh plagued her senses, and Julius's laughter still echoed in her ears. But it was a brutal end her mother's killer
deserved, and so much fucking more.

Festivities swirling around Venus. An hour ago, a portal brought the
party to the Grand Witcher's home.

Her head shook to shoo away that misconception.

North of downtown, Kalorama, an exuberantly wealthy neighborhood, had no homes. Homes were warm and full of character. In
Kalorama, mansions and town houses costing seven figures had the finest
things money could buy but lacked heart. A neighborhood so bougie it
was fit for ex-presidents and embassies to set up shop.

In the grand living room, music played energetically, and liquor flowed freely.

Venus, however, stood out like an odd jigsaw piece that didn't match the rest of the puzzle.

She played with a delicate ruffle on her borrowed dress to keep her hands busy while shifting uncomfortably on the velvety chesterfield.

Kiwi soared over the heads of the guests and landed on the chesterfield's opposite armrest. Moments later, Nisha emerged from the crowd with a lazy roll of her eyes, joining Venus.

"Your adolescent sulking is quite a buzzkill. You played a hand in bringing your mother's murderer to justice, and you've proven you're the rightful successor to Clarissa Stoneheart's legacy. A remarkable feat for such a young age."

Venus tucked a strand of hair behind her ear, watching inseparable girls gyrating to the music and showering one another in kisses. "I didn't have much choice."

Once upon a time, a young Venus asked her mom about a normal future and received a sour laugh: *"A brewer marries their work and rears their apprentice."*

Nisha clucked her tongue and leaned in, genuine amusement glinting in her chestnut-brown eyes. "Choice is an illusion. A brewer that bottles illusions of love should know that by heart."

Choice is an illusion. The words twisted like a key within her and unlocked an unalloyed truth that manifested as unnerved shivers.

"If choice is an illusion, then what's real?" Venus mused.

"Fate is real," Nisha said. "Our fates are beyond our control. Sewn into the fabric of reality long before we came to be. Why else do The Sisters show witchers glimpses of the future, warning us about what's in store for us?"

Regret seeped into her muscles, a heaviness pooling in her chest.

Leave it be.

Leave it be.

Leave it be.

As the words resounded in her head, she winced and squeezed her eyes shut.

It had to be done. It had to be done. It had to be done, Venus chanted inwardly to combat the shame eating away at her.

A white woman in her late thirties with a heart-shaped face and ash-blond curls emerged from the crowd. Venus winced slightly at the intense glint of her rainbow sequin dress and matching high heels.

The woman plopped into Nisha's lap with a giggle. One ravenous kiss later, she pulled back with a happy sigh.

Nisha arched her dark eyebrow, amused. "Are you satisfied, my love?"

"Of course. Being here is much more fun than working double shifts at the hospital," the woman said, swiping traces of her lipstick off Nisha's lips. Then she swiveled her attention to Venus. "Outstanding work, brewer. Watching that fucker burn was the icing on the metaphorical cake. I'm Chelsea, by the way."

"All in a long day's work," Venus muttered dully, uninterested in the festivities.

Or making acquaintances.

The crowd parted for the Grand Witcher's guard dog.

Venus's throat tightened in memory of what he had done to her earlier.

"Her Grandness seeks your audience," Ilyas informed temperately.

About damn time.

She rose from the emerald-green chesterfield, ready for this.

"Tread carefully," Nisha said, coiling her arms around her girlfriend's waist.

Venus didn't doubt that for a moment. Though the Grand Witcher handed her the opportunity for closure, she couldn't neglect the fact she was deceived and dragged here against her will.

Ilyas ushered her to a corridor, guards lining the walls, prepared to defend and punish.

A stony gaze met hers as he opened the door to a study.

"Play nice, you two," Madame Sharma cautioned motherly from her office chair, fingernails tapping on a keepsake box's lid.

Venus had to remain standing without a chair, making her feel helpless. Having done all she had tonight, hadn't she proven she deserved a seat?

A smile smoothed across Madame Sharma's painted lips. "You've pleased me greatly tonight, Miss Stoneheart."

"Thank you for the honor, Your Grandness." Venus inclined her head, laboring to remain collected under the Grand Witcher's dissecting gaze.

"Hard work and dedication earn a handsome reward. You'll find three hundred grand in the trunk when you return to your car."

Venus sucked in a gasp, blinking her eyes in bewilderment.

"That's far too generous, Your Grandness." The lie spilled from her lips, conveying a guise of modesty. A monster of greed took its first breath inside her, feeding her brain spoonfuls of dollar-green dreams.

"Clarissa negotiated the fee and the terms."

"She did?" Venus's momentary excitement shriveled away, surprise sprouting instead. "So, is that why you have a Stoneheart grimoire and one of my health potions? You got them from my mom?"

As Madame Sharma leaned back, steepling her fingers, she replied, "Yes, tonight's been in the making for a long time. My office investigated the witcher serial killings for months. Once we identified Keller as the culprit, we knew the WCTF would protect him if we made it public. His victims deserved justice. I knew about Davina's grimoire of vengeful love potions and contacted Clarissa about booking you." A pause. "It may come as a surprise, but your mother and I were close in college."

"Actually," Venus said, "Miss Florence filled me in at the funeral."

A muscle in Madame Sharma's jaw twitched before she brushed her tongue along the edge of her teeth. "Oh, is that so? How kind of her."

In Venus's skull, the Grand Witcher's irritation hammered like a headache, forcing her to realize that she should've kept her mouth shut. Her mind flashed back to the day of the funeral when Madame Sharma showed up. She remembered how potent and steadfast Miss Florence's hate was until the uninvited guests left.

Venus understood now that both parties disliked each other. She suspected an oldhead like Miss Florence wasn't a fan of the Grand Witcher's *ways.*

And she couldn't deny the Grand Witcher had a way of doing things.

A night like this wouldn't have been possible otherwise.

Madame Sharma continued. "We needed Keller's blood. Clarissa volunteered to get it herself, but he caught on to her and—"

"Killed her," Venus finished, shock nudging her a tiny step back from the desk. From the truth. Clarissa Stoneheart lost her life for money. Because, of course, she would. It followed her 3-B philosophy to the letter. Get your *bag, brew,* and *bounce.* And now the thing she died for sat in the trunk of her eldest daughter's car.

Numbness inched along Venus's skin. She drew herself into the theater of her mind, flicking off the lights. Moments and details she paid no mind weeks ago came back to haunt her, leading to theories that gave way to answers. If her mom had volunteered to get Julius's blood, she would've sent Patches to spy on him first. The night Venus received Mr. Mouse's payment was the first time she had seen that cat in days.

"Show me everything you saw." Venus overheard her mom say to him

after he reported back home. At the time, she didn't think anything of it. That interaction—that command—seemed like business as usual.

On the last night Clarissa Stoneheart was alive, Janus warned that something was dead-ass off. A warning Venus was too exhausted and mad to give a fuck about.

"She's always pissed at someone about something." She then said as a brush-off, not knowing that night would be her mom's last.

Now, far too late, Venus realized something had been off.

Only two things could've bent Clarissa Stoneheart out of shape like that:

1. Plans that didn't stay in place.
2. Folks that stepped out of line.

A murderous cop on her tail would've set her off twofold. Someone should've warned her. Someone should've talked her out of it.

Or maybe, someone already tried.

Venus remembered the phone call that put Clarissa on edge. A call Janus eavesdropped on, not sure if their mom was yelling about a *he* or *she*.

I don't care if he knows.

That must've been what she said.

He, as in Julius Keller.

How the fuck was Venus supposed to know her mom had her eyes on a serial killer?

"What would you've done if you had, hm?" It mocked. *"Absolutely nothing."*

No, she would've—

"Choice is an illusion." Nisha told her that only minutes ago.

Surrendering to another truth, Venus flared her nostrils, tears rimming her eyes.

Fate intended for Julius Keller to kill her mother.

As it was destined for Venus to kill him.

Like a hound, Madame Sharma sniffed out her anguish. "Having you as Keller's executioner was poetic justice, but your potion was also a test. Clarissa and I agreed that if your work pleased me, I'd hire you for another job. A much bigger job for two hundred and fifty grand to brew—"

"Five trinary-note potions," she finished quietly, deflating. Now, it all made sense. The extra money in her trunk wasn't a generous tip at all. The money was for more potions.

For more of her.

Madame Sharma drove out a sigh, pity clouding her eyes. "Come now, Miss Stoneheart. You thought you'd walk away with that much money and that'd be the end? Blood money always comes with veins."

Blood money implied a future of more blood.

"That sounds like a wonderful plan," It said.

As the reinforcement potions' potency waned, *Its* sway over her would wax.

Like a natural predator, blood enticed *It.*

More could trigger *Its* bloodthirst.

More could put her at risk of being overtaken.

"It's only a matter of time," It whispered.

Fear burrowed into her spine.

"My duty as a Grand Witcher in the nation's capital is to fight for witchers across the country." Madame Sharma displayed two manicured fingers to count her points. "In this world, you have to yell in the streets or whisper in ears to be heard. Back in the day, I used to shout at the top of my lungs to make my point, but with age, I learned I could get farther than ever imagined by whispering in a politician's ear."

Venus's brow bunched up. "You're a lobbyist?"

"Correct." Madame Sharma gave her soft brief applause. "For all these years, I've managed just fine on my own with charm and bribes, but with the Registration Act up for a vote, I fear that won't be enough. That's where you come in. Five swing senators are on my radar, but to ensure my plan is successful, I need them to fall in love with my ideas."

Blindsided, Venus squinted her eyes at the scheme's brilliance. "You want peitho potions to rig the Registration Act vote?"

As the Grand Witcher shook her head, a soft chuckle bubbled in her throat. "Surely, you don't think these indecisive politicians will vote in our best interests?"

"Not at all, Your Grandness."

"I have secured two places on the guest list for Senator Winston Mounsey's party tomorrow night. One for me and one for my intern Dionaea, which will be you. Senator Cavendish will also be in attendance," Madame Sharma said. "While I mingle, you'll look for the necessary ingredients to make the potions."

"And the other senators?"

"You'll be responsible for filling their vials on your own time."

A rigged vote meant Janus wouldn't pop up on the WCTF's radar, but five trinary-note peitho potions would drain every bit of her magic and destroy her.

"And if I decline your offer?" Venus posed, a soft quaver in her pitch.

"It wouldn't be in our best interests," Madame Sharma advised, shifting her attention to the ever-vigilant Ilyas posted near the door. "If I let you walk out that door, it could jeopardize my title as Grand Witcher. Commissioning a brewer for a controversial potion and overseeing a human's execution isn't very becoming of one in my station. If what happened tonight got out, I would lose everything I've worked for."

Madame Sharma tacked on, "Declining our arrangement would undo all the hard work your mother did on your behalf to ensure you and your sister live comfortably."

"Clarissa knew you were too pathetic to take care of yourself and Janus. Accept the deal," It hissed.

Her breath shallowed as a thickness gathered in her throat. "I would never say a word, Your Grandness."

"Of course, you won't." Madame Sharma eased open the wooden box's lid and pulled out a dagger with a polished bone hilt. "No one ever does after I'm done with them."

Venus recoiled a step, her heart beating wildly against her rib cage.

Madame Sharma cocked her head to admire the blade. "Did Clarissa ever teach you the surest way to gain another's absolute loyalty, Venus?"

She licked her lips nervously. "Yes, ma'am."

"So, it is safe to assume you understand what must happen?"

"Your Gr—"

Madame Sharma gritted her teeth as she sliced her palm. "I gave you the bastard that took your mother away from you. Am I not worthy of your loyalty? For a blood oath to work, your heart must have a sliver of willingness. What shall it be?"

The question hovered in the air as she presented the weapon stained in her blood.

Blood-tethers, such as the one Venus and her sister shared, fostered a need to protect each other. An ordinary knife sufficed, the magic in their blood weaving the tether. But a blood oath enabled the roles of dominance and submission until one's last breath.

Such a grave gesture required a ritualistic dagger forged in magic and fire by a Smith. As witchers and humans alike could abuse its magic, it was banned in all fifty states and twenty-three countries.

Memories of Julius burning and Janus asleep intertwined, forming the driving force behind Venus's solitary nod. She snatched up the blade and ran her thumb across the polished hilt's gold-embossed root mark of a letter *g* within an octagon.

A root mark was a distinct symbol akin to an artist's signature, so you always knew who bled and sweated over a creation. An ownership no amount of money could erase.

Much like the scar of a blood oath, Venus realized.

She eyed the engraved spell:

Sharp is this blade
Its cut sure and true
Magick will give aid
To see thy burden through

She slit her palm, clasping the Grand Witcher's hand in a viselike embrace.

Mingled blood wept onto the desk.

"Say the words," Madame Sharma ordered.

All this was for Janus.

The money.

The oath.

"I pledge myself to thee," Venus said as instructed. "My loyalty shall never flee. Measure my servitude with every heartbeat and breath. To which, this bond will sever by your tongue or upon my death."

She gasped sharply and twisted her face as an undeniable pain invaded her blood slit, infecting her innards. An ensnaring force tangled her hand with the Grand Witcher's, refusing to let her go as she hunched over the desk.

Her heart seized, and her knees gave way, but the blood oath was still at work, weaving their fates into an indestructible bond.

A false sense of freedom overcame her as the oath cut her loose.

Venus collapsed to the floor on all fours, wheezing as she attempted to crawl away from her agony. She toppled defeatedly. Hot tears blurred her sight.

"Clarissa told me you're a scrapper, Venus Stoneheart." Madame Sharma rounded her desk and strutted to the girl's curled body. "And I like scrappers. They claw and bite their way out of everything. Even if it means biting the hand that feeds them."

Madame Sharma squatted and crooked a bloody finger against Venus's sweaty brown cheek. "I've been bitten too many times before. With a protection locket and blood oaths, no one can hurt me ever again. I have too much to do to worry if you'll bite me too, dear. You will tell no one of this night or my wrongdoings. Every time you so much as think about going against me, the blood oath will bite you instead."

"What do you want from me?" Venus heaved, flinching at the gentle strokes.

"I already told you, Miss Stoneheart. I want love." As Madame Sharma rose and walked away, she added, "Ilyas, be a dear and give Miss Stoneheart her last gift of the night. Then ensure she returns to her vehicle safely. I think she'll find it useful for what's to come."

"As you wish, Your Grandness," Ilyas enunciated dutifully, bowing his head as she departed. He advanced toward Venus, dropping a velvet jewelry box within her bloodied fingers' reach.

"Get up," he delivered coolly. "Or you'll get blood all over the floor."

Even as Venus lay at his feet, weak and spent, she mustered up enough strength to retort, "I see that you like to bully other kids on the playground when Mommy's not looking."

Grabbing her gift, she struggled to get up but managed.

"Are you in any position to speak on mothers?" Ilyas said.

Venus couldn't help but wince at his cutting comment.

His lumbering stature exuded brawn and menace as he approached her. "That's what I thought."

"Don't come any closer," she warned, standing her ground.

"I know better than to do that."

"Scared of me?"

"No, I just know what's inside of you." His eyes lowered to the jewelry box in her hand. "The quicker you put that on, the quicker you and that thing inside can leave."

Venus parted the lid to reveal a silvery twisted rope ring and plucked it out, tingly pulses seeping into her skin. A Smith had forged and charmed it, but she was uncertain what it had been charmed to do. Wanting Ilyas to make good on his word, she put it on.

"*Every union needs a ring,*" It whispered in a legion of voices.

This wasn't a union.

This was captivity.

―――

Venus wanted to go home and scrub off her skin as if that would make all her fuckups go away, but she couldn't. *I'll stop by your crib when I'm done.* Hours ago, the most difficult challenge she thought she'd face was Presley. Then she ended Julius Keller's life and pledged hers to the Grand Witcher. When compared, the unfinished business with Presley seemed a lot less daunting now.

Walking around the white-brick house's left corner, Venus stopped at Presley's bedroom window. She rapped her knuckles against the glass. As she waited, her exhaustion made mere moments feel like an eternity. To keep track of time and avoid wasting any more, Venus counted Mississippis in her head and set her limit at sixty.

She whispered tiredly, "Fifty-six Mississippi, fifty-seven Mississippi, fifty-eight Mississippi, fif—"

Presley came around the back of the house. "Venus."

She looked away from her reflection in the window and toward them. Each took note of the other's differences. Presley in a durag, short satin pajamas, tube socks, and Jordan slides. Venus wore an extravagant gown that smelled of woodsmoke and sweat and was stained with blood. *Her* blood.

As she moved closer, her gown's train scraped across the grass behind her. "I know I'm late."

"For good reasons, I'm sure," they said.

She shook her head, a confession rising up her throat. "I—"

Agony radiated from Venus's freshly cut palm, splintering through her nervous system. Her knees gave out and she collapsed to the ground. Her spine bowed in a painful arch while her marred hand convulsed.

"*You fool,*" It hissed. "*How could you forget?*"

How could she have? *How?*

"Venus!" Presley dashed to her, dropping to their knees beside her.

Venus's mouth stretched into a silent scream as a warning rang through her bones: "You *will tell no one of this night or my wrongdoings.*"

"Breathe through it," Presley whispered, stroking her hair. "Just breathe."

She took desperate gulps of air, tears flooding her cheeks. The pain bled out of her, leaving her spent and breathless.

Presley didn't bother to ask what the hell had just happened. Instead, they scooped her up in their arms, carrying her inside the house.

They brought her to their bedroom, setting her on the bed. Venus fell back and rolled onto her belly, burying her face in the rumpled sheets. She screamed out all her frustrations.

Then her muffled screams gave way to muffled sobs.

Venus attacked the mattress with weak, pathetic punches.

"What do *you* need, Venus?" Presley asked. "I don't know what you're going through right now, but I want to help."

She lifted her head in response, her voice raspy and quivering. "Please get me out of this fucking dress so I can shower."

"Gotchu." Their fingers tugged down the zipper that ran along her spine.

Relief streamed down her cheeks at that word—that assurance. Presley ran her a shower in the hallway bathroom as soon as she was free of the gown. As she scrubbed her skin furiously with a washcloth, scorching water pounded on her head and coursed down her body in rivulets.

Her mother warned her to *leave it be.*

If Venus *had* done as told—

If she *hadn't* killed Julius Keller, no one could force her into a blood oath.

Or maybe, it didn't matter if she had or hadn't.

Nisha said choice was an illusion.

That fate was real and beyond her control.

Venus *didn't* want the Registration Act to pass, but she didn't want to be a pawn, either. In the Grand Witcher's endgame, she was a discardable piece. A game *her mom* helped design.

As the realization sank in, she stopped scrubbing her shoulder.

Venus didn't have a choice because Clarissa Stoneheart had already decided for her.

After her shower, she found a towel and a 3XL shirt on the counter. She dried herself and put on the shirt that swallowed up her 5'3" frame. Tiptoeing barefoot back into Presley's room, she dropped her damp towel into their hamper.

Presley pulled back the sheets. Venus slid in and snuggled up against them, resting her cheek on their chest. Pale morning light poured from the window. Birds chirped. Upstairs, feet thumped about as Mr. Jerome and Miss Florence began their day.

"It wasn't supposed to turn out like this," she whispered, blinking her heavy eyelids.

"Which part?" Presley leaned their chin against her crown.

"All of it."

CHAPTER
THIRTEEN

There are impostors out there that want to be us. Humans that'll drink potions to replicate witcher auras and give them a fleeting taste of our birthright. Imitation isn't the greatest form of flattery. If these humans think they can be us, they won't just use their power to speak over us. They'll pave over us.

—Megan Villanueva, a witcher activist

AS A RAP TRACK BLARED, VENUS WONDERED IF THE MUSIC drowned out her knock or if her sister chose to ignore it. Two days ago, she threatened to poison Janus with a love potion to protect her because exacting vengeance didn't make anyone a hero.

Payback had a cost and most couldn't afford it.

Venus thought she could, but robbing Julius Keller of his life didn't settle a score.

It only put her in lifelong debt.

Only hours ago, the Grand Witcher ordered, *"You will tell no one of this night or my wrongdoings."*

An order Venus had to obey. Or the blood oath would teach her a painful lesson of obedience. Earlier this morning, it schooled her right in front of Presley. She didn't want a repeat, but obeying Matrika Sharma wouldn't bring her peace, either.

Harboring that truth from her sister was a form of torment itself.

Venus lifted her knuckles to knock again, but the door yanked open.

Janus's annoyance slapped her face and she winced slightly at the sting. Curled into a ball, Patches napped on the bed.

"What do *you* want?" Janus crinkled her eyes into accusatory slits, crossing her arms.

"I just wanted you to know I'll be leaving soon," Venus informed.

As soon as the words left her mouth, Janus sized her up from head to toe. After she redyed her hair pink with leftover droplets of a beautification potion, she had to wear a wig to hide it. For makeup, the last thing to do was lipstick. Her robe covered her strapless bra and underwear.

Janus frowned, her concern as clear as day. "Where are you going?"

"Out," Venus said, hoping the answer would be enough.

It wasn't enough.

"Just like you went *out* last night"—Janus tilted her head, her voice thickening with suspicion—"and didn't come back until almost noon?"

Venus's tongue had a mind of its own. "You sound like Mom."

The observation wasn't an accusation or a dig. It was more like a tiny grain of musing that slipped through the sieve between Venus's mind and mouth.

They both shot a look down the hall to their mom's door, then back at each other, palpable silence and unsaid words hanging between them. Words steeped in grief.

"I won't be gone that long," Venus promised, but it felt empty. Only the Grand Witcher had a finger on tonight's pulse and how long it'd beat on.

"You're a homebody through and through, Vee. Yet twice in twenty-four hours, you've left home *willingly*." Janus held up two fingers and crossed them together, her tone hesitant as if she were bracing herself for the worst. "Are you and Pres...hooking up?"

The fact that she actually bothered to ask was so unlike her. She almost never wanted to know about stuff like that, which meant she was worried as hell. Not like her stubborn ass would admit it, though.

"What? No!" Venus reared her head back, her mouth flopping open. "We're trying to work things out, but *not* like that."

"*The ultimate sign of commitment is committing murder together,*" It chuckled.

She fought the urge to roll her eyes.

Janus pressed her lips, humming *mm-hm.* "If y'all aren't together, then what aren't you telling me?"

Venus shuttled out a breath. "I can't talk about it, Janus."

"Why not?" her sister pressed.

The Grand Witcher's command scraped across the pink folds of her brain. "*You will tell no one of this night or my wrongdoings.*"

Then a word stood out to her.

Tell.

Maybe Venus could *show*, but she wasn't sure.

If she couldn't, the blood oath would punish her for trying to be clever.

Venus held out her palm and braced herself for pain. When the blood oath didn't stir, relief swept over her.

Then came a foreign tide of regret through her veins.

Her sister's regret.

As Janus examined the scar, her eyebrows gathered. "I should've listened to it."

"What do you mean?"

"Last night, the blood-tether wouldn't let me sleep for shit. The pain kept me rolling around the bed in agony, but I was too stubborn to do anything about it. About you. I just figured you'd come back to me like you always do. I can't believe I took that for granted, especially after Mom's—"

Venus shook her head. "There was nothing you could've done."

Choice is an illusion.

She swallowed the four heavy words, deciding they were too bleak to say to a little sister who had high hopes for the future.

"You're wrong. I could've tapped into our blood-tether and used it to make a doorway to you."

"You can do that?"

"Well, I haven't tried it, but that doesn't mean I can't. You know I can only make doorways to places I've been. Your blood is inside me and mine is inside you. You're a part of me and I'm part of you. Maybe, wherever you go, I've been there, too. I've been doing my research."

Venus blinked. "Research?"

Janus widened the door for her to enter, gesturing for her to sit in the desk chair. The computer screen had a Witcherpedia page, but Venus got distracted.

"Why do you have so many damn tabs up?" she asked.

Janus sucked her teeth, pointing to a woodcut illustration of Sister Nature and Sister Magick. "*Girl,* just read what I found."

Nature draped in vines, flowers, and fur, wearing a crown of ram horns and gripping a shepherd crook. Magick garbed in constellations, a sunburst crown, and an embossed wet moon on her forehead, tipping a chalice to pour out stars.

No, not stars. Magic, Venus corrected inwardly.

Underneath the vintage artwork was a passage:

BLOOD, ANIMA, AND CHANT (BAC) WAS AN OLD MAGICK TECH-
NIQUE USED TO DISPEL MISFORTUNES. BLOOD PLEASES SISTER
NATURE. ANIMA IS A FIT OFFERING FOR SISTER MAGICK. A CLEVER
CHANT CAN SWAY BOTH IN YOUR FAVOR. FOR STALWART SPELLS,
TRY ALL THREE, BUT YOU MAY FIND VICTORY OR TRAGEDY.

In theory, it seemed tempting, but the risk wasn't worth it to Venus. She stood up, unimpressed. "Sounds like a death wish."

Witchery had bendy rules, but loopholes were a different breed altogether. If you didn't know what you were doing, a backfired loophole could turn against you before you even knew what hit you.

Venus was an expert at backfires.

"Our blood and fates are intertwined. I think this is the loophole I need. How else am I going to protect you from—?" Janus stopped herself short, but the unsaid implication thickened the air.

"Something awful will happen to me, won't it?"

Janus intentionally avoided her gaze, minimizing the browser window. "That part doesn't matter. What matters is I'll be there at your side."

"There's no stopping whatever you're trying to protect me from, Janus. Whatever's meant to be will be," Venus said, then changed the subject. "Before I have to go, can I get a hug?"

Earlier this morning, while in Presley's bed, Venus could not remember the last time she had been hugged or kissed by her mother.

Last night, a trinary-note potion nearly took her life.

Although attending a senator's party seemed safe, Venus wanted to hold her sister one last time because tomorrow wasn't promised to anyone.

"Stop being so dramatic. You know we're both going to grow old together and die in a cottage full of black cats with Patches as their leader," Janus snorted as they hugged, adding matter-of-factly, "And just for the record, I'm *still* mad at you about that peitho potion threat."

"I know. I'm mad at me too," Venus said.

As they broke apart, Venus pecked her sister's forehead before she returned to her room to finish getting ready. She slipped into a black high-low taffeta dress the Grand Witcher had left for her in a garment bag in her car trunk. With it, she wore a pearl-beaded body chain shawl that molded to her chest.

In the doorway, Janus stopped to watch her tuck her hair into the wig cap.

"Wow, you look different."

Venus put on her wig. "That's fitting, because I haven't been myself in a long-ass time."

She clocked her sister's changed attire for the night, from pajamas to street clothes. A low bun headwrap shielded her hair.

She pursed her lips to apply a matte black shade. "Weren't you in pajamas?"

"I decided to head out." Janus adjusted her bag's drawstring strap onto her shoulder.

Venus clocked the accessory in the reflection and the heavy book-shaped thing's contours screaming against the fabric. A suspicion slithered its way underneath her flesh. Janus always seemed allergic to any reading material not conveniently accessible by technological means. Whatever was in her bag had more embarrassing girth than a leather-bound dictionary.

She turned halfway with a pinched expression, her tongue ready to pop off. "Need I remind you that there's a *whole-ass* bounty on your head? So, I gotta ask. You're not trying to get yourself killed tonight, right?"

"No, but if I did, good thing I'll be at Epione," Janus teased as she sat down on the edge of the bed, plucking up a plush turtle and stroking it in her lap. "I can't tell you how many times I wanted to go there, but I was too scared to. Mom said no good would come if I did, and I believed her. I have to do this, Vee. I need to go see my dad."

Epione Hospital was the only witcher-friendly hospital in DC.

For the last decade, Malik had called it home.

Venus's agitation dissipated, but her curiosity held fast. "What's the book?"

"It's one of the albums from Mom's early WASP days," Janus sighed, her mood dampening.

Venus nodded slowly. "If I have any energy left after this party, would it be cool if I stopped by?"

"Yeah, I'd be down for that," Janus said, a notification chime from her jacket's pocket overlapping her words. She pulled out her cell and read the text message received, indecisiveness wrinkling her brow.

In Venus's mind, a conflict erupted when the two choices her sister struggled with fought it out. From all the violence, an ache pulsated against her temple.

She grimaced, asking a trick question. "Let me guess. Another party invite?"

Pocketing the phone, Janus hesitated to respond.

"There's a Registration Act protest tomorrow and"—she paused, swallowing hard—"the organizers want me to come."

Every part of Venus stiffened in alarm. "Janus—"

"I didn't say I *was* going!" Janus raised her palms in defense.

"Well, you didn't say you *weren't* either, Jay." Venus shifted on her bench, straddling it to face her sister. "I'm an *empath*, remember? I can *feel* how you're at odds with yourself. Promise me you won't go."

Janus sucked her lower lip between her teeth as she thought, bouncing her knee.

"Promise me, Jay," Venus urged.

"Your ride's here."

The doorbell chimed promptly after the words left her sister's mouth.

"This conversation isn't over." Venus slipped on velvety black gloves and grabbed a clutch she borrowed from her mother's vast collection.

"You borrowed nothing if she's dead. It's yours now, you idiot," It reminded her.

Thankful for the reprieve, Janus slumped her shoulders. "For now, it is."

The stretch limo glided down the winding driveway of a Tudor-style mansion. The warm amber glow from its windows whispered promises of the American Dream.

Madame Sharma drank her champagne. "You should know better than to get swept up in it."

"In what?"

"The illusion and that," she paused, tilting her glass toward the approaching mansion, "is merely the stage."

The Grand Witcher's cell lit up and hummed. She read a text message, a jumble of irritation and disappointment radiating from her pores.

Venus considered asking if something was wrong but concluded it wasn't her place.

Madame Sharma exhaled lengthily through her nostrils, then drained the rest of her champagne, washing away any trace of emotion. She peered inside the empty flute, deep in thought.

"Blood never mixes well with business, Miss Stoneheart."

Blood as in family, Venus realized.

Blood, as in Nisha.

Before bloody oaths, cop burnings, and her mother's burial, Venus often wondered how the Sharma sisters got along. She wondered what kind of love they had between them. Not all siblings had relationships steeped in storge, a familial love. Or philia, a friendship love. Some love had *no* name, only defined by complications, complexities, and consequences.

Business brought out the worst in others.

Venus learned that by working underneath Clarissa.

Maybe, that's what the Grand Witcher meant, too.

"Speaking of business…" Madame Sharma trailed off, tapping a knuckle against the partition. It hummed as it rolled down. A guard's gloved hand offered a rose-gold foil box tied with a satin pink ribbon.

She obtained it, then extended the gift to Venus.

But Venus wasn't eager to accept this gift because Matrika Sharma *always* made her pay.

One way or another.

"Take it, Miss Stoneheart," Madame Sharma instructed, a smirk springing to her mouth.

Dread writhed in Venus's belly like a pit of snakes as she obeyed.

She stared at the small rectangular box now in her possession.

Madame Sharma arched a delicate eyebrow. "Well, aren't you going to—"

"Thank you, Your Grandness." Her tone sounded mechanical as she spoke.

"I don't want your *fictitious* gratitude, Miss Stoneheart," Madame Sharma said, her lips tightening at the interruption. "I want you to open the damn box."

And so, Venus did with shaky fingers.

Her face went blank when she saw what was inside: a new phone. She was so determined to get revenge that she had abandoned her broken cell on the counter in the Swadesh kitchen's restrooms. It was a tiny detail that got lost in all of last night's chaos.

She hadn't even thought about it, but when she touched her gift's black shiny screen, she realized what she had left behind.

A keepsake of a memory.

Not the ones immortalized in photos, videos, and text messages, sitting safely in cloud storage. A peachy corgi phone case her mom got for her eighteenth birthday this year. She remembered Clarissa's rare amusement when she pulled it out of a dog-themed gift bag stuffed with tissue paper.

It was the last gift Venus ever got from her mom. And she left it behind to burn a cop at the stake. She should've taken the damn phone case with her even if the trinary-note potion's recoil busted it.

But she didn't.

She *fucking* didn't and now it was gone forever.

Suddenly, Venus wanted to cry over a *fucking* corgi phone case. Stinging pressed against the backs of her eyeballs.

How pathetic was that?

How pathetic was she?

"Given how long you've stared at it, I assure you it's a suitable replacement." Madame Sharma arched an eyebrow.

She cleared her throat, restraining her tears. "Yes, it is. Thank you, Your Grandness."

Silence.

"I'm not your foe, Miss Stoneheart."

"But you're not my friend, either." Venus put the gift box's lid back on.

"You're right. I'm not." The Grand Witcher nodded. "I'm *your* client with *high* expectations."

The limo eased to a stop underneath an impressive portico. A suited car attendant opened the door and presented a helping hand.

Venus hesitantly accepted, worrying about what her deviation could do. The last thing she needed was a bloodbath in a place like this.

Then again, the residents of the gated Montgomery County suburbs like this one only enjoyed the color of blood if it was the hue of their foreign cars, creamy lipsticks, and high-heel soles.

Her deviation fluttered at the thought of blood.

After the car attendant ushered the Grand Witcher out of the limo, she swanked ahead of Venus, her gown's sweep train rustling after her on the ground like a puddle of molten gold.

Venus trailed behind the imposing woman like a lowly servant. Still, when they stepped into Senator Mounsey's home, iciness melted away. A charming smile brightened the Grand Witcher's face as she encountered acquaintances, sprinkling warm hellos, friendly hugs, and dramatic cheek kisses.

Madame Sharma introduced her as Dionaea.

Venus smiled accordingly, shaking each hand offered to her. A dizzying whirlwind of politicians, their spouses, and wealthy backers. Glinting diamonds from tennis bracelets caught the opulent light as women plucked goat cheese and beet puff pastry bites from butlers' trays. Men adjusted the lapels and silky ties of their expensive-ass tailored suits, the kind with price tags that rivaled someone's college tuition.

There was jazz music, good laughter, healthy arguments, and fizzy champagne all around her, but underneath the veneer of enjoyment, she knew it was all fake.

All the guests had the power to make a difference, yet here they were, swapping *rich-people-shit* stories, like yacht mishaps in the Mediterranean and ski trips to Aspen.

Weeks from now, senators would vote on the Registration Act, yet no one here dared mention it. Maybe bitter truths didn't pair well with the caviar-on-a-spoon and puff pastries. Yet watching the human-hating Matrika Sharma pose as a charismatic ally among these people was like watching artistry in motion.

Senator Mounsey eventually addressed all his guests, his speech earning claps and more laughter. Venus wondered how much of it was genuine.

She took it as the perfect opportunity to excuse herself and slinked away upstairs toward the west wing, where Madame Sharma said the senator's bedroom was. She eased open one of the double doors and slipped inside quietly. All the while, her deviation thought it best to vocalize the *Mission: Impossible* theme song.

"You can cut it out now."

"*It isn't no secret everything looks ten times cooler with a background song,*" It replied.

"I highly doubt a background song will make sneaking into some dude's bathroom and collecting his hair cooler in any capacity." She flicked the bathroom's light switch and unzipped a leather toiletry bag on the marble sink counter, pulling out a fancy wood-handled razor. She tapped it gently on the hard surface for stubble fallout.

"Shit."

Nothing.

"A background song only enhances anticlimactic moments like that one," It boasted in a singsong voice.

Venus rolled her eyes hard and returned the razor to where it belonged, retrieving a wooden brush instead. Dark hairs hid in the stiff bristles. She sighed in relief.

Her deviation began, "Would've been a lot cooler if—"

"Oh my god, shut up," Venus snapped, her words bouncing off the marble and opulence. Immediately, she clamped a hand over her mouth at her fuck-up.

"Shit, shit, shit," she chanted in a whispery panic, hoping she hadn't given herself away.

She plucked off a velvet glove to pinch away a few strands and drop them in a glass vial. After putting everything back in its proper place, she adjusted her purse strap and escaped.

A familiar voice made her halt. "What are you doing?"

An ill Mister Mouse adjusted his spectacles as he shuffled toward her in his pajamas and slippers.

"Uh-uh-um, all the other bathrooms are occupied, so I figured I'd have a better chance of trying the senator's bathroom." She laughed bashfully to punctuate the lie.

"I completely understand." Mister Mouse squinted his eyes, tilting his head. "You seem very familiar. You're one of my son's interns, yes?"

"No, I'm a plus-one, but with a face like mine, people often mistake me for someone else."

Mister Mouse pushed up his glasses. "It's your voice. I feel like I've heard it before somewhere."

"Well, that's a new one," Venus teased. "I better get back to the party."

"Yes, yes. Of course," Mister Mouse agreed, unblocking her path to freedom. "Please, enjoy yourself."

It took every ounce of Venus's strength not to bolt. She had always known Mister Mouse was a pseudonym to protect his identity. Nearly all of her clients did that, but never once did she think that the son he so desperately wanted to reunite with was *so fucking important.*

Halfway down the stairs, a realization fell like a ton of bricks on her head. Her trot hastened, and she found the Grand Witcher chatting with Senator Mounsey himself.

Madame Sharma used an appraising glance to regard Venus in mid-laugh of a senator-delivered joke. She washed down the bubbly sound with a sip from her champagne flute, then teased warmly, "I was starting to wonder where you wandered off to."

"Wandering off is easy. Finding your way back is the hard part," Venus returned, earning Senator Mounsey's deep-chested chuckle. She presented a tight smile as her flag of forthcoming bad news.

If she brewed that trinary-note peitho potion, it wouldn't sway the senator to vote against the Registration Act.

It would straight-up kill him.

"And you going to introduce us, Sharma?" he asked, arching an eyebrow.

"Forgive me. Where are my matters?" Madame Sharma smiled, gesturing between Venus and the politician. "Winston, this is my intern Dionaea."

He extended his hand, but all Venus did was stare at the familiar watch of worn leather and dull gold on his wrist.

"Dionaea, don't be rude," Madame Sharma uttered.

The name startled her, rooting her back into the moment. She jerked her gaze up, embarrassment coloring her cheeks for not staying on task.

"I'm sorry." Venus accepted his offered hand, giving one good shake.

His grip was firm, absolute, and robust.

"That's quite alright," he assured, his smile friendly.

His gaze was kind even though he knew what Venus was.

But she knew what he was, too.

One of the indecisive senators who held the fate of all witchers in his hands.

"It's a gift from my father. He wore it for fifty years. Now, it's my turn." He adjusted his wristwatch, peering at it with pride. An emotional forgery she shaped and molded in her kitchen with a stove's heat and her agony.

Within 24 hours, she'd seen her handiwork in the flesh for the second time.

"It suits you well," Madame Sharma said, clicking an impatient nail against her glass. "Wouldn't you agree, Dionaea?"

"Absolutely," Venus lied, her smile as fake as the familial love he felt and the Grand Witcher's pleasant warmth.

Two of them were liars, and one was living a lie.

He nodded his thanks at the compliment.

"Speaking of watches, have you had time to think about our discussion regarding the Registration Act, Senator?" Madame Sharma asked, cocking her head.

His smile dimmed. Other guests in earshot aimed unapproving glances.

He slipped his hands in his pockets, his tone disappointed. "Tonight's about pleasure, Matrika. Not politics."

"Dionaea and I are witchers in a room full of politicians who intend to vote on an anti-witcher bill soon," Madame Sharma said smoothly. "I don't find much pleasure in mingling with senators who support it, but don't count me as naive for thinking you're nothing like them."

She raked her eyes over his form, cold and unimpressed.

Venus's eyebrows shot up, lips pressing tight to cage her smile and cork the laugh in her throat.

Senator Mounsey's face fell blank with shock. Madame Sharma presented her half-gone champagne. He took it, stunned.

"We'll keep in touch, Senator," she said, sauntering away with the grace of an empress. Partyers made way for their departure, throwing whispers and glares at their backs.

Venus tossed Senator Mounsey a final glance, noting his paling skin. Once outside, she felt like she could breathe again.

"As I said before, don't let the illusion fool you." Madame Sharma smirked.

As they waited for the limo to pull around, an angered voice drew their attention to the right.

A man paced on his cell, his face reddening. "You said you'd only be gone thirty minutes. It's been two hours!"

"Maybe, tonight will be pleasurable after all," Madame Sharma noted, a smile reaching her eyes before she prowled over.

Guests of extravagant parties often walked away with a party favor or two. The Grand Witcher walked away with a man. A senator, to be exact. Senator Harold Cavendish lay sprawled on the limo's carpeted floor. All it took was an offered glass of wine. After a few sips, the senator grinned sleepily and slumped over.

It proved difficult for Venus *not* to stare at the unconscious man.

"Hothead Harry should be the least of your worries, my dear," Madame Sharma stated, propping her feet on his back. "Now, explain to me what's the matter."

Venus took a deep breath, lacing her fingers on her lap. "A few weeks ago, a client named Mister Mouse came to me in need of a binary-note for familial love. He said he wanted his estranged son to love him again."

Madame Sharma smirked. "Let me guess, Mister Mouse is the long-lost father who miraculously came back into Senator Mounsey's life, and you're the one who made the reunion possible."

"Senator Mounsey's already been poisoned by one potion. His human body can't handle two. If you give him that trinary-note peitho potion, the brews will cancel out and he'll die from an overdose." Venus fidgeted in her lap, nervousness edging her voice. "Which jeopardizes your plan."

Madame Sharma laughed, shaking her head. "Who says it jeopardizes my plan?"

"Um, without the potion, you can't use him."

"Potions aren't the only things that bewitch"—the Grand Witcher dug a needle-point heel into the unstirring Senator Cavendish's back—"these disgusting creatures, Miss Stoneheart. In fact, it's the most intoxicating substance on Earth. Care to take a guess?"

Venus tilted her head. "Money?"

"Very close, but money will only get you so far. Money won't work on men like Winston Mounsey. The answer is power." Madame Sharma replenished her empty flute with chilled champagne. "There's a difference between magic and power, Miss Stoneheart. Power earns you respect. Power puts you above reproach. Power is what makes you rich."

"If a bribe won't work, then what will?"

Playfulness gleamed in the Grand Witcher's dark eyes as she sipped her champagne. "I'll handle Senator Mounsey myself. In the meantime, Cavendish will have to be our first victim."

CHAPTER
FOURTEEN

A well of magic, also known as a magic well, is an internal source of strength that sustains a witcher's magic. If it dries or over-flows, health and magic may suffer. Or, in extreme cases, a witcher may die.

—Witcherpedia, an online witchery encyclopedia

A VIAL OF FRESH BLOOD ROLLED AROUND INSIDE VENUS'S CLUTCH with her every step. The limo whisked away behind her, and the Epione Hospital's automatic doors whooshed open.

With Senator Mounsey no longer a target for a peitho potion, Venus gave his hair away to the wind on the ride here. Senator Cavendish's thin-ning mane would've worked just fine, but Madame Sharma said she never wasted a chance to make a politician bleed.

Venus regarded blood both as a necessity and a nuisance. An ingredient for potions or a stain to scrub out of her clothes. Never something to *relish*.

She felt a key twist within her as the Grand Witcher handed her a switchblade, unlocking a tiny part of her that *liked* hurting Hothead Harry. A part untouched by *It*. But as soon as she stepped out of the limo, her enjoyment's drug-like high came crashing down.

Resentment stabbed her as punishment, twisting its knife.

As Venus took an elevator to the eighth floor, an ICU, she wore a pained expression. She passed the understaffed nurses' station and gently pushed at an ajar wooden door.

She found a man comatose in his hospital bed, with IVs in his dark veiny arms and a feeding tube in his left nostril. Medical machines hummed and beeped. Flowers, balloons, cards, letters, and teddy bears covered nearly every flat surface in the room.

Janus's bag and the leather-bound photo album sat together on an olive-green sleeper sofa for visitors.

Seeing Malik in such a fragile state was so odd as he was one of the world's most influential and recognizable witchers. As the last surviving WASP founder, he served as the face of the witcher rights and species equality movement. He inspired millions and enraged twice as many.

His intended murderer believed that WASP would perish if he did. However, the organization continued to prosper even after he took a bullet to the head for it and survived.

Malik's calling to projection allowed him to exist in an intangible form separate from his body. He appeared and vanished as he pleased. He chose who was worthy of his presence. His well of magic still very much filled, considering how often he made public and television appearances.

"He's a ghost, haunting whoever the hell he pleases," Uncle Bram used to say whenever he read a newspaper story about his ex-brother-in-law. Yet Malik Jenkins hadn't visited his only daughter since she was *six*, only a few months after the shooting.

Venus wasn't sure whether it was her mom's doing, his, or simply the last thing they could agree on before their marriage imploded. His absence molded her sister into a little girl who wanted her daddy to notice her at all costs.

Even if it meant screaming in the streets to be heard.

Even if it meant becoming a martyr.

No, not on my watch, Venus thought, gripping his hospital bed's railing. Then tiny hairs rose on her nape as a sharp, uncanny sensation washed over her.

A warning bell not to be ignored.

"You're being watched," It warned.

Venus glimpsed around the room. Within an eyeblink, he appeared, standing before the hospital window. She clenched her chest, sucking in a loud breath.

Her heart's rhythm filled her ears like a wild drumbeat.

"It's good to see you, Venus," Malik greeted in his deep, rich voice.

"Good to see you too, Malik," she hissed, fighting the urge to punch at his unconscious body's shoulder. "Also, what the fuck? Warn a bitch before you decide to project yourself like that."

She got an amused sideways glance from him. "Duly noted."

A moment passed between them, the air heavy with something she couldn't quite put her finger on.

"I don't have much time, so I'll keep this brief," he said, looking to the hospital door. "Thank you for keeping an eye on Janus."

Venus frowned, crossing her arms. "I don't need your gratitude. I'll always do what needs to be done for her."

He nodded, glancing at the door again. "That girl's my world, Venus."

"Have you told her that, Malik?" She tilted her head, her tone as sharp as a knife.

Tapping a finger on her chin, she pretended to think. "My guess is no. Or you wouldn't be on the lookout because you're worried she'll come in and see you."

"I have my reasons, Venus. But make no mistake. I love my daughter."

"Then show *her* that because the only reason she does the things she does for you is to get your attention," Venus said, all thorns and venom. "She wants to go to that fucking protest tomorrow because she loves you. And if *you* don't tell her not to go, she will get herself killed. And if she does, I swear on my mom's grave, I'll kill you. You damn well know what I can do."

She glared at his helpless body in the hospital bed. His eyelids twitched, followed by a flinch.

Behind her, disappointment darkened his tone. "If Darius were here and he heard you talking like that—"

She swirled around to face him, interrupting. "That's the difference between you and him. If he were still alive, he'd *be* here for me."

He stared at her blankly, but his anger jumped into her, *his* shade of red flaring across her eyes.

"Did I hit a nerve, Malik?" Venus asked, smirking.

"You didn't hit a nerve, baby girl. That's blunt force trauma," It said proudly.

Malik shook his head as if she were a lost cause. "You're only acting like this because Rissa taught you to."

Venus rolled her eyes at that accusation. "I'm acting like this because I love my sister. If you do, too, you'll *tell* her not to go to the protest tomorrow."

She jerked her attention to the hospital door as it opened.

And just like that, Malik was gone, proving he loved *his pride* more than the girl he said was *his pride and joy.*

"Holy shit, you're back from the party early." Her sister ambled in, finishing off a soda. "So, how did it go?"

"It *definitely* went." Venus cleared her throat, claiming a spot on the sleeper sofa by the window Malik had stood by moments earlier. "How's the father-daughter bonding time coming along?"

Janus tossed the can into the trash and moved to her dad's bedside. "He hasn't come around yet. As long as his physical anchor is safe, he has no reason to. I'm just happy to be here."

"You're a *legit* reason." Venus picked up the dusty album and plopped it onto her lap, aching to relieve an itch to see photos of their mom, young and hopeful. "And don't ever think any different, Jay."

A ghost of a smile graced her lips as she turned the thick pages, admiring memories that weren't hers. Candid and carefree pictures gave way to staged and serious ones.

Of her parents, of Matrika, of Owen, of Malik.

Photographs of WASP unfolded right before Venus, from her mom's college sophomore year in 2000 to her dad's expulsion from Georgetown in 2002 to the day WASP opened up its first headquarters in 2003.

"My dad has a *purpose*, Vee." Janus gestured to the excess of gifts left by admirers. "He's out there on the grind, making a difference and trying to change the world. That's *more* important than midnight chitchats and photos of old glory days."

"Well, my schedule is wide open for a midnight chitchat." Venus paused at a group photo of her parents, Malik, Owen, and Matrika. On the left, her parents held hands. On the right, Owen had his arms around the future Grand Witcher's waist. Malik stood in the middle among his friends, yet he was alone.

Squinting, Venus tilted her head.

Presley's dad and Madame Sharma dated? Did it end badly? Maybe, so. Throughout the 2003 photos, Matrika's presence gradually waned until she was nowhere to be seen at the album's end.

If those two had a bad breakup, that'd explained the bad blood Venus sensed between the Grand Witcher and Miss Florence.

Coincidence or planned, being your ex's mom's boss was *wild*.

Janus threw her hands up, shoving an exasperated sigh out of her mouth. "You just want to talk about tomorrow. I'm done with that. Before you got here, me and Ty argued for nearly an hour on the phone. All that back-and-forth gave me a headache and made me thirsty. How many times do I have to tell y'all I *never* said I was going?"

"*Never* said and a promise *not* to are two different beasts, Jay. You're not slick. There's no loophole around us looking out for you."

Silence.

Then Janus slumped her shoulders and gathered Malik's limp hand, whispering a dejected *fine*.

A wave of Janus's resignation swooshed and churned in Venus's skull, making her dizzy. She cradled her forehead, squinting to concentrate.

Janus's eyebrows squished together as she examined her dad's hand.

"What?" Venus asked. "What's wrong?"

Janus tilted her head, curious. "His palm has a scar, and it looks sorta new."

A night shift nurse knocked and entered, her expression soft with sympathy as she informed them their after-hours visitation privileges had ended.

———

JUNE 27, 2023

Venus found more ease in an empty bathtub than in her own bed. She wanted to lie against something unforgivingly hard to keep herself awake. Lulling herself back to sleep wasn't an option when all her nightmares had her dead mom and Julius Keller's burned corpse in them.

Not that she needed to be asleep for nightmarish things to visit her. However, it was a choice. Her *choice* was a rarity, since puppets were at the mercy of whoever pulled the strings.

Mermaid pajamas, a familiar comfort, replaced taffeta and pearls. She wore a headscarf over her hair.

When she chipped away her façade , it brought her a fraction closer to some remnant of who she once was before all the bad came rushing in. Her deviation coiled meanly around her sense of self, squeezing her like a boa constrictor would its prey.

Even though Janus resided a doorknob twist away, Venus couldn't deny the heavy loneliness compressing her like a second gravity. Her new cell glowed brightly against the darkness as she stared at the number pad.

It squirmed inside her, a secondhand impatience infecting her. *"Here you are, drowning in your own self-pity. If you aren't careful, I just might…"*

Her thumb gave a rolling flex. A dead giveaway of *It* trying to override her will. A messy mix of dismay and determination burst within her. She wrenched back her freedom, burrowing her deviation *down, down, down.*

She heard *Its* string of profanities wane as she labored.

Her chest heaved and her lungs burned.

Internal silence greeted her, but deep down, *It* bucked and gnawed at her imposed prison. She flinched as *Its* tantrum rippled through her in feverish, achy waves, but she endured.

For how long, though, she wasn't certain.

She couldn't keep on like this, walking around like a ticking bomb with nothing to hold back the explosion. She wanted to be around someone who made her feel safe from herself.

Venus gathered the nerve to dial a number she knew by heart now.

Her heartbeat kicked up as each ring went unanswered.

On the last one, a tired raspy voice finally answered. "I was wondering when you'd call."

"I need a friend, Presley," she admitted.

Presley hummed a soft *hm*, then asked, "Is that what we are? Friends?"

"To be honest? I have no damn clue," she said softly, wondering if it was best for them both if she didn't.

"And that terrifies you, doesn't it?"

Her bitter laugh bounced off the bathroom walls. "You have no idea."

It writhed. Venus squeezed her eyelids shut, sharpening her concentration to pin *It* in place. *It* weakened further, but her might dwindled, too.

"Alright," Presley said. "Meet me at our old hangout in thirty."

Venus braced herself on the billboard's ledge, peering down at the world below her dangling feet. As dawn neared, shades of blue stained everything. Graffiti and scorch marks marred the billboard's *REPORT ILLEGAL WITCHER ACTIVITY* advertisement. The distant song of fire truck sirens filled the night.

It shuddered in delight at the prospect of fiery deaths.

Memories of Julius Keller's burned corpse leaked through her tight internal grip.

She struggled to gather her fraying composure, hugging herself for strength—for comfort.

A foreign hand touched her shoulder, startling her. She jerked away, darting an alert gaze at the intruder breaching her personal space. Her alarm stepped aside for shame as she registered the concern on Presley's face.

As a pathetic apology, she muttered *my bad.*

Presley retracted their hand, taking a generous swig from a flask.

"When'd you take up drinking? I thought you hated alcohol."

"Three years ago," they answered. "Grew a taste for it."

Venus stiffened. "So, I drove you to drink."

"I never said—"

"You don't have to, Pres. I already know the truth."

Toward the end of her brewer training, a fifteen-year-old Venus grew anxious to brew unsupervised. She got told she wasn't ready for car ride consultations or deliveries, either. So, her mom did those instead, passing off Venus's blood, sweat, and tears as her own.

While Clarissa was making a delivery one night, the rotary phone rang. Venus took the call and nearly penciled the consultation into the appointment book, but a plan spooled inside her mind.

1. Keep the meeting secret.
2. Pick up the client from the Hideout by lying to Mom that you need the car to do supply runs.
3. Double the price for which love potion the client wanted.
4. Brew the potion and do the delivery under Mom's nose.
5. You're a clever rich bitch, Venus Genevieve Stoneheart.

Cue smug nail buffing.

However, the client, Baldwin Tillery, had his own plan, too.

1. Procure an illegal love potion.
2. Use said love potion on Heloise, the ailing Tillery matriarch, to get back in her good graces after he stole millions.
3. Wedge his name back into the will before she croaked.
4. Ka-ching.

However, he did not know that another had *already* given Heloise a love potion. Nor did Venus know she had brewed *that* love potion as well. Weeks prior. She didn't know because her mom kept her in the dark about clients. Back then, patrons were just vials of blood to her. Their desires just another ingredient to add to a cauldron.

Had she known she had helped a member of the Tillery clan claim Heloise's love, she would've said no to Baldwin.

But she didn't know.

So, Heloise overdosed when she sipped tea poisoned with love for her estranged grandson.

Which made Baldwin a murderer. A clumsy murderer, at that, because he *left* the potion bottle at the crime scene. Hours later, he called Venus's burner, claiming he wanted to tip her for her *excellent* services. With no car, she asked Presley for a ride to a nature preserve trail in Alexandria.

"Just park over there and lie low," she instructed that night, pointing to a far corner of the parking lot.

In her eyes, all she saw were dollar signs, but Baldwin's fear and desperation made her see the truth. A terrible thing had happened. If he was going down for it, so was she. He used a gun loaded with iron bullets to coerce her toward his car. A force picked Baldwin up and catapulted him against a tree, making his skull crack open.

She was shoved out of her memories and back into her present as Presley's anger splintered through her blood.

Presley snapped, jabbing a finger into their chest with each *my*. "It was *my* choice to throw that bastard, and it was *my* idea to burn him in the woods! It's *my* fault we're deviants. Not yours. That's why I left. All of this is on me."

Tears swelled in her eyes, refusing to fall. "If I hadn't—"

"Stop it, Vee. Enough," Presley cut her off quickly, anger tautening the lines of their neck. "You wanted me to admit the truth. There it is."

Venus now understood it did not matter whose fault it was. They were both bound by and stained by the blood of Baldwin Tillery.

A deep, profound bond much like a blood oath or a blood-tether.

Venus snatched their flask, taking a big gulp. She coughed at the recreational brew's potency, liquid magic gliding down her throat and straight to her brain.

"A week after you left, I snuck to the pharmacy to get some snacks after school. Mom grounded me for sneaking behind her back. It makes me wonder what would have happened if I had just gone straight home, because that day some robbers busted in and held Aunt Key at gunpoint." Her lips quivered as she let out a shaky exhale. "I hid at the end of an aisle, but one of them found me and put a gun to my head."

She sniffled, taking a swig to wash down a lump of guilt. "A voice in my head said it could help. All I had to do was let it out, so I did. *It* infected the robber and made him turn on all his friends."

Venus flinched as those three gunshots echoed in her head. "Then he shot himself. And you want to know the fucked-up part? *It* convinced me that I liked what happened."

A gust of wind licked at her face, cooling her bothered flesh.

To her, the relief seemed undeserving.

"You saved lives," Presley said.

She returned the flask, using her hoodie sleeve to erase her tears. "But I've ruined more lives than I've saved, and *It* wants even more."

"*Tick-tock, tick-tock,*" *It* whispered to her.

"As punishment for what I did, I never went out or had fun. So, I had a lot of time to think about *why* I did it." Melancholy rewrote Presley's face, their eyelids drooping halfway in thought. "Would I be different if my mother kept me?"

The only thing anyone knew about Presley's birth mother was that she left her newborn in a car seat on Owen's doorstep months after a drunken one-night stand. No one knew her name or what she looked like. Not even Owen remembered.

"I'm not mad at her for doing it. I'm sure she has her reasons, but I just want to know why." Presley put the flask away, their tone soft. "I keep telling myself it'll fix one of the broken pieces inside me, but for all I know, she could be dead."

"Maybe, she's not." She tiredly propped her cheek on their shoulder. "You could look in the Black Book for trackers."

"Looking isn't cheap. Trackers have to destroy something precious, like her personal belonging or a memory of her. I have neither." They leaned their head against hers, sliding an arm around her waist. "I was only three when my dad died, so I don't remember anything about him, either, but at least I have his photos, videos, and interviews. I studied them all to feel closer to him."

Their sadness weighed heavy on Venus like a burden. She gave a lone nod, having studied her dad, too. Back then, she wanted to understand him better, thinking it'd help her understand herself.

But all it did was bring more questions. Serious questions she didn't dare ask her mom, like what he most feared or what kind of life he wanted to have before the Great Discovery and WASP. And dumbass questions she felt silly asking Aunt Key, like what his favorite TV show was growing up or if he was as mischievous as the smiles in his childhood photos hinted.

So, she decided it was best not to bother asking at all.

"I've also convinced myself I *feel* his love for me. So, for him, I learned to love myself. That helped me control my deviation." Presley's words rode on a whisper as their lips brushed her forehead, warm breath stirring her hair. "You got to love and respect yourself. It's the only way to keep your deviation in check. If you can't do that for you, then do it for Janus, Ty, and Bram. They all need you, Vee."

Venus closed her eyes, her flesh coming alive with goosebumps.

That task seemed more challenging than washing her dead mom's body or binding herself to a blood oath with Madame Sharma.

A heavy doubt stuffed her stomach.

But maybe, she could at least try.

After exchanging pity-party stories on a billboard ledge, the two tiptoed into her bedroom. Shutting the door behind her, Presley sat on her bed, their forearms propped on their thighs.

"Make yourself at home," she sighed tiredly, hanging her hoodie on the door hook.

Presley glanced around. "Nothing's changed."

"No point in fixing what's not broken," she said. "All these things make me happy."

Presley's shoulders shook with quiet laughter.

She frowned, moving to the bed. "What's so funny?"

While holding a purple octopus plushie, their lips curved into a smile. Then they unzipped the back and pulled out a stuffed satin heart with black marker writing.

P+V

BFFS 4EVA

"I got this to ask you out on a date, but before I could even get the question out, you took the plushie and called me the *bestest* friend in the world."

"*You* wanted to date *me*?" Venus blinked, sitting beside them.

Presley gave her a *be-for-real* look as they returned the heart and zipped up the plushie's back.

She chewed on her bottom lip, contemplating their words. Retracing her steps down memory lane. Moments when Presley's smiles and gazes didn't radiate philia love, *friendship* love. Moments where she wondered if Presley wanted more. Moments of denying herself the possibility of more because she didn't want to ruin what they both had.

"I guess you're right." Venus reclined on the bed to stare at the constellation of glow-in-the-dark stars on her ceiling. A strange question crawled onto her tongue the more she thought.

They unscrewed their flask, lying back as well.

"I need to know something." She lolled her head to watch them take a gulp.

A thin stream of bewitched liquor trickled from the corner of their mouth. "Aight, spill it."

Venus reached over, erasing it with a thumb swipe.

"Why didn't you hesitate"—she paused—"to kill Baldwin?"

"What the hell kind of friend would I be if I hadn't?" Presley countered.

Venus stared at the ceiling again. A *thank you* didn't sound like a proper response. Everything she could've said sounded wrong in her head and tasted wrong on her tongue.

She was in Presley's debt as much as she was the Grand Witcher's.

Grasping her chin, they navigated her eyes back to them. "Like I said, it was my choice. You've put up warning signs and caution tape all around you to keep everybody away, but I'm not everybody, Venus. What I did that night is proof."

"You're right, Pres. You're not," she concurred. "If you're not a stranger or friend, what *should* you be to me?"

"After everything we've been through, more."

Her heart wedged itself in her throat, its pulse creeping up.

"And what exactly does that entail?"

"Anything we want." Their fingers caressed her jaw. "What do you want, Venus?"

Her eyelids fluttered shut. She bit her bottom lip, a trail of blooming warmth following their touch.

A touch that felt like the promise of more.

And she wanted to explore it.

"I want to forget. Just for a little while." Venus blanketed her hand over theirs as they cupped the nape of her neck.

Presley brought her closer. Their nose brushed against hers, warm breaths tingling.

"And I want to remember everything."

CHAPTER
FIFTEEN

My daughter is named after the Roman goddess of love
because I wanted her to know love can exist in this cruel world.
I don't want her to see the world through rose-colored glasses.
I want her to feel loved and love who she chooses.

—Darius Knox, WASP cofounder

VENUS SWALLOWED PRESLEY'S MOAN WITH A KISS. FINGERNAILS BIT
meanly into her hips and guided her to go faster and harder, increasing
her collection of fresh and hours-old nicks.

She broke the hungry kiss and pressed her forehead against theirs.
Her eyes rolled back from bliss, her eyelids beating like butterfly wings.

A loud moan rippled in her throat.

Presley unleashed a sharp gasp, succumbing to another peak of
euphoria.

Their bodies stilled, their hurried breaths tangling.

"I can't think straight for shit," they panted.

"That's the whole point," Venus remarked unevenly, a sprinkle of
humor flavoring her delivery as she cascaded back to earth. She climbed
off them and collapsed beside them, studying her orgasm's residuals as
globs of color pigmented the air.

Presley slid off the bed to discard the spent protection in the waste
bin by her vanity. Prismatic blobs awaited her when she closed her eyes,
dancing and swirling for her entertainment.

The bed dipped, knees parted her legs, and hips separated her thighs. They trapped her against the mattress, their slick flesh and addictive warmth as her sky. Their mouth bestowed a soft, damp kiss on her neck's wild pulse, then suckled there as if to tame it to submission.

Venus pouted as their lips left her neck.

They reclaimed a spot at her side, exhaling.

Brown, slender fingers embraced hers, positioning the union in the morning light.

"I got you, Vee." A thumb stroked hers. "Always have, always will."

Their scarred palm pressed against hers. At the auroras party, Venus asked the story behind the scar, pouting a spoiled brat when they told her no.

Now, she realized that maybe Presley *couldn't* tell. Like hers, maybe a blood oath ensured they didn't. Maybe, that's why they returned after so long, convinced that *distance* would bring them *deliverance*.

Venus pushed the theories out of her mind to make room for a truth.

Being close to Presley Carter made her feel free.

***

The front door flung wide open as Venus and Presley ate cereal at the kitchen table.

"Janus!" A bewildered Tyrell rushed in, his fear scraping down her spine.

She clattered her spoon into her bowl. "She's asleep. What's wrong?"

Tyrell cursed loudly, pounding a fist against his temple.

"No, she's not," he growled. "I told Jay not to go."

A panicked Venus raced into her sister's room, only to find Patches on the bed, still as a statue.

She dropped to her knees and leaned close to address him, her whisper a desperate quaver. "Patches, where is she?"

Her words flipped a switch inside him, and he touched her forehead with his.

Closing her lids, a vision filled her mind through his eyes.

Janus wore an all-black outfit. FIGHT POWER WITH MAGIC graced her shirt in bold white letters. She had her hair in a coarse, bushy ponytail. Crouching down, she softly lifted Patches' chin, her eyes peering into his to address Venus.

"I've left this message with Patches and told him not to move until you speak to him." Janus began hesitantly, but as she went on, her voice became more confident. *"If you're seeing this, you either realize I'm gone or Ty snitched on me. I'm sorry, Vee. I know I promised you I wouldn't go, but I've got to do this. Y'all can cuss me out when I get home."*

With an air kiss and an I-love-you, the message ended.

Venus blinked slowly as the scene faded. Only the darkness in her head remained. She felt dread creep in, her breath got thicker like sludge in her lungs, and her belly sank like a stone.

Vivid scenes of witchers and militant Swiggers clashing clouded her mind. She could almost sense *Its* smug smile stroking her insides.

She felt ill as she walked back into the kitchen.

"I'll handle it," she breathed, trying her best to remain calm. "I'll go get her."

Tyrell shook his head, using a cut gesture across his throat. "Naw, you ain't going by yourself. We both going together."

"Ty, you can't go as you are. Plus, if you did change shape, we all know you can't keep it!" Her fingers coiled into fists, quiet anger festering into something worse. "It's safer if everybody stays here. I'll bring her back myself."

Offended, he sucked his teeth, patting his chest. "Let me worry about me, aight? Jay might not be my blood, but she is my kin. And I damn well know you ain't the one to talk about me holding my shape when you got a whole-ass supervillain tryna break outta you."

Venus recoiled at the insult, then ground out, "What did you just say to me?"

"I said what I said." Tyrell clapped out each word with emphasis.

"Aye, *both* y'all need to pump the brakes." Presley intervened, their gaze flitting between her and Tyrell. "Fighting won't get anything accomplished."

"You're *absolutely* right. I don't have time for this bullshit." Venus stalked out of the kitchen, tossing her hair over her shoulder. "Be ready in five minutes!"

"Bet!" Tyrell countered.

She marched into her bedroom, itching to suit up for war.

She slipped a pink-and-black checkered hoodie over her pajama tank top. She wore jeans, combat boots, and a sharp-toothed mouth mask.

"You got room for one more in your posse?"

She turned to face Presley. "I couldn't ask that of you. This is my problem."

"You don't have to fight this on your own, Venus," they said. "What do you have to lose by letting me come along?"

"You'll mess this up. You always do. We need them," It cooed, hosting a feast for her insecurities. Self-doubt ravaged her body, picking its fangs with the bones of her confidence.

"I won't take no for an answer, Vee. Now, do you have another one of those cute mouth masks?"

Venus realigned her attention to what mattered most.

Finding her sister.

She handed over a teddy bear one.

As her car sped through the streets, the blood-tether's silence gave her the assurance she needed to know her sister wasn't in harm's way. Yet. It was best to park at the nearest Metro station and hop on a line to get to Pennsylvania Avenue.

A body heat sensor clocked the trio's descent into a Metro subway station. Another did the same as they boarded the subway train. A digital counter's red digits and three chimes announced their arrival. A faint whiff of iron greeted them as humans fled to the next train car.

Tyrell, shaped as a young white guy, staggered to a vacant seat, collapsing into it with a wheeze. Presley claimed a spot beside him, coughing violently.

A sharp sting clawed at Venus's throat as if tiny needles pricked her airways. Her body trembled, but she was too antsy to sit. Her fingers gripped the handrail like a lifeline.

A gray-haired lady stayed put, her face of wrinkles set in a defiant scowl. She proudly pulled out an iron-infused pepper spray can, revealing herself as the culprit for their suffering.

Venus's watery eyes burned into the old woman.

"Give her something to be afraid of," *It* encouraged gently.

Its words sparked a tiny urge within her to obey.

Her hand tightened on the stationary rail as she fought against the suggestion. Yet she entered a silent contest of wills with the old biddy, refusing to back down from the challenge of winning a subtler war.

A war she wasn't sure who won. One moment she stood in a standoff for the ages, and in the next, she and her crew flowed into an engulfing river of witchers, human allies, choroused chants, and protest signs. They all maneuvered their way through the crowd, their eyes scanning and searching for any signs of a Black girl and her distinct mane of gray-black ombre curls.

The abundance of witchers in one place gave Venus a heady dose of sheer power, her magic scratching and whining uncontrollably for release.

The tsunami of violent intents sloshed around inside her.

She held *It* back, caging *It* in as best she could.

Opposing the peaceful demonstration were troops of Swiggers suited in their anti-witcher riot gear. Their monstrous tanks and barricades showcased a disgusting display of authority. Instructions to disassemble and disperse pierced the chants for peace and unity. Helicopters hovered above the rooftops, ready to coat the streets in iron dust. The Iron Watchers in chain mail lined the sidewalks, taunting peaceful protesters and rattling chains behind the militant police's protection.

"*Here it comes,*" *It* hissed with a twinge of bliss.

Venus didn't need to ask what *It* meant.

She felt the birth of war in her bones, a sounding trumpet no one else could hear.

"No!" she screamed defiantly as if the impending apocalypse would cease on her command.

It didn't.

An Iron Watch–made Molotov cocktail whizzed over the Swiggers' helmeted heads. Flames lapped the concrete, attacking innocents.

One witcher extinguished the fire eating away at the writhing bodies on the ground. The other retaliated by hurling a fireball in the direction from where the grenade came.

Pop! Pop! Pop!

Cans shot out into the crowds, bellowing out tear gas.

Witchers summoned wind gusts to thin out the intensity, but it didn't do much good. Tear gas had little effect on witchers, which the police knew. It was merely a tactic to weed out humans, forcing them to abandon their witcher friends to save their own necks. Swiggers on horses galloped with anti-witcher batons, striking masterfully at heads.

The suffering of others sought Venus out, trying to cram inside her. If it wasn't hers, she didn't want that shit. She ground her back teeth, shoving it *all* out, building a wall inside her even if it meant tearing her strength apart.

Walls consumed too much energy and never lasted, so Venus never used them. But now, she had no choice. A choice she'd pay dearly for later when the wall came crashing down.

The blood-tether yanked her roughly northbound toward the protest's front lines farther down Pennsylvania Avenue.

Damn it, Janus, she growled in the depths of her mind.

She caught Presley's eyes and jerked her head toward where they all needed to go.

They nodded and followed her.

"We have to keep moving!" She grabbed an utterly distracted Ty's hand, tugging him along.

It was hard for her to stay focused, too.

Emotions ambushed her, biting and clawing her skin to get inside.

But she had to keep going.

She had to—

Swoosh!

The twisted rope ring on her finger thrummed to life, coating her body in a translucent shimmery defensive shield. The barrier curved the bullet's trajectory to hit another victim.

A boy, not much older than her, fell to the ground from the force, shrieking and convulsing as blood bloomed across his green T-shirt. Tangles of smoke erupted from an entry wound as an iron bullet meant for her ate at him.

Protected due to his proximity to Venus, Ty gaped at the wounded boy in shock.

Someone rushed to the boy's aid and hauled him off.

"The fuck," Venus panted, gawking at the ring as its radiance petered out.

Now she knew why the Grand Witcher gave her this.

It was a protection ring. She wore a ring designed to protect her from the recoil of a trinary-note. Today, however, it saved her from bullets, too.

She whipped her head around, trying to pinpoint the bullet's origin. Momentarily, her deviation tugged at her internal puppet strings, guiding her to look up at a sniper's gun from a high rooftop.

"I can taste your bed buddy's anger," her deviation whispered, pleased.

She could taste the sharpness of it, too. Presley glared at the destruction and violence. The fine hairs on her skin stood on end as their aura blazed and swelled, saturating the charged air. Then they slammed their fist into the street. A tidal wave of radiant magic surged forth, with the three of them standing at its very heart. As it collided with bodies, white light bled from witcher eyes.

Protesters' callings flared up. A juiced-up witcher lifted a car, sending it soaring like a paper airplane. It headed straight for a marching flock of Swiggers. They were in tight formation, their iron shields raised, protecting officers who were firing riot control grenades from their launchers.

Horror, awe, and truth rallied together to ram into Venus.

Her alarmed gaze confronted Presley as she grasped their deviation's magnitude.

Tyrell plopped a hand on his blond head. "I ain't know you carried that kinda heat, Pres!"

Venus winced as the blood-tether plunged an invisible knife into her stomach, twisting hard. She bent over and let out a hoarse cry, snapping Presley out of an enraged trance.

Her cousin looped her arm around his neck, ushering her through the chaos.

"You good, Vee?" Tyrell asked.

Venus shook her head, wheezing out, "She's close."

"Where?" Presley urged, joining her other side.

She grimaced. "This way."

As she pursued the blood-tether's merciless guidance, she noted small clusters of witchers escaping down a specific alleyway.

The connection between her and Janus pulsed accordingly.
There.

In the passageway's mouth, the blood-tether's pull slackened and crumbled away. Janus stood with her back to them, feet set wide and palms outstretched. Escapees dashed through the five swirling doorways she kept open.

"Janus!" Venus broke away from Tyrell, racing toward her sister.

Janus tossed a startled glance over her shoulder, her eyes reddened and her nose bleeding profusely. The strain of maintaining the doorways was too much.

As the last trickle of witchers hurried through the portals, Venus grabbed her sister's shoulders and swiveled her around.

"Stop it now! You'll kill yourself!"

The portals dissolved when the concentration broke.

Janus yanked free, staggering back. "Dammit, Venus! I had it under control! I've never called up so many doorways for that long, and I could've gone longer. I'm getting better. I'm getting stronger."

"No, Janus! Presley's calling gave you a power boost," Venus said, pointing to them.

Presley nodded, taking a step closer. "My calling's influence isn't permanent. If you would've kept going, you'd be dead."

Janus shot Tyrell a glare. "At least I'd die doing what's right!"

Tyrell threw his hands up, snapping, "You stay tryna get yourself killed, J—"

He screamed as his back hunched into a grotesque bow. Bones shifted, jerked, and broke. The white skin he wore disintegrated as he became himself again, bit by bit. He hacked flu-like lung-quivering coughs, struggling for breath.

Presley reached him, holding on to him as he unfurled into himself.

"You good?" Presley asked.

Tyrell hung his head, nodding weakly. "We need to go, y'all."

Venus reached for Janus's arm, but her sister took a step back, defiant.

"I can handle myself." Janus spread her arms apart, preparing to summon a portal. "*Ya'll* the ones that need to go. I'll make a doorway."

"No, Janus! We're not leaving without you." Venus's tears rushed down her cheeks, everything becoming too much to handle. The wall within her collapsed under stress, her strength lying in the rubble. "You're my goddamn beating heart. If you die, what do I have left to live for?"

Venus limped to her sister, framing the girl's bloody face with her hands. "We promised each other we'd grow old together. Nowhere did I agree to early graves for the both of us. If someone's going to die first, it's going to be me. You'll have Bram and Aunt Key. Ty and Hakeem. Even your father will take care of you as best he can."

Janus's bottom lip quivered as she choked out a sob.

Venus tugged off the protection ring, slipping it on Janus's finger. "This will keep you safe."

"Don't move!"

Venus's blood ran cold.

Terror splayed across her sister's teary eyes.

Venus turned her head to follow the officer's movements as he cautiously entered the alleyway. His assault rifle's aim bounced between everyone as if he didn't know who to shoot first.

"*Stop brainwashing yourself into thinking you're a helpless runt, you stupid girl. You aren't powerful. You are power. Make him fear you,*" It screeched, ramming itself against the walls of her pathetic vow of abnegation. Walls no longer fortified by her reinforcement potions.

"*If you won't, I'll do it myself!*" It declared.

Venus released a pained gasp as she felt her vow break from *Its* brutality, cracks splintering the final stockade. She quivered in sheer agony, trying to keep herself from folding over. She gritted her teeth, caging her scream.

Tearily, she glanced at Janus, who mouthed the word *don't*.

It flexed her fingers, horror brewing inside her as it became her puppet master.

Violence beyond the alleyway strengthened and emboldened *It*.

"Let me show you how it's done."

She secreted black tentacles of inky magic.

"Venus!" Presley shouted.

In a panic, the Swigger shouted, "I'll give you until the count of three to retract your magic! One!"

She struggled to rip back the reins of her will, but *It* was a diligent fighter.

You can't do this, Venus begged internally.

"Two!"

"I can and I will," It returned, *Its* manifested corruption zipping toward the Swigger.

"Vee, control yourself!" Tyrell encouraged.

I'm trying, she wanted to scream, but her deviation seized her tongue.

"Three!"

Just as the officer's finger pulled the trigger, *It* struck him. Infected, he tramped off, turning his weapon on his own comrades like *It* wanted.

A force hit Venus.

She staggered into her sister's arms with wide eyes, making them both fall. Janus shrieked. "VENUS!"

Venus touched her chest's wetness. When she pulled back her shaky fingers, she realized the wetness was blood.

Her blood.

The bullet shot clean through her.

Shock overpowered the pain and she heaved frantically as the truth sank in.

She was dying.

"Ty, she's bleeding," Janus sobbed. "She's bleeding!"

Tyrell dropped to his knees, taking hold of her bloody hand. "Stay with us, Vee."

Dashing over, Presley instructed. "We need to get her to a hospital. Now!"

Rocking back and forth, Janus cried as she cradled Venus. "I'm so sorry. I'm so sorry. Please don't leave me. Don't leave me."

"It'll be okay," Venus lied shakily, giving her cousin's hand a weakening squeeze.

The fear of others filled her to the brim, spilling over.

"Give her to me, Janus," Presley reached down to scoop her up. "I need her now."

Tyrell grabbed Janus' shoulders, tears streaming down his face. "You gotta call up a doorway, Jay. You got to."

"Stay with us, Venus. You hear me?" Presley asked.

She nodded weakly, but her life seeped away gush by gush.

Janus summoned a portal to the entrance doors of the Epione Hospital.

Presley barreled into the ER lobby, shouting for help.

Time skipped beats.

One moment she was in Presley's arms. The next, she was on a gurney, surrounded by garbled visions of nurses and doctors working to keep her alive.

But it wasn't working.

"Janus," she whimpered, her sister's name tasting like blood.

The hospital equipment went haywire as her body did. "We're losing her!"

"*I hate you,*" *It* whispered.

Good, I hate you too, she whispered to *It* weakly as the world dissolved into nothingness.

CHAPTER
SIXTEEN

Sacrifice tells us much about ourselves. If you sacrifice for others, you're a treasure. If others only sacrifice for you, you're nothing more than a thief.

—Malik Jenkins, WASP cofounder

JUNE 28, 2023

VENUS AWOKE WITH A CHOKING GASP, HER NAILS CLAWING AT HER neck. Her eyes flitted around in a panicked frenzy, taking in her pastel surroundings too fast for her muddled brain to process.

Then three realizations pealed through her like a bell, vibrating down to her marrow.

Home. Safe. Alive.

She could only conclude her deviation orchestrated a fucked-up nightmare to make her think she had died. Sometimes, *It* painted her dreams with garish strokes of blood and violence, but the terror she reeled herself from was so *lifelike.*

It stirred slowly at her unvoiced accusation. *"There's only one way to find out."*

Its sheer exhaustion added weight to hers, heavying her sore limbs.

"You're only saying that to fuck with my head." Venus's words came out in a rasp, her throat swollen with thirst.

"And yet there's a tiny part of you that wonders," It countered.

The callout made her flinch with shame.

"Go on," It mocked.

Venus gave in to the urge, reaching underneath her tank top. She drew a breath as her fingertips found a knot of healed flesh. Her heart dried up in her chest. Her hand jerked out as though she had touched fire.

She whispered the word *no* as she got out of bed. Like a tot learning to walk, her wobbly legs shuddered under the universe's weight. She took a tragic tumble.

Venus reached for a bedpost and hauled herself to her feet with a laborious grunt.

She stumbled to her vanity and flumped onto the cushioned bench, yanking up her top. The soft yellowish light of morning unveiled a healed bullet wound.

Rapid-fire blinks of memory fragments splintered through her mind.

"Janus!" she screamed, staggering out of her room.

She braced herself against the walls and furniture for support.

A surge of determination drove her every step.

Venus froze in the kitchen's archway, her blood running cold.

"I'm glad you've finally decided to join us," Madame Sharma greeted from Bram's chair, lifting a WORLD'S BEST MOM mug in salute.

Clarissa Stoneheart's mug.

An upset Janus sat in her usual spot, using a fork to toy with her fluffy eggs. Her fear reached out to Venus, seeking an embrace.

By the kitchen back door, a heavyset stoic guard stood watch.

"Sit," the Grand Witcher ordered. "I insist."

Not wanting to rebel against the blood oath, Venus obeyed. Crisp bacon, scrambled eggs, and buttery biscuits adorned the breakfast table. An empty plate rested in front of her, but an odd coldness spread through her innards, spoiling her appetite.

Madame Sharma took a sip of coffee. "I suppose you have questions. I'll be generous and allow you three. Choose them carefully."

Venus squeezed her eyes shut as she tried to sort through the questions rushing through her mind like a whitewater rapid. There were *so* damn many.

As she decided what to ask first, anxiety churned in her stomach. Not because she thought it wasn't a good question, but because she feared the answer.

"How am I alive?"

Madame Sharma's expression shifted to contemplation. "Well, there are only two ways to bring back the dead. The first method requires a necromancer. The second method is *more*..." she paused, mulling over an appropriate word choice, "...*controversial*. As a brewer, you should be quite familiar with its infamy."

Venus clasped a hand over her mouth as the truth shone through the vague confession.

She spoke around her palm, her voice muffled. "You gave me a sacrificium potion?"

Someone *sacrificed* their life for hers. No brewer in their right mind would brew such a thing unless by coercion.

Nausea lurched from her belly, forcing her to stumble to the sink. Janus came to her aid and held back her hair. Puke spiraled down the drain. She flushed away the awful taste by slurping faucet water, not caring that it trickled down her chin.

Catching her breath, she clung to her sister, who guided her back to her seat. Janus refused to budge from her side and stroked her hair softly.

"We have an arrangement," Madame Sharma reminded as she sawed a piece of her biscuit, unperturbed, "which I've invested a pretty penny into. The ring should've protected you from a bullet if you had worn it, but instead, it graces your sister's finger."

Janus spoke up meekly. "Your Grandness, she only did it because—"

"I *know* why she did it," the Grand Witcher interrupted, her voice sharp with an edge, "but I didn't invest in *you*. Only her."

The rebuke made Janus's hand tremble in Venus's hair.

She wanted to shield her little sister from it but feared the blood oath would punish her. And if the blood oath taught her another lesson of obedience, she could only imagine how the burly guard would school Janus.

Madame Sharma's fractured mask restored itself to its original glory, her eyes slicing to the kitchen's archway beyond, then back to Janus. "Leave."

As Janus turned to leave, she bowed her head reluctantly.

Remembering something, the Grand Witcher snapped her fingers. "Oh, yes. Didn't you forget to give something back to your sister, dear?"

"Yes, Your Grandness." As instructed, Janus removed the protection ring and handed it over before she went. A warmth vibrated into Venus's skin as the ring united with her finger.

Madame Sharma put the fork down and used a napkin to dab her lips. "Now, what shall your last question be?"

Venus parted her lips to speak, but her question tripped on her tongue as an intense headache struck her with the subtlety of a runaway train. The world constricted around her in rhythmic pulses. Freedom. Suffocation. Freedom. Suffocation.

Being alive felt *undeserved* and *wrong*. She knew the cost of going to the protest, but another brewer paid her toll.

She hugged herself tightly, letting out a pained exhale. "How did you know I was dead?"

Madame Sharma hummed, nodding. "We learned of your passing from Nisha's girlfriend, Chelsea, who was one of the ER doctors on duty yesterday. She knew how much you meant to us."

Only the blurry faces of diligent doctors and nurses filled Venus's last memories. She did, however, remember how she *felt* on that gurney as her life seeped away.

Fear, hopelessness, acceptance.

The Grand Witcher opened a newspaper and settled on an article of interest, amusement coloring her voice. "A rogue Swigger takes the lives of seventeen fellow officers."

"I would've killed to have seen such a glorious show," It sighed longingly.

Venus chewed the corner of her lip. "I wasn't myself yesterday."

"Ah." Madame Sharma lowered the paper, arching an eyebrow. "So, we have your deviation to thank for this splendid feat?"

"See? She appreciates my handiwork," It huffed.

"Yes, Your Grandness." Venus turned her watery gaze elsewhere, ashamed.

Madame Sharma frowned. "You have the potential to be something great, Miss Stoneheart, but you let your weaknesses get the best of you. You look like a sad kicked puppy because you lost control, but sixty-four witchers also died yesterday. Those of greatness don't wallow in self-pity. They turn their flaws into weapons and their mistakes into milestones."

Venus winced as the words stabbed her.

"If not for your deviation, the witcher body count could have been *much, much, much* higher." The newspaper crinkled in Madame Sharma's increasingly firm grip, a muted ire pervading her demeanor. "My only complaint is that the Iron Watch death toll didn't exceed all others."

The Grand Witcher quickly folded and discarded the newspaper, recovering her measured composure. "Yesterday proves more than anything why the Registration Act *cannot* pass. We hired you for a job, Miss Stoneheart. You're no good to us dead. You have Cavendish's blood, but there are three senators to go. I'll deal with Mounsey myself."

The guard unglued himself from his post and stalked up to Venus, breaching the line between close and uncomfortably *close*. She flinched at his quick movements when he yanked something from his suit's pocket.

"Eat up." He dropped a glossy black booklet on her empty plate.

In bold white font, the title read:

THE UNOFFICIAL GUIDE TO POST-RESURRECTION CARE

The guard rounded the table and slid out of the Grand Witcher's chair.

"Nisha insisted I give you that to help you adjust." Madame Sharma rolled her eyes as she stood up, smoothing her palms over a lemon-yellow sheath dress's skirt. "Regarding your first solo mission, Ilyas will be here shortly to provide you with all the necessary information. Due to your delicate condition, I'll permit you to acquire additional help. And one more thing, Miss Stoneheart."

Venus tensed. "Yes, Your Grandness?"

"*Don't* disappoint me again." Madame Sharma walked out of the kitchen, her guard following.

Soon, they were out the door.

Venus hesitantly picked up the unofficial guide, prying it open to the middle pages. She read a single paragraph:

Sacrificium potions can revive the dead but can't replenish the Revived's magic. Resurrection is unnatural and traumatic to the Revived's mind, body, and magic. It takes time and a regimen of restoration potions and/or teas to rebuild magical strength.

That explained why her deviation fluttered pitifully inside her like a dying heart. Punishment well deserved. Her resurrection did something neither reinforcement potions nor immature vows of abnegation could do: incapacitate *It*.

What a sweet, fucked-up twist of irony.

Patches joined her in the kitchen, leaping into her lap.

"Jay sent you to check up on me, huh?" She gathered him up in her arms. He nuzzled his cheek against the hollow of her throat and purred.

Venus stared off into space, absentmindedly scratching the familiar's chin. She struggled to process the fact she shouldn't be *here*. She shouldn't be able to *pet* a familiar, *sit* at the kitchen table, or *exist*.

"*Be grateful,*" It said.

"All of this is your fault," she whispered angrily. "All of it."

"*I saved lives. So many lives.*" The vigor in her deviation's voice waned as It succumbed to fatigue, going utterly still in her bones.

"Yes, and ruined many more."

The breath in her lungs and the anima within her didn't belong to her. And yet it was expected of her to keep on keeping on.

Elder Glenn once told her: "*Instead of facing your problems, your mother taught you how to bury them.*"

He regarded that as a problem within a *bigger* problem, but it glinted like a key and caught Venus's eye.

Burying everything gave her a sense of control because she got to decide how deep to dig. She wanted to bury all the memories, thoughts, and feelings leading up to the moment she took her last breath.

That was the only way to get through this.

To try and make it to the other side.

Venus buried misfortunes like a pro. She buried what she and Presley did to Baldwin Tillery. She did the same for what her deviation did to those robbers. Now, the events of yesterday and her reason for breathing were just two more things she had to lay to rest in her graveyard of skeletons.

Just like Clarissa Abigail Stoneheart taught her.

Clamping her eyelids shut, she shoved all those painful things into that hollowness inside her that grew bit by bit each day.

As the back door flew open, Ilyas entered, carrying a glossy wooden box and a manila envelope.

His arrival not only made her jump in her seat but irritated the fuck out of her, too.

The door shut on its own accord.

Patches got onto the table, watching every move of their new visitor closely. She would've shooed him off any other day since *anything* with paws had *no* business being on a table meant for eating.

But probably having smelled the bad blood between her and Ilyas, he sat protectively in front of her.

So, she let him stay even though her protection ring made her untouchable.

"Please, come in." Venus made a sweeping gesture of the kitchen. "While you're here, would you like something to drink? Bleach? Drain cleaner?"

Ilyas lent no remnant of emotion at her offer.

She slowly stood, her knees a little stronger now. "Fine, have it your way. Don't say I wasn't a gracious host."

"The Grand Witcher instructed me to deliver this to you," Ilyas stated, putting the items on the table, "as well as a message."

"I'm all ears."

Patches stepped over a plate of bacon to get near the Grand Witcher's favorite guard. He crouched low, rearing back his hind legs. He observed Ilyas the same way he watched prey.

Ilyas moved back, narrowing his eyes. "Control your familiar."

A thin ripple of his fear squirmed in her veins.

"My familiar *is* under control. If he weren't, he would've got your ass already." Venus arched an eyebrow at his unease, amused.

"Her Grandness has given you until the twenty-first of July," Ilyas said. "No exceptions. The Senate will vote on the Registration Act on the twenty-sixth."

Twenty-three days wasn't enough time to shake down senators for their blood and to brew four trinary-note peithos. Also, according to *The Unofficial Guide to Post-Resurrection Care*, she was screwed *mentally, physically,* and *magically.*

The protection ring would save her ass from a potion's recoil, but it couldn't save her from the brewbug. Chronic brewing led to overexertion, which led to the brewbug, an illness like the flu but on magical steroids. Venus had it once. She was bedridden, feverish, and delirious for two weeks, coughing up blood and choking on gallons of restoration tea.

She promised herself never again.

A promise she'd break within these next twenty-three days.

Venus nodded. "I'll try my best to meet it."

He reiterated in a detached tone, "Try?"

"I said what I said." She twisted her lips, annoyed.

"It would be in your best interest to do whatever it takes to meet the deadline. Her Grandness won't be pleased if you don't adhere to it. She'll punish you for it. After the blood oath does."

"For a moment, it almost sounded like you cared, Ilyas, but we both know your heart's capacity can't handle that." Venus crossed her arms, tapping a foot.

He neared her, dipping his head close enough to say, "That's where you're wrong. I don't have a heart at all."

She nailed him with a brave glare as he passed her by. "Let me guess. You burned it some time ago."

"Those like me don't have one."

"If there are *others* like *you*, I'll steer clear."

Ilyas cut his eyes over to Patches. "They're closer than you think."

And with that, he left her be.

Opening the manila envelope, Venus extracted a report of the senator that the Grand Witcher and Nisha wanted her to target. The report included a biography and a schedule of Senator Edward Hoage, *husband of Helena Tillery-Hoage*. In other words, he married one of Heloise Tillery's daughters.

And in a town as small as DC, Venus wasn't surprised she would run into this damn family again. Making the senator bleed, however, would be the *least* egregious of her crimes after what her potions did to Heloise and what she did to Baldwin's body. Now, she only wondered which Tillery she'd face next.

Venus unlocked the box's lock and revealed a letter atop a collection of vials, three empty, one filled, each marked with a name: *Westbay, Hoage, Radliff,* and *Sharma*.

She opened the envelope and pulled out a slip of paper.

The handwritten note read:

> *Obey Matrika's plan to save our nation.*
> *Her words should be your salvation.*
> *Or this country will fall into ruination.*

A notion for Venus to forge these peitho potions.

She grazed a finger down Madame Sharma's vial of blood.

A substantial responsibility she couldn't fuck up, but she couldn't do it alone.

She left the kitchen and went to her sister's bedroom. Emotions seeped through the wood to reach her. Guilt and sorrow tasted like salt and blood. Her entry intensified the flavors. In the closet, Janus hid with her legs huddled to her chest, wetness staining her cheeks.

As Venus crawled in, her sore bones protested.

They sat in silence for a while, simply existing.

Something that shouldn't have been if not for the sacrificium potion.

Janus propped her damp cheek on the ball of Venus's shoulder. "No apology will ever be good enough for what I've done."

"I don't need one."

When she turned on her phone, she saw thirteen missed calls from Tyrell. Each time, he left a voicemail. Her chin trembled as she listened to his words, fat tears rolling down her cheeks. His last voicemail message wrenched a sob out of her.

She parked in front of his crib, wiping at her stinging wet eyes.

"Get yourself together, Venus. You can fall apart later," she told herself, yanking down her sun visor to examine her pitiful reflection. After a few deep breaths and self-prescribed cheek slaps, she got out of her car.

With a manila envelope tucked under her arm, Venus used her key to get into the house. Hakeem lounged on the couch, watching an anime and slurping from a cup of ramen.

"Hey, Vee," Hakeem greeted with a mouthful of noodles.

The bruise on his neck was nearly gone.

Guilt held her tongue hostage.

She cast him a weak smile in passing.

Leap chilled on a knobby driftwood branch in his terrarium.

She beelined to Tyrell's bedroom door, knocking their secret knock rhythm they came up with as eight-year-olds. Halfway through it, her eyes bulged as the door swung open.

Tyrell yanked her inside his room. As he slammed the door shut, he body-slammed her into a gigantic hug.

Hakeem's voice traveled through the wood. "What did Mom say about slamming doors?"

Tyrell ignored his brother, squeezing her tighter. "I was so goddamn worried about you, Vee."

"I know. I listened to all your voicemails," Venus wheezed out, "and cried my eyes out."

He eased up his embrace and she took a much-needed breath.

"My bad," Tyrell apologized, releasing her completely. He took a step back, rubbing the back of his neck.

She pulled him into another hug, propping her chin on his shoulder. "Naw, that's cool. I'm sorry about everything."

"Yeah, you should be. Not answering my calls after your resurrection is mad disrespectful," Tyrell delivered flatly.

With her cheek propped on his shoulder, he couldn't see how her face crumpled into a grimace at the word *resurrection*. He didn't know hearing that word felt like fingers ripping open a wound she was trying to mend one stitch at a time.

She forced out a soft one-note chuckle.

After giving each other one last squeeze, they broke apart, the manila envelope falling to the floor.

He squatted down to pick it up, cheesing from ear to ear. "What's this?"

"My last will and testament," she replied, copying his dry tone from earlier.

His smile dissolved, his deep dimples exiting stage left.

She pasted her palm over her mouth to muffle her snort.

Tyrell sucked his teeth, handing the envelope back to her. "Stop playing games, girl. Forreal, though. What is it?"

"I've got a big gig, and I need your help," she said, plopping down on the edge of his bed.

He took a spot beside her, giving her an uneasy look. "Aight. Then, how can I help?"

"Well, about that…" Venus trailed off.

He scrunched his face as she pulled out the report, handing it to him.

"This is a senator," he stated, his grimace deepening. As his brain connected the dots, the realization beckoned shock. "Is this another game?"

"No, Ty. I'm not playing. You're a chameleon. You can blend in anywhere," Venus said, curling her arm around Tyrell's shoulders to draw him closer. "Plus, it'll be good practice. The more you practice, the longer you'll keep shape."

Tyrell squinted at the floor, losing himself in thought. He smoothed his thumb across his bottom lip, then pinched at it, shaking his head slowly.

His fear carved out a home inside of her, tightening her nerves.

"I need to get better. But…" Tyrell cut himself short.

"You don't trust yourself," she finished softly, giving him a teasing nudge. "I have a damn PhD in that."

The edge of his mouth curled up.

"But unlike me, you've got a teacher, Ty," she added.

His slight smile flatlined. He lobbed Venus a sideways glare, shrugging her arm off his shoulder. "Naw, that ain't happening. I ain't asking her for shit."

Venus heaved a sigh. "Aunt Key is the GOAT at shifting. You know that."

"Now, Vee. If she's at the top of her game, you damn well know I'mma always fall short." Tyrell said hotly, rising to his feet. He claimed his computer chair. Though only a few feet divided them, it felt more like oceans apart to her.

Brooding, he stretched out his long legs, swiveling from left to right.

Silence stretched on and on until he spoke up, his gaze hard and challenging. "I'll help you, but I gotta do this my own way. Aight?"

She considered his terms, then said, "Fine, but if your shape slips while we're working, you'll ask for Aunt Key's help."

Tyrell opened his mouth to protest, but she held up a palm.

"Don't fumble a bag trying to be hardheaded, Ty."

He tipped his head to the side, his eyebrows climbing in surprise. "Hold up. Run that back."

Venus smirked. "I've got two-hundred-fifty racks. We'll split it."

"You'd split a quarter mil with me?" He straightened up in his chair, poking a finger at his chest. "Me? Tyrell Xavier Kennedy?"

"*Only* if Tyrell Xavier Kennedy agrees to my terms," she reminded him matter-of-factly.

He cursed under his breath, dragging a hand over his face. "When do I need to be ready?"

"Getting ready requires homework," she said. "A research project."

"And what exactly am I researching?"

"Not what. Who."

CHAPTER
SEVENTEEN

OPPORTUNE TIME FOR EXTRACTION:
    Dines alone at Micah's every Monday and Wednesday evening with a 7 p.m. reservation. On rare occasions dines with wife Elena Tillery-Hoage. He enjoys his drink. Exploit this by any means necessary.

—Excerpt from Target Profile of Senator Edward Hoage

JULY 3, 2023

VENUS PRODDED HER TONGUE INTO HER CHEEK AS SHE LAID Janus's baby hairs, delicately sculpting the final swoop. According to a text, Tyrell was minutes away from arriving. A trip to go meet him out front took a detour when she saw a frustrated Janus in the bathroom trying to perfect her edges. A task that was as easy to her sister as breathing air, but lately, easy things were becoming tough to do.

For everyone.

"All done." Venus pulled away the purple toothbrush, lime-green gel glistening on the bristles.

Janus turned halfway on the counter she sat on, peering at her reflection. An immaculate part ran down the middle of her scalp, her ombre hair sleeked and styled in two voluminous puffs. Her expression more contemplative than content.

"You don't like it?" Venus asked.

Her sister's somber gaze found hers in the mirror. "No, it's just lately I only ever look my best for funerals."

Tomorrow, one was to be held for one of the protest organizers. A funeral the deceased's family asked her to speak at because she was Malik's daughter first and a hero second.

Janus saved lives at the protest. A protest Malik was nowhere near because of optics. Yet somehow, being his kid crowned her as an avatar of his greatness. She believed it was a token of respect.

More proof she walked in his footsteps but hid in his shadow.

A receipt Venus didn't have the heart to pull out.

"You're too young to be doing eulogies," she sighed, screwing the cap back on the hair gel.

"Both of us are too young for a lotta crap, Vee," Janus returned, wrapping an edge scarf around Venus's handiwork. She hopped off the counter, and her slippers clapped as they landed on the floor.

As Venus straightened up the array of hair supplies, she muttered, "Facts."

"I should've stayed home that day." Janus shook her head. "Like I promised."

"Your portals saved lots of lives, Jay. That should count for something."

She felt Janus's sadness before the matching smile showed up. "But I couldn't save the one that mattered to me most. You. When that Swigger shot you, I was so distraught. I didn't know what to do or how to think. Pres picked you up and told me to open a doorway to Epione. Ty had to shake sense into me because I was *so* fucking useless."

Venus shoved every little painful, bloody moment her sister's words invoked into the pit within her as she stared blankly at the fuschia-pink toothbrush holder. Her chest's center tightened and ached in remembrance.

Push, push it, *push* it all in.

Bury, bury it, *bury* it all down.

"Pres texts me every day asking about you."

With a slow blink, Venus came back to reality. She pretended not to hear that tidbit of information, organizing the bathroom counter. Busying her hands sticky with hair product, not blood.

A ball of emotion ballooned in her throat.

Venus hadn't seen Presley since the day of the protest.

By her choice.

As if shit wasn't already complicated, she made things *worse* when she kissed them, then kissed them again and again until kisses weren't enough. Until Venus got greedy as hell and wanted *more*.

After she returned to life, a clock began to tick, reminding her she was on borrowed time. She didn't have time for *more* or unpack what the fuck *more* even meant. Something had to give. Something had to go. So, she decided to put aside whatever she had with Presley.

The problem was she hadn't told *them* that.

Janus folded her arms, her head tilting. "When are you gonna call them, Vee?"

"When I'm ready," she lied to her sister, shrugging. Hoping her manufactured display of indifference would expedite this utterly uncomfortable topic's conclusion.

Venus *never* committed to anything beyond that night that bled into morning.

Great, now she was lying to herself.

Soon, she'd leave with Tyrell in tow on a mission to make a politician bleed.

By any means necessary.

Otherwise, her *personal fuckups* would have *nationwide consequences*.

The front door announced Tyrell's arrival with a slam.

"Ayo, it's time to go!" he called out, clapping his hands.

Hard soles clicked on the floor, the sound growing louder as he neared.

He appeared in the bathroom doorway, standing before them dressed in a white sixty-six-year-old man's flesh. Iron-gray hair styled in a neat combover. Dark beard, short and tamed.

Tyrell's shape was named Wilbur Edwin, a real estate mogul who had made his millions by swooping in like a vulture to gentrify the skeletal remains of witcher neighborhoods *he* killed. He *also* had a reputation for being Senator Hoage's most generous benefactor.

Tyrell looked the part, but was he dressed the part?

Hell naw.

Not dressed in a wine-and-navy argyle tailored suit, trilby hat, and caramel wingtip oxfords.

A stunned Venus slapped a hand to her mouth while Janus belted a laugh.

Tyrell cocked his bearded chin up, giving his lapels a confident tug. "Don't laugh at my drip, Jay."

"The only drip you got is the IV drip you left back at the nursing home."

He scowled, his wrinkles deepening. "So, you got jokes, huh?"

"Plenty, but I'll stop while I'm ahead. I don't want to disrespect my elders," she teased, squealing and ducking behind Venus as he tried to grab her. "Stop, Ty, before you break a hip!"

Tyrell growled, "I'mma break loose on you if you keep on playing with me."

Venus crimped her lips, annoyed. "Jay, cut it out."

He craned his neck to make sure Jay could see a full view of his satisfied smirk. He hummed a cocky *mm-hm* as if Venus had picked to fight on his side of the war when she was merely a referee.

"As for you, Ty," she began, inciting Janus to toss out her own *mm-hm*. "What the hell are you wearing?"

"Men's Wearhouse," Janus answered, earning an elbow to her gut. She hunched over with an *ow* tangled in another belly laugh.

Offended, he blinked at them, scrunching his face.

"First off, hush your mouth, Jay," he said. "Second off, I worked real hard on this, Vee. Swapping this fit out for another one will burn my energy and our time."

"Fine, you can keep it," Venus sighed, knotting her arms over her chest, "but remember our deal."

His gaze stiffened, a touch of resentment lurking in ice-blue eyes that didn't belong to him. "How could I possibly forget?"

"What deal?" Janus peeked nosily over Venus's shoulder.

"Mind your business," he warned testily.

"Alright, okay. I'll leave y'all to it," Janus assured, lifting her hands in surrender. "As long as I'm allowed safe passage."

Tyrell didn't budge an inch.

"Venus," Janus whined with a pout.

"Ty, just let her by."

He stepped aside, gesturing to the door all gentlemanlike.

Janus crept around Venus, her eyes cautiously snaking up and down their cousin. As she went to pass him, she nimbly knocked his hat off. He caught it quickly midway into his impending counterattack, two warnings tangled together.

"Don't you mess up her hair!"

"You better not touch my hair!"

He killed his speed enough to reposition the trajectory and swatted her forearm.

"Thank you," Janus said, rather pleased. "Oh, and Ty?"

He shot her a fed-up glare. "What you got to say now?"

She took inventory of his oxfords, nodding her approval. "You made the right choice on those Rich White Guy 3000s."

The compliment cracked open his guardedness.

"You see the vision?" He turned on his heels, wearing a very not-Tyrell smile that suited a viper.

No dimples or charm.

Just pure predatory.

"Very clearly, but I'd prefer *not* to see that smile again."

While Venus drove, Tyrell studied video clips of Wilbur Edwin on his phone, clearing his throat between each attempt to replicate the man's voice. It took a fist thump to his collarbone to iron out the quavers and errors. By the time she parked the car, he wore the timbre of a business-man well.

Whether he'd be able to *act* like one was another matter entirely, but she believed in her cousin.

Because if you made a Venn diagram of hustlers like her and chameleons like him, you'd find the abilities to adapt and survive in the overlap.

At their core, they were survivors.

Survivors always found a way in the end, even if it meant taking a thorny path.

Venus pulled down the sun visor to look in the mirror, examining her loose water wave wig. Its wet sheen looked caught in the dying sunlight.

Tyrell pulled some mints from his pocket, popping one in his mouth. A faint tart-yet-sweet aroma of magic tickled her sensitive nose.

He held the tin out to her. "Take one. It's a make-do."

Make-dos were the outcome of make-doing, an ill-advised boot-leg version of brewing. With no brewer training or disposable income to spare for potions, crafty witchers turned to make-doing, cooking up enchanted edibles for quick fixes that didn't fix a damn thing.

While brewing punished the brewer, make-dos had a reputation for causing more harm than good to whoever ate one. Potions were tailored to the drinker, which made them expensive, but anyone could eat make-dos. Yeah, the price tag was cheaper, but the cost of having a bad reaction was high.

"What's the flavor?"

"Catch a Cold," he said. "They lower your body temperature to make it past the heat sensors undetected. It can last up to an hour or two."

"But what's the catch?"

"Body chills, a brain freeze, hypothermia, or it could trigger your cryokinesis," he rattled off nonchalantly as he smacked on the make-do.

Cryokinesis. Also known as ice manipulation.

"So, let me get this straight," she said, rolling her eyes. "It'll help us fool the heat sensors, but there's a possibility you'll accidentally turn a server into an ice sculpture, which might give us away."

"That won't happen. I've tried one before." He snapped his fingers and pointed at the crystalline tablets. "I swear this is high-quality stuff right here."

Venus pursed her lips, unconvinced. "*High-quality* make-dos are an oxymoron."

"Would I steer you wrong, Vee?" He hiked a bushy, dark gray eyebrow.

She chewed on his question even though she already knew the answer.

No, he wouldn't.

Heaving a sigh, she went to pluck one out of the tin but stopped short as a thought dawned on her realization. "Who did you get these from?"

Tyrell sucked his teeth, looking ahead. "I took them."

"From?" she pressed.

He gave her a *don't-play-games* side eye.

Aunt Keisha. The unspoken answer made sense. Shapeshifters would need make-dos like these to milk shapeshifting for all its worth and go undetected by humans sans ones that liked iron.

"Oh," she uttered, eating one. A refreshing spearmint flavor brightened her senses, followed by a deep shudder and goosebumps pebbling her skin. The symptoms weren't as drastic or uncomfortable as she'd thought they'd be. At least not yet. There was plenty of time for her reservations to be proven right. A draft breezed around her bones. An unfamiliar sensation no blanket or fire could alleviate. Yet she still wanted to wrap herself into a blanket burrito.

It wasn't unbearable. Just *odd*.

Once out of the car, she smoothed her hands over the off-shoulder midi-wrap dress the color of hot mustard. Everything she wore on this mission belonged to her mom, right down to her confident stride. Because the rule to dining with wolves was to never put your fear on the menu.

The hot teeth of Tyrell's fear bit into her, warming her up a little as the make-do had its way with her.

She glanced at Ty as they neared the restaurant. "No turning back now."

"Don't want to." He fixed his cuffs with an undeniable swagger.

Stepping into the lobby was like stepping onto a stage after the curtains opened. They were no longer cousins. He was real estate mogul Wilbur Edwin and she was Aaliyah Grant, a young entrepreneur from Building Up Bright Businesspeople. A mentorship program the *real* Mister Edwin founded himself.

They both had parts to play now.

The two traded glances as they passed through the heat sensors. Venus swallowed around the violent throbbing in her heart, staying collected when no foreboding chimes announced their arrival and the digital counter held on to its big red zero.

But the host still greeted them with a round-eyed expression, his jaw unhitched and quivering.

"Mister Edwin," the host laughed nervously, beckoning a server over, "we weren't expecting you tonight. A party is currently seated at your usual table, but that can easily be fixed."

The host harshly whispered a command in the server's ear, pointing toward the occupied table. As Venus scanned her surroundings, she realized the *usual* table was far from Senator Hoage's.

She covered her mouth as a fake cough came on, getting Tyrell's attention. Then she cocked her chin toward the section they needed to go.

"That's quite alright," he said, holding up a hand.

Shock painted broad strokes all over the host's and server's faces.

"It...is, sir?" the host asked, which only meant the *real* Edwin would've wilded out in this situation.

A glower crawled onto Tyrell's face, his voice firm. "Must I repeat myself?"

"No, sir. Not at all, sir," the host assured rapid-fire quick, checking his computer screen. "Uh, we have an available—"

"I'd like to be seated over there by the fountain," he interrupted swiftly, his gaze sharpening.

She wrestled a smile. Not at the host's mistreatment but at how masterfully Tyrell adapted, molding himself into the heartless man they expected.

Code-switching was a survival tactic.

"Yes, of course. Right this way," the host said, stepping from behind the lobby counter. As they strolled behind him, Venus mouthed *nice*. Tyrell buffed his nails on a lapel.

Their target sat alone, enjoying a drink, as his file said. Draining his wineglass, he waved two fingers at his waiter for a refill.

He blinked at Tyrell as the host led them by, his brow wrinkling. "Will? Is that you?"

"Eddy?" Tyrell tested out, carrying a tone of pleasant surprise.

A smile broke out on the senator's face as if the nickname unlocked it. "You normally give me a ring when you're in town."

"Maybe I'm not the man you once knew."

"You've changed that much in four days, huh?" Senator Hoage scanned Tyrell's choice of attire. "Well, one thing's for certain. Your taste in fashion has changed. A nice change."

Tyrell puffed out his chest at the compliment. "Change is inevitable, my friend."

His actual voice sashayed into Venus's mind, smug and excited. *"Told y'all this fit did what needed to be done."*

Venus resisted the urge to roll her eyes.

Senator Hoage pinned his sights on her next. "And who might this be?"

She enthusiastically offered her hand, her smile white and broad. "Aaliyah Grant, sir. It's an honor to meet you."

Senator Hoage accepted the handshake.

"I've taken Miss Grant under my wing for this mentorship cycle." Tyrell patted her shoulder proudly.

"And what's tonight's lesson?" Senator Hoage asked, his tone carrying a note of interest.

"Trust no one," she answered, her smile easing wider. Senator Hoage ducked his chin in approval.

"Well, unless they donate to your campaign," he joked, winking at Tyrell. A rumble of a laugh came from the depths of his chest, inciting Venus, Tyrell, and even the host to join in.

All three laughed their fake laughs because sometimes your survival depended on convincing a *powerful* jerk to believe you liked their *weak-ass* joke.

"Well, why don't we kill two birds with one stone? Both of you will join me for dinner. I've got a tale or two you can learn from, Miss Grant,"

Senator Hoage offered, picking up his wineglass instinctively to sip before realizing it was empty. "What do you say, Will?"

Tyrell stroked his beard, considering. "I suppose so. As long as you don't put the poor girl to sleep."

"I'm only boring when I'm sober." He then looked at the host, unpleased. "My waiter not refilling my glass on time is giving *me* trust issues, Tobias."

Tobias pulled out a chair for Venus, handing out the two menus tucked under his arm once they were seated.

"I'll locate him immediately, sir." Tobias bowed politely and then dipped.

He enjoys his drink. Exploit this by any means necessary.

Despite what the file said, Venus couldn't lace his drink with a sleeping pill crushed in her purse if his hand kept hold of the glass. His server, Donovan (according to the name tag), arrived tableside with a bottle of red wine, apologizing profusely.

The weight of his fear crushed her chest, leaving her slightly breathless. The senator stared at him unamused, a finger *tink-tink-tinking* impatiently on the glass.

"Don't hold back, son," Senator Hoage ordered when his drink was halfway full. Donovan nodded, tilting in more wine too slowly for his liking. He took the bottle and waved the server away.

Donovan took down their drink orders, promising to be back.

"Yes, let's hope for your sake you are," Senator Hoage commented.

Tyrell's growing hate for the senator poured over her bones like lava.

"You love to torment defenseless things, don't you?" he asked once Donovan left, his smile sharp with a hue of cruelty. Knowing her cousin inside and out, she highly suspected a fantasy of him slapping the taste out of Senator Hoage's mouth was playing out in his head.

"You say that as if you don't normally enjoy it when I do," Senator Hoage said lightheartedly, lifting his glass in salute.

After a deep gulp and a satisfied sigh, he looked at Venus. "Much like the world of business, Miss Grant, DC is a war zone, and in war zones, the concept of friends doesn't exist. There are only allies and foes. And some foes become allies because they're the lesser evil. The key to trusting no one is relying on your greatest ally: *yourself*. Your judgment is your compass. Your bloodhound. In fact, I have a reputation for being an excellent judge of character."

Laughter welled up in her throat at how highly he spoke of himself, but she bit it back.

Her eyebrow rose in a slow arch. "Well, Senator. What do you make of me? Am I an ally or a foe?"

"An ally, of course. I can tell there's not a bad bone in your body, Miss Grant," he said.

An ally? *Far, far, far* from it.

He had no idea he was their prey, which pleased Venus.

The one or two stories he promised turned into a rant session of who he couldn't stand on Capitol Hill and a list of grievances to back up the why. The more he drank, the more his tongue loosened and the more his composure slipped.

He repeatedly wrangled Tyrell into his storytelling, spouting off those *do-you-remember-when* questions and *tell-her-about-the-time* insistences.

To which, Tyrell laughed his *oh-how-could-I-forget* laughs and paired his amused headshakes with *no-no-you-tell-it-so-much-better* assurances.

He enjoys his drink. Exploit this by any means necessary.

Maybe, she couldn't drug the senator and cut him like she had planned, but she realized she could bleed something else out of him. Something just as valuable as his blood.

More tea.

"What about Senator Mounsey?" she asked innocently, spearing one of the cherry tomatoes in her salad with a fork.

Senator Hoage snorted, shaking his head. "Ah, the Senate's crowned prince. A future presidential candidate. Adored by all."

Venus blinked. Senator Mounsey was going to make a presidential bid? Did Madame Sharma know that?

"All except you, Eddy," Tyrell tacked on.

"Do you not trust him?" she asked.

"It's not that I don't trust him. I just don't trust who he invites into his company." Senator Hoage gazed down into his nearly empty glass, brooding. "An aide told me he had contacted Sharma and offered her a meeting on a silver platter. He wanted to hear her out, but knowing her, she'd only try to bewitch him with her money. I'm sure I'm her next target."

Venus and Tyrell exchanged sideways glances.

Tyrell grabbed the second wine bottle of the night.

He tsked as he filled up the senator's glass. "Mounsey sounds like a fool."

He enjoys his drink. Exploit this by any means necessary.

"It sounds like you know exactly why Sharma shouldn't be trusted, Senator," she pointed out gently, egging him on.

"According to a trusted source, Sharma drank Ironskin potions and joined the Iron Watch, pretending to be human in her early days." After taking a long sip, Senator Hoage put his drink down long enough to dab his mouth with a napkin. "Apparently, she's the one to blame for the Iron Nail Bombing."

Tyrell's shock rattled alongside hers.

She couldn't wrap her brain around such absurdity.

Owen was the sole target of the iron nail bomb, a death sentence placed right on his doorstep. A tragedy that the Iron Watch unofficially claimed as their handiwork.

Despite her methods, Matrika Sharma wanted the same things as WASP did. What could she have *possibly* gained from being the bombing's alleged mastermind?

Plus, Owen was her ex-partner.

"She used the bombing to curry favor when she entered the Grand Witcher election as an unknown. An election she won by a landslide, mind you, against some hag who owns a grocery store." Senator Hoage continued, swirling the wine in his glass in that *pretentious-rich-folk* way.

Venus blinked. A hag who owned a grocery store? Florence Carter? So, they *ran* against each other?

That added yet another drop to their puddle of bad blood, but that didn't mean Madame Sharma was behind Owen's murder.

Senator Hoage leaned in, a fucked-up amusement kindling his gaze. "Do you know what her slogan was, Miss Grant?"

Venus swung her head in a no.

"Tough as nails," he informed.

Oh, shit.

She stiffened, her mind racing.

If Madame Sharma was willing to poison politicians to rig a Senate vote, was her orchestrating a WASP founder's assassination to influence an election too far of a stretch?

No, it wasn't, Venus thought after a long moment.

Madame Sharma had coerced someone to sacrifice their life for Venus. Having a graveyard of her own, she couldn't exactly judge the skeletons the Grand Witcher had. Especially when the Grand Witcher gave her one to burn to a crisp.

If Matrika had done the Iron Nail Bombing and if she did use a campaign slogan to hint at it, then Miss Florence's hatred made sense.

A lot of fucking sense.

But Venus doubted that a young, idealistic Matrika Sharma would sacrifice her ex to win an election against his mom. Maybe the Grand Witcher didn't have much of a heart now, but she had a very big one years ago.

Venus *remembered* her in that old photo album.

A chronicle of her good deeds and good nature captured in candid photos.

"Why didn't the Iron Watch out her then?" Venus quizzed, not entirely convinced. "I mean, didn't they have more to gain by her losing the election?"

"Shame, I imagine. A farmer would never admit that he had accidentally welcomed a fox into the henhouse," Senator Hoage said with a cough, lifting his blasé shoulder. He took another swig, but it didn't alleviate anything. He emptied his fit into a fist.

Tyrell retrieved his tin from his pocket, flipping open the lid. "Sounds like you need a mint to clear that right up, Eddy."

Venus snapped her attention to her cousin, her heart freezing in midbeat. She only wanted to incapacitate the senator long enough to squeeze a few drops out of him; he'd be of no use to her if he *froze* to death.

"Thank you, Will." Senator Hoage popped a make-do in his mouth, crunching on it eagerly. Too drunk to realize his breath came out as gray huffs. "Woah, this is some strong stuff."

"You have no idea," Tyrell said, his grin skewed. She slyly dug her heel into his foot to wipe it off his face. It did, crumbling in a heap.

A dazed Senator Hoage wagged his head to clear the icy fog, massaging his temple.

"Is everything *alright*, Senator?" she asked, emphasizing the word *alright* through gritted teeth.

"Nothing a little warm water to the face can't cure," he decided, standing up with a wobble.

"A trip to the gentlemen's room doesn't sound like a bad idea." Tyrell stood as well, slinging his friendly arm around Senator Hoage's shoulders to keep the man from falling.

Venus's teeth worried her bottom lip as they walked down a corridor to the restrooms. A sign above the entryway showed an icon for men, women, and unisex. Standing calmly, she straightened her dress and followed.

She was going to whisper-tell her cousin to take the senator to the unisex restroom, but he was already one step ahead. His head peeked out the door, waiting for her arrival. She hurried inside, locking the door behind her.

Senator Hoage was slumped over the restroom sink, gripping the marble top for support. He stared into the mirror hazily, his eyes wafting over to her reflection.

"What…is…she…doing…here?" he slurred with a violent shudder, fighting to keep his head up.

"She thought nobody was in here, and I forgot to lock the door. Just splash some water on your face, Eddy." Tyrell twisted on the faucet and rained encouraging pats on the senator's back.

She levied a *what-the-fuck* glare at Tyrell, fighting the urge to beat him. "This wasn't part of the plan."

"I had to improvise." He threw up his palms, frustrated. "Ol' dude wasn't gonna let his spirits outta his sight for nothing."

She stamped her foot. "Improvising generally doesn't end in *murder*, Mister Edwin."

"He ain't dead *yet*, Miss Grant." Tyrell sucked his teeth and trained his finger at the drugged senator, utterly oblivious to their bickering as he splashed water on his face.

A loud *clunk* drew their grazes downward as Senator Hoage fell unconscious. He looked low-key blue but alive. Venus crossed her arms as Tyrell tilted his head back, sighing at the ceiling. He dragged the senator to where the hand dryer was, propping up the limp man underneath. Senator Hoage sat upright like a rag doll against the wall. His head hung down. A roar of hot air poured down on him when Venus punched the START button.

She needed to work quickly before he warmed up and woke up.

She reached into her purse for a sewing needle and a vial with his name on it. Dropping to her heels, she got his hand and jabbed his finger. He stirred for a moment and there was a loud groan, but it wasn't from him. It was from Tyrell. As she squeezed blood into the vial, she looked over her shoulder to see her cousin doubled over, hugging himself.

Bones rippled and shifted under his skin as he struggled to hold his shape.

"Venus," he grunted pleadingly, falling to his knees. She capped the vial with a cork, tossing everything into her purse. She crawled over to him, and he collapsed into her.

"I thought I could make it to the end," he panted, his face twisting in pain. "I'm sorry."

"Don't apologize, Ty," she whispered, embracing him from behind. "Nobody planned for him to gossip for as long as he did. You were amazing. Absolutely fucking amazing."

He hissed, grinding his teeth. "A deal's a deal, though. I'mma have to ask for Moms's help, but maybe it's for the best. I can't keep living like this."

"We'll handle that later, but we gotta get the hell outta here, Ty," she said. "I need you to hold on for one more minute."

Tyrell swiveled Wilbur Edwin's blue eyes up to her, unshed tears brimming at the edge. "Just one?"

"Sixty seconds to get to the entrance door." Venus nodded, pulling out her cell. She put on a timer for exactly one minute, showing him.

Tyrell fought to his feet.

"Start the timer," he rasped out, his face a mask of determination. She obliged.

He wheezed through his nose as he carried himself to the door one hellish step at a time. Senator Hoage's eyelids drew up drowsily, a pinkish color coming back to his skin as the make-do's effects began to subside.

Venus hit the hand dryer's START button again as a farewell gesture.

The countdown inspired Tyrell to walk faster, even if it brought him more pain again. Sweat sheened the pale wrinkly skin he wore. His knuckles coiled tight. Chimes filled the air as they passed through the heat sensors, but the digital counter stayed at zero.

They made it back to the car with eight seconds to spare.

CHAPTER
EIGHTEEN

A brewer's pledging day is a rite of passage. The ceremony contains three acts: debut, demonstration, and devotion. First, a master brewer debuts the pledgling into brewer society. Then, the pledgling will brew a potion to demonstrate mastery. To conclude the sacred occasion, the pledgling will devote themselves to a discipline before an audience.

—Witcherpedia, an online witchery encyclopedia

THAT NIGHT, VENUS'S NIGHTMARE DRAGGED HER BACK TO THAT alleyway. She did everything right, but it all still went wrong.

"Venus!"

Janus's shriek jolted her awake.

Her teary eyes gazed down at her trembly hands.

No warm sticky blood.

Venus flopped backward and took deep breaths to shrink the pain mushrooming in her chest. Her skin felt feverish and tight; all she wanted to do was peel it off to be free. She kicked off the covers, spreading her limbs out like a starfish across the pink bedspread.

As her pulse steadied, she listened to the beat like a lullaby, calmness creeping through her.

Until a blinding light flooded the room.

She flinched at the intensity and shielded her sleepy eyes from its cruelty. She stumbled about, unpinning the source from her corkboard. Its brilliance petered out like a dying star, revealing what it was. She bowed her head back, her frustration manifesting into a raw scream at the ceiling.

She tossed aside the invitation as she marched to her closet.

A panicked Janus jerked the door soon after with a fireball at the ready in her palm, her words tumbling over a drowsy tongue. "What is it? What's wrong?"

"Life, *that's* what," Venus sneered as she searched for something to wear.

The fireball snuffed out and left a thin smoke in its wake. "What's going on now, Vee? Are you having symptoms?"

Anxiety knotted her stomach. "No, not yet."

"Then what's up?"

"I have to go to some idiot's pledging ceremony." Venus plucked free a zipper-front green-and-purple plaid dress.

Her blood fell onto the invitation like a punctuation mark, and a chemical reaction occurred. A soft radiant light sprang from the inked cursive words, swirling into a door. A Gothic cathedral towered before her in all its glory as she stepped through.

Venus recognized the church immediately: she was northeast of Deanwood. She rolled her eyes, irritated that she wasted blood when she could've driven twelve measly miles.

She climbed the steps, going against her better judgment.

Religious folk and witchers had been natural enemies for centuries. Though the accused in historical witcher hunts were overwhelmingly human, actual witchers still viewed the Church as a formidable foe. Even now, people wield religion against witchers to justify irreligious deeds.

By law, religious establishments didn't have to abide by anti-witcher regulations, making them a perfect sanctuary for witchers in need, but most chose not to.

Most, but not all.

Shadows bathed her as she passed underneath the covered archway and approached the blossoming archivolt, which framed a pair of ornate doors. Hinges groaned as the right door opened.

"Welcome to the Cathedral of All, my child. Rest assured, you'll find no ill intentions beyond these doors." A priest smiled kindly as he welcomed her, gesturing for her to enter.

Venus nodded hesitantly and slipped inside. Moonlight filtered through the stained-glass Rosetta window, painting patches of vibrant colors on her brown skin.

"The others are waiting downstairs," he informed as he guided her through the nave, passing rows of cushioned pews beneath a sky of the ribbed ceiling.

Vibrant clerestories depicting saints, angels, lambs, Mother Mary, golden chalices, and red roses ruled from above like silent gods. He led her to a spiraling staircase hidden in the south transept, journeying deeper and deeper into the church's bowels. Amber lanterns lit the way through the gloomy crypt as they weaved through a sea of carved pillars until they reached the intimate gathering.

The total in attendance nearly impressed Venus. There were eighteen nonincarcerated brewers within the South Atlantic region. After tonight, there'd be nineteen, but something still didn't add up.

Excluding the pledgling, she did another head count, matching faces to a mental catalog of names. Surprise arched her eyebrows as she solved the mystery.

Elder Glenn hadn't come.

Yes, he was bitter, but he followed brewer traditions to the letter.

She leaned her shoulder against a pillar and crossed her arms as she watched.

Memories of *her* pledging day overlaid the present.

Her mom had debuted her with a curt speech. Then she brewed a binary-note philia potion called the Nectar of Friendships as her demonstration, her daffodil-yellow dress torn and bloodied from the degree of recoil. During the act of devotion, she slit her young palm with a ceremonial knife and pledged to the discipline of love, planting her handprint into the Book of Brewers.

Or as Clarissa Stoneheart liked to call it, the Book of Fools.

She half smiled at that.

A round of applause cut her trip down memory lane short.

As the beginnings of a headache infected her, she decided it was time to leave.

"Clarissa was never one to stick around at these things, either. You inherited that habit from her." A redhead woman neared, wagging a finger.

Venus massaged her temple as her headache dialed up a notch. "I figured my presence wouldn't be missed, Elder Leslie."

Leslie snorted at the formal address. "Let's cut the formalities and stick to first names, kid. Now, how's life been treating you?"

"Poorly. You?"

"Richly, I suppose. With the Registration Act on the table, brewing Ironskin is more lucrative these days," Leslie said vainly, examining her expensive pedicure. "I'll make you a batch if you'd like. On the house."

If anyone had an Ironskin supplier, Venus bet all her money it was Leslie.

She stifled a laugh to keep it from bouncing off the subterranean walls. "So, if I catch an iron bullet, the iron won't kill me. The fact it's a bullet will. I appreciate the offer, but I think I'll pass."

Sympathy darkened Leslie's cyan eyes. "I'm sorry for your loss. Rissa was one of a kind."

Venus shifted uneasily, rubbing her arms. She had never quite figured out what to say to people who gave their condolences.

Especially when the condolences were gift wrapped in pity.

Leslie encroached further, saying softly, "I remember your pledging day like it was yesterday. Rissa was so proud of you."

A bitter smile broke across Venus's lips. "That's surprising."

"Why? She was your mom."

"Because I never really felt like her daughter."

Leslie's face softened. "Venus, talking about you to me always smoothed her edges."

"Yet mine sharpen every time she's talked about to me." She exhaled slowly to bear through the acute burst of pain inside her head and the agony of this conversation. "It's time for me to go, Leslie. Good to see you again."

As she turned on her heels to flee, the world's weight punched her in the gut, emptying the air from her lungs.

The universe contracted around her rapidly. Torment detonated inside her head. She stumbled from the fallout and braced a pillar for support.

An awful hum stuffed her ears.

Venus squeezed her eyes shut. The stolen anima within her delivered secondhand sorrow, regret, and guilt through her veins as surely as blood.

Suddenly, all the pain and emotion vanished.

A constricting reality stopped its coil, letting her go.

Letting her breathe.

Venus panted madly, her wide eyes flitting around to satisfy her paranoia.

She was here.

In the cathedral's basement.

She was exactly where she needed to be.

Was this body hers?

No, it wasn't.

Yes, yes, it was.

It was hers, hers, hers, but she felt caged in her skin, wanting to claw it all off.

"Whoa there, honey." Leslie's voice pierced through the episode, hooking Venus's arm across her shoulders. "Let's get you some fresh air."

Somebody asked, "Hey, is she alright?"

"Yeah, we're just gonna go upstairs to be with God for a bit," Leslie informed as she ushered Venus away.

The two rested on the steps leading up to the altar and the apse. An effigy of a crucified Jesus looked down on them sadly. Leslie pulled out a vape pen, sucked at it, tilted her head back, and breathed a plume to the ribbed heavens.

Venus cradled her pounding head. "Are you seriously about to do that here?"

"I bet Jesus has bigger problems than me and my vaping." Leslie took another puff for emphasis. "Now, you ready to confess?"

"There's nothing to confess."

"If you're trying to get into Heaven, lying in God's house has more damage than my smoking habit."

Venus had hoped that Leslie would take the hint if she kept quiet.

Leslie took another hit, vapor fluttering out her nose. "I'm waiting."

Well, that didn't work.

"Life is shit." Venus admitted one truth, but not the one Leslie desired.

Another puff. "That's true, but I know you're lying to me."

They locked unfaltering gazes, agreeing to an unspoken rule: Blink and lose.

Time ticked on by.

Leslie finally turned her gaze to the rosette window that baptized Venus with colors, situated at the far end of the nave.

For some odd reason, it felt wrong to lie in a church even though she didn't believe in what it stood for. "You know that rally that turned nasty a few days ago?"

Leslie partook another drag, nodding. "Yeah, didn't sixty-four of us get killed? What of it?"

"Actually, it was sixty-five," she corrected.

Once more, they regarded each other before Leslie pocketed her vape pen.

"I don't have time for your lies," she said, rising.

Venus cocked her chin to gaze up at the redhead. "I'm not lying."

Leslie rolled her eyes. "Good seeing you, Venus."

Venus shot to her feet and yanked down her dress's zipper. She snapped up Leslie's hand and parked it in between her breasts. Leslie tried to pull away, but Venus escalated her grip.

"What in the hell are y—?" The words crumbled in Leslie's mouth as her fingertips discovered the truth. The taste of copper flushed Venus's mouth. The struggling ceased.

"You still think I'm a liar, Leslie?" She released what didn't belong to her.

Leslie plopped down on the cold stairs, leering in disbelief. "I knew something wasn't right when he didn't come tonight. What did you get him mixed up in?"

Venus grimaced, zipping up her dress again. "Who are you talking about?"

"Oh, don't be so dense, Venus!" Leslie flashed, her anger echoing through the church and Venus. "Glenn wouldn't have made that goddamn sacrificium potion for you unless someone forced him into doing it! And that someone had to be dangerous and powerful!"

The allegation slammed into Venus so hard it knocked the air from her lungs.

As her mind raced for answers, words fumbled out of her. "Elder Glenn didn't—No, he couldn't have—"

Leslie cut her off, her voice raw. "And *you're* in denial, kid. As of tonight, there's nineteen of us in this region. Four have a discipline in healing and only three showed up." She fished out her vape pen again with quivery hands, bringing it to her mouth for a desperate suck. "Do the math."

Venus already did that at the ceremony's start. She added up the heads and only found *one* missing. Rerunning the numbers was unnecessary. As was jumping to conclusions. Elder Glenn's absence tonight didn't mean he was dead.

He probably had to make a delivery or fulfill an order.

Maybe his old bones just needed a rest.

But that didn't mean he was dead.

Right?

She tried to shove that tiny speck of doubt—that possibility—out of her head, but it refused to budge. Then that speck grew into a dot split into two, then three, and more.

The South Atlantic region only had *four* brewers of health, but *only* one lived in DC. *Only* one was in Matrika's reach, living in her dominion. Venus only died for a few hours. Dying in the afternoon, waking up alive the next morning. *Only* one could've brewed that dangerous potion so fast with so little preparation.

Elder Glenn.

It all led back to *him*.

Venus shook her head, whispering, "You're wrong."

Yet her body betrayed her, agreeing with Leslie. Guilt oozed into her bloodstream. Salty tears swelled in her eyes, her breath quickening.

Her heart protested violently, throwing itself against her chest.

She bit her lips to cage a thick sob in her throat.

"Venus," Leslie spoke softly, her expression one of pity. "I don't know what you're going through, but—"

No, fuck that.

Venus pivoted on her heel, fleeing down the stairs. As she raced through the nave, Leslie called after her.

She didn't stop.

She couldn't stop.

Her palms pitched the twin doors open.

She ran, and the world whipped past her in a blur.

After a few blocks, she staggered to a halt, collapsing against a closed convenience store's wall. She slid down until her ass hit the ground, crying uncontrollably. Her phone vibrated in her little purse and she pulled it out, accepting the call.

Janus freaked out on the other end. "Are you hurt? The blood-tether went berserk."

Venus wiped her tears away, failing miserably at steadying her voice. "I'm okay."

"You don't sound like it. I'm using the blood-tether to get you. This is the perfect time to practice. I've been studying hard."

"No, Janus. Now's not the time," Venus barked as her fingernails gouged her palm, trying to control the tsunami of emotions within her. "Put some clothes on."

"Why?"

"I need to find out the truth."

A thorny, static sensation washed over them as they breached Elder Glenn's property. Venus had goosebumps all over.

Janus shuddered, hugging herself. "You feel that?"

"Yeah."

A heavy-duty defense spell designed to keep others out unless invited in by its conjurer.

It gave Venus hope he was inside.

"I hate to break it to you, but we might have to abort the mission, Vee," Janus said as they pressed on. "I don't wanna find out how the defense mechanism deals with trespassers."

Venus knocked. "Elder Gl—"

The back door opened on its own accord, cutting her off.

The two sisters exchanged surprised glances.

"Elder Glenn?" Venus called out, refusing to budge.

No one answered back, hope curdling in her stomach.

Janus peered in apprehensively, crinkling her nose. A pesky fly buzzed around her head, forcing her to swat at it. It attempted to enter the house, but an unseen shield zapped it.

She pointed to the dead insect somewhere at her feet. "Exhibit A is why that's a no from me, partna."

A cold reminder crept over Venus.

If Leslie was right—

If Elder Glenn was truly gone, then that meant—

"If he sacrificed himself to brew the sacrificium potion, he gave all his anima, which means I have it inside me," Venus reasoned. "I think that's why the door opened. The defense spell *thinks* I'm him."

Remorse washed through her bloodstream, unable to fathom his pain in those last moments.

If she were wrong, she'd suffer.

But if her hunch was correct—

She reached out, her hairs rising as her trembling hand eased through the barrier. Her lungs released a shaky exhale as a gust of relief licked her. She proceeded inside.

Venus stuck her hand out the door for her sister to take. "I got you."

A gentle tug of encouragement allotted Janus an entry, a ghost of a smile on her lips.

They split up to cover more ground. Venus remained in the kitchen while Janus explored the rest of the house. Nothing seemed out of place.

No evidence that a man sacrificed his life as an ingredient for a potion.

"He didn't do it here," she told herself as she paused at the stove. He probably got carted off to Swadesh while the Sharma sisters waited safely elsewhere, listening for an explosion to let them know the deed was done.

Exactly like they did for Venus.

Venus balled her hands into fists, discarding any seeds of ill thoughts before the blood oath punished her.

She wandered over to the alcove bookcase and rose to her tiptoes to reach the top shelf, grazing her fingers against the red volume she fought Elder Glenn for on the day of her mom's funeral.

"You know you want to," *It* breathed.

"Shut up," she hissed.

It chuckled, then quieted.

But that tiny ember of encouragement was enough to light her curiosity's fuse. She bit her bottom lip as she pulled the heavy grimoire down, laying it gingerly on the book stand like a priceless artifact.

Venus glanced over her shoulder, half expecting him to barge in and stop her. But he couldn't. While she lived on borrowed breath, that heavy truth hung over her.

She turned to the spot where she clawed out the recipe, but all she found were the torn edges left behind. She flipped and flipped, becoming more desperate with each page turn. She flipped the grimoire face down, shaking the pages. Nothing.

She grabbed another and did the same.

And another and another and another.

Nothing, nothing, nothing.

But Venus couldn't stop, because stopping felt like more defeat. More failure.

Pulling the last leather-bound book from the shelf, she threw it open. She frowned as she looked at dates, potion names, prices, and patron initials separated into columns. When Venus realized what she held wasn't a grimoire but a ledger, disappointment, anger, and frustration swept over her bones like a hot gale.

Before she snapped it shut, two entries stuck out to her. Entries dated on the night of her mother's murder. On that same night, Venus picked up the reinforcement potions. An order Elder Glenn documented.

06/16/23—Reinforcement—$60,000—CS
06/16/23—Healthy Glow—$100,000—GWMS

"CS," she read aloud, frowning. "Clarissa Stoneheart."

According to the ledger, another patron paid Elder Glenn a late-night visit after Venus left.

She wagged her head, shaking her questions away. Questions that had *nothing* to do with why she came here.

"Vee, I found this plugged in his—" Janus paused, her jaw falling at the mess Venus made. She forgot about the cheap cell in her hand as she stepped over discarded volumes.

"Dammit!" Venus chunked the ledger aside. "It's not here!"

She gritted her teeth, slamming her fists onto the counter.

"What's not here?" Janus asked, soft and cautious.

"The potion recipe Mom used to break her pledge. It's missing," she said.

Janus's face twisted into a pained grimace. "Why are you even looking for it?"

"Because," she growled.

"Because?" Janus probed, easing closer.

Venus threw her hands up. "Because I want to know what potion she thought was worth losing her magic over!"

A blanket of silence draped over them, thick and smothering.

Then Janus said, "You can't fool me, Vee. This ain't about how she lost her magic. It's about who she became after losing it. Isn't it?"

Her sister's words chiseled away at the strength of her legs until she dropped to the floor, propping her back against cupboard doors. She hugged her knees.

A tear rolled down her cheek. "I never understood her, Janus, and I wanna know why. Elder Glenn once told me Mom didn't come to him alone when she broke her brewer pledge. He said *they* were persuasive."

"Sounds like *they* were desperate." Janus joined her on the floor.

"So desperate Mom was willing to forfeit her magic." Venus nodded slowly as she stared at the kitchen's back door, trying to envision the scene of Elder Glenn, a younger Clarissa, and faceless company.

Janus picked up a grimoire to examine it. "Well, if all his grimoires are accounted for, maybe, he took the recipe with him."

Those words made Venus pause. She gazed at the sea of grimoires she mistreated, her brow puckering in thought.

If Elder Glenn only took the recipe he *needed* and she couldn't find the recipe she *wanted*, then that meant—

"No." She shook her head slowly, stopping that train of thought in its tracks. "Because if he did, then that means..."

"That means what, Vee?" Janus pressed gently.

Venus snatched her lip between her teeth, not wanting to say the theory out loud. But the more it seeped into the folds of her mind, the less abstract it felt.

"The only recipe Elder Glenn would've needed was..." she paused, her expression somber, "...the sacrificium potion."

Disbelief glazed Janus's face. "Wait, are you saying—?"

"I *don't* know what I'm saying," Venus snapped out a lie. "I don't understand shit."

Even though she couldn't bring herself to say it, she couldn't deny the truth:

Clarissa Stoneheart brewed a sacrificium potion.

"I understand completely," Janus laughed tearily, wiping at her wet face. "It proves Mom had a fucking heart and cared enough to forfeit her magic."

"But who did she do it for?" Venus whispered.

"I don't think it matters who she did it for, Vee. Actions are receipts of true character."

"When did you get to be so wise?" Venus reached for her sister's hand, lacing their fingers together.

"I got that from a daily motivation app called Chant," Janus said proudly. "Uncle Bee put me onto it."

The edge of her mouth lifted a tick at the thought of their uncle, a 6'6" tower of muscle and fearsome strength, reading motivational quotes.

"Speaking of phones, I found this charging on Elder Glenn's night-stand," she said, forking over a cell. A notification of seventeen missed calls and thirteen voicemail messages haunted the lit screen. All from customers, probably. There was no point in taking your burner phone if you knew you'd never be able to use it again.

Venus turned it off.

An act that felt like she was putting Elder Glenn to rest.

"There's a locked room down the hallway, too. Could be something important on the other side," Janus informed, eyeing her worriedly. "Unless you wanna call it a night. You look exhausted as fuck. We can pick this back up tomorrow."

"No, I want to finish this." Venus stood up, tugging her sister onto her feet.

They went to the locked door. Janus donated simple magic to act as a key. On the other side of the door, a cozy bedroom awaited them. A four-post bed dressed in a beloved quilt and assorted pillows populated much of the space. Paintings and antique family photos cluttered the floral wallpaper. Quaint nightstands housed vases of withered Valeriana and browned water.

Be strong and *be healthy* uttered the flowering plant.

Venus grazed a finger on a shriveled blossom.

"Look at this." Janus brought over a framed photo of a woman gardening with High Witcher Florence and handed it to Venus. "This must be his sister's room. The one that died of cancer."

The name *Yolanda* awoke an instinct in Venus's heart like a kneejerk reaction. *Love.* Elder Glenn's love for his sister endured even after his death.

Venus considered the picture of Yolanda in a thriving vegetable garden with Miss Florence. Both wore overalls, one holding a watering can while the other had a spade. Both smiled under the shade of their wide-brimmed sun hats.

But while sunny joy shone in Miss Florence's smile, Yolanda only had the dawning of one. She looked so at peace. A peace that only came when you accepted your fate.

As Venus settled back on Miss Florence again, an old question filled her mind.

Did you know this would happen?

But the question wasn't the right one, she realized. The right question was, did Yolanda want to know?

She imagined Elder Glenn's sister sitting in Miss Florence's writing room, watching her fortune unfold pen stroke by pen stroke. Surrounded by bookshelves filled with journals of the many who looked to Miss Florence for answers.

Answers wrapped in riddles.

Venus blinked as a realization stole over her. She sat on the bed, old springs creaking under her weight.

During her mother's funeral, Miss Florence offered to pen her fortune. Though Venus didn't outright reject the offer, she refused to go for herself.

But if she went to that writing room, she'd find the journal with her mother's name on it. Though Venus had no desire to know about her future, she *needed* to know her mother's past.

And if she got her hands on that journal, she could study Clarissa Abigail Stoneheart's life like a history book.

JULY 4, 2023

Patches used Venus's ankles as a gateway into the house. With an *I love you* and *good night*, Janus shuffled down the hallway, yawning.

Venus squatted down to scratch the familiar's ear. He nuzzled his crown into her palm, purring.

She pulled out her cell phone with a free hand, clocking the time. It was ten past midnight, which only meant one thing.

"Happy hundred-fifty-first anniversary, you old cat," Venus said, her voice soft and raspy with exhaustion. Then she smoothed her hand over his head as a farewell before she headed to bed.

Or at least, that had been her initial intention until she eyed her mom's bedroom door. A messy tangle of longing and sorrow hooked into her, reeling her toward a realm she actively tried to avoid.

Venus took off her shoes. Then climbed into her mom's bed, burying her nose in a pillow.

Clarissa Stoneheart's scent haunted her senses like a fading ghost. She wished it *would never go* away. Her shoulders shivered as she emptied her sobs into the pillow.

Crying for her mom.

And Elder Glenn, too.

CHAPTER
NINETEEN

A familiar's supernatural durability is often mistaken for invul-
nerability. A familiar's years of servitude play a pertinent role
in how they can withstand magical or nonmagical harm. Young
familiars are more susceptible to injury or demise. Familiars
over a century old, known as antique familiars, can endure dangerous volumes of magic. Only their fruit of loyalty is left when
a familiar's physical form is destroyed.

— *The Familiar Manual*, 2009 Edition

VENUS SLEPT ALL MORNING LONG, ONLY ROUSED BY NEARBY
sirens. A shower washed the crumbles of sleep away and coffee livened
her up. As she stepped out into the July heat, a tingly eerie sensation
inched across her skin. On her nape and arms, tiny hairs stood on end.

She felt eyes on her, but she wasn't sure from where.

Patches sat on the front lawn, his tail's tip twitching. His gaze fixed on
a tree at the yard's edge, thick with green. As a soft breeze stole over the
block, he broke into a gallop, vaulting up into the foliage.

A flock of birds took to the skies at the intrusion.

Feline screams, squawks, and branches snapping filled the air.

Seconds later, a parakeet ablaze in wild anima burst out of the tree,
flapping away. Patches hopped to the ground, his mouth full of lime-green
feathers.

Venus stood there, shocked.

Her mind wrestled with the information her eyes took in. She crouched when Patches came to her, plucking out one of the plumes.

Pinching the quill, she turned it between her fingers.

Venus glanced at the sky, looking for the answer to a question that rang through her bones like warning bells.

Why the hell was Nisha's familiar *spying* on her?

Venus stepped aside as a pack of children flew down the porch steps with daydream lollipops.

"Well, I'll be," Miss Florence said from behind the screen door, drying her hands on a kitchen towel. "Is that who I think it is?"

"The one and only." Venus marched up the steps.

Miss Florence opened the way into the house. "I already know what you want."

The house smelled of sandalwood and thyme, which Venus always found comforting. Pictures of neighborhood and coven children decorated the fridge in the kitchen.

Venus grazed her fingertip on a photo of her eight-year-old self and six-year-old Janus peering out the windows of their yellow playhouse. Pictures of Tyrell and Hakeem were also there, too. And then, of course, one of Presley, maybe thirteen or fourteen, with corkscrew curls and glasses.

Looking over her shoulder, she wondered and worried if they were home.

Venus suddenly felt like a soldier in enemy territory. She needed to get what she came for and get out as soon as possible. She only wanted to face whatever truth lay in her mother's premonition journal.

Not whatever truths Presley might ask of her if they knew she was here.

Florence asked teasingly, "Did you come here for your future or to reminisce about your past?"

The journaling room was a parlor offshoot from the kitchen.

They flowed through airy white curtains hanging in the doorway. Bookshelves lined with journals adorned every wall. The room's heart held an intimate circular table with a fountain pen on its rosewood and leather stand.

Miss Florence grabbed a new journal and told her to sit down.

Venus dropped her bag to the floor and tapped her fingers anxiously, sweeping her eyes around to get a lay of the land.

Which shelf had her mother's?

A reminiscent smile spread across Miss Florence's lips as she glanced affectionately around the room. "This is where I wrote premonitions for your Granny Davina back in the day." She turned her kind eyes to Venus. "A tradition I've continued with your mother, uncle, and sister. Now it's finally your turn."

Venus's mouth parted in shock. "You penned Janus's future?"

"Yes." Miss Florence tapped a finger on her cheek as she recalled. "Janus came for a visit nine days ago. She left our session very upset."

Venus nodded, thinking back to that Witcherpedia page on magical loopholes and the conversation that followed. A discussion that occurred *before* Venus took a bullet to the chest and bled out on a hospital gurney. *Before* Elder Glenn sacrificed himself to bring her back to life.

"Something awful will happen to me, won't it?"

"That part doesn't matter. What matters is I'll be there at your side."

Was her death the awful thing Janus wanted to prevent? No, if it was, her sister could've easily prevented it by not going to that damn protest. No magical loophole necessary.

Which meant it was something else awful.

Which meant whatever Miss Florence wrote upset Janus enough to make her want to bend magic's rules and risk provoking one or both of The Sisters' wrath.

Somewhere in this room, Janus's journal held an upsetting truth.

A *tiny* part of Venus wanted to steal that one, too.

But being greedy would only get her caught.

"You alright, honey?" Miss Florence's voice dragged Venus from that moment in Janus's room.

She cleared her throat, forcing herself to smile. "Everything's fine."

Miss Florence believed her, cracking open the journal. A blank page gazed up at her. She retrieved her fountain pen, extending a hand to Venus.

"Let's b—ah!" Miss Florence flinched and recoiled her hand, using it to massage her forehead. She rose with a stumble, her chair clattering to the floor. She stumbled toward the doorway, pushing the curtains aside hastily.

Venus snapped up to help. "Is everything okay, Miss Flo?"

"Don't mind me. I just need my migraine remedy, is all." Miss Florence flailed a wrist dismissively at her. "Elder Glenn made the best health potions."

Made. As in past tense. As in, Miss Florence knew Elder Glenn was dead. She would've only known if Elder Glenn sat in this room to have a premonition penned.

Guilt preyed on Venus, sinking its teeth deep. The strength in her knees faded away and she plopped back into her seat. Frantic thoughts bubbled up in her mind. Did Miss Florence know how he died? Or why he died? Did she know who was behind it? Was she aware of who inherited his anima? What the fuck did she know?

Miss Florence's footsteps *thunk-thunk-thunking* up the stairs shattered Venus's rising panic, reminding her *why* she was there. She stalked to the west-facing bookcase. Her gaze flitted from name to name etched on the journal spines. She furrowed her brow as she tried to make sense of how Miss Florence had organized them.

Ardelia D.

Edwin G.

Taylor Q.
Aisha O.
Phillip B.

The journals weren't alphabetized by first or last name. Venus could only describe the organization system as random.

She pulled Phillip B.'s off a shelf, examining its exterior cover for clues. Nothing, nada, zilch.

Opening it, she found a date scribed on the front pastedown.

January 5, 1970

She tested a theory by taking a gander at Aisha O.'s journal.

January 5, 1968

To be sure, she tried Taylor Q.'s, too.

January 5, 1965

Miss Florence organized the volumes by birth dates. She moved along the shelves, quickly checking inside different ones in search of October birth dates.

A thrill raced through her as she found one.

October 8, 1989

Bingo.

Venus ran a finger along the rows of spines until she hunted down the name she needed.

Clarissa S.

She brought it to her chest, closing her eyes in relief.

"Yes," she whispered. "Fuck yes."

She hurried back to the table, shoving the book into her bag.

"Venus?"

Her pounding blood went utterly still. She turned halfway to find Presley in the curtained doorway.

They caught her not only stealing but also in a moment she'd been avoiding. That moment when she had to face them.

"Presley, what are you doing here?" When the question drained off her tongue, Venus nearly facepalmed because, *of course*, Presley was here.

They lived here.

Fortunately, Presley had a different interpretation of the question.

"Mama Renny wanted me to ask you if you wanted some lemonade or sweet tea while she took her remedy." Their regard sank to her bag, judgment bright as day on their face. "But I doubt you'll have enough time to drink either if you've already got what you came for."

Venus pointed a finger at them—at their audacity. "Don't you dare, Pres."

"Don't I dare what, Vee?" They arched an eyebrow.

"*Judge* me." She roughly shrugged on the bag's straps. "You're the last person on this entire fucking planet that should be judging me."

Their anger sparked to life behind her ribs.

Presley jabbed a thumb over their shoulder. "Oh, I'm sorry. Let me get my pom-poms, so I can cheer you on for *stealing* from my grandma."

"I appreciate the thought," Venus replied, advancing toward them and the doorway they blocked, "but I'd rather you just look the other way."

Words like hers fanned *that* spark of their anger into a flame.

Presley popped off, "What does it look like I've been doing since the day you—?" They stopped short, a *let-me-calm-the-fuck-down* exhale rushing out their nose. Their tone softened in volume but stayed taut and strained. "I *know* you've been avoiding me, Venus."

"If you knew *why*," she said, narrowing her eyes, "then we wouldn't be having this conversation."

Presley stepped forward, erasing the distance between them. "Maybe, I want to hear you say it aloud."

She cocked her chin up to nail a glare. "You're in my way. That's why."

"It's alright, Presley," Miss Florence rested a comforting hand on her grandchild's shoulder. Presley clenched their jaw, moving aside to let her pass.

"I've known for quite some time you'd come for Clarissa's journal, Venus." Sympathy painted Miss Florence's face as she shuffled by in her slippers. "To make sense of what happened to her."

Venus frowned, her gaze following the old woman. "You never penned my fate. So, how could you know that?"

"Because it says so in my journal." Miss Florence claimed her seat. "It's paramount you take it."

"Why?" she pressed. "Why is it paramount?"

Miss Florence folded her hands on the table. "Read it, make sense of it, and let your fate unfold."

"So, you did know, didn't you?" Venus growled, aiming an accusatory finger at her. "You knew she was going to die?"

"Venus." Presley grabbed her forearm to hold her back.

"No, Pres." She ripped her arm out of their hold, stalking over to the table. "She knew what would happen. I bet she hid it in some dumbass riddle because life's a big fucking game to her." Venus slammed a fist down, making everything on the table clank, clatter, and bounce. "That's it, isn't it? You like playing with folks' lives. Don't you, Miss Florence? Is that why you can't stand Madame Sharma? Because she bested you?"

Miss Florence's expression soured. "There's more to Matrika Sharma than you know."

Venus leaned in dangerously, her glare poison tipped. "More like what you think she did to Owen?"

"What?" Shock saturated Presley's words. "What do you mean?"

"*Do it,*" her deviation instigated. "*Set it off.*"

Retreat. Venus needed to retreat, but bright red anger shoved her to march onward past a point of no return.

No blood oath could punish her.

No bullet could stop her.

Venus was free to be mad as fuck.

"Mama Renny thinks the Grand Witcher has something to do with your dad's death, Pres." Like a bomb, she dropped a rumor like it was truth, hoping the words would cut like shrapnel and make everyone hurt like she *hurt* and *hurt* and *hurt.*

Miss Florence's eyes widened slightly, but she wore an armor of reserve so impenetrable Venus couldn't sense *anything.*

"Isn't that right, Miss Flo?" She pressed on, determined to see what'd it take for that armor to crack. Miss Florence drew a thin line on her lips as she digested Venus's words.

But Venus only served an appetizer. More hurtful words swelled at the back of her tongue. Old Venus would've swallowed them down and minded her business, but New Venus was petty, angry, and reckless.

Behind her, Presley asked, hurt, "Is that true?"

"Presley, go to your room." Miss Florence kept her eyes trained on Venus as she spoke to her grandchild, shaking her head like a parent used to toddler tantrums.

Presley began, "But—"

Miss Florence held up a palm, her tone cold. "Don't make me ask again."

Venus couldn't bring herself to look over her shoulder and see the damage she'd done, but she *felt* the ramifications.

Her ruthlessness stabbed Presley deep.

It stabbed her, too, right in between her ribs. That knife of guilt remained lodged in her heart even after Presley left.

Miss Florence adjusted her glasses. "You've gotten what you've come for, Venus Genevieve."

"No, I don't think so." Venus plopped into the opposite chair, defiant. "Write my future down."

The old crone frowned at the insistence.

Venus thrust an open hand at her. "You told me there's a journal with my name on it. I'm taking you up on that offer."

A journal sailed off a nearby shelf and quietly landed on the table, opening itself to Miss Florence's eyes. She leafed through it. Putting on her chained glasses, she settled on the intended page, her face clouding with confusion.

Her reaction dampened the fire inside Venus, flames of anger giving way to wisps of worry.

Miss Florence shook her head. "This doesn't make a lick of sense. I foresaw you taking the journal and leaving. You weren't supposed to stay this long. You weren't supposed to ask to have your future penned. If you were meant to, it'd be in this entry."

Venus frowned. "So, you made a mistake. No one's perfect."

She sure as fuck wasn't.

"My plotline never changes, chile. If I was meant to pen your future, The Sisters would've made this known to me through a premonition. Something's terribly wrong." Miss Florence snatched up Venus's offered hand. Her eyeballs rolled back to the whites, her eyelids fluttering as she searched for a glimpse of the future. Her lips twitched and quivered.

Venus looked on in horror.

A spare hand picked up the fountain pen, scrawling into the blank journal.

Not legible words. Just childlike scribbles.

Miss Florence let go of her hand, panting wildly.

"That's how my future looks?"

"No, Venus. You don't have one. You lost yours, and now you have another's. Sister Nature and Sister Magick don't know what to do with you."

CHAPTER
TWENTY

Society only saw our differences because I got my father's human nature and Owen inherited our mother's witchery. Because of his compassion, he earned enemies. They thought taking him from us would stop his life's work. All it did was win them millions of lifelong enemies.

—Lamonte Carter, brother of WASP cofounder Owen Carter
Transcription excerpt of eulogy

VENUS STAGGERED OUT OF THE HOUSE, THE SCREEN DOOR CLAP-ping shut behind her. As she stumbled down the porch steps, she grimaced at the harsh daylight. Saliva pooled in her mouth, nausea kicking her in the stomach. She draped herself over the railing, watering the bushes with her vomit.

She wiped her mouth with the back of her shaky hand.

"Sister Nature and Sister Magick don't know what to do with you."

Venus tried to escape Miss Florence's warning, but her wobbly legs and dizzy head couldn't keep up. She should've peaced out when she had the chance, but she got reckless and ruthless.

She took the journal and got greedy.

And now there were *more* things she had to shove into that dark pit inside her. As the days went by, her pile of skeletons grew and grew and grew. She dug all she could and it *still* wasn't enough.

The word *survive* echoed through Venus, switching her addled brain to autopilot mode. Her consciousness drew into herself. Her feet carried her home. Her mind hazy, everything around her a blur. Miss Florence's words followed her home, making her feel even more lost.

"Sister Nature and Sister Magick don't know what to do with you."

The moment Venus's shoes landed on the front door's welcome mat, she snapped out of her daze. She went inside.

Uncle Bram emerged from the kitchen with a cheesecake slice on a floating plate, wearing a mouse-ear party hat. "Aye, where you been, Pinkie? We already sang happy anniversary and cut up the cheesecake."

Venus closed her heavy eyes, muttering a curse word.

She completely forgot about Patches's anniversary celebration.

"I'm sorry," she said. "I lost track of time."

She lost her appetite.

She lost her mom.

She lost whatever the fuck she had with Presley.

And according to Miss Florence, she lost her future, too.

So many damn losses.

"You aight?" Janus joined their uncle's side and raised an eyebrow, her voice edging with concern.

"I'm not sure anymore," Venus admitted as she passed by, too tired to lie. The two left her be, but their worry gnawed at her, wanting her attention.

Her tired footsteps led her into the room at the end of the hallway. She locked the door behind her.

As Venus sat crisscrossed on her mom's bed, she held what she hoped would be answers in her hands.

Even though those answers hid within riddles.

She started on the first page.

November 1999

> *You'll stand at a door, knock to be let in, and face a dare.*
>   *Be prepared to fall.*

Venus chewed her lip, staring at the date. Clarissa would've been eighteen then in her freshman year at Georgetown.

She closed her eyes, picturing a teenaged Clarissa standing at a door, knocking to be let in. Questions invaded her mind, crowding in at the edges of her imagination. *Why* did fate give Miss Florence a glimpse of that moment? *What* was so important about it?

She thought hard but snapped the volume shut, blowing frustration through her nostrils.

Venus hated riddles. She thought of them as jumbled knots she could barely untangle. She liked solutions as plain as day.

Explicit, unmistakable, clear-cut.

But quitting on the first page wasn't an option.

She returned to that entry.

> *You'll stand at a door, knock to be let in, and face a dare.*
>   *Be prepared to fall.*

On her second try, little things stuck out to her.

> *Knock to be let in. Face a dare. Be prepared to fall.*

Knox. Darius. Love.

The truth pieced itself together in her head. During her studies at Georgetown, her mom met the love of her life, Darius Knox.

Venus *knew* that, but her frustration clouded the obvious.

That's why Miss Florence penned it.

With another page turn, she employed a strategy she should've used the first damn time.

Trust herself.

Venus might've not known *everything* about her mom, but she knew *more* than she gave herself credit for. She remembered little stories Uncle Bram and Aunt Keisha would recollect with cackles and backslaps when they both had one too many.

Little stories that were big moments back then. The kind of moments you tell with humor to make scars easier to look at.

May 2003

You'll find a safe nest
But you must defend it with stings.

After the WASP founders got expelled, her mom bought a house that turned into their headquarters, casting a shield spell that stung and stunned those with ill intentions.

Another page turn.

June 2005

You're a gardener with a growing seed of love.
Water may protect it from fire.

When Clarissa went to labor with her, the Iron Watch planted iron nail bombs in various parts of Epione. Uncle Bram punched a hole through a wall as an escape route and brought his little sister back home, where she gave birth in a bathtub filled with water.

Venus kept reading, matching riddles with all the stories she knew of her mom. Until she came across the first one to make her heart twist.

November 2007

A harvest will come too soon.
Yielding your own fruits could restore cut roots.

She knew this one too, but she didn't learn it from Aunt Keisha or Uncle Bram. Elder Glenn gave her the breadcrumbs, and it took his death for Venus to understand what he meant. Miss Florence's riddle was merely a receipt at this point.

A harvest. A death.

Come too soon. Died suddenly.

Yielding meant to provide, but it also meant surrender.

Your own fruits. Magic, brewing.

Could restore cut roots. Bring back to life, resurrect.

Her mom broke a pledge, brewed a sacrificium potion, and gave up her magic.

Venus just didn't know who her mom did it for.

Bringing the journal up to her face, she squinted hard, like she could intimidate it into elaborating. She turned the page as if she'd find the mystery identity on the other side, but only the last entry waited for her.

June 2023

Dip your thoughts in ink and air them to dry.
For what your seed tilled has levied

Venus couldn't make out the crossed-out words behind the wavy scribbles.

Frustration seeped into her voice. "Why the hell did Miss Florence do that?"

Was it a mistake? Or a choice?

Theories rattled her skull, distracting her. Leading her astray. She shook her head to clear her mind and focus on the only completed line.

"You'll dip your thoughts into ink and air them to dry." Her eyes darted over to her mom's writing desk and its wooden holder of pens. "A letter. She must've written a letter."

A burst of determination fueled Venus as she climbed off the bed, rushing over to the desk. She hunted for the letter.

She rummaged through drawers. Nothing.

She foraged in the closet. Nothing.

She lifted the cumbersome mattress, but she found absolutely fucking nothing.

Defeatedly, she collapsed on her ass at the foot of the bed, out of breath and hope. A sense of familiarity crawled underneath her flesh, giving her goosebumps. Clarissa sat in this exact spot the night she handed over a letter written by a dead man.

An inheritance that sat in a box for years.

A box Venus hadn't come across yet unless—

She looked underneath the bed, reaching for it. Her relief overflowed. She dragged the box from the bed's underbelly, surprised by how heavy it was. Metal scraped the wood floor.

A four-digit combination lock secured the box. Unlike Miss Florence and her riddles, Clarissa Stoneheart was a practical woman, so Venus took a practical approach.

Birth years.

Hers and Tyrell's, 2005. Janus's, 2007. Clarissa's, 1981. Her dad and Aunt Keisha's, 1980. Uncle Bram's, 1978. As well as Hakeem, 2012.

In a last-ditch effort, Granny Davina, 1957.

Nothing worked.

No way in hell would her mom pick Malik's birth year as the key to this box, so Venus was out of options.

Again, she underestimated Clarissa Stoneheart.

"Damn it," she growled, wanting to bash the box against something until it cracked open like a skull.

"*Like Baldwin Tillery's skull?*" It chuckled.

Her grip tightened on the box. "Shut up."

"*Go beg for help. Magic can solve this.*"

But doing that would only show Janus and Uncle Bram the depths of her desperation.

Of her obsession.

Venus squeezed her eyes, listening to what went on beyond the door.

Uncle Bram gave a toast to Patches. "Thank you for putting up with us for hundred fifty-one years, you old cat. My nieces' descendants will be lucky to have you for hundred fifty-one more."

"Pump the brakes, Uncle Bee. There won't be any kids from *moi*," Janus said matter-of-factly. "So, I guess he'll be stuck with *Vee's* descendants."

Hundred fifty-one years.

In Venus's mind, that three-digit number sparked a tiny realization. She had tried the birth years of Clarissa's family.

But not the year a familiar swore to protect and serve the Stonehearts.

Hesitantly, she selected the numbers.

1-8-7-2.

The lock gave way with a soft *click*. She lifted back the box's hinged lid, her heart clambering up her throat.

Venus found an envelope addressed to her on top of neat stacks of banded Benjamins. When she picked it up, she realized it had something else inside besides just a letter.

As she unfurled the folded paper, a gold coin humming with magic fell into her lap. The coin could've only come from one person. The king of Washington, DC's witcher society's underbelly. The owner of the Golden Coin. The keeper of the Black Book.

Prospero.

It was like a harbinger of bad news for Venus.

She didn't dare pick it up.

My dear Venus,

I'm not the perfect mother, but I love you and Janus more than you'll ever know. I'm hard on you both because the world's hard, but I now realize I should have been softer. Darius's death broke me, and marrying Malik didn't mend me. I only wanted you both to be stronger than I ever was to survive.

Darius believed every witcher had two gifts: magic and heart. A heart is a safe for your passions and freedom, which makes it worth breaking into for those who intend to wrong you. For those who want to break you. For those who seek to own you.

I thought that was corny for a long time, but I now see truth in his words. There are folks who will stop at nothing to get your heart, Venus. I've tried to protect you from them, but all options have been exhausted except one. You have to run.

Run before they threaten you, throw money at you, or lure you in with what you desire most. Run before they are desperate enough to use Janus or Bram against you.

Or me, Venus. They'll use me in their lies. Just run. Cash in Prospero's coin, find a doorkeeper in the Black Book to take you far away from here, and don't look back.

Love,
Mom

The paper trembled in her hands, tears blurring the words. Sorrow tore through her and she tipped over in defeat, hugging her mom's words to her chest like a teddy bear.

Grief shattered her yet left her intact. For her, that was worse than a trinary-note potion's recoil.

Venus was too weak to crawl to the kitchen and gulp down a mending potion to see if it'd piece together all the jagged shards, splinters, and slivers she had carried within her since those homicide detectives arrived at her doorstep.

But, in truth, no potion could fix her.

Grief was a poison with no remedy.

So was confusion.

I've tried to protect you from them, but all options have been exhausted except one. You have to run.

Her mom wanted her to run away, but from who? Not Julius Keller, right?

Venus didn't even think he knew she existed until she stood before his unlit pyre with a torch. But Madame Sharma did say Julius caught on to her mom tailing him. Did he do the same? From afar, did Julius stalk her mom back home like a predator, taking note of those she loved? Maybe, he did know of Venus, but that didn't mean he would've wanted *her heart.*

A serial killer like him would simply want her *dead*.

No, the warning her mom wrote wasn't about Julius Keller.

Venus had inherited a different enemy from her mom.

"*Now, she wants you to be a coward and run away,*" It hissed.

"No, I can't," she whispered tiredly, her throat tight and raw from bottling up all her sobs and screams.

Like a weight against her chest, the letter pinned her in place.

Run before they threaten you, throw money at you, or lure you in with what you desire most. Run before they are desperate enough to use Janus or Bram against you.

She couldn't leave her flesh and blood behind to save her own skin.

Leaving wouldn't protect her heart. Leaving would only corrode it. Just the *thought* of running skinned ribbons from her heart.

Please, do as I say, Venus, a voice of reason encouraged gently, dressed in Clarissa's voice. She gave a closemouthed laugh that sounded like a drawn-out hum, amused by grief's trickery.

Venus sat up with slumped shoulders. She stared at the words, wishing they'd rearrange into different instructions. They didn't, of course. But the longer she considered her mom's cursive, the more her thoughts and sense rearranged themselves instead.

She straightened up, squinting as she reread the letter.

Run before they threaten you, throw money at you, or lure you in with what you desire most.

Venus lost her grip, the paper fluttering down to her lap.

Her scarred palm awaited attention.

A memory stormed into her head.

The shrill of a rotary phone in the night. The scent of roasting human flesh. The promise of a lot of money in a car trunk. The warm slickness of entwining blood. The torment ruining her from the inside out as an oath sealed itself.

Venus's chin quivered. In the theater of her mind, the Grand Witcher gritted her teeth as she slit her palm. *"I gave you the bastard that took your mother away from you. Am I not worthy of your loyalty? For a blood oath to work, your heart must have a sliver of willingness. What shall it be?"*

Venus's breast rose and plummeted as her uneven breaths quickened.

Or me, Venus. They'll use me in their lies.

The numbness started in her fingertips and then roared through all of her. She shook her head, disbelief knifing deep into her chest. "Mom didn't negotiate any terms. She wanted me to run."

It tsked. "You carved out your heart and offered it to Matrika on a silver platter."

"Matrika had me at knifepoint," she said, burying her face into her hands to hide from her shame. "Nothing makes sense. Why would the Grand Witcher lie?"

Her memories answered for her.

"What do you want from me?"

"I already told you, Miss Stoneheart. I want love."

She lifted her head slowly, her blood an icy sludge.

The Registration Act.

"Mom hated politics," she whispered, her voice raw and quivering. "She didn't want Jay or me anywhere near it."

"Yet here you are, about to brew peitho potions to rig a vote on Capitol Hill. Auntie Politics Clarissa was barely cold in the ground when Matrika came for you," It instigated. *"How convenient."*

Too convenient, Venus realized. She remembered the last night she saw Clarissa Stoneheart alive. She remembered how Janus tried to eavesdrop on that phone conversation. What if Janus had been right the first time? What if their mom had said *she*? What if Matrika Sharma was that "she" their mom spoke of?

What if—?

Venus grabbed fistfuls of her hair, yanking at the roots as if that'd rip *that* thought right out of her mind.

"*Go on,*" It urged.

What if Matrika Sharma killed Clarissa Stoneheart?

No, she couldn't have done it herself. A witcher couldn't shoot a gun bearing iron bullets, which meant a human would've done the deed for her. Maybe, one bound by a blood oath, too.

Did she use Julius Keller as her triggerman? Did she use him to take out other witchers? Or was he just a fall guy to make Venus willing to give her heart away?

Something her mom warned her not to do. A treasure Matrika believed was worth killing for. A prize Matrika thought was worth coercing Elder Glenn into brewing a sacrificium potion.

If Clarissa Stoneheart wanted her daughter to be used to rig the Registration Act's vote, she wouldn't have left behind a one-way ticket out of town.

Prospero's coin.

And the only way to get to Prospero was through—

"Nisha," she whispered. "She must've warned Matrika."

A perfect motive for murder.

Venus teemed with rage. In her mind, she pictured the blood of the Grand Witcher on her hands. She wanted to bathe in it. She ached to choke on the scent of it.

Her deviation squirmed in delight at her murderous thoughts.

Venus waited for the blood oath to punish her.

To teach her a lesson in obedience for daring to *think* about going against Matrika Sharma.

But it never came.

I pledge myself to thee

My loyalty shall never flee
Measure my servitude with every heartbeat and breath
To which this bond will sever by your tongue or upon my death

The revelation drove a dagger of shock through Venus's healed bullet-hole scar. The blood oath dissolved when she took her last breaths on that ER gurney.

"*She brought you back to life to be her puppet but gave you the power to strangle her with your strings,*" It pressed. "*Kill her for what she's done.*"

Venus balled her mom's letter up, her fist trembling.

"No, not yet. If I kill her now, it'll jeopardize rigging the vote. Me and Ty have worked too hard to stop now. But afterward," she ground out, her molars scraping together, "she's mine."

She wasn't going to run.

According to Miss Florence, she was a girl with no fate.

So, at that moment, she set the terms of her destiny.

She was going to kill Matrika Sharma.

CHAPTER
TWENTY-ONE

Because familiars are mostly stoical beings with a pain immunity, there's a belief they lack feeling entirely. This is incorrect. Familiars possess emotions, amusements, disappointments, desires, and fears. They do not fear death itself as they've already died once. If a familiar perishes, only the fruit of their loyalty remains.

—*The Familiar Manual*, 2009 Edition

SINCE THE RESURRECTION, WHEN GUNSHOTS RANG OUT NEAR OR far, Venus would go rigid, suck in a breath, and grimace. Each time she heard them, her heart startled into a crazed gallop, her chest aching. It was a new normal she had no choice but to accept.

Venus *expected* the fireworks. Fireworks came with the territory of Independence Day. The difference between fireworks and gunshots was their cadence. A fact she had known since she was little, but in the dark of her closet, her body still acted up at the celebratory *pop-pop-pops* and *boom-boom-booms*.

She hugged herself tight, clenching her teeth. Fear and rage ravaged her. In her head, she was back in that alleyway the day of the protest, staring at her blood-stained hand. But in her heart, she desired only Matrika Sharma's blood on her hands.

Her deviation egged her on, whispering *Its* approval.

A tiny part of her appreciated the encouragement, wanting to hear that what she wanted was right. To want *vengeance*. Even if it came from a voice only she could hear. Even though she knew her magic was only using her. Since the protest, *It* struggled to replenish its strength, having hemorrhaged so much.

She knew she'd find no peace or closure in avenging her mom, but she *had* to do it. The Grand Witcher *would* be punished for her treachery.

Her phone vibrated beside her, its black screen lighting up as an incoming call came in. She spared a glance to see who was bothering her, but she found no name or even a number. Just the words NO CALLER ID.

Only six folks had Venus's personal number. One was dead now, and the rest preferred text messages over calls.

So, she chose not to answer, instead taking deep breaths. Seconds later, she heard a text notification chime. She picked up her cell with a shaky hand and read the message.

Answer your phone, little Stoneheart.

Only one person ever called her that. A person who was also on her two-person-long *it's-on-motherfucking-sight* list.

When the device went off again alongside another firework, Venus growled the word *fuck*.

"Nisha. To what do I owe the pleasure?" She slathered artificial sweetness all over her greeting. Surprised, all her trembling didn't bleed into her tone.

"Well, the profiles of our last two targets are waiting for you here at the Golden Coin." When Venus heard Nisha's mellow, amused voice, she wanted to reach through the phone and *strangle* the Grand Witcher's sister.

She glared at the slit of pinkish light that bled through the crack of her closet doors. "I thought they'd be delivered to me."

By Ilyas or another one of Madame Sharma's guards.

Nisha chuckled, the melody crisp but brief. "That was the initial arrangement, but I miss seeing your little face. I have a soft spot for you."

Venus bit back the word *bullshit* at that lie.

It was obvious what Nisha was up to now. First, her familiar spied on Venus this morning for her. Now, she issued a last-minute mandate for Venus to come to the Golden Coin. Which only meant she *believed* Venus was guilty of something.

She just didn't know what yet.

But Venus knew, though.

She was guilty of knowing the truth.

A tremor of hatred ran down her spine before a symphony of fireworks stiffened it.

She tightened her grip on the phone. "I'll be there soon."

"Good. Come through the back entrance. I'll be waiting for you in Prospero's office." Then Nisha ended the call.

It took *everything* in her not to chuck the phone against the wall.

If it weren't for Janus's noise-canceling headphones and a playlist of songs with 808 basslines turned up loud, Venus would've broken her promise to be at the bar soon. On the way there, she slipped into her mind's theater, picking at the meat and bones of every moment she shared with the Sharma sisters since her mom's funeral. Those two bitches fed her lies, and she swallowed down every spoonful because she trusted them.

A curtain spell hid the bar's location and noises. Passersby saw only a boarded-up abandoned building. The old chain-link fence surrounding the property had a crooked NO TRESPASSING sign. Ironically, a glowing, body-sized incision was located to the sign's left. Most humans couldn't see the entryway, but desperate, determined ones always found it.

One way or another.

Venus's fingers danced across the digital keyboard as she sent Tyrell a text, asking him if he was down for whatever was next.

He replied within moments:

as long as I ain't shaped like somebody's granddaddy again.

Her lips curled slightly around the cherry lollipop in her mouth, a white stick poking out. She smiled for the first time all day. After realizing that, it crumbled off her face.

Firecrackers went off nearby during the momentary pause between songs. The headphone muffled the sound, but it set Venus on edge. She flinched and gritted her teeth, crunching hard on the sugary red bulb. She swallowed the jagged shards and clumps of cherry candy, a faint tinge of copper tainting her taste buds.

Venus slipped through the glimmery gateway a mere second before the cruiser turned onto the block, unknowingly driving by the entrance to the Underbelly. A nickname given to DC witcher society's underworld. The cop warningly flashed their siren lights at a witcher pushing his toddler down the sidewalk in a stroller. The threat forced him to up his pace, his fear spiking into Venus's heart.

"Asshole," she spat under her breath, narrowing her eyes at the patrol car passing by.

Outside the bar, kindred gathered, drinking bottled beer, chatting, and vaping. Out of blown smoke, they made animals and mythical creatures. The gravel crunched under Venus's sneakers as she walked around to the back as instructed.

The rusted back entrance opened up for her. She came in, her stride cautious. She took off her sister's headphones, letting them hug her neck.

Thanks to the holiday, a biblical flood of patrons had flooded the Golden Coin. Venus could tell by how boisterous it sounded in the bar area beyond the dim corridor.

She imagined the stone-cold expression most likely adorning her uncle's face as he used magic to tend to the thirsty, noisy crowd. Even though only hours ago, he wore a mouse-ear party hat and happily chowed down on strawberry cheesecake to celebrate *a cat*.

It was loud enough here to bury the outside's festive explosions. Loud enough to drown Venus's screams if this turned out to be an ambush. Loud enough to devour Nisha's screams if Venus gave into the deep-seated urge to wrench answers out of her.

To her left, the office door yawned for her, light spilling out the doorway and onto her. Nisha sat in her boss's high-backed chair, with her bejeweled heels propped up on his desk, her ankles crossed. She toyed with a dagger-like letter opener. Her familiar sat on the chair's crest, his neck missing a patch of feathers.

A dark shade of delight sliced through Venus at her cat's handiwork.

"Do come in." Nisha wielded the letter opener like a royal scepter, aiming its tip at one of two empty chairs.

"Don't mind if I do," Venus said flatly as she came in, scorn enflaming her throat.

Suddenly, the door closed on its own, blocking out all the noise in the bar. A soundproof enchantment coated the walls to ensure privacy.

Venus ignored the gesture to sit, heading straight for the two manila folders on the desk. She needed to get what she needed and head right on out. Venus had little patience to play a game of pretend with this woman for longer than necessary. She also doubted she had the restraint to *not* stab Nisha in the throat with that letter opener.

Because she wasn't entirely sure what role Nisha played in her mom's death *yet*, she could only hate the bitch for being guilty by association.

She snatched up Senators Martha Westbay and Blanche Radliff's profiles and shoved them into her bag, flashing a fake-ass smile. A quick *thanks a bunch* flicked off her tongue.

"I want to have a little chat with you."

"I'd love to," Venus began, hitching a thumb over her shoulder, "but I've gotta—"

Nisha held up a palm. "I wasn't asking."

Her warm brown gaze glided over to the quilted leather seat to Venus's right.

Well, fuck.

A reluctant Venus spared a glance at the door she wanted to fling open and escape through before she plopped into her assigned chair.

Nisha's head tilted as she eyed her with muted curiosity. "Has Bram ever mentioned my calling to you?"

Venus blinked at the odd question, then nodded. "You're a medium."

"Yes, but I don't commune with the Spirits to help my patrons find closure. I summon Spirits from behind the Veil and turn them into familiars. Much like the art of brewing, familiar-forging is very grueling work." Nisha cocked her head back to admire Kiwi still perched on the executive chair's arched ridge. "The ones patrons pay for I simply regard as my creations, but the ones I keep for myself, like Kiwi, I consider as my children. And like all good mothers, I'm protective of my children. Your old little kitty cat left *quite* a mark on my Kiwi this morning."

Venus refrained from rolling her eyes. Patches only taught Kiwi a lesson and confiscated a few feathers, but he could've done much worse. Nisha should've been *grateful* her little birdie returned to her at all.

"Kiwi seems to be handling his ass-whooping *quite* well." As soon as the words left Venus's mouth, she expected Nisha's anger or annoyance to barge inside her.

But she only felt her *own* anger boiling in her veins, her patience threadbare.

"But I have no one to blame but myself." Nisha favored Venus with a sober gaze, her expression contemplative. "I should've known better than to send a youngster into an antique familiar's territory. You've spent the day wondering why I made the choice I did, haven't you?"

Venus bounced her knee as she balanced on a blade of indecision, swaying between attacking Nisha or listening to her. If she chose the former, she'd have to use the coin in her back pocket to call a doorkeeper and run like hell, just as her mom wanted. That, or she'd have to go straight to the Grand Witcher's home in Kalorama and take out that bitch, too.

Which both jeopardized gutting the Registration Act.

If she chose the latter to sit and listen, what if Nisha gave her another lie?

"What's one more lie?" It whispered.

Venus nodded. "Yes, among other things."

"I wanted to check on you." Nisha set aside her letter opener. "Resurrection is just as traumatic as a violent death. Being a big sister can be traumatic, too. Big sisters carry the world's weight on our shoulders so that burden doesn't weigh our little sisters down."

Venus's brows creased, her lips faltering. Although her brain tried to detect deception in anything Nisha said, it couldn't.

"Seven days ago, *you* took a bullet for your sister, little Stoneheart," Nisha replied, her voice soft and compassionate like a therapist.

Or a teacher.

Venus *knew* how many days it had been. She couldn't shove that knowledge into that abyss inside her filled with a growing heap of *I'll-deal-with-it-laters*.

And yet when she *heard* it aloud, tears suddenly distorted her world.

A sob tightened into a painful lump in her throat. She swallowed it down hard, wincing as it sunk to her chest, pain lurking about her ribs.

Venus averted her watery vision to the silver ring she wore, recalling the bullet it deflected at the protest. Then she thought of the bullet she caught in her chest and the moments afterward.

How life gushed out of her.

How Janus sobbed.

How Tyrell, stunned and helpless, stared at her.

How Presley carried her into the emergency room.

The moment she slipped that ring onto her little sister's finger, consequences fell like dominoes, creating a disaster she couldn't clean up.

But Nisha wasn't supposed to say shit like that. And Venus wasn't supposed to cry, but she couldn't stop. Her hurt justified every single tear. She let out a shaky exhale, wiping madly at the streams of wetness on her face.

Then she felt Nisha's guilt crawl across her flesh.

She wanted to scratch her skin raw.

Nisha's mouth sank into a frown. "After the resurrection, the Revived requires immediate care and attention. Neither of which we gave you, even though it was *our* choice to bring you back to life. It was lazy of me to give you that unofficial guide. You deserved—"

"*I* deserved what?" Venus snapped, shooting to her feet. She jabbed a finger into her chest, pointing at her heart—at stolen anima. "What about what Elder Glenn deserved? What about him?"

Nisha didn't seem surprised that Venus knew what had happened to him.

A question stuck out in her mind like a splinter. Did Kiwi spy on them when she and Janus went to Elder Glenn's house last night? She pictured him flapping his little wings back to Nisha to report everything he saw.

"Your value to us outweighed his."

Venus knew that, too. She'd be six feet under if she were that dispensable to the Sharma sisters. She understood why she had a second chance.

If she were to die, it'd be on their terms.

Not hers.

Venus pushed her way into the restrooms, nausea wringing her stomach. She made it into a stall just in time to vomit into a toilet. She braced the walls, panting heavily over the bowl. A string of spit fell out her mouth. She flushed and stumbled out to the sinks. Venus cupped her hands underneath a faucet spewing cold water, bringing it to her lips for a slurp. After a rough swish, she spat out the horrid aftertaste of her puke.

She splashed water on her face, too, for good measure.

Hanging her drippy face over the sink, she blindly reached for a paper towel and yanked one out of the dispenser fixed to the wall beside her.

The restroom door opened, then closed. After Venus patted her face dry, she looked in the mirror, seeing her uncle in the reflection.

He pressed his broad back and shoulders against the door's wood, which creaked at his weight, untucking a charmed cigarillo from behind his ear. He always enchanted them to protect them from his brute strength. His teeth clutched the wood filter gently as he lit the end with a finger snap.

As he breathed out the sweet-smelling smoke, a question fluttered out, too. "What business you got with Nisha?"

Venus crumpled up the damp paper towel, tossing it in the trash. "I wouldn't even call it business. I played a stupid game and won a stupid prize."

Uncle Bram shook his head. "I know you eighteen and all, and you wanna handle business your way, but I've already lost Rissa. And I ain't losing you *again*, either."

She flinched.

"Who told you?" she asked, her voice small with shock.

"Jay," he sighed, shaking his head. "You got the right one to guard your bread box, Pinkie. She only gave me a few crumbs to get a taste of things. A bit of the why and the how. To prepare me for who you are now, so I know when to give you space and when to love on you."

"Who I am now, huh?" she whispered to herself, staring at her reflection.

He tapped his nails on his scalp to rectify an itch. "Maybe, those ain't the right words for it."

"No, you're right, Uncle Bee. I *have* changed."

Not all at once, though.

Venus felt like a lump of wet clay on a pottery wheel. The world blurry as she spun while life had its way with her, molding her into something unrecognizable.

Making her more and more of a stranger to herself.

"It's a fragile time for you," Uncle Bram said.

She laughed at that, imagining the word FRAGILE in red stamped all over her. Like she wasn't already messed up, damaged, ruined.

The love, patience, and understanding of others wouldn't be enough to piece her back together. It'd only teach everyone else how not to get cut when handling her.

She didn't correct him, nodding to his words.

"I should've been there for both of y'all the morning those cops came, but..." he stopped himself, choosing to suck on his cigarillo over spitting out what was on his mind.

Venus snuck a sideways glance. "But?"

"Truth be told, I ain't been at the house much 'cause I was afraid. Still am." A contemplative plume eased from his nostrils. "Rissa always made me promise her that I'd take care of y'all two if something ever happened to her, but deep down, I hoped I never have to. I knew I'd be lost without her."

She planted her hands on the restroom counter, blinking back tears.

"I'mma always regret not being there to protect her," Uncle Bram continued.

"It's not your fault."

"*But you know who's to blame. Go on, Pinkie. Tell him who took Rissa away from us,*" It whispered, including *Itself* among those who mourned for Clarissa Stoneheart. *It* always respected her in *Its* own way, never going against her. Even though magic-less, she had a calling of putting everyone in their place like a general.

And *It* loved being surrounded by those who reminded *It* of war.

She wagged her head at *Its* insistence.

Matrika was hers and hers alone.

"Guilt don't give a damn about whose fault it is, Pinkie. You know that."

"All too well."

They both welcomed a beat of silence.

"I need to keep my promise to Rissa, which means if whatever you got going on gets outta hand, I'm tapping in. You feel me?"

Venus snapped him a look, panic storming through her bones.

Her uncle's bladed gaze slit the objection out of her throat.

"It's a yes or no question, Venus Genevieve. And it betta not be no."

Suddenly, she felt like a little kid again. "Yes, sir."

"Nisha done lost her damn mind if she mistook my employment here as submission and complacency. If something happens to you, nobody gone like what happens next."

"Be careful what you wish for, Uncle Bee."

"Naw, *she* needs to be careful. If something big is happening in your life, I don't wanna find out from a newspaper or Jay. Or even Ty's goofy self. I wanna hear it from you," Uncle Bram paused, a thick eyebrow edging up. "Is there anything else I should know?"

Matrika Sharma killed Mom.

The words queued up in her throat, but she swallowed them down with a hard gulp. Her breath snagged on something within her chest as she gathered the nerve to look at her uncle.

Venus fortified her expression so it wouldn't crack.

"No, that's it." The lie dove off her tongue smoothly.

A notification bell's chime from Uncle Bram's pocket punctuated that lie. Seconds later, knuckles knocked on the opposite side of the restroom door.

He nodded, pleased. "Your escort is here."

Venus frowned. "My who?"

CHAPTER
TWENTY-TWO

Sacrificium potions can last for years, unlike most potions. Because animas do not age, the Revived inherits the Willing's anima but not their remaining lifespan. Sacrificium potions often let the Revived live until old age, tragedy, or disease strikes.

—Witcherpedia, an online witchery encyclopedia

"YOU FIRST."

Presley gestured to the fence's aglow doorway, their glittery cotton-candy-pink nail polish catching in the light.

After everything today, what went down in Miss Florence's writing study seemed like forever ago now. Back then, Venus was too busy stealing shit and firing off heard rumors as truth to notice anything about Presley beyond their judgment and subsequent shock, then hurt.

Hurt she wanted Presley and Miss Florence to join her in.

Now, they both stood in the aftermath of what she'd done.

There were only two options.

Step around it and pretend like it never happened.

Or pick up the shards, even if it meant getting cut.

"Cute color. Am I rubbing off on you?" She hugged herself, tensing up at every *boom*, *pop*, and *crackle* that filled the night air. Despite not wanting to retreat to the Golden Coin, being there bought her time away from fireworks.

"In more ways than I can count," they said.

Venus walked through, Presley following right behind. Once on the other side, she grabbed onto the chain-link fence for dear life, stuttering, "Give me a minute."

In her chest, her heart hammered as if trying to escape the fireworks, too.

She feared for the integrity of her trembling knees.

"Get on my back."

Venus scrunched her face, swerving her attention to Presley. "What?"

"I *said*, get on my back. It's the quickest way to get your ass home," they paused, arching a light eyebrow, "unless you want to message Janus to open a—"

"No," she interjected.

Janus witnessed her dying.

Janus saw her dead.

But Venus didn't want her sister to see her like this, absolutely terrified of fireworks. Nisha said it best: *"Big sisters carry the world's weight on our shoulders so that burden doesn't weigh our little sisters down."*

Venus had to bear this burden.

For her sister's sake.

For her dignity.

Presley gave her a piggyback ride home. The fact they didn't drop her ass along the way surprised Venus. Her arms around their neck were tight enough to be called a chokehold.

But it didn't faze them one bit.

They carried her through the front door, down the hallway, and into her bedroom.

As she clung to Presley, they pressed a palm on her door, whispering an incantation.

"To give me the peace I desire, these four walls must hush the world's choir." Magic bled from Presley's hand, spreading across the door and the walls like wildfire. A soundproof spell, Venus realized, but theirs was more like a Band-Aid when compared to the immovable one in Prospero's office.

Still, it silenced all the noise beyond her door.

Venus didn't relax right away, her body not yet catching up to her relieved mind.

She slipped off Presley's back, shrugging off her bag full of senator profiles. "How long does the spell last?"

"Until I open the door." They turned to face her, their gaze falling on hers.

"So, that means…" she trailed off.

"It means *I* want answers." Presley sat down on the bed, loosening their boot laces, "*And* you want quiet." They halted briefly to rub at their neck, wincing.

So, her unintentional chokehold *did* cause some damage.

Today, she caused Presley much more damage than just a sore neck.

"You need help with that?" Venus asked hesitantly, kicking off her shoes.

Their hand dropped away. "Be my guest."

She got on her bed and kneeled behind them. When her fingers touched their neck's crook, goosebumps covered their flesh as her caress journeyed to the bothersome knot of tension.

As she kneaded, they melted in her palms as the moments dripped on.

Her eyes crinkled with slight amusement. "Do you like that?"

"Don't ask questions you already know the answer to." They pulled off their boots, their tone warm and relaxed.

She kept on until their hand crept up to blanket hers.

"You good now?" she asked.

They grasped her wrist and eased it forward over their shoulder, drawing her front against their back.

Like a half-done hug.

"Now, I am."

She gently curled one arm around their neck while they studied the blood oath's scar on her other palm.

Propping her head against theirs, she rested against them, her wall coming down brick by brick. A wall not even Uncle Bram could scale to see what she hid on the other side.

"Matrika gave it to me." The confession came swathed in a shred of a whisper.

Presley stiffened against her. "As in the Grand Witcher?"

She nodded.

"Tell me everything you know about her and my dad." A violent flare of Presley's quiet anger burned her veins. *It* sniffed deep as if savoring a flower, shuddering in delight.

"They dated in college, but I think they fell out after our dads got expelled," Venus whispered, sewing together her assumption with a definite fact. She remembered the memories from her mom's old photo album. She remembered how the last few pages of 2003 photos didn't show Matrika anymore. She suspected that the breakup was to blame.

With caution, Venus repeated the rumor Senator Hoage told her and Tyrell. More and more, the allegation felt like another long receipt detailing the cost of Matrika Sharma's ruthless ambition.

Her deviation wheezed out a chuckle. *"And what did Clarissa use to say about ambition?"*

Ambition is only greed with a business plan.

"If Mama Renny knew the truth all this time, why didn't she do anything about it?" Presley sprung off the mattress, pacing. Their turbulent aura fattened and darkened.

"Because she can't prove it. Everyone thinks the Iron Watch did it, and the Iron Watch never said that they didn't," Venus said, tasting out the words with an expression of uncertainty.

Presley rooted their feet. "Did your mom know?"

The question knocked her back on her ass, her eyes widening in shock. Never once had she considered that.

"I"—she paused, her voice growing small—"don't know."

"What if she did, Vee? What if she kept quiet because Matrika forced her into—"

"I'mma stop you right there." Venus cut them off, jabbing a finger at them. "*That* didn't happen."

"What if you're wrong?" they countered, shaking their head.

She snapped, "My mom would *never* commit to a blood oath, Pres."

"How do you know that?" they pressed.

"Because I washed her dead body myself. All by myself. That's how I know! Dammit!" She jabbed her index finger into her collarbone repeatedly, her lids beating back a tide of tears. "She might've had old scars from her brewer days, but *not* that kinda scar."

Her body trembled as she held in a sob that fought to lash out.

"Is that good enough evidence for you, Presley?" Venus scrambled off the bed, shoving her shoes back on and knotting the laces tight. "Unless you want to dig her up to see for yourself. She hasn't been dead long."

She snapped her fingers as if a lost thought had returned to her. "Oh, and let me go to the garden shed and get a shovel."

Presley captured her forearm. "Venus, wait."

"Let me go." She snatched it back, edging away.

Her wall back up again.

"I'm sorry." They crept closer, empty palms up. "I didn't mean to go that far. It's just I keep telling myself if I know everything there is to know about him, I'll have some fucking closure."

Venus shoved around on the ball of her foot, cramming her eyes shut.

Her shaky breaths sawed in and out as she tried to calm down. She pressed the heels of her palms against her temples as she tried to make sense of everything.

In her mind, bits of information sat in a pile. She tried to fit them together to form the bigger picture. Some puzzle pieces, however, had tabs and blanks that didn't quite fit, leaving her with a half-solved conundrum.

Leading Venus to wonder if they were all lies or half-truths.

A tiny seed of a theory sprouted, grew, matured within her.

She put her hands on her head. "What if the rumor I heard was only half-right?"

"Then which part is right?" Presley asked, their tone soft but cautious.

Now, it was her turn to pace.

"I think Matrika *did* infiltrate the Iron Watch, but—" Venus cut herself off, disgusted that she even considered giving her mother's murderer *any* benefit of the doubt.

Presley pressed gently, "But what?"

"But she wasn't behind the Iron Nail Bombing," she finished. "I couldn't help but wonder why the Iron Watch took the fall for it and didn't retaliate. Senator Hoage believed they were too ashamed to admit a witcher tricked them."

"*You* don't believe that, though."

She shook her head. "I think the bombing *was* their retaliation."

"But why would they target my dad?"

Venus interjected, "Matrika and Owen got back together. Just not sure when they got back together, but I think they were dating during Matrika's spy mission. If the Iron Watch caught on to her, they would've been spying on her, too."

In silence, they both stared at each other.

Presley backed away from her slowly, their knees hitting the bed's edge.

"I think I know why my dad and Matrika broke up in the first place." They sank to sit down, their expression unreadable. "I'm the reason."

"What?"

"Think about it, Vee." Presley shook their head slowly, their disappointment and sadness weighing down Venus's heart. "I was born February 13, 2004, which means—"

"Your mom was pregnant when your dad and Matrika were together," she finished, her voice barely above a whisper.

Presley stared right through Venus, their eyes unfocused. "If Matrika wasn't behind the bombing to gain an edge in the Grand Witcher election, why the fuck would she even want to infiltrate the Iron Watch?"

"The Iron Watch's beef with WASP goes all the way back to when our dads and Malik started the movement at Georgetown," Venus said, joining them on her bed. "They had Matrika's help from the beginning. Maybe, she did it out of loyalty to the movement."

"Makes sense." Presley slumped their shoulders, their sigh somber and heavy. "Then, on November 4, 2007, my dad paid with his life."

That date punched Venus square in the face, her head rearing back. The remembrance mural at Carter's Pantry had shown it to her more times than she could count, but she had seen it elsewhere, too. Well, sort of.

Today, she didn't see that actual date, but she did come across that month-year combo.

"Wait." Venus crawled toward the mountain of plushies on the far side of the bed, shoving a hand underneath. She hid the premonition journal there to keep the truth close to her.

Once more, Venus sat beside Presley, holding the thing she needed. After cracking it open, she flipped to the entry.

Miss Florence's penned words dripped off her tongue: "November 2007. A harvest will come too soon. Yielding your own fruits could restore cut roots."

"What does that mean?" Presley took the journal from her hands, their brow furrowing as they examined the riddle their damn self.

"I think it means *my* mom brewed a sacrificium potion for *your* dad, Pres. She wouldn't break her pledge and forfeit her magic for just anyone." She tapped a finger at the page. "When Elder Glenn told me she used one of his potions, he said *they* were very persuasive in convincing him."

Venus's throat tightened as a question gripped her.

That meant Miss Florence foresaw her son's death, if she was right.

She reread the premonition:

Yielding your own fruits could restore cut roots.

Her gaze grew more and more focused on the word *could*. A word that made the riddle's final line seem more like a suggestion than a certainty. Did Miss Florence try to undo the tragedy by planting an idea in her mom's head? A tragedy she blamed Matrika for? Had she set up a scheme where others would pay the price to resurrect Owen?

Venus's shame washed away the idea of an oldhead she respected trying to toy with fate like that.

A confused grimace carved lines into Presley's face. "They as in her and Matrika."

Chewing her lip, Venus nodded. "It's gotta be, but something must've gone wrong because if she had succeeded—"

"My dad would be alive," Presley finished.

Clarissa Stoneheart broke a pledge, botched a brew, and couldn't save a friend. Even if she failed in the end, she still would've followed its recipe to the letter.

So, what the fuck went wrong? And who loved Owen enough to hand over their life as an ingredient?

CHAPTER
TWENTY-THREE

OPPORTUNE TIME FOR EXTRACTION:
   Out of the country with wife for wedding anniversary.
Nephew Tanner Jensen will do. A part of a five-person ultra-
violent Iron Watch faction called the Iron Hand that congre-
gates on weeknights. Use violence if necessary.

— Excerpt from Target Profile of Senator Martha Westbay

JULY 5, 2023

TO KEEP THE SOUNDPROOF SPELL IN PLACE, PRESLEY STAYED FOR
the night. Venus told them everything as they sat side by side on her bed,
with their backs propped against pillows and the headboard. She started
with the night she burned Julius Keller alive, and she kept going until her
voice was hoarse and nothing was left to tell. Then she propped her cheek
on their shoulder, surrendering to her exhaustion.

When Presley attempted to leave in the morning, Uncle Bram insisted
they stay for breakfast. He whipped up one of Venus's favorite meals out of
pity. She tried to enjoy her strawberry crepes drizzled in chocolate sauce
and dusted in powdered sugar. Key word: *tried.*

But Venus could only stomach a few bites, still digesting yesterday's feast of secrets, truths, and lies. Nor did it help that Uncle Bram
kept a steady eye on her and Janus kept aiming concerned side-eyes at

her. A pair of babysitters she didn't ask for. Their guest, Presley, was a witness.

Even though she struggled against the weight of their shared concern, she did what she did best: *pretend.*

As an out, Presley asked her if she could hook them up with cornrows.

She kept her cool when she agreed. Having an excuse like that was all she needed to avoid her sister and uncle. If just for a few hours. She also needed something to keep her hands and mind busy to keep her anxiety at bay.

Because by nightfall, it'd be time to make another politician bleed.

Well, sort of.

Venus dragged Presley to the bathroom, getting right to work. Wash, condition, detangle, and blow-dry. Then she sat them on her vanity's bench. She watched their lids come down in the mirror as she sectioned and braided, calmness pinwheeling across their face.

Presley broke the silence. "I want to come tonight."

"Can you clarify which one?" She arched an eyebrow.

They cracked a smile, opening one playful eye. "Get your mind out of the gutter."

"*Don't* be vague, then." Venus popped their crown with her comb.

"I want to come with you and Ty tonight."

All humor drained out of her.

Immediately, she resumed her work. "Naw, that's not happening."

"I read that senator's file last night, Vee," Presley said, wincing as she braided a row a little too tightly. "You two can't handle a domestic terrorist group alone. You'll need more help."

"I said what I said, Pres." Venus narrowed her eyes, pointing her comb at the door. "If you don't like it, there's the door. Miss Florence can finish your head."

Her heartbeat spiked as Presley stood.

She gulped and backed away until her back hit the door. Presley encroached on her, their stride eating up all space except for an intimate sliver. Her pulse thumped a quickening rhythm in her throat, their closeness shackling her breath.

Venus trailed her gaze to their face, exhaling thinly as their knuckles brushed her cheek. Her skin sparked with goosebumps.

"I'm coming with you, Venus." Presley dipped their head low. "I'm not losing you again. You understand?"

"Affirmative," she breathed out. Her eyelids fluttered shut as they kissed her forehead tenderly. A rush of want tore her veins, testing the levee of her restraint.

Presley pulled back slightly, their warm breath fanning her skin. "I care about you, Vee."

"That's *very* bad for your health."

An hour after sunset, Tyrell barged into the house thirty minutes late. In the living room, he found Venus and Presley waiting for him.

Crossing her arms, she glared.

"I already know, so don't even start," he said, putting his palms up to ward off any complaints queued on her tongue. His annoyance rippled through her.

"Change of plans." She rolled her eyes, lifting her chin in Presley's direction. "Pres is tagging along."

"Aye." Tyrell's mouth split into a grin as he swaggered up to the couch. "Love that for us."

Presley chuckled as they both dapped each other up. "Glad you approve."

Janus entered the room, rubbing her palms giddily. "Are we ready to go?"

"What do you mean by *we?*" Venus flitted her gaze between Tyrell and Janus.

A harsh whisper oozed through her sister's teeth. "You said you were going to tell her."

Presley brought a fist to their mouth, hiding a laugh in a fake cough.

"It slipped my mind," Tyrell growled. "A lot's been going on. Aight?"

"Hello," Venus said in a singsong tone, waving to gather their attention. "Hi, there. What the hell is going on?"

Tyrell glared at Janus as she pushed him toward Venus like a sacrificial offering, muttering, "Do it now, Ty."

"*Yes,* Ty. Do it," Presley encouraged, thoroughly amused. "Whatever that may be."

He sucked his teeth and shot the bird.

Venus clenched her jaw, irritated as fuck as her cousin and sister's negative emotions struggled for dominance inside her.

"Aight, check it, Vee," Tyrell clapped his hands to commence his presentation. "The Iron Hand ain't nothing to play with. Violence and destruction are their religion. I can't risk losing my shape while tryna dodge bullets."

It stirred awake, unfurling in her veins at the mention of *violence* and *destruction.*

Venus's gaze homed in on her sister. "And where do you come in?"

Janus took a confident step forward, fully prepared to present her case. Having most likely worked on it in secret.

"The Iron Hand earned a spot as one of WASP's top three threats to DMV witchers. They've been monitoring the jackasses for a while now. As the faction is super active, their cars have tracking spells on them, so WASP sends out text alerts when they hunt in witcher neighborhoods." Janus took out her cell, her thumbs working the screen. "But I have access to this."

Next, she handed the device to Venus, who stared at a live-time threat-tracking map with filters set to the Iron Hand's location. A blood-red dot traveled along a colored road, then stopped. Within a minute, it abruptly took off, rounding a corner.

So, Senator Westbay's nephew had already clocked in his night shift as a domestic terrorist.

Presley leaned over for a closer look. "They're in Lincoln Heights right now."

Barely a mile south of Deanwood.

Good, that makes it easier to hunt them down, Venus thought.

"Yeah, they've already set an old lady's car on fire tonight," Janus said, a sharp edge to her voice. "And knowing them, that's *only* the appetizer."

"So, you want her to be our compass," Presley said to Tyrell, arching an eyebrow.

Venus's mouth set into a line of worry. "In case you forgot, the last time all four of us were together outside this house, we were dodging bullets, Ty."

"What I want is for us to have the upper hand on the Iron Hand," he said, jabbing a thumb at Janus. "With Jay's hookups, this time won't be like last time."

"And if things get hairy, we can use my doorways to escape," Janus added, making dramatic hand gestures like she was about to open one, "or push those bastards into one. WASP would love it if the Iron Hand spent a few days lost in the woods."

Venus and Presley exchanged knowing glances.

So, *that's* why her sister wanted to tag along. Tonight would be just another opportunity to perform a heroic act to get Malik's attention.

To make Malik proud of her.

Sighing, Venus used her fingertips to massage the corners of her eyes.

"Jay, we're not going after the Iron Hand to punish them. So, if that's why you want in, you're wasting your time. We only have one target."

"Yeah," Janus nodded, her mouth sliding into a sly smile. "Tanner Jensen, Senator Westbay's nephew."

Venus's eyes rounded in shock, darting over to Tyrell. "You told her?"

He backed up, shaking his head. "Hell, naw. Not me. No, sirree."

"He didn't need to. After the Grand Witcher kicked me out of the kitchen, you *seriously* thought I wasn't gonna eavesdrop?" Janus confessed, pointing at her ear.

At the mention of the Grand Witcher, Presley shifted, uncomfortable. Venus laced her fingers with theirs, squeezing their hand.

They squeezed hers right back.

"I know why she resurrected you," Janus continued, "and I also know why it's okay to use Tanner's blood for Senator Westbay's potion. Westbay donated her bone marrow to him when he was ten because he had leukemia. The media ate it up. Bone marrow transplants can sometimes change a recipient's DNA and blood type to the donor's."

"Word?" Tyrell draped a hand over his forehead, surprised and impressed. "The more you know."

"Tell me I'm wrong," Janus urged, sloping her head matter-of-factly.

"You're not," Venus admitted softly.

"So, can I go?" Janus clasped her hands, putting her puppy dog eyes on full display. "Please, please, please?"

"You've already denied her the chance to taste revenge by claiming Matrika for yourself. If the girl craves fresh blood, give it to her. She deserves at least that," It said.

She grimaced, hating how right *It* was. "Fine, you can go."

"This is going to be so much fun!" Janus jumped up and down excitedly, clapping.

"No, it won't," Venus, Tyrell, and Presley chorused.

Once everyone piled into Tyrell's 2004 Honda Civic, he fished out three ski masks from a crinkled brown paper bag. Two pink ones for Venus and Janus. A black one for Tyrell. Presley borrowed a full-head latex panda mask Janus wore last Halloween.

Tonight, they all were on a mission to make Tanner Jensen bleed, even if it meant being villains in his story. A deep monstrous part of Venus—the part that wasn't *It*—relished that reality.

But she couldn't admit that aloud.

From the front passenger seat, Janus spewed directions to Tyrell, guided by her tracking map app. The app updated them on which witcher residences caught fire. The precise jerks in his wheel as he weaved through traffic radiated determination.

The group stalked the Iron Hand into Fairfax, parking adjacent to a gas station. There, the bastards made a pit stop for fuel and grub, carrying on like rowdy college kids after a big win.

Venus named the other four: Baldie, Green Polo, Square Jaw, and Backwards Hat.

"I could set them on fire with one little spark," Janus snarled.

"I'm down for that," Presley concurred.

"Sounds like a plan to me." Tyrell choked the steering wheel with one hand.

All their combined hate doused her insides.

"Only *one* target," Venus said, needing to be the voice of reason before another mission went haywire. A drunk senator was one thing, but dealing with five *very* sober and dangerous humans wasn't only a different ball game.

It was a completely different *sport*.

Once the Iron Hand had their fill, their Jeep peeled off from underneath the gas station's lit canopy. They roared victoriously out their windows.

Tyrell was careful not to tail them too closely but ended up behind them at a stoplight.

"I think they're headed to the Iron Watch's Fairfax branch. It's only a few blocks west," Janus said, unbuckling her seat belt. "This might be our only chance."

"Jay, don't!" Venus panicked, grabbing her sister's shoulder. "Stick to the plan!"

"This is me sticking to the plan, Vee!" She wrenched herself out of Venus's grip, climbing out of the car.

Venus snapped her hand to the door handle, yanking it.

"If you go after her, it might put her in more danger," Presley warned.

Tyrell shook his head. "Pres is right, Vee."

She gritted out a curse, stamping her foot.

Janus boldly blocked the four-way intersection.

Tanner honked at her intrusion, but she rooted her feet, glaring them down. As she began to summon a doorway, he revved his engine. Tires shrieked and smoked as the bastard's car surged forward to hit her. Venus's heart dried up in her chest, her mouth stretching into a silent scream.

Presley gripped her shoulders. "*Trust* her, Vee."

The doorway yawned wide enough for Tanner's car to race through. Tyrell slammed his foot on the gas pedal, chasing their target across the swirling threshold. The Jeep crashed into a derelict brick building.

Tyrell veered to avoid a collision. Venus twisted halfway around, frantically looking for her sister out the back windshield. Janus sauntered through her portal, unscathed and unbothered.

Venus sagged against the backseat, relief skittering down her spine.

They all joined Janus outside as the Iron Watchers spilled out of their car, bleeding, crawling, and delirious. Janus gagged and clasped a hand over her mouth, backing away.

Tyrell and Presley recoiled, too. Their fear of the horrid scent warded them both off, promoting Venus to the helm.

She refused to budge, shivering in reaction to the iron. The fear and anger of others hummed through her, *feeding* her boldness and magic.

Tanner let out a bloody-toothed laugh, struggling to his feet. "We're protected by the iron and an ironclad brotherhood, witcher-fucks."

Venus reached around to lift the back of her shirt, extracting the loaded gun tucked away in her waistline. Her mom taught her how to use it for consultations and deliveries that went sideways. She only ever used it for target practice, but she always excelled at hitting her marks.

Unable to rely on her magic, Venus had no choice but to be good at shooting.

"Let's see how much you love your brothers. Remove all the iron jewelry and throw it down that gutter," she ordered, her hand shaky as she aimed at him.

Stupidly, he mistook her trembling grasp for hesitation or fear.

He spat a red-tinged glob in her direction. "You don't tell me what to do, stupid bitch."

"Not a smart idea calling the bitch with a gun a bitch to her face." Venus shot one of his ironclad brethren in the shoulder. Green Polo cried out, curling into a ball.

Tanner flinched at the gunshot, balling his fists. "We're not afraid of you."

"All iron jewelry. In the gutter. Now." Venus fired another shot into Square Jaw's hairy calf. He yelped in agony and crumpled to the ground, pressing a palm against his fresh wound.

"Just do it, Tanner," Green Polo wheezed.

He barked, "You cowa—"

Pop!

A bullet whizzed by his head, purposely missing him. The gun's recoil resonated with her every time she tugged at the trigger. The only type of recoil she liked. Spilled blood and the pain of others attracted the natural predator within her.

She wanted more.

"If you weren't starving me, I'd gladly give you more," It hissed.

"That's no way to talk to your ironclad brother," Venus mocked. "Do as I say or I won't miss next time. I'll do Baldie, then Backwards Hat until it's only you left."

Taking off his iron possessions, Baldie held them above his head in his fist. His surrender earned a poison-tipped glare from Tanner.

"Don't look at me like that. Dammit!" Baldie snapped, spittle flying out. "Tan, I've got a kid on the way!"

"Just do what the bit—I mean—what she says." Backwards Hat followed suit swiftly, correcting himself when Venus swiveled the sidearm's aim toward him.

Tanner conceded begrudgingly.

Hatred fueled his compliance as he confiscated all the iron jewelry and disposed of it in the gutter. The group of four closed in on their prey, forcing them into the abandoned building. Trash crunched underneath their feet. Piss stained the air. A museum of graffiti improved the walls and framed a masterpiece quote dripping like blood:

BE WARY OF LAMBS WITH LION TEETH

None truer.

Presley shoved Square Jaw onto a filthy mattress in the corner.

"Please, I need medical attention," Square Jaw panted, nursing his wounded calf.

"I think I can help with that." Presley's palm glowed a dangerous hot red, smoke rising like a bad omen. They pressed their hand against his bullet wound to cauterize it.

Flesh sizzled. Shrieks of agony bathed the room.

Green Polo tumbled backward, clutching his bleeding shoulder. He crawled backward to escape a prowling Tyrell, but his back hit the wall.

"You want some medical attention, too?" Venus heard the smirk embedded in Tyrell's voice. A frightened Green Polo shook his head, gawking up at Tyrell like a mortal would a god.

Backwards Hat and Baldie cowered from Janus in a corner as she stood guard over them. She crossed her arms, pleased.

Venus stood toe-to-toe with Tanner in the center of the room. He carried himself like the pack leader, fierce and unflinching. The same energy discharged from her as well.

Two opposing fronts set to collide like Sister Nature intended.

It fidgeted with excitement at the prospect of witnessing a war's onset.

"What do you want from us?" Tanner flared.

"I want your hand," Venus said, tucking away her gun.

She reached into her purse, pulling out her switchblade.

Tanner spat out a barbed laugh. "Ran out of bullets, so you're gonna cut me now? Huh?"

She flicked her wrist to open the weapon. "Hand. Now."

He obliged, offering his palm.

Venus slit his fingertip deep.

He didn't flinch, only stared his hard-as-hate eyes at her. "What are you going to do with my blood? Use it to lay a curse on me?"

"You don't need a witcher to curse you, Tanner Jensen. You already are a curse." She caught his blood in the vial and capped it.

"You're a plague on the American Dream," he hissed resentfully. "All four of you. When the Registration Act passes, being registered won't protect you from us. We'll know where to find you, so you can get the punishment you deserve."

Venus and her crew all glanced at each other before bursting into laughter.

"We already know the Registration Act won't protect us, but if it passes, it won't protect you from us witchers either," Presley said.

"We're getting very, very fed up," Tyrell chimed in, squatting down to Green Polo's level to show off his taunting smirk.

"That's how revolutions start," Janus said, walking to him, "and everyone knows revolutions spread like wildfire. Nothing, not even your precious iron, can stop that."

"Sounds like something that rotten vegetable Malik would say, kid," Tanner goaded. "It ain't healthy eating the shit he fe—"

Janus unleashed a guttural roar as she punched him square in the face. He flattened from the blow, collapsing with a heavy thunk. No magic. Just pure rage.

She straddled his waist, pummeling him. "Keep Malik's name out your mouth!"

It shuddered in delight, feasting on Janus's fury that galloped wildly in Venus's heart. Envy speared her as she witnessed her sister dish out retribution.

While Matrika was somewhere in DC, breathing.

But not for long.

Tanner choked on his blood as Janus got off him. He lolled on his side, a medley of spit and blood dribbling from his lips. Sticky scarlet stained her hand.

Janus squatted down to grip his chin, steering his gaze in her direction. "Witchers don't ruin dreams. We bleed them."

An unbridled fear etched into Tanner's face.

The gang filed out of the building, passing by the wrecked Jeep.

Presley stopped to face it. "Y'all up for giving these fuckers a taste of their own medicine?"

Tyrell swiveled on his heel, perking up. "What's the flavor?"

"Hot, I hope," Janus growled.

"Great minds think alike." A fireball flared to life in Presley's palm.

Venus stood back and watched, admiring her squad's handiwork as smoke bellowed and fire flailed. She clasped the vial of blood.

Two down, one more to go.

CHAPTER
TWENTY-FOUR

Let this heartache ebb.
Let the numbness swell.
Untangle from sorrow's web,
In peace, you shall dwell.

—The "Relieving a Grieving Heart" potion's notion

JULY 13, 2023

VENUS SUNBATHED AT HER MOTHER'S GRAVE. THE SUN'S RAYS dripped through her closed eyelids, creating a kaleidoscope of warm reds, yellows, and oranges. The stiff patch of dirt beneath her blanket made her back ache. A wooden cross, a temporary grave marker, cast its shadow on her face. There'd be a headstone in a few months after the ground settled. If only she knew what to engrave on it. Maybe:

CLARISSA STONEHEART

OCTOBER 24, 1981–JUNE 16, 2023

MOTHER OF WILD, VICIOUS DAUGHTERS

ALL BEWARE

Or:

CLARISSA STONEHEART

OCTOBER 24, 1981–JUNE 16, 2023

HER HEART TRULY WAS STONE

BUT SHE LOVED HER DAUGHTERS DOWN TO THE BONE

Yes, that'd do.

A feeling of serenity filled Venus, even though it was fleeting. She came here to pick a fight with the dead, after all.

"You told me to leave it be," she said, a warm breeze playing with her hair as she spoke. "But now that I know the truth, I can't just leave it be."

She quieted, waiting for a voice that'd never come.

"At the séance, you only had to spell out her name. Were you worried we'd be trampled? You shouldn't have been," Venus continued. "I'm gonna prove Matrika isn't invincible. I swear I'll prove you wrong, Mom. When I'm finished with her, there won't be anything left of her to bury."

Now, Venus only had nine days to brew all the potions.

But after she finished her job—

After the senators voted against the Registration Act—

Matrika Sharma would be hers.

Venus relaxed a little longer, wanting her promise to seep through the earth and varnished wood to rest alongside her mother. Eventually, she stood up and folded the blanket.

Her feet took her a few rows north to pay a rare visit to her father's grave.

DARIUS KNOX

MARCH 5, 1980–JUNE 10, 2006

HUSBAND, FATHER, HERO

Venus stood there with nothing to say. What do you say to a man you didn't know? She should've felt love for him because his blood flowed through her veins, but all she felt was understanding. She understood now why he did what he did. She now understood why he chose to fight for others even if it cost him his life.

Seventeen years later, she'd carry on where he left off, but unlike him, she'd survive. She had to.

It wasn't an option.

A chill crawled across her flesh, her hairs standing on end as a presence approached her.

"Darius was a wonderful man, Venus."

Her attention turned to a pale, college-aged human man wearing a botanical chart shirt, holding a cluster of black-eyed Susans.

Every flower had a meaning. In tribute to an unjustly killed man, the ones in the stranger's hand symbolized *justice*. She blocked his path to the gravestone out of protectiveness, maybe a little possessiveness.

The voice sparked recognition, but nothing else matched.

She glared at him skeptically, then asked with a sharp tongue, "Do I know you?"

He bonked his palm against his forehead, chuckling, "Of course, you don't know me like this."

A freakish mitosis unfolded before Venus, an organism toiling to divide into two. As she stared in shock, her brain glitched to process everything.

Her stomach twisted as a spectral body successfully uncoupled from its generous host.

Her jaw hung down, lips quivering. "Malik? How the fuck—?"

"It's a layer of my calling. I use it sometimes so I can remember what it's like to feel again," he said, gesturing to his companion, "and there is a willing volunteer nearby to let me. Venus, meet Levi, a WASP intern." Callings contained layers, abilities that built upon each other with time and age. No witcher was ever truly sure when they would get one, or what the layer would be. Or it'd be of good use or only do harm. Malik's layer, however, seemed to do both. It was of use to him, yet if his daughter knew the truth, it'd cause harm.

Levi extended his hand for a handshake, a scar staining his palm. "It's an absolute honor to meet the daughter of the legendary Darius Knox."

Venus cut her narrowed eyes back to Malik, anger brewing underneath her words. "So, let me get this straight. You can possess people's bodies, but you can't hitchhike with one of your corporeal rides to see your only daughter?"

Levi sidestepped her and deposited the black-eyed Susans in the gravestone's flower holder, moseying off to give them privacy.

"I'm the only founder left to lead WASP, which makes me and those close to me a target." Malik sighed. "Darius and I wanted you both to have the Stoneheart name to protect you both, but that wasn't enough. So, Rissa and I came to an agreement when we divorced. I'd take care of WASP and she'd take care of Janus."

Venus scoffed. "I'm not stupid. I know there's more to it."

"I don't want Janus to get used to me being around," Malik confessed. "Any enemy of mine can walk into Epione and end me. It's only a matter of time. I don't want my daughter to mourn for me. It's best if I was never there at all."

"Don't you get it, Malik? She already mourns for you!" The words flew off her tongue, echoing across the cemetery.

Malik tilted his face to the sky, resigned. "I didn't come here to argue, Venus."

"Why are you here, Malik?" Venus cocked her head, suspicion staining her tone. "I'm going to go out on a limb and say you're not just here to pay respects to your best friend, either."

"I'm here because of him." He paused. "And Rissa. She asked me to watch over you and Janus if anything ever happened to her."

Venus clasped a hand over her mouth, muffling a giggle. "Like a guardian angel? Oh, wait, wait!" She snapped her fingers as a better taunt came to mind. "Or maybe a fairy godfather? Is granting wishes another one of your layers, too?"

"This isn't a laughing matter, Venus Genevieve," he said grimly, his face unreadable.

"Watch me as I laugh all the way to my car, Malik," she rejoined, sauntering past him.

"I know about your *arrangement* with Matrika."

Venus froze but refused to turn around, unwilling to let him witness her dumbfounded shock.

"And you've come all this way to talk me out of it?" she asked, proud of herself for ironing out any quivers in her voice.

"No, I think you should go through with it," he said.

She blinked, facing him once more. "You do?"

"It's dangerous to assume these politicians will do the right thing by our kindred. It's up to us to stop the Registration Act from passing in Congress," he said, "even if it means using your...*talents*."

Her eyebrow rose in a slow arch. "But?"

"Matrika's power has gotten the best of her." Malik wagged his head, disappointed. "Since Owen's death, she hasn't been the same."

"Yes, I'm aware they had an on-and-off thing."

"An on-and-off thing? No, Venus. The only thing that broke them apart was the Iron Nail Bombing."

"Matrika goes from being all *rah-rah* at WASP events"—Venus shook her fists like pom-poms—"to being a no-show for most of 2003. I've seen the pictures. If not because of a breakup, then what?"

"Because WASP functions were no place for a pregnant woman."

Shock reared her head back, her lashes beating a stunned rhythm. "I beg your pardon?"

"Back then, the Iron Watch realized they could turn peaceful WASP events violent by conspiring with the cops. When Matrika became pregnant, she no longer could attend."

"Did she lose..." Venus hesitated "...the child?"

"Not until much, much later."

"So, Owen got two women pregnant. Matrika and Presley's mom."

Malik threw his hands up, irritation crimping his lips. "I'll never forgive Florence and Jerome for spreading that damn lie. You can't have a *drunken* one-night stand if you don't drink."

Even though Venus wasn't a big fan of Malik, dealing with only his projection made her feel slightly more normal. Without his physical body, she could only witness how he felt, but she didn't have to worry about feeling it.

"What if *Owen's* the one that lied to save face?" Venus shrugged, unconvinced. "If he and Matrika stayed together until the end, he could've just said he got drunk as an excuse for sleeping around."

Malik fired off, "A woman cannot get pregnant if she *doesn't* exist."

"Wait a minute." Her face puckered in confusion. "What?"

The thoughts and questions jumbled in her head, tangling into something monstrous. She didn't know how to unravel or make sense of it. Not knowing which thread would loosen her confusion or make it worse was hard.

If Owen didn't knock up a one-night fling, that only left one possibility that Venus would've never guessed in a million years. A possibility she hoped wasn't true because that possibility *murdered* her fucking mother.

"Matrika is Presley's mom?" She scrunched up her face, hating the taste of that question. When Malik nodded, her heart froze midbeat.

Venus closed her eyes, cutting her voice low, "Please say sike, Malik."

"I'm sorry, Venus, but that's the truth."

"Why the fuck would Miss Florence and Mr. Jerome lie about the identity of their grandchild's mother?" She pressed a hand to her belly, trying to stomach this moment. "Do they think Matrika engineered the Iron Nail Bombing, too?"

Malik arranged his mouth in a sour line, his tone accusatory. "Who the hell told you that bullshit?"

"Senator Hoage," she answered.

His laughter lacked humor. "Of course. Whenever that lush considers someone a threat, he'll have their name in his mouth more than his favorite wine."

"That still doesn't explain why Presley's grandparents would lie to them for their *entire* life, Malik."

"Back then, the Iron Watch would send spies to our headquarters, pretending to be human allies. Every time we made a move or made progress, they'd strike back to knock us back. Always one step ahead of us." Malik approached his best friend's sun-kissed headstone and smoothed a hand over its curved edge, unable to feel its warmth. "Darius figured it out. We all agreed we needed our own spy. Matrika volunteered shortly after Presley was born. She remained our insider for years."

"So, for years, she and Owen had to keep their relationship and their family secret." Venus hated herself for caring enough to have a morsel of sympathy for Matrika Sharma.

"Yes, for their loyalty to the cause. To protect Presley, she stayed away, but they grew up without her and didn't know she was their mother. The Iron Watch eventually found out she was our operative and sent that postal bomb to Owen's house."

"And Owen lost his life."

"No, another lie. That day, Owen did die, but not for that," Malik countered. "The public *believes* he was naive enough to pick up that package from the doorstep. He would've *smelled* that iron and known immediately it was a trap."

"Then who—?"

Those words withered on her tongue as something clicked inside her brain. Owen, or any witcher old enough, would've known nothing good would come of a package *reeking* of iron.

But a very young witcher wouldn't.

A toddler witcher wouldn't.

"Earlier, you asked me if Matrika lost the child. And I told you—"

"Not until much, much later," Venus whispered, a cold tremor of shock rattling through her. She clasped a shaky hand to her mouth as she envisioned a young Presley squatting down to retrieve a packaged death warrant. A violent burst of fire and iron contained within her skull made her flinch.

A tear cascaded down her cheek.

"But Presley survived," she said, brushing the wetness away.

Dangling a lie in Malik's face to see what he'd do with it.

"No, they didn't. That's why Rissa brewed a sacrificium potion Glenn wouldn't to bring Presley back to life."

So, Clarissa Stoneheart *did* successfully brew it, after all.

A thin stream of pride trickled through Venus.

Presley was living proof of her mom's sacrifice and another's.

"You said Owen still died that day," Venus said, crossing her arms as a disguise to hold herself for comfort. "He willingly sacrificed himself for that potion, didn't he?"

"Yes." Malik nodded. "As would any good parent."

Would you do the same, Malik? Venus opted not to ask for fear he'd get pissed and cut this history lesson short.

Venus poked her tongue into her cheek as her mind chewed on a partial fact she couldn't figure out how to make whole. "After everything that went down, why didn't Matrika raise Presley herself? I mean, there was no reason to stay away anymore."

"She tried, but the odds were stacked against her." Malik's mouth forged into a frown, his expression pained. "Her *revived* three-year-old lost the only parent they knew and suffered from the resurrection's consequences. Presley only wanted their grandparents. Florence and Jerome tried to get her to stay, but she walked away from being Presley's mother to—"

Venus cut in, "Become a Grand Witcher."

"Exactly. Florence tried to intervene by running as an opponent to force Matrika to come back, but she lost the election."

So, Miss Florence didn't blame Matrika for her son's death. Her hatred for Matrika stemmed from choosing a political career over Presley.

"Then Presley won't miss her when she's gone," It whispered.

Presley's entire life was a lie.

A lie all the grown folk kept alive and gatekept the truth, some of which included her own kinfolk. An actuality she now regretted that she knew. Because if she told Presley, she had no doubts the truth would break them.

Telling could also jeopardize the plans she had for Matrika.

Plans she had already told Presley.

If she told, what if they asked her to show mercy?

Or would they step aside to let her do what needed to be done?

Venus didn't want to know which one Presley would choose.

Maybe, she'd tell them after the deed was done and she washed off the blood.

Maybe.

"You didn't have to waste a trip here to convince me to brew the potions." Venus glanced at Levi reading gravestones in the distance as she spoke to Malik. "I was going to do it, regardless."

Venus had already begun gearing herself up for brewing again.

On Sunday, she recommitted to a vow of abnegation, and on Monday, she started her restoration regimen. Three times a day, she choked down entire teapots of restoration tea. Morning, noon, and night. Hell, she even had a half-full thermos in her car today, waiting for her to polish it off. She had more fresh flowers in the fridge than food for her nighttime Purification baths.

As Venus tried to replenish her well of magic, her deviation slurped up all the pampering, fattening *itself* up bit by bit. After realizing that the Grand Witcher wouldn't die until *after* the Senate vote, It pledged temporary compliance last night, not wanting to ruin the planned feast of blood and violence.

She refused to think about what It had in store for her afterward.

"Though it's reassuring to know you will, I'm not here for that," he said. "Matrika's out of control. A fact known for quite some time. Julius deserved a trial for his crimes, but not the one Matrika gave him."

"If you know Matrika was his judge, then you know who his executioner was." A dare arched Venus's eyebrow. "Am I outta control, too?"

"Venus, you're many things," he admitted, "but out of control isn't one of them. You have Rissa's self-restraint. You had a hunger for retribution. Matrika exploited it. We have decided she needs to step down from her position."

"We?" she reiterated, her eyes popping wide.

He nodded. "Yes, we. Myself and the capitol's Grand Witchers."

The Grand Coven, an executive board of Grand Witchers.

Venus suppressed her disbelief, wearing a mask of reserve. "You want to stage a coup."

"We want to stage an *intervention*," he corrected. "The public won't care if Julius Keller is a murderer if a Grand Witcher orchestrated his execution. They'll care witchers gallivanted around him as he burned alive. They'll think we're all monsters."

Venus tittered dryly, "They already think that."

"Matrika must step down," Malik said, "but she won't go peacefully."

A silence flourished between them as Venus weighed the conversation's undertone for its true worth. "You want me to brew a peitho potion to make her love an idea."

He appeared pleased by her inference. "An early retirement would be for the best, but we recognize it would be unwise not to use her political connections to our advantage."

Basically, Matrika was too corrupt to be Grand Witcher but not corrupt enough to not be a lobbyist.

"Who would replace her?" she asked, her voice tightening in anticipation.

"I would step in as her replacement"—Malik gestured to himself—"until we have a proper election in her dominion."

His announcement made her roll her eyes into the back of her head. "How generous of you. I've had enough of this. Bye, Malik."

Venus went to leave but stumbled a step back as Malik manifested before her, obstructing her escape.

"Say you'll think about it," he implored.

Venus strolled right through him, not looking back or saying another word.

Malik and the Grand Coven wanted to send Matrika into an early retirement, but she was destined for an early grave.

Venus returned to her mom's grave for a goodbye but paused at a purple hyacinth left on the mound. Squatting, she picked it up and examined it.

Flowers had something to say, and this one had three:

Sorrow.

I'm sorry.

Please forgive me.

CHAPTER
TWENTY-FIVE

OPPORTUNE TIME FOR EXTRACTION:
As a fierce blood donation advocate, she donates hers every eight weeks at the Blood Line Center. Strike at night. Overnight security guard is an ex-SWIG sharpshooter.

—Excerpt from Target Profile of Senator Blanche Radliff

PING!

As Venus pulled up to the curb outside Aunt Keisha's house, she got a text message from Tyrell:

vee, where the hell are you?! moms done lost her damn mind!

She closed her eyes and cocked her skull back against the headrest, groaning, "Not another fight."

Before her visit to the cemetery, Venus promised Tyrell that she would be by his side when he asked Aunt Keisha to teach him her ways. But Malik made her late, upset, and confused. During the drive over, she tried to untangle and sort her thoughts.

About Matrika, Owen, and Presley. About the impending coup and the role Malik wanted her to play in it. About what that meant for her plan to reap Matrika's last breaths.

If it meant anything at all. Dwelling too long on it meant Venus cared enough about Malik to consider his proposal. A reality not even a cross-country road trip was sufficient time to dissect and examine the innards.

Yet alone a twenty-minute drive.

So, she decided to put it all on the back burner to simmer until she was ready to deal with it. Until then, there was one more vial to fill and four peitho potions to brew. Eight days remained until the deadline. Five days after that, the Senate would vote on the Registration Act.

Then, Matrika was *hers*. No one—not even Malik and the Grand Coven—could stop that.

Her deviation gently nudged a vision into her mind for a split second.

Her body splattered in blood.

Red crusted and lumped under her nails.

Another *ping* drew her out of her head.

Another text from Tyrell:

keem says your car outside!! i need backup!!!

Venus killed the engine and got out, jogging up to the front door. Hakeem opened it on cue. Her arrival lured irritations and frustrations to her. She grimaced as the bad vibes chased over her skin like a prickly wave.

"About time," Hakeem said dully, jamming a thumb over his shoulder. "Them two won't stop fighting."

"I'll handle it, Keem," she promised, patting his head of sleek braids in passing.

Tyrell and Aunt Keisha stood in front of the terrarium, both pointing at it while they butted heads.

"Naw, not happening. I ain't that desperate," Tyrell snapped.

"Boy, if you don't man up and do the damn thing," his mom tossed back. "I did it. Your granddaddy did it, as did your great-granddaddy and all those before him. It's family tradition."

Before Venus could even referee the argument, Tyrell's glare drilled into her face.

"Tell her I ain't eating Leap. Family tradition or not."

Her eyebrows launched up. "I beg your pardon. Eat as in a fealty feast?"

"Basically."

Aunt Keisha rolled her eyes. "Stop being so dramatic."

Venus bounced her shocked gaze between her cousin and her aunt. "Uh…"

"You're not eating Leap. You're swallowing him," Aunt Keisha corrected tightly, her patience wearing thin.

Tyrell threw his hands up, frustrated. "Same thing!"

"No, it's not." Aunt Keisha reached into the glass tank to retrieve the familiar, exhaling a gust of irritation. "Leap'll stay in your throat the whole time. His loyalty will help you keep shape and balance out your calling's stamina by giving your magic what it lacks. Our ancestors called it swamping."

Tyrell sucked his teeth at that.

Unconvinced, unmoved, unwilling.

"So, Ty's gonna have a frog in his throat?" Hakeem fell over onto his side on the couch, holding his belly as he laughed. "You need some cough drops, Ty? There's some cough syrup in the bathroom, too!"

Venus gagged on a giggle, earning another daggered look from Tyrell.

"Our ancestor, Delphine, called upon Leap to help her escape from the South in 1890 after she killed a white lady in self-defense," Aunt Keisha said, tenderly stroking the frog's head with two fingers. "He helped her keep shape to avoid bounty hunters for three weeks and over eight hundred miles."

"I ain't know that." Tyrell blinked.

Now, it was Aunt Keisha's turn to suck her teeth. "Boy, what do you mean? I've told y'all that story a hundred times."

Venus muttered under breath. "More like a couple thousand if we're being honest."

Tyrell frowned. "Well, it's hard to pay attention when you always be yelling at me."

As if the words punched her, Aunt Keisha jerked her head back. She fixed her lips to deny it, but a whirlwind of emotions pinwheeled across her features. Anger swirled into doubt and doubt swirled into regret, muddling together to make a shade of stubbornness.

As each heavy feeling fell on Venus, it weighed her down like rocks in her belly. She feared her knees would buckle if she carried any more feelings that weren't hers.

Aunt Keisha cleared her throat. "All I'm saying is Leap'll take good care of you. You'll forget he's even there."

"Trust me. I won't forget," Tyrell said flatly, eyeing the creature who earned the one thing he could never have.

His mom's respect.

"Me either!" Hakeem sputtered out another laugh as he rolled off the sofa's edge, falling to the floor with an *oof* and a *clunk*.

"I think Aunt Key should come with us," Venus said, causing her little cousin's hysterics to shrivel up at the suggestion.

Tyrell and Aunt Keisha stared at her as if she had lost her damn mind.

And they weren't wrong.

Old Venus wouldn't have put her nose into business that wasn't hers.

But Old Venus was dead now, and New Venus was tired of the fractured relationships all around her, unsure of where to step. Now an orphan, she felt like a visitor in a museum, looking at glassed-in exhibits of fucked-up familial relationships. Powerless to fix the displays.

Janus and Malik.

Tyrell and Aunt Key.

Presley and their family.

All around her, *parents* were the root of everyone's problems, every single one too prideful and hardheaded to clean up the messes they made. To ice their offspring's bruises and nurse the cuts they caused. To just be there. Her cousin said a lot while saying little, a language Aunt Keisha should've been an expert in but wasn't.

Most likely, half waiting for English subtitles to materialize out of thin air.

So, Venus took it upon herself to be the translator.

"If Aunt Key comes with us, it'd be like on-the-job training. Training you're getting *paid* for, Ty." Her eyebrows hiked up as she added emphasis to the word *paid*. She sprinkled in a little more flavor by rubbing her fingertips, the universal hand gesture for money.

Tyrell cocked his head back, blowing out his cheeks in surrender.

"Paid?" Aunt Keisha blinked. "How much are we talking about?"

"One hundred twenty-five racks," he answered reluctantly. "I wanted to surprise y'all with it."

Surprise struck his mom's face, her mouth falling open.

"Keem, go to your room," Aunt Keisha instructed. "Now."

Not wanting to be told twice, Hakeem dipped, mouthing *rest in peace* to his brother and Venus along the way with a clasp of prayerful hands and a head bow.

Once it was only the three of them, Aunt Keisha cupped Tyrell's cheek. "Thank you for thinking of Keem and me, but your money is yours. Period. I'mma help you get it, though."

Then she smoothed her tongue across her gold grill, lacing her arms over her chest.

"Alright, tell me everything I need to know, and don't y'all dare leave anything out."

Venus smiled. "I won't. Trust."

Aunt Keisha's bag of tricks was an old-school traveler's trunk in the garage. Worn black leather, rusted studs, dull metal buckle. Its hinges cried when she tossed back the lid.

Venus and Tyrell stood over her as she pulled out a crystal-clear quartz.

As Aunt Keisha turned the crystal in her hand, she wore a reminiscent smile. "Growing up, when Darius and I snuck out of the house and changed shape, y'all's granny used this to find us."

Briefly, Venus considered asking a question about that fact—about her dad. However, the door of opportunity slammed in her face when her aunt gazed into the quartz cluster and uttered a scrying spell.

> *Crystal, crystal*
> *Wistful, blissful*
> *Reveal to me what I desire*
> *This request is all I require*
> *For as long as I cradle thee*
> *Thou shalt honor my plea*

Venus dug her fingernails into her palm as punishment for not acting faster.

Senator Radliff appeared within the crystal's faces, prismatic colors weaving into a real-life scene of her walking her giant schnauzer at Rock Creek Park. With a calculating squint, Aunt Keisha moved the cluster around to examine the woman from all angles.

Blood donation banks didn't label blood bags with names, so they needed something precious of Senator Radliff to find *her* B-positive donation out of hundreds at the Blood Line Center.

Aunt Keisha tilted the quartz downward, homing in on the senator's hand that held the leash as her dog that led her down a winding path.

"We ain't stealing the dog," Tyrell made known.

"I ain't looking at the dog." Aunt Keisha pursed her lips at the comment, shaking her head. She crooked a finger for her son and Venus to come down to her level.

They both obliged, leaning in for a peek.

"I'm looking at that," Aunt Keisha said, pointing to the ring on the senator's finger. "Antique. Art deco. Asymmetrical. Emerald-cut centerpiece. Baguette diamonds."

"A family heirloom?" Venus asked.

"Most likely." Aunt Keisha nodded. "We'll have to use a diversion to switch it out."

"With what though, Moms?" Tyrell questioned.

Aunt Keisha chuckled, pulling out a wooden ring.

A stressed Tyrell paced around his room, holding Leap.

"Just close your eyes, pinch your nose, and swallow the frog," Venus coached calmly, sitting in his computer chair.

"Aight, aight," he chanted nervously, following her instructions. But as he brought Leap to his mouth, the familiar expelled a timely croak. A sound that bugged Tyrell out, making him choke a gag.

Low-key, Venus wondered if the familiar was yanking her cousin's chain.

She blew out her cheeks. "Ty—"

"Gimme a countdown," he growled.

She began, "Three, two—"

"One!" Hakeem concluded from underneath the bed.

Cramming his lids shut, Tyrell opened wide and tossed the frog in.

Venus used the rearview mirror to adjust her shades and her wig's bangs. Aunt Keisha and Tyrell, shaped like two soot-black Labrador retrievers, sat in the backseat as she drove to Rock Creek Park.

Her cousin's fear of fucking up again swarmed her chest like a surge of wasps. The emotion stronger and more potent as they neared their destination.

She rolled down the right rear window to distract him, looking into her rearview mirror. "Stick your head out the window. You might enjoy it."

A growl built up in his throat, working its way around Leap. "I'll bite you, Vee."

She bit her bottom lip to fend off a laugh while his fear gave way to irritation.

"And I'll drop you off at the pound," she countered.

He bared his teeth at her, but she knew he was all bark and no bite.

"Act like y'all two got some home training." Aunt Keisha wagged her head, expelling a sigh from her snout. "Let's go over this plan from the top. First, Vee will take us for a walk until we find this ol' broad, then...."

"We'll act rowdy and tackle her ass to the ground," Tyrell added.

Venus pulled out the wooden ring from her pocket. "While I help her up, I'll slip off her ring and offer her the ditto."

Dittos mimicked what the fooler wanted the fool to see. Despite their various sizes and shapes, dittos could only replicate things of a similar scale. Once upon a time, a thieving great-uncle with a penchant for diamond rings used one Venus had in her palm.

By the time they arrived in the parking area, Senator Radliff had finished her evening walk. Her well-behaved pet led her to a cherry-red sports car.

Tyrell smeared his wet nose on the window. "We're too late!"

"No, we're not." Venus pulled into a parking space. "There's always plan B."

He snapped his attention to her, his floppy ears flailing along for the ride. "Plan B? What plan B? We ain't go over a plan B!"

"Boy, if you don't calm down." Aunt Keisha lifted her heavy paw, plopping it on Tyrell's back. "All ain't lost. Just because she's 'bout to drive off doesn't mean she's leaving. You feel me?"

As his gears churned, Tyrell tilted his head in confusion before he reared it back in shock. "Wait? What?!"

When Venus opened the rear passenger door, Aunt Keisha and Tyrell leaped out, galloping to cross the path of the senator's car. A raw but practiced *no* tore from Venus's throat, her feet pounding the asphalt to chase after them.

A sharp honk pierced the air and tires screeched.

Paws skidded to a halt, too, coming face-to-face with a front bumper.

A handful of inches spared Aunt Keisha and Tyrell from impact. Aunt Keisha's magic nudged at the car, giving the illusion of something hitting it. Tyrell's eyes rolled into the back of his head as he collapsed, all theater and drama. His long pink tongue rolled out of his mouth like a red carpet.

Venus mustered up tears and sobs as she dropped to the ground, cradling him.

Senator Radliff hopped out of her car, panicky *oh-my-lords* tumbling around in her Louisianian accent.

"I didn't see 'em coming at all! Is he alright?"

Aunt Keisha watched on with a whine, tucking in her tail.

"I don't know!" Venus choked out, rocking him.

One Mississippi.

Two Mississippi.

Three Mississi—

Tyrell's eyelids flipped full open, throwing her countdown off-kilter. Her entire being drew in a pained gasp as the sensation of war rammed into her rib cage, invading her chest. His back hunched, then bowed in an unnatural arch.

Senator Radliff screamed in horror, stumbling until she fell into her car's hood.

"No! Fight it!" Aunt Keisha barked like a drill sergeant, prompting the senator's shriek. "Shut the hell up, lady!"

Bones shifted, jerked, and broke. His glossy coat cleaved apart like ripped seams, his actual flesh and clothes breaking free. He convulsed out of her arms, his face contorting halfway between a dog and a boy. He hacked flu-like quivering coughs between his screams, struggling for breath. Every stitch of Venus felt the fight within him.

That damn frog and his nature were at violent odds.

Leap dragged himself from Tyrell's jaws, covered in blood and spit.

Venus scrabbled backward, finding her feet as her cousin became an oscillating mass of mismatched extremities and features.

Flesh, fur, scales.

Person, animal, monster.

Fluidly, Aunt Keisha reshaped back into herself. As best she could, she looped her arms underneath Tyrell's evolving limbs, hauling him away.

Leap hopped after them.

Venus spotted movement from her peripheral vision. Senator Radliff inched around the car hood, trying to get to the open car door. Their gazes shackled together.

"Keep away from me, you jinxmonger," the woman hissed as she clenched her fists, unknowingly keeping her ring safe. "Do you know who I am?"

Venus had been called all sorts of things, including that slur Senator Radliff so easily wielded. On any other day, it would've rolled right off her back.

But today wasn't one of those days.

"Make her bleed!" It demanded.

Venus's legs ate up the ground. Her hand hoisted high.

Senator Radliff tried to retreat in a clamber, but nothing could save her from the strike across her face. Or the three nails that scored deep into her cheek. She shouted, tumbling down.

All the commotion inspired some wannabe heroes to rush their way.

"Hey!" somebody shouted.

Aunt Keisha revved up the engine, peeling out the parking spot. She accelerated toward where Venus was and whipped the wheel, pumping the brakes to make the car drift to a shrilling stop. Its rear passenger door flung open like welcoming arms.

Venus leaped in, yanking at the handle as Aunt Keisha sped off.

Tyrell lay across the backseat, propped against the opposite door.

Six pairs of eyes crowded his distorted expression, colliding and spinning.

Flecks of pain glittered in each iris.

"Get down!" Aunt Keisha ordered.

She did as told and hunkered down over her cousin, cringing at the distant clap of a gun. The tinted rear glass shattered. Her molars scraped as she clenched her teeth. Dark shards rained on them, but Venus's back and the protection ring shielded them both as he writhed, changed, and cried out.

Her heart gunned into overdrive, fear maddening her blood. Her chest rose and fell to a panicked rhythm as she took heavy, open-mouthed breaths to calm the fuck down. But memories of June 27th she hid in that deep pit within her crawled out, *demanding* her attention.

Tyrell's repositioning bones jabbed into her as if she were a pincushion, reeling her out of her head and back to the present.

Venus's cell vibrated in her pocket.

A call from Janus, no doubt, all in thanks to the blood-tether's snitching.

A sharp splinter of a memory protruded in her mind. *Awry protest, shadowy alleyway, blood blooming, numbing shock.* She quickly wedged it back in place, braving the sting.

"What's wrong with him?" she shouted over the roaring wind as Aunt Keisha broke all sorts of speed limits and traffic laws.

"He's bent outta shape!" Aunt Keisha answered, jerking the wheel to zoom around a corner. "Overexertion triggers it."

Venus and Tyrell careened, but she gritted her teeth, anchoring herself to keep them from tipping over the backseat's edge.

"I thought Leap was supposed to help him so that wouldn't happen!" she growled.

Somewhere in the front seat, Leap issued an offended croak at the accusation. The audacious sound got under her skin, igniting the urge to chuck him out the window. Not that it'd hurt him anyway. Plus, a familiar's unwavering loyalty acted as a compass, always leading them back home.

Loyalty.

At that word, three realizations pealed through her, too loud to be ignored.

Tyrell didn't trust Leap's help, and Aunt Keisha was to blame for all that. For waiting too long enough to cultivate a bond. That's why back at Rock Creek Park, Tyrell rejected Leap. Venus didn't need to call her aunt out because her aunt *already* knew.

As proof, hot tendrils of Aunt Keisha's anger and fear braided tight around Venus's spine.

But the third truth was Venus was just as guilty. She laid down the breadcrumbs to lead Tyrell to the brink, damn well knowing he'd fall so his mom could catch him.

She just hadn't expected him to break like *this.*

So used to him piecing himself back together.

"Will he be okay?" Venus demanded, sitting upright.

"He won't be if we don't get him to a brewer of health!" Aunt Keisha admitted. "I'm taking him to the best one in the DMV!"

Venus tensed up, dread knotting her stomach.

Don't say his name. Please, don't say his name, she pleaded in her head.

"Elder Glenn will get him back into shape!" Aunt Keisha said.

Her lids came down hard as she whispered the word *fuck.*

After a beat, she asked, "What if he's not there?"

"For all our sakes, he better be," Aunt Keisha replied.

But he won't. Venus swallowed those three words down.

Tyrell's screams died down to nothing, which terrified her. He lifted his hand, paw, talons weakly out to her. She took hold of him, even if it made her grimace and bleed.

"*Wars have casualties,*" It said. "*You're naive to think otherwise.*"

She shook her head, refusing to accept that. Her vision grew watery.

Even though he was her ride-or-die, he *wasn't* dying today.

Not on her watch.

Not for a bag of blood money.

And sure as hell not for Matrika Sharma's master plan.

So, Venus came up with a plan of her own. A plan that would cost her magic for it to pay off. Maybe, even her life, but she wasn't afraid of death. She took its hand once.

Facing Elder Glenn's cauldron, she'd have terrible odds stacked against her. Four days' worth of restoration tea put a shallow pool at the bottom of her well of magic. Having a resurrected body that ran on borrowed breath did her no favors, either.

But she didn't give a fuck.

"*You wouldn't,*" It hissed.

Watch me.

CHAPTER
TWENTY-SIX

The inheritance syndrome is a condition where those resurrected by a sacrificium potion inherit the Willing's memories, emotions, magic, and, in some cases, magic-forged commitments unaffected by death.

— *The Unofficial Guide to Post-Resurrection Care*

AN EVENING AUDIENCE WATCHED FROM PORCHES AND OUT WINDOWS as Venus and her aunt carried Tyrell to the back of Elder Glenn's house, like soldiers would a wounded comrade. Minding one's business was unofficial witcher law, so she could do whatever she needed to without worrying about WCTF. On the ride here, she weighed all consequences, but her selfishness tipped the scale each time.

"We've come too far for you to ruin everything," It nagged. But Venus couldn't be stopped. She was too much like her mom, following the same path right to Elder Glenn's kitchen.

The back door opened to her as a greeting.

Aunt Keisha didn't question why as they hustled inside, lobbing Tyrell on the table. His sweat glistened as he furrowed his brow, his six pairs of eyes overrun with tears.

She rushed to the sink, snatching a dish towel off a cabinet's towel bar.

Delirious, he lolled his head from side to side.

His mouth, snout, beak freed a shaky wheeze. "Vee?"

"I'm here, Ty," she assured, returning to his side to dab his face clean.

Aunt Keisha stalked toward the kitchen's cased opening. "Glenn, get your ass out here! Glenn!"

"He's not coming. He's dead." Venus locked eyes with her aunt from over her shoulder. "I'll brew. Ty'll die if I don't."

Tyrell whimpered, "I don't wanna die."

His fear sparked alive in her belly, weak but very much felt.

"That's not gonna happen." She wiped away a fresh tear of his. "I'm not gonna let that happen."

Her aunt blinked in shock. "You'd break your pledge and sacrifice your magic, just like Rissa?"

"Of course, I would. I can live without being a brewer and my calling," Venus snapped, "but I can't live without Ty."

Tyrell shuddered, whispering, "Moms, I'm so damn cold."

"Shh, baby boy." Aunt Keisha scooped up his hand-paw, sandwiching it between her palms. "It's OK. I got you."

Aunt Keisha addressed her again, "I know this is my fault."

Venus shook her head. "It's *both* our faults, Aunt Key. I'm just as much to blame as you. That's why we can work together to make it right. What's the name of the potion?"

"Renovatio," Aunt Keisha answered.

Tyrell hacked a cough, blood dribbling down his chin. The sight of it should've worried her, but the brewer in her was glad she didn't have to *make* him bleed to brew the potion.

Aunt Keisha snatched up the towel to clean him up, her voice edged with panic. "We don't have much time."

"Well, we need to think of something, because I *need* time," Venus said, retrieving a pewter cauldron from the overhead rack. After filling it with water, she set it on the stove and twisted a knob to high heat.

"I think he's weak enough for Leap to overpower him and lull him into hibernation," Aunt Keisha proposed. "It won't stop his shifting, but it'll slow him down."

Leap croaked at the mention of his name.

They both pitched their eyes to the wide-open back door. The familiar lingered just beyond the threshold and Elder Glenn's zappy home security spell. Only with her permission could he enter.

With a nod, she granted Leap entry.

He hopped in, vaulting onto Tyrell's chest.

Leap's skin secreted a glowing mucus that oozed off him, slathering over Tyrell like quick-moving lava. Ty's eyes rolled back as the frog engulfed him in a slimy incandescent cocoon.

"How long do I have left?" Venus asked.

Leap croaked again.

"Forty-five minutes at least," Aunt Keisha said. "Fifty minutes at most."

"Alright, everyone out. Now," Venus ordered, marching over to Elder Glenn's alcove bookcase. Invisible hands lifted Tyrell and Leap off the table, ushering them out of the kitchen with Aunt Keisha following closely behind.

Venus plucked volumes off the shelf, riffling through pages.

"Where is it, where is it, where the hell is it?" she said, slamming yet another grimoire shut to snare another. A spruce-blue book flashed through her overwrought mind. A reminder Elder Glenn was a part of her.

She fetched it, combing through the pages. A gush of relief washed over her as she found the Renovatio recipe, muttering *thanks* to the old man.

In the recoil's aftermath, Venus folded over in pain, hugging her midriff. Agony blistered her insides. Her lungs burned as she gulped down smoky air. She wasn't entirely sure if the pain was from siphoning what little she had in her magic well or from breaking her brewer's pledge to the discipline of love. Or maybe, both were the cause.

The protection ring's bubble shield dissolved away.

Venus spread a shaky hand across her chest, the drum of her heart pounding frantically against the palm of her hand. She wanted to shove her fingers through her flesh and rib cage to rummage around for *any* sign of her deviation.

Tears of relief flowed down her cheeks alongside the ones from pain.

Was *It* actually gone?

Was she finally free?

A gurgling laugh rang deep in her bones, soaking into her marrow. *"Sike."*

"I broke my pledge," she whispered, shocked. "You shouldn't be here."

It tsked. *"Venus Genevieve Stoneheart has failed yet again."*

Her mind foraged for an explanation. She, a brewer of love, concocted a health potion. Without Elder Glenn's memories, she wouldn't have found the Renovatio recipe. Having his anima left Venus with the love he felt for his sister, too.

Then she remembered something she learned from the unofficial guide Nisha gave her as a *welcome-back-from-the-dead* gift. A gift she had read from cover to cover on nights she was too afraid to close her eyelids, which was *most* nights now. She knew the booklet nearly by heart.

The inheritance syndrome. That's what Venus must've had. If she had his anima, did she inherit his pledge, too? Did that mean she was bound to two pledges? One for love and one for health?

If her magic was still here, it must be true.

Suddenly, her stomach revolted at the truth, forcing her to totter to the kitchen sink and heave.

Every single time she discovered something about the sacrificium potion's repercussions, she wondered what was worse:

Feeling like a grave robber or being Elder Glenn's grave.

Venus poured the sappy potion into her cousin's mouth with a shaky hand, afraid she'd spill a precious drop. His eyelids blinked rapidly as he regained consciousness, his chest heaving. With widened eyes, he arched his back and hollered at the ceiling, floundering as the potion worked on him. Bones righted themselves. His limbs reverted to factory settings. His extra eyes submerged into his skin, the pair she'd known all her life drifting back into place.

Bit by bit, he became himself again.

Then he curled into a ball on Elder Glenn's bed, quivering.

Though Venus wanted to comfort him, Aunt Keisha *needed* to.

She turned to go, limping away.

"Thank you, niece," Aunt Keisha said carefully, gratitude glazing over her face.

After closing the door behind her, Venus pressed her back against it, sliding down, down, down to the bottom. Exhausted and pained, her shoulders sagged and her head drooped.

"You shouldn't have done this," It hissed. *"You have too damn many trinary-note potions to brew and too little time! We'll die!"*

"Wars have casualties," she uttered softly, noting Senator Radliff's dried blood under her nails. "Isn't that what you said?"

It fell silent, unable to fight *Its* own logic.

CHAPTER
TWENTY-SEVEN

Lies are useful in a place like DC, where your truths are used against you.

—Malik Jenkins, WASP cofounder

JULY 19, 2023

ON THE SEVENTEENTH, VENUS BREWED SENATOR HOAGE'S PEITHO potion. The day after, she did Senator Westbay's. As for Senator Cavendish, she made his today. Only two days remained until the deadline, and she had one more potion to go.

But as expected, the brewbug forced Venus to her knees.

Literally.

She crawled out of the smoky kitchen, Patches trailing after her. Due to her protection ring, she didn't need his assistance to combat a potion's recoil. Despite that, he helped her in other ways by giving her ingredients, fetching heart-shaped vials, and stirring the cauldron as the brewbug gnawed at her.

Her eyesight grew fuzzy, darkening around the edges.

"You should've started your restoration regimen sooner, but no, you had to be stubborn," It mustered, just as affected as her.

She was glad no one else saw her like this.

Uncle Bram's next check-in visit was later this week. Janus had gone to a coven meeting at Miss Florence's to go over what to expect if the Registration Act passed. An hour ago, while Patches tended to the bubbling cauldron, Venus had pressed a bag of frozen strawberries against her temple to soothe a headache and listened to her sister's reason for wanting to go.

"I know the bill won't pass," Janus said, shrugging, "but Miss Flo makes bomb-ass cookies."

As Venus's little sister munched on cookies a few blocks away, nausea frothed in her stomach, vomit crawling up her throat. Tears of relief filmed her as she left behind the marred hardwood floors for bathroom tiles. She gripped the toilet bowl, emptying her stomach until it had nothing left to give. As she hawked a wad of spit to expel the aftertaste and flushed, Patches sat on the bathroom counter, watching.

Rising, Venus tottered to the sink to swish around some bubblegum-flavored mouthwash. She doused her face in cool water to combat her fever, bracing the counter to let droplets drip off her face. Patches grabbed a hand towel off a wall rack, bringing it to her.

Her tears mixed and dripped with the water on her face. She took the towel from the cat and blotted away the moisture, wishing it were enough to stop her tears.

But they continued to pour and pour.

Since summer began, Venus had brewed one binary-note potion and five trinary-note potions, carving out slivers of herself to sweeten the flavors. Though it was no secret brewers liked to dance with death, Venus was tap-dancing on the Grim Reaper's last nerve.

But she still had one trinary-note potion left to brew: Radliff's.

Having exhausted all her strength, her will to remain standing tumbled.

Venus crumpled onto the tiled floor, rolling onto her side.

Weak and defeated from a won battle with no victor.

Venus was sprawled across her bedspread in her underwear. The ceiling fan whirred above her, but it wasn't enough to combat her fever. Patches laid curled up on her belly, his anima seeping into her clammy skin, attempting to quell some of her sufferings.

But shivers echoed through her, skittering over her pained bones. Her hair clung to her flesh. Her skull felt too tight for her brain.

A door's slam vibrated the house's bones.

Somebody came home.

No, two somebodies.

She listened with half an ear to familiar voices and laughter.

Janus brought Presley home.

Then she stiffened.

The door.

Venus needed to close the door so that she could suffer alone. Her body screamed at her as she brushed Patches off her and got off the bed, but she didn't get far as her legs gave out. Pressing her palms against the floor, she tried to get up, but she crumpled, dizziness rushing in.

Darkness preyed on her.

And she surrendered to it.

A desperate thirst coaxed Venus awake. Peeling back her eyelids, she found herself in bed. Janus was sleeping beside her. Curled in a loose ball, Patches slept in the narrow valley between them. Slowly, Venus sat up, biting back a groan. Though her fever had petered out, the brewbug was far from done as pain splintered through her.

Venus eased out of bed, tiptoeing over to her discarded 4XL shirt she always wore as a nightgown and putting on her pink monster slippers. Her palm braced the walls as she journeyed to the kitchen.

Then she froze in the arched doorway.

Uncle Bram sat in his chair, lifting his flask to his lips for a sip.

He wasn't supposed to be here for three more days.

The four potion bottles stood in a line on the table.

His simmering anger made her feverish all over again.

Fuck.

Venus pretended to ignore him as she fixed herself a glass of water, grimacing with her every move. After guzzling it down, she placed the cup in the sink.

"Why are the names of the undecided senators on these potions?" he questioned.

Halfway to her exit, her barefoot stride came to a halt. She turned slowly, but light-headedness still swept over her like a tide. She gripped the counter's edge to anchor herself, having made acquaintances with the floor too many times for her liking.

"What?" She blinked.

"Don't play dumb, Venus Genevieve." He narrowed his eyes, searching her face. "You damn well know I read the paper every day. I see one for Cavendish, Hoage, and Westbay, but one is missing a name. Who's that one for?"

Venus lowered her gaze in guilt, rubbing her tongue's tip against a canine tooth. "I think you already know."

"I've got two guesses," Uncle Bram said, "but I want you to tell me. You promised me no more secrets and lies. You told me ain't nothing big happening in your life, but here you tryna tamper with that Registration Act's vote. Seems like a pretty big fucking deal to me."

Her head snapped up at his audacity. "You want to talk about secrets and lies, Uncle Bram?" She took a bold step forward from the counter, too angry to worry about a fall. "What was the last potion Mom ever brewed?"

"What?" Uncle Bram's eyebrows lifted in surprise.

Aggravation sharpened her tongue. "I didn't stutter."

A thickening silence clotted the air as she stared her uncle down.

"A sacrificium potion," he answered, his voice empty of emotion.

"Why?" Venus pressed, impatient.

Uncle Bram drooped his head to break their stare-off, stealing her earlier reply for himself. "I think you already know."

"But I want you to tell me," she hissed, throwing his own words back at him.

Silence.

"For Presley," he admitted, slumping his shoulders, "because of the Iron Nail Bombing."

"That's right." Venus nodded. "And who asked Mom to do it?"

A frown darkened his face. "You've proved your point."

"Who asked Mom to do it?" she repeated, ignoring his directive. "Or are you too scared to say Presley's mom's name? Fine, I'll say it for you. Matrika, Matrika, Ma—"

"I said enough, Venus!" Uncle Bram's fist struck the kitchen table, causing it to snap in half and collapse. His magic caught the potion bottles mid-fall. A spur of his anger slammed into her, knocking her back. She fell against the counter, her heart drumming violently against her ribs.

Like a tide, silence rushed back in, washing away his temper. His magic gently carried the bottles to the stove and sat them down on the windowsill.

"I've seen and done a lot of bad things, Venus," he admitted, quiet. "I helped Prospero gain power by causing a lot of hurt. I made his name a name to be feared. But nothing prepared me for the night Matrika and

Owen came here, crying and begging for Rissa's help after that old bastard refused to brew that fucking potion.

"I'll never forget Presley wrapped up in a bloody blanket." His eyes fell to a particular spot on the kitchen floor a few feet away. "I'll never forget how Owen held on to them for dear life. All I could do was just stand there."

Venus's lips trembled as her uncle's words painted a vivid heart-wrenching scene in her mind, stroke by agonizing stroke. Visions of tears, desperate pleas, spilled blood, a life lost, a potion's recoil, a resurrection, and...an owed debt.

If her mom broke a pledge and forfeited her magic to brew a health potion that Elder Glenn wouldn't, offering his potions at dirt-cheap prices was too low a cost to settle the debt.

"Lately, that's all my life has been," he continued. "Standing around. I can't stand by anymore, Venus."

Then Uncle Bram muttered a repairment spell for the broken table. It pieced itself back together, splinters and all. Then he stood at the same moment the table did.

He pulled out a folded square of inky black from his pocket, offering it to her.

Hesitantly, she took it. "What's this?"

"Me stepping up."

Venus unfolded it, flinching as a burst of light hit her face. She sucked sharply at the air as she realized what she held in her hands.

The Love Witcher ad, ripped from the Black Book.

"You took this?"

As the ad's brilliance shined up on them, he acknowledged with a glance. "After everything I've done for Prospero, I earned that page and more."

Her regard slid to the peitho potions on the windowsill above the sink, soft moonlight filtering through her sacrifices the hue of blush pink. The pale glow bleached the delicate green tendrils and tiny pastel buds.

Next week, the country would watch the Senate vote fail, and they'd never know it was all thanks to her. For years, she had gladly accepted the facelessness that came with every gig, but this time was different.

Too much blood had been shed.

Two too many lives had been taken.

Suddenly, she recognized where she stood in the food chain.

The prey for the wolves and vultures.

No gratitude given for the feast.

"You deserve rest, Pinkie," Uncle Bram said tenderly. "That page can no longer work you to the bone."

Then he left her be, going out the front door.

Moments later, Venus hissed in pain and hunched over as the rage of another surged through her blood like thousands of needles. Her hand balled into a fist, crinkling the ad. She struggled to lift her head as Presley stepped into the kitchen, rubbing their palms as if they had found a treasure trove.

"I'm glad Jay and I agreed to take turns looking after you. I was in Bram's old room, waiting for my shift to start. I heard everything. You're a liar, Venus."

Her lips trembled around her words. "Presley, I didn't lie to you."

"Withholding the truth is the *same* thing as telling a lie." Their rage coiled around her tightly, holding her hostage as they closed in on her. "How long have you known?" They asked, their gaze glittering with ire.

"Not even a week," she wheezed, straightening up. "I swear."

"You swear, huh?" Their voice hoarse with desperation. "Then swear to me on Clarissa's grave that you intended to tell me the truth."

Venus shook her head, tears burning at the borders of her eyes. "I can't do that, Presley."

"So, you do think I'll interfere with your plans for"—they broke off, then gritted out—"her." As the last word drained off their tongue, venom and acid dripped with it.

"Then prove me wrong and swear you won't."

Presley's nostrils flared at her ultimatum, a bulge spasming as their jaw clenched.

Silence.

But their anger spoke volumes to Venus, confirming something she already knew. Even as a girl with no fate, she knew this moment was inevitable.

"You want to hurt Matrika for what she's done, Venus? Go report her to the Grand Coven," they pleaded. "They'll strip away her Grand Witcher title. They'll take away her power."

"Yes, they can take away her title, but they'll never take away her power. Not when she has blood oaths, connections, and lots of cash." Her body screamed at her as she turned halfway to grab a paring knife from a wooden holder. "I know you want answers, Presley."

Venus drew a step closer. "So, I suggest you squeeze everything you can out of Matrika because when that bill fails next week, I'm killing her."

"Let me guess," Presley said, glancing down at the knife. "If I refuse to do as you say, you'll stab me?"

"No, Pres. Not at all." Venus slipped the polished handle into Presley's hand and closed their fingers for them. A blank, unreadable mask covered Presley's face, but she felt their unadulterated shock congealing in her belly.

The knife's point prodded her navel. "If you can't accept what I'm about to do to that bitch, the only way you can stop me is by killing me yourself."

They glared at her like they hated her fucking guts.

No, not like.

Did.

At that moment, Presley did hate her.

At least they both could agree on something.

Their dagger-sharp resentment sunk into her, hitting bone.

As Venus grimaced, her words rushed out, winded and pained. "I've already died once." She lifted her watery gaze to the ceiling to keep her tears at bay. "What's a second time?"

The knife clattered to the kitchen floor.

A devastated Presley backed away from her with a slight limp, pressing tight fists against their temples. "Fuck, fuck, fuck!"

Venus squeezed her eyes tighter, tighter, tighter as that word stabbed at her, hurting her in ways a knife could never.

Their shoulders heaved with every harsh breath. "You've poisoned me with one of your love potions, haven't you?"

"No, Presley," Venus assured, shaking her head. "Never."

"Then why the fuck do I still love you, Venus?" They barreled toward her and grabbed her shoulders. "Tell me why." They shook her once, but once was just enough to get her tears to fall.

In her tight, achy chest, a seed of sob grew like a weed, robbing her strength. It burned the back of her throat as she choked on it.

"I warned you I was bad for your health."

Presley's grip tightened on her shoulders, their eyes wild with hurt. The kind of hurt that came with heartache or heartbreak. "No, don't you dare shove the blame on me. How could I keep away?"

"Maybe, I should've tried harder at pushing you away for both our sakes," she whispered, tears sagging her words. "You're too good for me, Pres. I've known that since day one."

"Do you love me, Venus?" Their hands framed her face, thumbs wiping away the wetness that stained her cheeks. As if their anger couldn't override the need to care for her like it was etched into their DNA. "And don't fucking lie to me."

"I don't know. Whatever it is, it terrifies me. You'd think that because

I brew love, I'd know what it is I feel, but I don't, Presley. But if I'm willing to kill Matrika even if I know it'll hurt you, it doesn't sound like love to me. And if you refuse to understand why I have to do it, maybe you don't love me the way you think you do."

As the last word left Venus's mouth, she didn't know what to expect. Presley's anger, hatred, a sense of betrayal, or resignation. Or maybe, all four would chase her down as a pack, ravaging on the scraps of her that the brewbug hadn't come back for yet.

But as the angry light went out in Presley's eyes and blankness settled onto their face, something worse echoed through her. Not an emotion but a word. A realization that terrified the fuck out of her.

Done.

Done with this.

Done with her.

"That's *if* you can kill her." Presley let her go, backing away. "I can't stop you, but that doesn't mean someone else won't."

As they exited the kitchen, her feet faltered as she followed. She squinted tearily as her vision throbbed a wild beat.

Blurry, clear, blurry, clear.

"I can handle Matrika's goons." Venus shook her head, trying to dispel her symptoms. She collided into a corner of the couch, gripping the armrest to stop herself from fumbling forward.

"No, Venus. I'm not talking about them." Presley's magic flung open the front door. "You're not the only one with plans."

Shock jarred every atom in her body, her voice quivering. "Do you know something I don't?"

They halted, squaring their shoulders. "Yes, and I have no choice but to keep it that way."

Then they left her behind.

The door slammed shut, punctuating their departure.

Janus's rage announced her arrival, barging right into Venus. "I guess it's *my* turn now, huh? Don't worry. I think I'm last on the list with a bone to pick with you."

Venus's weak knees gave way, unable to withstand the intrusion.

Unable to stand her ground in yet another war.

Of course, Janus had heard everything. She was the queen of eavesdropping. A queen who had come for Venus's head.

Her sister stood over her. "How long have you known, Venus?"

"Long enough," she admitted raspingly, the truth scraping the back of her throat raw. Having told so many truths tonight, she was surprised her voice hadn't given out yet.

Janus wiped wildly at her tears, her tone hitching. "The moment you found out, you should've told me!"

"I wanted to tell you everything."

Wanted to but didn't.

Couldn't because she was greedy.

"When I wanted to find Mom's murderer, you held me back," Janus sobbed, distancing herself further and further. "All this time, I thought you did it to protect me, but now, I see you and that thing inside you wanted revenge for yourselves."

Venus shook her head, sniffling, "I *am* trying to protect you."

"I fucking hate you!"

She felt her sister's sharp spike of hatred and mistakenly believed it was her own at first. After all, war and hate went hand in hand.

As Janus stormed out of the house, Venus lowered her watery sights to the floor. She expected a path of blood from having her heart clawed out and stolen.

Panic inflated, then imploded in her chest, sending her into a fit of hyperventilation. She hugged her belly and fell over, wanting the world to devour her one chomp at a time.

She gulped in air like an antidote.

Her fever sunk its hot teeth into her consciousness.

Her eyeballs bowled back as the dark rushed in.

Down, down, down she went as she fell through memories masquerading as nightmares and nightmares masquerading as memories.

Blood, bone, fire, smoke.

The Swadesh kitchen.

Screams and last breaths.

Elder Glenn's final moments.

Its voice bled through the madness: *"Claw your way out!"*

But she couldn't.

Nor did she want to.

CHAPTER
TWENTY-EIGHT

This potion's purpose is to ensure or maintain a healthy aura. A well-balanced aura generates the reliability of a Patron's magick if witcher or enhances the overall condition of physical, emotional, and willpower, thereby heightening aura intensity if human. The potion's effects wear off in extreme stress situations.

—A Picture of Health: Recipes for Health Potions
Excerpt of Healthy Glow recipe

JULY 20, 2023

THE BLOOD-TETHER REELED VENUS OUT OF HER DREAMLESS SLUM-ber, the world welcoming her with a heated embrace. She winced at the brightness all around her as she parted her eyelids, groaning at her splitting headache. A wet Patches sat in her lap, leaning against her midriff. His anima was a cool relief soaking into her skin. He leaped out of the tub, landing gracefully on the toilet's closed lid.

Venus sluggishly lifted her cheek from the bathtub's rim, gazing at the milky bath filled with shriveled tulips. Through her feverish fog, she also realized she'd been stripped down to her underwear again.

"Janus," she rasped out as loudly as possible, but her scratchy voice didn't carry as far as she wanted. She plopped her cheek back in the warm spot it had previously rested on.

The bathroom door opened.

A pair of mint-green stiletto heels sauntered in.

Venus scanned upward. From pale ankles, calves, and thighs to the ruched dress and, finally, the familiar face of Nisha's doctor girlfriend.

"Chelsea?"

"So, you decided to live." A pleased Chelsea nodded, her glossy ash-blond hair in a crown braid catching the light. She wore a rose behind her ear. "Good."

In Venus's mind, memory fragments assembled themselves into an incomplete puzzle. Brewing the third peitho potion. Uncle Bram's unexpected visit. The Black Book ad. Presley's confrontation with her. Janus's discovery of how deep her greed ran.

"Why are you here?"

"Your little old cat came to the Golden Coin looking for Bram." Chelsea stroked Patches's head gently. "Unfortunately, your uncle was a no-show for his shift. So, he got Nisha's help instead, but she's not a doctor. You're lucky, though, because she dates one."

"My sister's in trouble. I need to find her." Venus tried to sit up, but she collapsed back into the tub. Water sloshed over the rim and onto the tile floor. She instructed Patches to look for clothes and her cell phone, lying to herself that by the time he finished, she'd actually have the energy to stand.

She suspected he knew that too, but still, he obliged her. He nodded once and vaulted off the toilet lid, exiting the bathroom.

"No need." Chelsea pulled a pen out of her purse. "I know *exactly* where Baby Stoneheart is."

"How do you know that?"

"I know because Nisha just left after getting a call that"—Chelsea crouched beside the bathtub—"*your* baby sister accused *her* baby sister of murder and tried to kill her."

Fear and shock ripped strips from Venus's heart.

That's why the blood-tether tugged her out of the oblivion's quicksand.

"No, no, no," Venus breathed out, wagging her head weakly.

"The operative word is *tried*." Chelsea clasped Venus's chin to keep it still, shining a medical penlight's beam at her bloodshot eyes.

Venus grimaced at the brightness, too frail to pull away.

"Being a furious teenage girl screaming bloody murder in broad daylight in Kalorama *did* get her inside the Grand Witcher's home, but she couldn't get past the guards." A thumb click killed the light.

"So, she wrecked the place. Now, *she's* in time-out, *you've* been summoned, and *I've* been instructed to get you well enough to go before Her Grandness." Chelsea took her rose and dipped it into the milky water as a test. Her face withered into disappointment as the flower withered. "But I'm not a miracle worker. You broke yourself. Badly. You've already had six Purification baths since two in the morning. I estimate at least a monthlong recovery time. If you brew more, you'll probably die."

"I don't have a month," she said, "nor do I have a choice. The deadline is tomorrow."

Chelsea shook her head, dropping the shriveled rose into the tub. "The *deadline's* tomorrow, but the reception is next Wednesday, and the Senate vote isn't until Thursday, the twenty-seventh, which is a full week away."

Venus winced as she worked her throat through a dry, painful swallow. "Reception?"

"Yes, the Grand Witcher is hosting a banquet as a guise to get all the senators in one place and poison them." Chelsea paused, her shoulders lifting in a shrug. "Well, sans Mounsey. He'll be there, but they have *nonpoisonous* plans for him."

"Why are you telling me all this?"

Chelsea pursed her lips in thought, smoothing out the pinkish-orange lipstick she wore. "Because, well, number one, I'm not bound by a blood oath, and number two, I'm not too prideful to admit that without you, this country is fucked." She pulled a naked prescription bottle from her purse. "And number three, I'm tired of presiding over preventable deaths that come into my ER. Like I did yours."

Venus lolled her head to stare at the tub's drippy faucet, her lips trembling. She forgot Chelsea was the last person to see her alive and the first person to see her dead.

Chelsea continued, "If that Registration Act passes, *our* privacy will be public knowledge. And the morgues will overflow with witcher bodies. When you go before the Grand Witcher today, ask for a little more time. Even with a blood oath, *you* have more leverage than you think."

Venus mulled over the word *leverage*. She'd always known she was a cog in a giant machine, but if a single cog no longer did its job, then the machine would grind to a halt.

She had this realization once before. It dawned on her when she brewed a health potion for her cousin, willing to forfeit her magic and crush Matrika's grand plans.

Using leverage, Venus could buy herself a few more days, whatever good that'd do. Using leverage, she could get Janus back, even though her little sister *despised* her to the very core.

Chelsea shook out a yellow octagonal pill covered in orange dots. "Now, open up."

Out of instinct, Venus hardened her face in distrust.

Chelsea rolled her eyes, blowing a long breath. "Don't be childish. I wouldn't have wasted nine hours of my life trying to make sure you don't die *again* just to do you in with a make-do. I use these to get through long shifts. I've stayed up four days in a row on one of these alone."

Venus finally complied, opening her jaws. The make-do tasted of grapefruits and tangerines, the bright flavors invigorating her taste buds.

Once Venus swallowed it, Chelsea added, "Oh, yes. Side effects include cardiac arrests and death. Either-or, but sometimes both. It will shorten your brewbug's lifespan but only by sacrificing some of its own endurance. So, who knows how long the make-do will last for you, but if I had mentioned any of that beforehand, you probably wouldn't have taken it."

"You're damn r—"

Her own gasp interrupted her as goosebumps frolicked along her skin and a burst of energy surged through her veins. She took open-mouthed breaths as if she had finished a marathon, but she had enough vigor to run ten back-to-back. Her heartbeat raced so fast, blood rushed into her ears.

As if Chelsea could hear its rhythm, she said, "Don't move until your heart calms. Once it does, we can leave."

Venus groaned at the command. That was like asking a snake not to slither or a great-auntie not to side-eye. She wanted to move.

No, she needed to move.

She needed to get to Janus.

Moments ago, she needed all the strength to open her mouth or lift her head. Now, she had to use all of it to be still.

Venus closed her eyes to concentrate, but waiting for her heart to calm was like waiting for paint to dry. It took too damn long. Or maybe, her racing pulse distorted her sense of time. She had no clock or cell to guide her.

So, she waited and waited and waited some more. When her heart steadied its pace, she sat cautiously in the bathtub, afraid of overexciting herself at the prospect of freedom.

Bump, bump, bump.

Nice and steady.

She rose slowly, stepping onto the fuzzy pink bath rug.

Bump, bump, bump.

Fuck, yes.

Chelsea dropped Venus off at the curb in front of the Grand Witcher's tan-bricked mansion covered in lush, green ivy. She marched up concrete stairs to the front doorstep.

Venus banged hard for entry, and the door obliged. An army of guards awaited her with hardened faces and dead eyes in the foyer. She maneuvered past them with no further regard, silently challenging anyone to try her.

She longed to unleash all that excess energy. She wasn't certain if the make-do poured a little *something* something into her well of magic or if it merely gave the illusion that it did.

Either way, Venus felt invincible.

Ilyas entered the foyer.

"Come," he ordered reservedly.

"A simple *please* goes a long way," she returned.

"Force goes even further."

She narrowed her eyes as a prelude to lashing out with all she had if he dared to give the wrong answer. "Is that what you did to my sister to stop her?"

"None required," he informed. "We convinced her with other means."

Though she despised Ilyas with every inch of her being, she could always rely on him to tell her the truth.

Venus cooled down but stayed alert as he escorted her to the Grand Witcher's study. Magic must've cleaned up any trace of her sister's tantrum in the immaculate house.

Ilyas stopped at the door, gesturing for her to enter.

Then he stood guard as Venus stepped inside. The last time she was here, she pledged herself in blood. Now, she was *free* of that blood oath. Only its scar remained now.

"I've been waiting for you," Matrika said, nodding her chin to a chair opposite hers. "Sit, Stoneheart."

That fated night, no chair was in sight. Almost as if the Grand Witcher deemed Venus unworthy to sit eye to eye. Now, as she sat across from the most powerful woman in all of DC, they were equals.

Maybe her worth was finally seen and acknowledged.

"You've been a busy girl."

"Yes, very." Venus schooled her expression, refusing to crack. "I'm nearly complete with all the potions."

Matrika arched an eyebrow. "You're fully aware that's not what I meant. Why did you tell your sister I killed Clarissa?"

"Because *you* did," Venus said. "Because you're a monster."

Mirth shook the Grand Witcher's shoulders. "I'll admit I am a monster, but so are you. You have too much blood on your hands. It's a stain that never comes off, Venus, but only monsters get things done. That's why I invest in them." She tapped her nail against the varnished box that contained the blade that scarred Venus's palm. "That's why you stood before this desk not long ago and pledged a blood oath to me."

Matrika's words fell on Venus like daggers, impaling the walls she'd built up as a defense.

Venus flared her nostrils, anger festering inside her. "A blood oath my mom would've *never* let me do. You told me she negotiated the terms, but she *never* would've agreed to me be a part of your master plan. She hated politics. As her friend, you knew that."

"Oh no, my love." Matrika tutted her tongue, amusement kindling in her warm brown eyes. "I don't think it's *me* she wanted you to run from, but yes, I tried to convince Clarissa many times. But she wouldn't budge and I respected her choice."

"There she goes trying to point the finger at someone else," It hissed.

"You respected her choice?" Venus spat out, curling her upper lip.

"You ordered her execution when it interfered with your plans since you knew you couldn't sway her."

"I didn't play any part in Clarissa's death."

"I'm beginning to suspect neither did Julius Keller," she retorted, crossing her arms. "No one can deny Julius was a murderer, but he wasn't hers. You sacrificed him to incentivize me into a blood oath."

"Julius terrorized my dominion. He deserved to burn, but I'll admit he had no responsibility for Clarissa's murder. I needed your undying loyalty, so I framed him in that regard. However, her blood isn't on my hands."

Venus shot out of her seat, slamming her palms onto the desk. "You're lying."

"I highly recommend you sit, or you'll be in a world of pain," Matrika ordered evenly.

"I already am," she sneered, not budging an inch, "*without* a fucking blood oath. It died when I died, but when you poured Elder Glenn's life back into me, you signed your death warrant."

"Oh, I'm *very* aware, but I know you'll do as I say, with or without the blood oath." Matrika relaxed in her chair, her finger *tap-tap-tapping* on the dagger's box again. "After all, I didn't need a blood oath to convince your sister to obey. I simply sent a guard to visit Malik's hospital room. To keep him safe, she won't leave here, which means she's under *my* care until you finish your job."

Deviants inspired fear, but as a brewer, Venus's vow of abnegation defanged her. Imprisoned in her bones was a power that could start wars and knock down DC like a house of cards.

But she was powerless by choice. A choice that others knowingly used against her. She was a foot soldier marching onward at everyone's command. But today, Venus Genevieve Stoneheart wanted to break rank, which was unfortunate news for anyone who stood in her way.

Fuck any tragedy or consequence that followed.

Within that split second, a war strategy formed in Venus's head as she registered the significance of what dwelled in that box. Her birthright rallied within her veins, a white-hot sensation pooling obediently under her palm's skin. Ripping away her fear like a Band-Aid, she growled as she broke her vow.

Agony scored her with its claws, shredding away the make-do's hard work. Tears sprang, blood gushed out her nose, and the brewbug frayed her strength.

Her magic jolted back the lid and fetched her the dagger.

"So, you intend to stab me to death? How personal and dramatic."

"*You* aren't the target," Venus swore, impelling the weapon to drive forward. As expected, its edged point and the Grand Witcher's incandescent aegis clashed. Determination nudged her chin high as she thrust magic at it, producing a fracture.

Sharp is this blade
Its cut sure and true
Magick will give aid
To see thy task through

The dagger was bewitched to cut *always*, its function a foe against Matrika's stalwart shield. It sunk deeper, the cleft growing, a thin slice of access forming.

Bingo.

Matrika's lips parted in horror, prompting her to call out: "Ilyas!"

Her fear *invigorated* Venus beyond measure, fueling her magic.

"Ready to come out and play?" she asked *It* as the door lurched open.

"*I thought you'd never ask,*" *It* replied giddily.

She reached within herself, liberating her deviation. For once, she trusted *It* to do right by her. An inky tentacle of energy sprung from her as she zeroed in on Ilyas coming to his mistress's defense.

It struck him furiously through the chest, infecting him. Ilyas froze, his eyes glossing black. No longer did he have fealty to Matrika.

He belonged to Venus now.

"End her."

"As you wish," Ilyas declared, his power seeping into her cracked shield. Gasps and gurgles bathed the air as he hoisted Matrika from her seat, choking her as he did it. The same punishment he used on Venus once upon a time.

She thrust her magic against the study door, holding it shut while others tried to get in. "You said I was a monster, Your Grandness. I'm just showing you how much of one I am."

A slew of violent intents emboldened *It*.

Matrika wheezed out. "Pl-please, don't. I'm h—"

"I told Presley I'd wait until next week to meet you," Venus interrupted, "but plans change, don't they, Your Grandness?"

Matrika's eyes gaped wider at the mention of Presley's name.

"H-how did y—" A high heel fell off her foot as she kicked frantically, her fingers clawing at the invisible immovable force constricting her neck. As her immense tempestuous aura dulled to a gray hue, it rapidly condensed until it clung to her body thinly.

Just like a human's.

Pure shock pulverized Venus's bloodthirst. Then the consequences rushed in all at once. Her hold on Ilyas decayed as the brewbug again infested her body, draining away her will to stay conscious.

A limp Matrika dropped to the floor, her fall dislodging the ritualistic dagger.

It roared *Its* frustration, famished for a kill.

Venus drifted out of consciousness, plunging into the choppy waters of the dark unknown.

CHAPTER
TWENTY-NINE

My wrongdoings, you must forgive.
Separate good times from bad like a sieve.
Cut this tension like a tie
So that we may see eye to eye.

—The "Forgive and Forget" potion's notion

VENUS WOKE UP INSIDE A WALK-IN FREEZER, HER WRISTS AND
ankles bound by unseen shackles. Frigid temperatures did little to witchers because their blood naturally ran hot, with her brewbug, being here
for too long wouldn't fare well for her. She didn't even know how long
she'd been in here. The brewbug loved to gobble precious time.

Had hours gone by? Or had it been days?

Venus huddled against the wall, shivering. Her eyes adjusted to the
darkness quickly. Wispy clouds formed from her breath. All the memories
leading up to her blackout encircled her head, regret crashing over her.

*"Out of all the places we could meet our end, I never expected it'd be a
freezer,"* It grumbled. *"At least last time, we died honorably."*

"We're not going to die," Venus snapped, her teeth chattering. Her
many brushes with Death showed how indecisive the grim entity was
about her.

But she didn't want to test her luck, either.

Venus needed to gather the last of her strength to get out of here.
She embraced herself as much as her shackles would allow and dug deep
within her innermost self in search of nuggets of magic. She groaned as

she came away empty-handed, having burned precious energy in pursuit of power.

Her need to see her sister again was the only thing keeping her afloat. Janus was *somewhere* in this mansion. Knowing that made Venus want to try another rescue since the first one went awry.

Since she tried to kill the Grand Witcher.

"No," Venus reminded herself, shaking her head. "Matrika's not a witcher at all."

"You should've let Ilyas wring her last breath while you had the chance," It hissed. *"She's human! You wasted an easy kill."*

Venus leaned her head against the icy wall in defeat. "You're right."

"That has a nice ring to—"

"Don't get used to it."

Angered by being cut off, her deviation growled, *"Rude, much."*

For a human to masquerade as a witcher, the easiest way was to drink a health potion to add vibrancy and vigor to their aura.

Venus hissed and pressed her fingertips into her temples as a memory gnawed at her brain. Her present, and a past not of her own, pulsed contradicting rhythms, colliding and battling for dominance.

The evocation trawled her into Elder Glenn's kitchen and into his skin.

Seeing what he saw.

Hearing what he heard.

Feeling how he felt.

Elder Glenn ladled a potion the color of green apples into a bottle, clenching his jaw as Ilyas entered his home. His annoyance sifted through him—through her—at the intrusion. He corked the bottle, placing it in a box with its brethren. Ilyas approached and closed the lid without regard to Elder Glenn's fingers.

He snatched his hand away in the nick of time, levying a glare at Ilyas's back.

He asked, *"How much longer does she expect me to support this charade, hm?"*

Ilyas didn't break his stride. *"Until you die."*

In a breath between two moments, Venus lived in Elder Glenn's memory.

Then she was back in the cold, dark.

Her mind drifted back to the ledger she found and the initials GWMS on every page.

Grand Witcher Matrika Sharma.

But why would Madame Sharma pretend to be a witcher for all these years? How was she able to stay undetected for so long? Perhaps, she knew that as the Grand Witcher, she'd possess something greater than magic.

A faint recollection timidly crept close in the back of Venus's mind, wanting its turn next. One where she had learned about power while an unconscious senator's body lay at her feet. But the memory slipped out of her reach, startled by the walk-in freezer's creaky door opening.

Light chased away the shadows and bathed her. She flinched and squinted at the silhouette. Polished oxfords tapped on the chilled metal floor.

The visitor squatted down, a trickster smile lingering before her.

"Venus," a tongue delivered playfully.

She croaked out, "Prospero."

"You've been quite naughty."

"Which is why I'm in time-out," she said. "Unless you're here to punish me."

He tilted a head, amused. "Inflicting punishment is beneath me. It's more entertaining to watch, but you needn't worry. No one's allowed to lay a finger on you."

She blinked in surprise. "By Matrika's orders?"

Then the surprise gave way to fear.

Venus understood her value, but after attempting murder, she assumed her worth only depreciated, amounting to nothing. However, if she wouldn't be punished, did they find someone to take her place? Did Matrika intend to hurt her by hurting one of her loved ones in retaliation? Or would she hold more hostages to ensure Venus's obedience?

All the questions in Venus's head boiled down to one realization.

She *hadn't* thought this the fuck through. Hadn't considered anyone or anything beyond herself. Beyond her wants, greed, and pride.

At the beginning of summer, she kept her head down. Along the way, she turned into a monster that *wanted* heads.

"No, my mother's." He stood and peered down his hawkish nose at her, offering his hand. "Come now. She wants to see you."

She didn't stir an inch beyond her trembling, untrusting of his gentlemanly gesture.

"Regardless of our little predicament, I haven't lost my manners."

"I'm in here because I lost mine," she said. "Who says I won't misbehave again?"

"You won't."

Venus begrudgingly accepted his hand, her cold skin soaking up his warmth. He helped her up. Her invisible restraints clattered as she shuffled and stumbled along. He led her up the basement stairs and into a luxury kitchen.

He lifted Venus easily as if she were as light as a doll, placing her on a barstool at the kitchen island. Nisha arrived moments later, heading straight for her. She flinched away in anticipation of an attack as Nisha reached for her.

But only a warm hand touched Venus's forehead, testing her temperature.

"We put you in the freezer to break your fever," Nisha said.

Venus lifted an eyebrow. "And the chains?"

"Well, *those* are because you tried to assassinate my sister." Nisha flashed a mocking little smile. "I hope you understand."

She then muttered an incantation, dissolving the chains.

Venus rubbed her bruised wrists, frowning.

"We need to get you better," Nisha said. Then she turned to address Prospero, "Did you make the restoration tea as I instructed?"

"Yes, ma'am." The Underbelly's king bowed like a royal servant.

"Excellent." Nisha clapped her hands, pleased. "Go make a cup for our guest."

Prospero turned on his heels, moving to the stove to complete his task humbly. It was difficult for Venus to conceal her confusion as she watched one of DC's most notorious witchers make her a cup of restoration tea and hand deliver it.

"Uh, thanks," she trailed off, the heated porcelain heating her palms. An audience of two watched her guzzle it all down. Strength dripped back into her as if dispensed by an IV. Slow and steady. Her tongue swiped her lips, gathering any stray droplets of flavor.

Then Prospero took back the mug, depositing it in the sink.

As Venus rubbed her cold hands together, she realized the protection ring no longer graced her finger. Someone must've extracted it while she was unconscious. A wise punishment for the girl who attempted to assassinate the *non-witcher* Grand Witcher.

However, going backsies didn't fit the crime. For what Venus had done, a death penalty seemed fitting, but with one love potion left to go, she was a valuable pawn. Maybe, they only kept her alive long enough to brew the final potion that would end her.

Killing two birds with one stone.

Still, she expected guards to flounce in and fuck her up at any given moment until she remembered Prospero's reassurance: *"No one's allowed to lay a finger on you."*

An order not issued by Matrika but by his mother.

Yet another player with skin in this game.

"Will that be all?" Prospero addressed Nisha.

"Yes, dear." Nisha cupped his cheek tenderly, casting him a motherly smile.

The exchange plunged a knife of perplexity into Venus's mind. Then within an eye blink, Prospero folded himself into a lime-green parakeet and perched onto Nisha's shoulder.

Shock threw Venus off-kilter. She fell off the barstool, landing on her ass with a loud *oomph* followed by a groan.

"This brewbug has got me tripping." Venus buried her face into her hands, massaging her closed eyelids as if to smooth crinkles in her vision and sanity. "Because I know I didn't just watch Prospero turn into—"

"Your sight is fine," he cut in.

"Let me get this straight," she spoke through gritted her teeth, using the barstool to heave herself up. "Kiwi *is* Prospero."

She draped her chest across the stool's cushion seat. As she struggled to catch her breath, she thought about all the times she'd been to the Golden Coin. Even though Venus could count on one hand how many times she had seen Prospero, she had only ever seen him in his office *with* Nisha.

Each time, Nisha's near-constant companion was absent.

Venus had heard of familiars that switch between animal and agathion forms, but she had never encountered one. Hell, she'd never even seen the latter. Or at least, she didn't think so. As beings of magic, a witcher's aura and an agathion's were alike. She could've passed one in a grocery store or on the sidewalk without even noticing.

"Yes," Nisha admitted, "but he prefers his animal shape."

"Flight and birdbaths are quite freeing experiences," Kiwi confessed, lifting his wings briefly.

"So, Prospero's just a puppet. A faceman." Venus grimaced. "Does my uncle know he's working for a bird?"

"Of course he knows." Nisha folded her arms, arching an eyebrow. "I brought Kiwi into this world nine years ago, making him my youngest child. Back then, I needed your uncle's brawn to help build me the Underbelly by protecting Kiwi while his magic matured."

Despite being honest about his role in the Underbelly's early days, Uncle Bram only told the abridged story. However, Venus couldn't blame him for withholding that his boss was actually a feathered familiar that enjoyed birdbaths.

"You call him your youngest," Venus panted, the accusation tasting all wrong, "which means you're the mother he spoke about. And if he's your youngest child, where the hell are the others?"

A smile edged Nisha's mouth. "You've met them all already."

Since when?

Before Venus could ask, she tensed as Ilyas entered the kitchen. His cold eyes settled solely on Venus as he passed her.

"He won't hurt you. I forbade him from doing so," Nisha assured as he positioned himself next to her.

A realization sparked through Venus.

"The guards. *They're* your children," she rasped out, straightening shakily at first. "You built Matrika an entire army of familiars?"

"Why wouldn't I?" Nisha tilted her head. "She's the most influential Grand Witcher in the country, which makes her a target for attacks." She paused, snaking her judging gaze down Venus. "And *assassinations*."

"Oh, right. Of course," Venus said, her tone harsh. "So, it has nothing to do with the fact she's *human*?"

Nisha scoffed, massaging a temple. "After all the good she's done for witchers, do you *truly* feel betrayed she is one?"

Nisha's annoyance blew through Venus, fanning at her temper's embers.

"How good are her deeds if they require blood and fear?" Venus seethed, every atom of her body uniting in anger. "*You* built her an army of goons. Not to just protect her but to make her untouchable. To make sure no one ever gets close enough or they'll see through the cracks of this deception."

"Matrika let you closer than she's ever let another in a very long time," Nisha said, her expression guarded. "You didn't see any cracks until *you* created them yourself."

"*We didn't crack anything,*" It said. "*We shattered her lie to pieces.*"

"I ruin folks. She knew that." Venus ignored her pain, faltering forward. "Letting me close was a grave error on *both* your parts."

Ilyas smartly blocked her path but did nothing more.

Still obedient to Nisha's previous command.

"I don't think so. I saw the love potions on your kitchen windowsill this morning." Nisha laid a hand on Ilyas's shoulder and he immediately stepped aside, freeing a course for her to sashay straight to Venus. "We are only one potion away from salvation. Otherwise, this country will spiral into chaos and ruination. Is that what you want for your sister, little Stoneheart? Because no doorway she conjures will save her from that future."

"Don't you dare bring her into this," Venus hissed, her nostrils flaring. "You know I'd do anything for her."

"Yes, I do. You can raise an army and start a war with your calling." Nisha stalked around her, assessing her from all angles. "What makes that any different from what I do for my sister?"

Despite Venus's best efforts, her legs trembled from fatigue. "Because your sister had my mom murdered. *That's* the difference. Matrika met with her the night she died."

To gauge Nisha's guilt, she forged a theory into a fact.

"Ilyas, is this true?" Nisha's stride jerked to a halt, her gaze flickering to her son. His single nod invoked surprise to bloom on her face.

"I guess I'm not the only sister with secrets, then."

Nisha composed her bearings quickly. "Alright, two old friends met, but that *isn't* proof my sister murdered Clarissa. After everything Clarissa sacrificed for us, Matrika would *never* hurt her."

"No, she would never do it herself," Venus said, exhibiting her palm scarred by the Grand Witcher's greed, "but that doesn't mean someone else didn't. It wouldn't be the first time she's let others do her dirty work. Or have you forgotten that she tricked me into killing Julius Keller?"

Nisha pursed into a grim line, her eyes downcast. "I didn't agree with her choice to use Keller as a scapegoat to entice you into a blood oath."

"Enticed?" Venus sucked her teeth. "Let's be for real, Nisha. She *coerced* me into one. If I had the choice, I would've brewed the fucking potions anyway."

"I told her that, too," Nisha admitted, "but she's stubborn and blood oaths are her way to ensure loyalty."

"No, not for loyalty. Because Matrika's human, it's another way to protect herself and her lies," Venus said, anger burning in her belly. "Without magic, blood oaths give her power over witchers and humans. Blood oaths put her above reproach. There's a difference between—"

"Magic and power," Nisha finished, her face unreadable. "Our witcher father reminded us of that often as we grew up, so Matrika didn't feel insecure for being human like our mother. It's also what he told Matrika to convince her to join WASP during her college sophomore year. If she hadn't…"

Venus filled in the blank, "Matrika wouldn't have met Owen."

"Yes, she was WASP's first human ally, but other witchers didn't trust her." Nisha footed across the kitchen, stopping at a ceiling-high arched window. "She worked hard to show them that she believed in the movement, but many were still unconvinced."

"So, that's why she infiltrated the Iron Watch. To prove herself."

Nisha half turned to face her, lobbing a cynical look. "What else has Malik told you?"

"Why do you ask, Nisha?" Venus mocked, cocking her head. "Are you worried he might've told me *too* much?"

"So, you do know about the child, then," Nisha said, her smile bitter.

"That *child* has a name," she asserted, instantly protective, "and their name is Presley, in case you forgot."

"Trust me, little Stoneheart, I haven't," Nisha replied, turning her attention back to the greenery beyond the window.

"Are you afraid to say their name? Do you not care about them because your sister gave them up to pursue politics?"

"Why do you think Matrika and I have done the things we've done? Everything we do, we do for them to make this world a little easier to live in. As Darius Knox's daughter, *you* should know that politics is a blood sport. Witcher, human, adult, child. Politics doesn't give a fuck whose blood is shed."

"If not for my mom, Presley would've *stayed* dead. She did the thing Elder Glenn wouldn't, even after Matrika and Owen begged and pleaded with him." Goosebumps prickled Venus's skin as a realization washed over her, cold and unyielding. "That's why he was so disposable. You and Matrika got your lick back by forcing him to brew the very same potion for me and sacrifice his life as an ingredient. Tell me I'm wrong, Nisha."

A weighty silence thickened the air. She took it as confirmation, her voice hardening, "My mom did what Elder Glenn wouldn't. And what did she get as thanks? Matrika ordered someone to gun her down."

More silence, then:

"I'll look into the matter," Nisha replied coolly.

Venus began, "But—"

"What do you expect me to do?" Nisha spun around on her heels to face Venus. The suddenness sent Kiwi flying to the top tier of a fruit basket. "Get out the guillotine? She's *my* sister. I'll deal with her myself if what you say is true."

Her anger flared bloodred in Venus's vision.

"What's your definition of *deal with*?" she asked, her voice on the verge of breaking.

"A blood oath."

The offered reparation brought Venus no solace.

"You had your chance," It said, disappointment permeating *Its* tone. Hot shame threatened to cascade down her cheeks, but she held back.

"Don't you dare give her the satisfaction of seeing you cry," It said.

Venus held back her tears and the scream that writhed in her chest.

Nisha calmed, brushing a tress out of her businesslike regard. "We'll give you until Wednesday to brew the last potion, but you have a very difficult choice to make."

"From what I understand, I have no choice." A bitter smile curved her quivering lips.

"Oh, quite the contrary," Nisha replied, approaching. "Because you broke your vow of abnegation to try and murder my sister, there simply isn't enough time for a new one to fortify, which means—"

"No," Venus whispered, every muscle in her body tensing in horror.

"Yes," Nisha countered. "Retire your little old cat with a fealty feast or your sister's never coming home."

CHAPTER
THIRTY

Your familiar's distrust is a gift, not a curse
Listen to it well or be unprepared for the worst

—A witcher proverb

HOURS AGO, DETERMINATION PUSHED VENUS TO FACE MATRIKA Sharma. Now, indignity drove her out. It was a mile from Kalorama's quiet streets to downtown's hustle and bustle. She merged into a river of foot traffic, hugging herself. Each step forward, she fractured, leaving shards of herself on the sidewalk.

A numbness crept over her.

A static plagued her ears.

Saliva pooled in her mouth.

Her heart slowed to a sluggish throb as the world's rhythm slowed to a crawl.

Her body pushed itself to its limit as she searched for a witcher-friendly haven that was dim enough to lick her wounds in peace. She found a café, its silvery bell jingling, wrenching her from a trance. The sound evicted her from the innermost spot she withdrew into.

Venus claimed a corner booth in the far back, a pendant light bathing her in deep amber. Then she felt. Regret, guilt, and shame preyed on her, sharp teeth sinking deep. Tears blurred her vision, teetering on the edge.

The blood-tether kept silent, but that meant nothing. As long as Janus remained in the care of enemies, she'd never be safe.

Venus turned on her cell. Its battery was at 4 percent. She chewed her bottom lip until teeth broke plump flesh, wrestling with who to call. Automatically, she eliminated Uncle Bram. He had left a mountain of missed calls, voicemails, and text messages. A telltale sign he found out *something* had happened.

With little battery juice left, there was no point in listening to his voicemails or reading his text messages. It was a sure bet that he was at the house right now, waiting for her ass.

Instead, Venus rang up Tyrell, keeping the call brief but urgent.

Thirty minutes later, his car rolled up to the curb. His irritation slithered underneath her skin as she got in. The source of his grumpiness sat on the dashboard.

Leap greeted her with a bark.

"Before you even ask," Tyrell began, his tone gruff, "after what happened at Rock Creek, Moms says I have to trust Leap for swamping to work. We gotta spend *quality time* together." With a souring face, he put air quotations around the words *quality time*.

It had been a week since the Rock Creek incident. Venus texted him daily to check up on him, but all he ever sent was an *I'm aight* text or a thumbs-up emoji. Now, with him in the flesh, she took stock of him.

His rich brown skin held a dullness. Dark circles hung underneath his hardened eyes like ornaments. Deep hollows disrupted his babyface's landscape, once ruled by dimpled smiles. That made him eligible to join the We've Seen Better Days Club, of which Venus served as president.

He peeped at her, too. They both looked like life had chewed them up and spat them out like bubblegum wads.

"You mind filling me the fuck in or naw?" Tyrell merged into traffic with a wheel jerk, cutting off another car. It earned him a prolonged aggressive honk. He flipped the bird and slammed his foot to the gas pedal, weaving in between dangerously narrow slices of room.

Venus bulged her eyes and gripped the *oh-shit* bar. Her stomach performed a limber somersault as he jerked around a corner. A morbid sense of impending death prowled on the fringes of her existence, inciting her to confess all that transpired. Her words flowed out of her choppy and unfiltered.

Tyrell hit the brakes as a stoplight impeded his *Fast & Furious* routine. Their bodies jolted forward as the vehicle skidded to a screeching stop.

"You should've called me. You ain't have to go there alone," Tyrell said as he snapped his scrutiny to her, his voice raw and livid. "Shit, Vee!"

A sharp horn slit through the palpable tension, alerting them that the traffic light had turned green. He released a frustrated growl and smacked the steering wheel, driving forward.

Silence clogged the car.

"It's my mess." Venus reclined her seat, staring at the interior roof. "I thought I could handle it myself."

Tyrell heaved a sigh. "Well, now we've got an even bigger mess."

"We?" Venus reiterated, frowning.

"Yes, we."

Worry wormed through her. Ty's struggle to hold shape nearly cost him his life. A mistake that was seven days old, rooting deep like a weed to absorb all his goodness. She had asked too much of him and now thought even less of herself.

Though the health potion mended his body, it didn't heal his hurt. Hurt like that never truly went away. It lingered in the veins. It festered in the marrow. It haunted the mind. So potent it possessed the power to corrupt you inside and out.

Venus knew that best of all.

An objection formed on her tongue. "No, Ty. Because of me, you're in no condition to—"

Tyrell slammed his palm on the wheel. "What are you afraid of, Vee? Do you think asking for help makes you a failure?"

His words struck her hard and she fought the urge to recoil.

"Not you being a hypocrite," she said, her tone tight.

"Yes, I admit I gotta work on me," he said, patting his chest, "but we're not the same. My problems only hurt me. Your problems hurt you and everyone around you."

She lifted an eyebrow, a muscle twitching in her jaw. "Yet you're confused about *why* I don't ask for help."

"You hate asking for help, but you don't like accepting it, either," Tyrell countered. "If folks offer a hand, they know the risks."

Venus couldn't find the words to protest. Too many mixed emotions crowded her chest, swarming her heart. Pressing against her lungs. The painful truth soaked into her skin as she lay there in defeat. Her eyes swam with tears. Her bottom lip trembled.

"I *know* the risks, so you can't talk me out of this, Vee." His tone brokered no argument. "You and Janus have saved my ass more times than I can count. Being afraid of myself is a curse I don't wanna live with anymore. Moms says I need time to heal, but I'll start the clock later."

Bram's ride was parked outside the house, just as Venus expected. However, she didn't expect a pickup loaded with potted plants to be there, too.

Tyrell circled the block, killing the engine a street over. To loosen his nerves, he careened his neck left then right, shutting his eyes. A palpable hesitation ebbed from him as he breathed into his cupped hands.

"You don't have to do this, Ty," Venus assured, resting a hand on his shoulder. "It might not even work."

"Naw, it's happening." His tone firmed with determination. When

Tyrell uttered Leap's name, the brown tree frog vaulted from the dashboard and into his opened palm. He and the familiar stared at each other. "Get out, Vee."

Once out, she propped her back against his whip, soaking in violent tremors as a metamorphosis transpired within the cocoon of metal. A symphony of misery, chaos, and the audible snap of bones rushed into her ears. His screams of agony struck her like a sledgehammer, but the awful, abrupt silence unnerved her most of all.

As her sister exited the car, her heart skipped a beat.

A bucket of ice-cold reason doused her head, reminding her it was all a lie. For a moment, she thought the only thing separating her from Janus was a car.

Tyrell rolled his shoulders and flexed his fingers, testing out his new shape.

Her sister's shape.

"You good?" Venus asked, worry etching her face.

Out came her sister's voice: "I'll live."

As they journeyed toward the house, she coached him.

"If Bram asks, *It* had a temper tantrum and you portaled me somewhere until I could get *It* under control," she said as they walked up the driveway. "OK?"

"*I beg your pardon?*" *It* huffed, offended.

Tyrell nodded. "I gotchu."

Patches slunk out of the bushes and nuzzled his head against her shin, purrs seeping into her jeans. He pawed her leg. A plea to be picked up. Her eyes narrowed at him, but she squatted to scoop him up.

"Did you snitch?" she asked.

Patches wagged his head.

Which meant someone else tipped off Uncle Bram.

She turned halfway to gauge Tyrell's readiness.

His nod made her sister's ombre curls bounce. With a doorknob twist, Venus entered first, limping inside.

The home was wrecked. Overturned furniture laid about like slain victims of a massacre. Shards of vases and framed photos mingled into a sea of glass, crunching underneath her soles. Craters indented the walls.

Two guests waited in the destroyed kitchen: Malik and Levi, his corporeal ride. Patches hissed at the two.

Malik scowled at the familiar's rudeness, then leveled his eyes on their arrival. "Welcome home, girls."

"I wondered whose pickup was outside." Venus's gaze veered from the mirage of a man before her to his willing vessel seated at the lopsided kitchen table, its wooden leg suffering a splintered bend.

A sacred staple desecrated again.

"I'm a botany major at Georgetown." Levi blushed, rubbing his nape. "I work at a plant nursery, too." An awkward chuckle. "And have a bad habit of taking work home."

His words sharpened her recognition into a weapon, plunging deep into her heart. Georgetown was where the WASP movement planted its roots, its greater purpose entangling followers in its vines. And her father was one of its three gardeners.

It made sense that Levi left black-eyed Susans at her father's grave.

Like her, he understood the language of flowers. During her cemetery visit, she found an offering on the barren lump of earth her mother rested underneath. *Sorrow, regret, I'm Sorry*, the flower whispered to her that day, leaving her to wonder who hand delivered the message.

Not once considering the culprits hid in plain sight all along. A purple hyacinth was a fitting choice for a mournful ex-husband, especially if his knowledgeable WASP intern acted on his behalf.

Her eyes sliced to Malik. "Where's Bram?"

"Resting," he answered, his hand motioning in an up-palm swipe to encourage them to take in all the damage. "I reached out to him, asking if he knew Janus's whereabouts. He tried calling you both, but it kept going to voicemail, which didn't improve his mood. You know how he gets."

That explained the holes in the wall. Bram's calling required immense restraint and patience, but the constant fight against his own nature fostered a swelling pressure within him. When a catalyst cracked him open, rage and destructiveness gushed, emptying out until he was hollow.

After every rare episode, his body demanded rest.

Malik eyed her expectantly as if she owed him an explanation. She didn't.

In between breaths, Malik dissipated, emerging out of thin air within inches of her. Though his physical form was at Epione, his phantomlike presence emitted a felt energy, beckoning her goosebumps to rise on her arms.

"Your silence is telling," he said.

"I hope you're getting an earful." Venus hissed in pain as she set Patches down.

He nailed his "daughter" with a look. "It's rare for you to be so quiet. What do you have to say for yourself?"

"Vee lost control of her calling. I portaled her somewhere safe, so she could rein *It* in," Tyrell-Janus said as rehearsed.

Its anger burned in her gut, still cold at being scapegoated.

"If that were true, Matrika's guard wouldn't be watching over my physical form at Epione. Or worse, waiting for the orders to kill me." Malik said to Tyrell, his stern eyes zeroing in on her. "You're free to be your true self again, Ty. There's no point in continuing this lie. I know exactly where my daughter is."

The charade crumbled apart, matching her kitchen's ruins.

Venus pinched the bridge of her nose, exhaling deeply as her fingertips massaged her tear ducts. "So, *you're* the one who told Uncle Bram."

Tyrell-Janus massaged the spot where Leap sat in his throat. His tentative gaze sought her approval.

"Thanks, Ty." She consented with a nod. He nodded back, then left, finding privacy in the hallway bathroom to undergo his undoing.

Levi grimaced at the potent screams, fidgeting in what she realized to be her mother's chair. A territorial itch bothered her, urging her to knock him on his ass. The feeling receded as he stood quickly and excused himself, escaping out the back door to distance himself from Tyrell's shrieks.

With no witnesses, Malik's voice adopted a harsher edge. "What the hell have you done?"

Venus walked away from him and picked up a dented copper cauldron lying among the destruction, cradling it to her chest. After laying it inside the sink, she turned on the faucet and filled the empty crucible. She debated whether or not to entertain his question as the water rose.

The blood-tether's stillness gave reassurance, but fear hummed within her like a very low frequency.

Quiet and dangerous.

She gritted her teeth as she hauled the hefty cauldron to the stove. With every step, water threatened to slosh over the rim.

"Now isn't exactly the time to brew, Venus!" Malik growled.

Anger yanked at her strings, impelling her to drive her fist down. "How else am I supposed to get her back, Malik?"

Pain splintered through her hand, sparking up her arm. She scrunched her eyelids shut and bowed her head, failing to restrain the stinging bitterness within her. A rivulet flowed down her cheek and droplets trickled into the cauldron, her tears becoming an improvised ingredient.

Tyrell's screams stopped. A leaden silence added to the air's density. It filled her lungs, seeped into her pores, and circulated through her bloodstream.

"You must've stepped out of line," he said, "which would also imply you've lost your damn mind."

Her shoulders quivered as a hollow laugh poured out of her.

Venus twisted a knob to bring the stove eye to life. "I didn't lose anything."

"You lost my daughter," he parried.

She flinched at the verbal jab, her rib cage impeding the blow to her distressed heart.

"If something happens to Janus because of your recklessness—"

His threat's onset baited *Its* interest.

The prospect of a confrontation was akin to blood in water.

It nudged Venus to whip around and face him, brandishing provocation. "You'll do what, Malik? What are you gonna do to me? You're about as real as a figment of my imagination. You can't touch me or hurt me."

Pity bracketed his eyes as he tilted his head, staring at her like she was a limping stray he couldn't help. "It must exhaust you turning everything into a war and everyone into an enemy."

Venus smirked, rubbing her tongue's tip on a canine tooth. "Trust me. You're not my enemy. That requires hate. I just don't fuck with you because I don't care about you."

"But you care about Bram. I can only imagine how betrayed he feels by the things you've done," he noted, jerking a thumb over his shoulder.

She followed the digit's trajectory.

Out the arched doorway.

Past the living room.

Down the hallway.

Through the second door on the left.

Behind that door, her uncle slumbered, aware of her mistakes and failures but oblivious to how she intended to fix them.

Venus wore a mask of contemplation, tapping a fingertip on her chin. "And I can only imagine how betrayed Matrika would feel if she found out about the coup you and the Grand Coven have planned for her. Or the peitho potion you want me to brew for her."

An impressed glint flashed in his eyes as he forced himself to appraise her in a new light. "You sound just like Clarissa."

Her regard drifted to the empty chair she nearly threw hands over. Fantasy flickered over reality as Clarissa Stoneheart sipped coffee from her World's Greatest Mom mug.

"I've been hearing that a lot lately," she said as the apparition faded away, soft sorrow infiltrating her smile, "and I'm starting to take it as a compliment."

Silence passed between them.

"I'll brew the peitho potions. Hers and yours."

Malik exhaled, "We both want the same things, Venus."

"Yeah, but for very different reasons." She turned to the cauldron, peering inside at the tiny clingy bubbles.

"Yet we both agree your potions are the only way to stop the Registration Act and Matrika. Otherwise, she'll always use Janus against you. Against us."

Her unease inflated within her chest, reluctant to pop.

Brewing could free her sister from being hostage.

Brewing could save the country from the Registration Act.

Brewing could carve Matrika the Puppeteer into a puppet as a punishment for abandoning her friend.

However, all of this was at the expense of Venus's life, even if it meant dying for something bigger than herself.

Like her father.

She couldn't decide if it was a generational curse, a legacy, or both.

The thought of death didn't frighten her.

Not seeing Janus one last time did.

"Yes," she whispered, her fingers curling tight.

"It's all for the greater good. Levi left a vial of my blood in the fridge," he returned. "I'm sorry it came to this."

She turned halfway to fire off a sardonic *are you really* but found no one to take the hit.

A fatigued Tyrell faltered in, fixing himself a glass of water. After he guzzled it down, he used his shirt to wipe away the stray droplets dribbling down his chin. Confusion puckered his weary face, gears churning.

Venus and a cauldron were a disastrous pair.

"What the fuck are you doing?" he barked as he marched over, killing the heat source. "Naw, you ain't dyin' today. Not if I have anything to do with it."

"So, me dying tomorrow is cool with you then?" she teased bitterly, reaching for the stove's temperature dial.

He seized her wrist to bar her. "You're not thinking straight, Vee. You broke your vow of abnegation today. You've gotta renew it!"

"I only have a few days to brew more two trinary-note potions, Tyrell."

One for a senator and one for Malik.

Telling him would only lead to him trying to talk her out of it.

She continued, "If I renew my vow, there's not enough time to fortify it. I'm dead either way. So, why bother postponing the inevitable? You know what's at stake if I don't do this."

"There's gotta be another way to get Janus back," Tyrell said. "You need Presley."

Her body went rigid. "No, absolutely fucking not."

He towed her to the bathroom and braced her shoulders to steer her. "Look at yourself."

The girl in the mirror observed her with jaded eyes. Although the restoration tea dripped some vigor back into her, she looked like death warmed over.

"You aren't in any condition to brew tonight, Vee," Tyrell said. "You need rest. Leap's gonna be there with Patches when the time comes for you to make those potions."

When his name was mentioned, Leap barked from somewhere in the house.

As the word *rest* hit her eardrums, a chemical reaction occurred, limbs growing heavy and her head light. Her determination's integrity failed to keep the curse of exhaustion at bay. His permission made her knees buckle under the weight of the world. He caught her, scooping her up.

He deposited her on her pillowy bed of pastels and plushies.

As he turned to leave, she captured his hand.

"Stay," she said, shimmying over, "like old times."

A half smile ruled his lips at the request, and he collapsed onto the empty spot she carved out for him. She huddled closer to him and coiled her arm around his, propping her cheek against his shoulder blade.

Together, they fit like a puzzle of incomplete nostalgia.

Their missing third piece elsewhere, out of reach.

CHAPTER
THIRTY-ONE

Power cuts you in ways magic could never. That's how politicians, cops, and the rich have ruled over us for so long, making
us bleed dry.

—Megan Villanueva, a witcher activist

VENUS'S NIGHTMARE WAS A MANGLED MEMORY. A SWIGGER FIRED
a gun. The bullet's impact pushed her backward into her sister's arms.
Ruby red soaked through her hoodie. Janus's tears rained down on her,
each fallen droplet weaving into a flood that engulfed them both. She
cradled her firmly, kicking toward the surface.

A trail of Venus's blood dyed the waters as they rose, but a hand curled
around her ankle, impeding their ascent. She peered down to see Presley
as the heavy burden. She gasped to dispel the distress in her throat, unwit-
tingly inhaling water. Screams erupted into a torrent of bubbles as they all
sank deeper into the unknown.

Venus jerked upright, wide-eyed and alert.

Her heart an untamed thing in her rib cage.

Pain wrapped its arm around her as punishment for daring to move.

Venus combed her digits through her tresses damp from sweat,
smoothing a palm down her slick nape. Another fever licked her insides
like flames. She flung aside her half of the covers to combat it.

Tyrell slept soundly through it all, hugging a penguin plushie.

Venus reclined and gazed up at the ceiling-sky of glow-in-the-dark stars, trying to decipher the meaning of her dream like an unfamiliar constellation. She thought of Janus as her lifesaver, but Presley was her anchor, dragging her down to the crushing dark.

Punishing her for what she'd done.

For what she tried to do.

Her cousin's words swam in her mind: *"You need Presley."*

Venus rolled onto her side to stare at her cell on the nightstand. She chewed her bottom lip, debating. In the car, Tyrell had been right. She *did* hate asking for help. Since childhood, her mom had programmed stalwart independence into her, but over time, independence became an excuse to push others away. Until this summer, she hadn't asked for help or accepted it from others for quite some time.

"You need Presley."

Yes, she did need Presley.

However, they didn't want anything to do with her. If she were them, she'd feel the same way.

"You need Presley."

Hesitantly, Venus reached out for her cell, but the rotary phone's urgent ringing made her stiffen. The metallic sound forewarned her of another's desire to use her. She smashed a pillow against her head to snuff out the noise.

Her tensed muscles surrendered to relief as it all fell silent, but the brief era of peace ended abruptly as the phone stirred awake again, calling out to her. The fluff muffled its neediness until it dripped into her ear canal, echoing insistently.

Annoyance came to a rolling boil in her skull.

She squeezed her shuttered eyelids tighter, flashes of bright dots dancing in the dark. Her nostrils pushed out puffs of air in a rough escalating tempo, stretching her lungs to a state of soreness.

Even after the phone stopped ringing, her rushing blood refused to simmer down as if in anticipation. The quiet baited Venus with a false sense of security, but she was too wary of falling for it. She sprung from the bed and darted to her mom's room. Her footfall slowed as she neared the writing desk. She positioned her palm over the phone's neck, waiting to strike with venom on her tongue.

As it sang out again, she snatched it up.

"We're closed for business indefinitely," she bit out, her grip coiling. "Go fuck yourself."

"Surely, Clarissa taught you some manners."

Her eyes widened at the sound of Prospero's voice.

Kiwi's voice.

Clarissa Stoneheart taught her many things, like seeing this phone as the heart of her hustle and fools who called as a bag secured.

But the Underbelly's king wasn't a fool.

He was a puppet, Nisha's creation.

Venus knew that now.

She smoothed away any wrinkles of malice in her voice. "To what do I owe the pleasure?"

"I come bearing gifts," he said, his tone genial.

Skeptical as hell, she pursed her lips at that. "Are they really your gifts or *your* mommy's?"

"It doesn't matter if we all signed our names on the greeting card."

Seconds later, Janus's voice trembled in her ear. "Venus?"

"Janus?" A mixture of shock and relief poured over her skin as frantic words tripped over her tongue. "Are you okay?"

"I'm fine." Janus's voice cracked the words.

Venus closed her eyes, her chin quivering. "I'm sorry, Jay. I'm gonna get you home. I swear on Mom's grave, I will."

"That's quite touching to hear," Kiwi-Prospero said, wearing a blasé mood like a crown.

Anger made the roots of her teeth pulse. "Why did y'all do this?"

"A little birdie told us Baby Stoneheart's a wanted fugitive."

Venus gripped the phone so tightly that her hand quivered. "Why does this feel like a threat?"

"Well, sometimes threats are reminders," he said in a singsong tone, "and sometimes reminders are threats."

"So, ya'll want to turn her in."

"Oh, no. Not at all." Kiwi-Prospero chuckled. "We'll *gladly* be her guardians in Canada while she attends that school you'd like her to attend. We're willing to uproot the Underbelly and settle down up north. She'll be well taken care of."

Her jaw went slack, fear prying open her heart with a crowbar. Only *one* other person aside from herself knew about that backup plan. Uncle Bram was the little birdie, and the forces that be wanted to rip apart their nest.

A breathless whisper rushed out of her. "You wouldn't."

"We can and we will, but you know exactly what you must do to prevent it."

After the line went dead, Venus slammed the phone back to its hook, crouching to dislodge its cord from the wall. An action equivalent to flipping a door sign from COME IN, WE'RE OPEN to SORRY BITCH, WE'RE CLOSED.

Her lungs emptied out fast and hard, panic thickening in her throat. She needed air.

Fresh air.

Her mind sharpened and homed in on that necessity.

She left her mom's room behind, stumbling in her slippers through the maze of destruction.

Patches lounged on the kitchen counter, lapping at his paw. He leaped down to the tiled floor, shadowing her exit.

She ended up in a lawn chair to think, breathe, exist.

Humidity smothered her.

Crickets played their night symphony.

Her nightmare yanked her back into its waters. A replay unfolded in her mind as Presley grappled against the crushing pressure to drag her down. Her brow wrinkled in thought.

Venus thought at first that the blaze in their eyes was spite, but now she realized she was dead wrong.

It wasn't spite.

It was unalloyed determination.

Presley wanted to breach the surface as much as she and Janus did.

Same goal, different motivations.

The realization forced her to recalculate all the factors, resulting in a master plan. It unfurled like a map, situating all the major players as pawns to be moved at her will.

Like a general in a war room, she shifted them about.

———

Tires screeched to sleep as Venus slammed her foot on the brake. She flung the car door open, hobbling out. Engine still running. Door stretching into the street. As fast as her spent legs could take her, she rounded the corner of the Carter family's house. She tasted her pulse in her throat.

At Presley's window, she rapped her knuckles, desperate.

"Presley," she whispered loudly. "Presley, please open up."

Time stretched on. Or maybe, her mind raced so fast it seemed like time had slowed. As her knuckles went the glass for the hundredth time, the window opened up. She shuddered as Presley's quiet scorn crept up her veins.

They braced against the windowsill, leaning forward. Blank, exhausted eyes stared at her. "What?"

"Last night, Janus overheard everything," she said, her voice frantic and wild. "This morning, she went to Matrika's house and tried to kill her. She was taken hostage. I went there to get her back, but then I tried to kill Matrika, too."

Presley's emotionless mask cracked. "What?"

Moments earlier, the first *what* was one of apathy.

The second one dripped with shock.

So pure it stole her breath away.

"I've fucked everything up. Janus won't be freed until I make the last love potion, but I can't wait that long, Pres. They even threatened to kidnap her and take her to Canada. That's why I'm here. I need your help in getting her back *tonight*."

"I told you not to do it." Presley tried to compose themself, their delivery low and concise. "I told you nothing good would come of this."

Her guilt cut deep as she whispered, "I know."

"What could *I* possibly do?" Presley leaned out their window a little more, cutting her with a glare.

"You wanted to face your mom. This is it. *This* is your chance." Venus placed a hand on theirs, bravely yet afraid, too. "You'll get a chance to ask questions. I get my sister."

They flickered their attention to her hand. She expected them to yank theirs away, but they didn't, giving her a tiny kernel of hope.

"If I remember correctly, I already got my answers last night." They paused. "From you."

She shook her head. "There's more, Pres."

"Maybe I don't want to hear anymore." Disinterest shrouded their face. "Matrika chose the Grand Witcher title over me. That's all I need to know, so I can move the fuck on."

"Today, I learned a secret that'll give you the power to not only take that away," Venus proposed, "but also *ban* her from witcher society."

"They're trying to hold themself together, but something is shredding them apart. I wanna see," It said.

Though a blanket of clouds blotted out the moon, Venus didn't need its pale glow to dissect Presley inch by inch. In the inky dark, her teeth pinned her bottom lip in concentration to use her deviation as a scalpel to slit them open, peeling back flesh and muscle to see the battle raging within them.

It was right.

She sensed Presley's logic and desires clashing for dominance.

Secondhand conflict reached out from the incision to aim for her throat, but she sutured everything back together, severing the connection.

Presley narrowed their eyes. "Tell me."

Presley banged on the entrance door, translating their anger and frustration into a singular force. Venus stood back.

"Open the fuck up," they demanded, refusing to relent.

One of Nisha's daughters answered the door. The tailored suit she wore paired well with the pageboy style her leather-black hair was sculpted into.

"The Grand Witcher is unable to entertain guests tonight," she said coolly, her face a neutral mask.

"Let me in now. I want to see—" Presley paused, then gritted out, "*Matrika.*"

Nisha's daughter bowed her head and moved aside.

Presley peered over their shoulder to Venus, surprise rounding their green eyes. Clearly, they had expected the opposite, but it made perfect sense to her. They were of Sharma blood, which gave them authority over all the familiars loyal to that bloodline.

Presley's hesitant steps carried them into the dark grand foyer.

Venus attempted to follow suit, but her audacity triggered an alarm, drawing troops from the shadows.

Nisha's daughter crinkled a steely gaze into dangerous slits, blocking Venus's path. "You're not welcome here."

A bubble of panic burst in her chest as Presley appraised her worth to them. After all, she gave her ex-best friend the key to both their problems. A tool they could use against her to lock her out. What more did they need of her?

A perfect punishment she wholly deserved.

As the door rushed toward her face, Presley finally said, "She's with me."

The woman halted midway and jerked it back open.

Relief came over her.

"Much appreciated." Venus entered with an uneven stride, brandishing a superficial smile.

A sea of inexpressive eyes flocked to Presley. They shifted uncomfortably at the attention and the weight of expectations that came with it.

"You." Presley pointed at a random guard. "Go tell Matrika her child is here to see her now." They flitted their regard to all the others. "Everyone else, go make yourselves useful elsewhere."

All the guards filed out of the foyer, splitting off in packs.

Once alone, Venus hugged herself, a *what-if* nibbling at the edges of her mind.

"You thought about leaving me behind, didn't you?" she asked, eyeing Presley carefully.

"Not at all."

She looked back at the front door. "Don't lie, Pres. I saw that look in your eyes."

"That *look* in my eyes was me picturing what I'd done if I had been in your shoes earlier today. I wondered if I'd do the same thing."

"Would you?"

Presley's eyes browsed her in a languid sweep. "Right down to the fucking letter."

Ilyas entered the foyer.

Venus frowned. "If you're going to be on the welcome committee, you could at least pretend to be happy."

Presley came behind her, addressing their final obstacle. "She's right. I don't feel very welcome right now. A smile goes a long way."

Unseen strings tugged at Ilyas's down-turned lips, lifting the corners into a forced smile. But hollowness still reflected in his stare.

Presley's blood, his puppeteer.

"Her Grandness has instructed you both to leave the premises."

"Take me to her now."

Ilyas bowed his head. "As you wish."

He led them both through an archway that led into a living room. A pair of glass doors opened to them. Humidity hit their faces as they entered a greenhouse solarium filled with trees and thick greenery.

Venus couldn't help but look up at the bright pink flowering vines that grew along the wooden beams. Mandevillas symbolized *thoughtlessness* and *recklessness*. Two words that perfectly summed up her dealings with the Sharma family tree.

Behind a lavish bar, Kiwi in his Prospero shape played bartender as he rattled a cocktail shaker.

"Following directions isn't your strong suit, Miss Stoneheart." Light amusement danced across his face as he poured his concoction into a martini glass.

"Hustlers don't follow directions. We make our own rules," she said in passing, earning his smile.

He rounded the curved oakwood counter, relinquishing the drink to Matrika, who lounged on a crushed velvet chesterfield the color of sunflower petals. She wore a gold choker that glinted in the chandelier glow.

No necklace of bruises on her neck in sight.

No evidence she nearly lost her life hours prior.

Mending potion, Venus thought, frowning.

A rainbow aura radiated off Matrika's skin, too, which meant she also had gulped down a Healthy Glow.

Draining it in one go, Matrika fished out the speared olive and polished it off measuredly. "Don't look so disappointed, dear."

"Nisha told me to bring your order or come back with a better idea," Venus said, gesturing to Presley. "Well, here's what I came up with. Who doesn't love a family reunion?"

"They shouldn't be here," Matrika sighed tiredly, draping her forearm over her brow.

Presley bared their teeth. "Is that any proper way to greet your child, Mom?"

She lolled her head to drink her child in, wincing as if they were too much to take in all at once. "You look so much like Owen."

The observation chiseled the anger off their face, a pained shock settling there. "Me being a dead man's doppelgänger haunts you too much, does it? Good. It's what you deserve."

"Maybe so, but at least you'll never know the feel of an iron nail bomb again." Matrika handed off her empty glass to a dutiful Prospero. "Everything we've done, we did for you, Presley."

"No, you two did that shit for yourselves," they fired back. "Venus told me the truth. I know my entire life's been a lie *you* architected."

A loud laugh glimmered in Matrika's eyes.

It spurred Venus to lash out. "Let me make this clear," she said. "I'm here for my sister, and I'm not leaving without her."

Matrika's tongue clucked motherly *tsks* as she wagged a finger. "Having a temper tantrum won't get you what you want." She swiveled her gaze between Venus and Presley. "You both want something from me but came here empty-handed. You know nothing in this world comes free."

The rejection jabbed *It*, provoking her magic to rise. *It* seethed within her like a loaded gun, waiting for her to cock the trigger. Her aura mounted in unruliness. A clue she intended to go apeshit, too.

Prospero and Ilyas drew closer, cautious.

Savage energy as black as night arose out of her palm like bellowing steam. "I'm *not* empty-handed."

"I'm all for games, but you've already played that hand." Matrika stood and prowled over. "Do you want to gamble and risk not seeing your sister again?"

Venus went rigid at the thought.

Matrika capitalized on her fear and touched her hand, navigating her fingers to curl inward to extinguish her flex of power. She suffered tremors of rage as she restrained herself. *It* raked claws down her insides and whimpered for a feast of violence, but she ignored *Its* hungry cry and her own bloodthirst.

Insincere pride gleamed in Matrika's eyes as she leaned in, whispering, "Smart girl."

The warm breath of her taunt fanned Venus's face.

Presley seized Matrika's wrist, severing the unwanted connection.

"Enough," they growled, letting Matrika go. "You might know what Venus wants from you, but you don't know what *I* want."

She walked to the chesterfield, trailing a finger along the contours of its crest. "I'm all ears."

"I'm not leaving here without a blood oath," Presley said, their tone confident and unmistakable, "and if I don't get it, major human news outlets will receive a tip that Madame Sharma, the country's most influential Grand Witcher, is an impostor. They'll eat it up because they can't stand you."

A blood oath? Venus's eyes widened with shock as Presley changed the war strategy they had agreed on together.

Matrika shook with mirth. "Is that so? What proof do you have?"

Nudging their plan back on course, Venus said, "Elder Glenn kept a secret ledger of all his orders. Your initials take up quite a few spots for it for Healthy Glow and other potions." She tapped a contemplative finger on her chin, battling a pained wince. "When I first looked through the ledger, I couldn't figure out who GWMS was, but then it clicked for me today. GWMS is *you*. Grand Witcher Matrika Sharma."

"First, you'll be ostracized by witchers," Presley said, showing off two fingers. "Then the WCTF will arrest you for purchasing illegal potions."

Matrika paused her footfall, her voice thick with suspicion. "*Neither* of you has the guts to jeopardize the Senate vote."

"I had a feeling you'd say that." Presley pulled out their cell. After a few thumb clicks, they revealed their screen.

"You took a very poor photo of the Golden Coin. Do you intend to upload it on GrubAdvisor and leave a scathing one-star?" Matrika's question garnered Prospero's textured chuckle.

"No point in leaving a bad review if the DC SWA gets a tip on the whereabouts of the Underbelly, the infamous Black Book, and so much more." Presley shrugged, their demeanor nonchalant as if they hadn't just threatened to set their family's empire on fire. As air faded from her lungs, Venus was left speechless at yet another creative liberty taken.

"*Oh, this is getting good,*" It purred, no longer salty about getting play-time taken away.

A perfect blankness matured on Matrika's face, her stare businesslike and shrewd. "You'd turn against your own blood?"

"We're blood, but we're not family." Presley splayed their hand over their collarbone. "Now, let Janus go and I'll consider postponing going to the media until after the Senate vote."

Venus watched with twisted glee as Presley's abrasiveness rubbed at the woman.

Matrika remained an expressionless statue, her voice tight and controlled. "You're bluffing."

"Am I?" They dialed a number, pressing the speaker button for everyone to hear the rings.

An automated voice answered: *"Thank you for calling the DC Suspicious Witcher Activity Reporting Hotline, a vital asset to the WCTF. To speak to a representative, please hit the pound sign."*

Their thumb hovered over the pound sign. "If I press this button, I won't stop at the Golden Coin. I'll bring them right here, too. Now, give Venus her sister or I'll give *everything* you've worked for over to the WCTF and media. Your choice, *Mom.*"

The last words rolled off Presley's tongue like a spiteful insult.

Venus felt the *tick-tick-tick* of an unannounced countdown in her bones. This threat wasn't like all the others she had heard from them. Presley Carter meant every word they said, which made them the most powerful person in the room.

In the Underbelly.

In DC.

Matrika's nails dug into the chesterfield, her practiced self-control wavering. She drew her eyelids close slowly, her jaw setting firm.

"So be i—"

"Ilyas, go get Baby Stoneheart," Nisha interjected coolly, sauntering in. "Prospero, go get the dagger."

Her sons dispersed at her command.

"Nisha!" Matrika snapped, slamming her palms down. "What are you doing?"

"For years, we've worked to build up the Underbelly and our reputations to do what must be done. We're *so* close to our goal," Nisha argued. "If the child wants a blood oath, I'll give them one."

"I promised Owen I'd protect our child." Matrika's face creased with anger.

"And we promised each other we'd see this through until the end."

The thunder of rapid footsteps filled the air, growing louder and louder.

Venus whipped around as her sister tore into the salon. Bolting toward her, their reunion was a collision of bodies. Cupping Janus's tear-stricken cheeks, her thumbs swiped away thin warm rivers as she frantically searched for bruises, cuts, any hint of harm. The quiet blood-tether guaranteed her sister's safety, but she couldn't help herself.

Tears blurred her sight as she rained kisses on Janus's temple, whispering *shh, shh, it's okay* brokenly. Her chest muffled her sister's sobs. Their embrace was unwavering even as they quivered in each other's arms.

Prospero returned with the dagger, giving it to his mother. Matrika advanced to her sister, but Ilyas coiled his arms around her waist, holding her back.

"Nisha," she ground out. "I'll never forgive you for this!"

"Lies," Nisha scoffed. "We always forgive each other. That's what sisters do."

Once, Venus believed the Grand Witcher was the closest she'd get to being near a god. But within a single day, she now knew Matrika Sharma was merely a human playing dress-up in holy garb.

Venus now understood why her mom and Matrika got along so well.

Without magic, they never let anyone close to protect their power.

Not even their own children.

Not out of trust but because they both knew offspring were a parent's greatest weakness. A weakness anyone could exploit. But that didn't make any of it right.

None of this was right.

"Ilyas, I think it's time for my sister to rest. She's had a very eventful day," Nisha quipped as she slit her palm unflinchingly, nearing Presley.

He hauled Matrika off, unfazed by her kicking and screaming.

Nisha sighed like an exhausted mother.

Venus threw a look at Prospero, imagining Nisha diligently molding a Spirit into a body and endowing breath and magic to forge a familiar—to birth a child. In a way, Matrika was Nisha's creation, too.

Bound by blood and sustained by magic.

Without the Healthy Glow potions, without Prospero, without Ilyas, without the guards, without the protective locket, a human Matrika had nothing.

Presley ended the call, squaring their shoulders as their aunt approached.

Nisha handed the stained dagger over. "I hope my blood oath will suffice."

"It'll do just fine." Presley's gaze sharpened as they sliced their palm.

Two bloody hands embraced. Agony forged the union as their aunt swore herself to them. They both trembled uncontrollably, breaths ragged and sweat gleamed. With ragged breaths, the pair shook.

Nisha fell to her knees as the oath devoured her strength.

"Now that that's out the way." Presley held her hand, crouching down. "I have a list of demands."

Faint amusement crinkled her tired, teary eyes. "I'd be disappointed if you didn't."

"First, you'll dedicate your little banquet to the WASP founders for their sacrifices to the WASP movement. Second, you'll reserve seats for us *and* our guests. Third, no harm will be done to Venus, Janus, or any of their loved ones in retaliation." Presley darted a glance at Venus and Janus, arching an eyebrow. "Anything y'all would like to add?"

Janus snipped, "You can tell that goon in my dad's hospital room his shift is *over*."

All eyes turned to Venus next. Vitriol planted rows of ideas in her mind. All the painful moments leading up to *this* moment watered them. She picked one and chewed on it, gnawing the pulp to get to the bitter, thorny seed.

"I'm pretty attached to *my* little old cat, Nisha." Her eyes slid over to Ilyas as he returned to the greenhouse solarium. "So, you have a difficult choice to make. Either give me *his* fealty to feast on, or no love potion."

A pained expression marred Nisha's face at the demand. Her quiet anguish crept through Venus's veins, appeasing *Its* appetite for suffering. *Its* delighted sigh fluttered up her spine and across her bones like a lukewarm breeze.

Venus smirked, refusing to hide her petty satisfaction.

Presley released Nisha's hand, rising up. "We'll give you some privacy to say your goodbyes. We'll wait in the foyer."

With a heel turn, they stalked away, shooting a *let's-get-the-fuck-outta-here* scowl at Venus.

Her sister huddled closer to her as they both followed right behind.

CHAPTER
THIRTY-TWO

A shared Purification bath is a sign of vulnerability and respect
between witchers.

—Witcherpedia, an online witchery encyclopedia

ILYAS'S LOYALTY LOOKED LIKE A BROWNISH-RED PLUM, PULSED LIKE
a heart, and flickered a glow like an ember. It rolled and swayed inside a
jar as the trio exited the mansion. As Venus held it against her chest, its
warmth seeped through the glass and kissed her skin.

Beyond the sloped front yard, Venus anchored her sights on the
familiar pickup parked behind hers at the curb. Her last sight of it was
just hours ago when it still had potted plants in its cargo bed. As they all
descended the steps, Presley remained at the helm, their body rigid with
aggravation. Once they all made it to the sidewalk, the WASP intern got
out of his truck.

"Venus, Janus, Presley," Levi greeted with a dimpled smile, waving
once, "it's good to see everyone again."

At the mention of their name, Presley stopped dead in their tracks.

Venus glanced between the two. "Y'all know each other?"

A tangle of terror and embarrassment painted Levi's reddening features. Her deviation gobbled up the two emotions as they poured into
Venus.

"Um, uh, I mean," He stammered, groping for words. "I'm sorry. I
get so flustered when I'm in the presence of legacies." His shaky hand

gestured nervously between him and Presley. "No, we don't know each other, but I wouldn't be a good WASP intern if I didn't know all the names and faces of the WASP founders' children."

Venus understood his embarrassment, but terror was an *extremely* negative emotion for a slipup like that.

It sniffled loudly as if catching a whiff of blood. *"Smells like a secret."*

"Right," Presley said, frowning.

Confused, Janus asked, "Levi, what are you doing here?"

"Malik sent me here for you," Levi said, rubbing his nape, "in case you'd rather decompress at a safe house instead of going home." Then he added in a choppy singsong tone, "It's stocked with all your favorite things."

That bastard, Venus thought. Of course, Malik waited for others to rescue his daughter so he could swoop in like a savior and whisk her away. Venus already knew she couldn't compete with her sister's idol.

Not when she was a villain for wanting Matrika for herself.

Still, she glanced sideways in hope. A hope that shriveled in her heart as indecision drew her sister's eyebrows together. Janus caught her bottom lip with her teeth, bouncing her troubled gaze between her untrustworthy big sister and Malik's likable, dorky intern.

Venus wore a mask of calm even though dread ripped her insides to shreds. She held back her own tears, her throat thickening with sobs she refused to let go.

Then Janus made her choice, her eyes misty as she gently edged away from her rescuers, hugging herself tight.

As her sister's sadness swelled, Venus lost herself in the waves, tides dragging her away. Their once-close relationship now just a speck in the distance.

"I can't go back home, Vee," Janus said, tears trickling down her cheeks. "If I do, it'd be like accepting what you've done, and I'm *not* ready for that yet. To be a hundred percent honest, I don't know if I will ever be able to. I appreciate both of y'all for getting me out of there, but I'm going with Levi."

Venus arrowed a teary glower of distrust in Levi's direction. "Do you even know him like that to be heading off with him? Or is Malik's approval enough for you?"

Janus walked to the passenger door he held open for him. "Right now, I know Levi better than I know you, Vee." She spared one final glance over her shoulder before she climbed into the truck.

As Levi waved goodbye, his pity swathed Venus like an itchy wool blanket.

When the pickup drove away, her heart abandoned her. A tightening hurt pressed against her ribs. A flood of emotions rose within her, pressing against her chest. Wanting out, out, *out*.

Presley stepped closer, their voice soft. "Ven—"

Malik emerged from the night air, his projection deepening its non-transparency and color.

"This is for the best, Venus." His mouth turned down in sympathy.

His voice dug its heel on her restraint, snapping it in half. Raw rage poisoned her veins, her eyelids flying wide.

"Fuck you, Malik!" Venus flicked the words off her razored tongue, spittle flying out. As she lunged for him, Presley grabbed her waist before she fell through an apparition and headfirst into concrete.

"You're a *user*!" she screamed, struggling against their hold.

"You don't mean that, Venus."

"Oh, I mean every word," she growled, glaring. "Maybe that's why Mom left your ass."

Nothing satisfied her more than to witness a bolt of anger flash across his face. If only she could actually feel it.

Ignoring her, he addressed Presley coldly, "I think it's in her best interests for you to get her out of her before these humanfolk call the cops."

"Your wish is my command, Your Highness." Their sarcastic reply seeped through gritted teeth.

"That's what I like to hear," Malik said.

Then he faded away.

Presley drove her car back to their house. After the gears shifted to park and the engine quieted, they sat there together in silence, blankly staring at the windshield. Venus couldn't feel anything. Not her emotions. Or Presley's, for that matter.

A telltale sign they had both fallen prey to numbness.

Venus inched her eyes over to them. Their bloodied hand rested in their lap, palm up. She retrieved a pack of alcohol wipes from her glove compartment.

"Gimme your hand," she instructed softly.

Presley obeyed, keeping a steady gaze forward.

As she gently cleaned away the crusted blood, it dawned on her that the fresh cut now laid diagonally over the old one.

The scar she had been curious about since the night of the auroras party.

"I shouldn't have done that," they said, their voice dull. "I wasn't supposed to do that, but I wanted to see how'd Matrika react if I demanded a blood oath. I convinced myself that if she agreed to it, then power's why she left."

Venus's brow creased. "But she refused. What does that tell you?"

"She couldn't swallow her pride." Presley tilted their head back, their body sagging.

"So, you set her up for failure then," she said, stuffing the used wipes into her cup holder for later disposal. "Damned if she did, damned if she didn't."

"Ain't that what she did to me?" Anger flew their eyelids wide, a vein ticking along their temple. Livid green eyes clashed with empathetic amber ones.

"I'm not saying she didn't." Venus closed their fingers into a fist for them. "No matter the outcome, it would've hurt like hell for you. I've been there and done that with my *own* mom, Pres."

A rogue tear rolled down Presley's face and she swiped it away. She cupped their cheek longer than she should've.

As she pulled her hand away, Presley said, "Don't."

So, she didn't.

For a long moment, they both regarded each other. The air thickened and her breath shallowed.

"I don't want you to go home, Venus," they said, unshed tears glimmering. "Not yet."

Venus froze, her pulse quickening. An ache unfurled in her chest from their raw, hoarse words. Their desperation clung to her, its nails digging into her needily.

Silence.

"Alright," she said, her voice almost a whisper. "Just for a little while."

<hr>

Accepting Presley's offer to share a Purification bath was a bad idea, but Venus's body had a mind of its own. She stripped down to her birthday suit, showing her flaws. As she wiggled her toes against the chunky rug, she calculated how she'd fit into a tub that barely fit Presley. In the milky Purification bath, lavender stalks floated, the aroma and wet heat massaging her tension as she stepped in.

Venus settled between their long legs. Immediately, the flowers went black. She extracted a stem and plucked away the black petals. The tiny act of destruction brought her some comfort.

Goosebumps peppered her skin as Presley brushed a finger along her shoulder's curve.

"Our lives are falling apart."

"You mean our *second* lives?"

Ilyas's ripe loyalty jar sat on the bathroom counter. Venus glanced at it. "If the fealty feast is too bland to replenish my well of magic, it's over for me when I step before a cauldron." Her pain was versatile, making her feel heavy and hollow all at once. "I'll never know who killed my mom." A rebellious teardrop broke free. "I'll never be able to make amends with Janus for being a liar."

But the worst part was she'd do it all over again.

For Janus.

Always for Janus.

An acute silence stretched between them. Unable to bear it any longer, Venus stood up, rustling and sloshing the water, not having enough fight to go toe-to-toe with her consequences.

"Don't you dare run away from me," Presley commanded, their tone too calm for her liking.

Venus closed her eyes and rallied all her courage as she turned to face them. She lowered back into the tub, hugging her legs.

Before, she was naked, but now, she was bare, exposed, vulnerable.

No armor, just skin.

"Then what do you want, Presley? I lied to you, too. Do you want me to apologize?" she asked, dreading a reply.

They propped their head against the tiled wall, their smile slight with a hint of sadness. "No, I don't, Venus."

"Then what do you want?" A restlessness infected her limbs, forcing her to coil her arms tighter to anchor herself in the opaque bathwater.

"You already know the answer."

"I warned you about me," Venus whispered.

Presley reached out and crooked a finger, brushing away evidence of a tear. "And yet that didn't stop me from catching feelings, did it?"

"I've given you the perfect reason to hate me." She turned her cheek away to reject the unwarranted tenderness. "Kick me out."

"No, I'll take you as you are, Venus," they said. "If you're a liar, then you're *my* liar. And I'm yours."

Now, they were utterly bare, too.

She looked at them saucer-eyed, taking shallow sips of air. "You've lied to me?"

"Yes, and now we're even."

If you're a liar, then you're my liar.

Those eight words drew her back to them again. She unfurled, her cheek on their chest and her chest against their belly. She stamped her ear over their heart. Presley's fingers combed her hair languidly, their fingernails scraping her sensitive scalp, making her eyelids flutter and her heart pitter-patter.

She didn't deserve this.

But she wanted it. And who was to stop her?

Venus entered the dark house. A *spotless* house. She pinched the bridge of her nose, groaning exhaustedly as the kitchen lights came on.

An overtired Bram ambled in, pointing at the kitchen. "Family meeting. Now."

She followed behind him, fatigue and pain flooding her legs. To buy herself some time, she placed the jar into the fridge, even though she was sure a familiar's fealty didn't need to be kept chilled.

Venus turned to face him. "Everything's my fault."

Bram's eyelids lowered to half-mast. "Why?"

Many reasons stewed in her mind, but she boiled it all down to one.

"I tried to kill Madame Sharma," she breathed out, looking at the empty spot at the table's head. Her mom's spot. "I wanted an eye for an eye."

His words traveled on a rough whisper. "Naw, that can't be the truth."

She tilted her head back against the fridge to stare at the ceiling, hoping gravity would send her tears backward—not onward. "I might be a liar, but I would never lie about this."

"Is this why Jay left?"

Ashamed, she closed her eyes, nodding. "She's with Malik now."

Silence.

Heavy hands draped her shoulders, pulling her closer.

Bram hugged her, his hold on her delicate.

Venus cried, his shirt gathering in her grip.

His fatherly response to her deception baffled her. She deserved his rage and screams, but she suspected his tiredness played a role. She clung to him tighter, nonetheless.

"I warned you this would happen, Pinkie," he sighed, chin atop her crown. "When you hold someone tight to protect them, you might be hurting them. I wouldn't preach it if I hadn't lived it."

Venus peered up at her uncle, spotting a secret of his own in his dark gaze.

An understanding passed between them.

"Who did you hurt?"

"Not who, but how many," he answered.

"How do I get her back?" she asked, uncaring of how pathetic she sounded.

"You can't get her back. Jay has to want to come back on her own terms. All you can do is wait."

Tyrell was dead to the world. Venus found him sprawled across the bed so comfortable in his resting place. She didn't mind his invasion of her side. Sleep evaded her, and lying awake only left her vulnerable to those nocturnal thoughts that made her get lost in the dark of her mind.

Venus sat on her cushioned vanity bench and closed her eyes, breathing deep through her nostrils to quiet the urge to scream. Her throat tightened painfully. She pressed the heels of her palms against her eyelids to seal in the building wetness, but beads escaped.

She cried silently until tears flooded and snot dripped.

A truth harassing her: *Janus'll never forgive you.*

Sniffling, she blindly got a tissue and wiped away any evidence of her woe.

But one wasn't enough.

As she reached for another, her forearm knocked over nail polish bottles and lipstick tubes. She winced at the light commotion, but Tyrell didn't budge. An envelope sat underneath the disorder. Inside, a message penned by her dead father. For weeks, Venus tried to ignore its existence. Or at least, she tried to. A few days ago, she gave in to the urge to pull it from the vanity's drawer but chickened out, throwing it to the side. Tonight, however, it whispered to her something she couldn't ignore: *It's time, baby girl.*

She wasn't ready but realized she'd never be ready for it.

Opening it meant facing Darius Knox.

Opening it meant missing and mourning a man she didn't know.

Her heart couldn't take any more hurt.

Brushing away the obstacles, she retrieved her inheritance.

Ripping open the envelope felt like tearing away a Band-Aid, but reading the letter felt like reopening an old wound that was new to her.

My dear Venus,

A week from now, I'll march and I won't make it back home. My dreams told me so. My choices will rob you of a father. My promise to read you your favorite bedtime story will be a lie to see you smile one last time. You have every right to hate me. I hate myself for the heartbreak ahead of you. I don't know if my death will put a dent in a hard hateful world, but I want it to be a lesson to you. Weaponize your love. Use it to protect you and those in your heart. It makes you brave to some and a monster to others, but not all monsters are monstrous. Be a love monster.

Let love drive you to do what needs to be done.

I love you, baby girl.
Dad

The words blurred as an onset of more tears rushed in, but his instructions glued to the backs of her eyelids, reluctant to be washed away by salt and stings.

Weaponize your love.

Weaponize your love.

Weaponize your love.

She delicately laid the note down on her vanity like a flower on a grave and left everything behind, setting herself on the warpath to oblige her father's final wish.

Doing what needed to be done.

Being the love monster he wanted her to be.

CHAPTER
THIRTY-THREE

This potion's purpose is to brew for a Patron that wishes a Drinker to believe a lie. Caution the Patron that 1) they must tell the Brewer the lie and the truth and 2) it must be a lie already told to the Drinker. Snapdragons symbolize deception and graciousness. Red dahlias represent betrayal, dishonesty, and perseverance. The more substantial a lie is, the more snapdragons and red dahlias the Brewer must use.

—*In Bad Taste: Deceptive Love Potions*
Excerpt of Not Gonna Lie recipe

JULY 23, 2023

VENUS COUGHED UP BLOOD INTO THE BATHROOM SINK, HER REAFfirmed vow of abnegation not agreeing with her. She had broken and mended the promise so many times its peculiar angles brayed her insides. Patches sat on the counter, watching. His worry and fear swam in her veins. An uneasy 151-year-old familiar as a brewing companion inspired very little confidence in Venus. She had never felt his concern before, so if she lived to see another day, she hoped never to feel it again.

She hacked another cough, blood dribbling down her chin. She sipped on cool water as it streamed out the faucet and swished it around, spitting out pink-tinged fluid.

"Chill out, Patches," she said raspingly. "It'll be fine. Let's go."

However, Patches didn't budge.

A disobedient familiar was an oxymoron, but his need to protect her might've overridden his pledge to be obedient.

After all, these could be her last moments.

Venus sighed, "I need you, Patches."

After a long moment, he nodded.

He followed Venus as she limped to Elder Glenn's kitchen. Leap waited by the boiling cauldron, his magic stirring it with a spoon. She approached the half-complete peitho. Venus half expected the old man to reprimand her for reclaiming his kitchen as a laboratory, until she remembered he was dead.

Guilt soured in her stomach, worsening her nausea.

Venus unscrewed the lid from the jar with Ilyas's loyalty. Even days later, it was still pulsing and aglow. She wondered if it was something you savored bite by bite or devoured. It had no particular scent, and she had no idea what it tasted like. It could've been poisonous for all she knew, given Ilyas's dislike for her.

But there was only one way to find out.

She took a bite, chewing on the pulp. His loyalty tasted like tart cherries, lemons, a drizzle of honey, and a comforting warmth. A warmth that slithered across her tongue and down her throat, seeping itself into her jagged, pathetic vow of abnegation, rehabilitating and nursing her bone-dry well of magic. It didn't squash her stalwart brewbug but gave her magic strength.

Venus ate and ate until there was nothing left.

Her limbs tingly, her head humming.

"Much, much, much better," It sighed, pleased.

Patches sat on her shoulder, still apprehensive.

Venus drained Senator Radliff's blood into the frothing brew.

Extracting the next vial, rage circulated through her at the scribed name.

Matrika Sharma.

Her hand trembled as she craved to clutch it until glass cracked and the blood of her mother's killer coated her fingers. Every droplet poured was retribution denied.

Obey Matrika's plan to save our nation.
Her words should be your salvation.
Or this country will fall into ruination.

Her enemy's notion fidgeted in her cupped palms, alive and antsy. She wanted to choke it to death and watch its tinged vapors ooze between her knuckle creases, but a reminder rang within her:

Weaponize your love.

Reluctantly, Venus dropped it in. Next came the sliver of anima. She had whittled away at Elder Glenn's anima so much, she worried how much of it was left.

She pricked her thumb and her deviation tensed up in apprehension.

"You think this will work?" It asked.

She glanced at the two familiars on her shoulders as magic radiated from them.

"There's only one way to find out," Venus said, adding her blood to the cauldron. As the degree of recoil began, a dribbling monstrosity surged from the pot, piercing the veil of periwinkle smoke to ambush her. Something fiery and forceful knocked her back, sending Venus flying until she hit a wall.

Patches and Leap hurtled toward it, colliding with her creation.

Her body sank to the tiled floor, clothes singed. Her head dizzy and throbbing from impact. She blinked, struggling to breathe in the smoky air.

The potion thrashed and twisted against their attacks.

With his radiant teeth and claws, Patches waged a fierce battle. Leap lashed his freakishly long tongue, whipping in a blur. Every strike and slash whittled away at the potion's endurance.

Patches parried the final slash of his radiant claws, dismembering the potion. Glops of blue fell back into its crucible.

Venus struggled to her feet, standing with a sway.

Adrenaline pushed through her.

One more potion to go.

JULY 24, 2023

Venus felt all kinds of wrong for sleeping in a dead man's bed, but fatigue pinned her down. She dreamed of fathomless portals to other worlds, darting from one to another in search of her elusive sister. She swam to the ocean's midnight depths, hopped across rivers of molten lava, and drifted helplessly into the universe's infinity.

Forever a failure.

Venus jerked awake, an alert bundle of jittery nerves.

Her eyes flitted around the room, still searching.

She drifted asleep throughout the morning, rousing laboriously in the early afternoon to stagger to the bathroom. Burst vessels in her left eye forced her amber iris to lurk in a pool of red. She took a shower to prepare for delivery, hoping the scorching water could forge her into something stronger than she was after brewing two trinary-note potions back-to-back.

Venus stopped at Epione's first, dropping off the first bottle at Malik's room. His projection didn't pay her visit, but she didn't expect him to after she cussed him out. Someone had left him a bouquet of fresh yellow snapdragons and red dahlias on his hospital nightstand, so she hid the bottle there.

Then she drove to the Grand Witcher's mansion, carting weapons of mass destruction in a salmon-pink backpack. Dark shades painted the sunny day dreary.

A guard answered her persistent knocks. "You're not permitted to enter."

"Fine by me." Venus shoved the book bag into his chest, potion bottles clinking.

"I'll permit it." A familiar voice asserted.

She weathered her surprise.

Taking a step aside, the guard allowed her to see Nisha, dressed in white attire fitting for a mother in mourning. Her sorrow submerged Venus's heart in a numbing, icy bath.

"Come on in, little Stoneheart," Nisha insisted, her bare face blotchy.

Venus narrowed her eyes, refusing to budge from the doorstep.

"I told you I'd look into the matter about your mother," she asked, a soft smirk forming over her lips. "Don't you want to hear my findings?"

Against Venus's better judgment, she allowed curiosity to beckon her in, remaining close to her only exit. She glared at the scattered army of guards lurking close by.

"You needn't worry. Presley made it quite clear no harm was to come to you," Nisha assured, coming near. "But if you prefer privacy, I'll respect that." She swiveled an even-toned directive over her shoulder. "Leave us, children."

The guards cleared out.

"So, let me guess." Venus lowered her eyelids midway in disinterest. "You've completed your investigation, and you've found Matrika to be innocent."

Nisha nodded twice. "On the night of Clarissa's murder, she did see Matrika. She wanted one of Prospero's coins for *you*."

Venus's gaze dropped to the floor.

"So, you found it, then." Nisha raised a brow.

She scowled. "Yes, I did. In a letter that told me to run away from folks like you and Matrika."

"*Like* us, but *not* us," Nisha said, wagging a finger. "Why would Clarissa ask for something from someone she warned you about?"

Silence.

Venus's brain mulled over that question until it tired itself out, which didn't take long. For a moment, her eyes grew distant with memories of that night.

"You're right. She wouldn't," she said softly, her mouth sinking into a deep crease of a frown. "Did Matrika call her after she left?"

A dark tendril of hair fell out of Nisha's chignon bun as she shook her head. She hummed a deep two-note tune that meant *no*, then said, "She didn't."

"Did you ask her?" Venus inquired, skeptical.

"If you're not convinced," Nisha said, "*you* can look into it yourself. If you're curious about the call Clarissa received, perhaps her call log will satisfy that curiosity?"

Venus widened her eyes.

A vision flashed across Venus's mind of her mom's phone, tucked away in a cardboard evidence box she hadn't touched since she had brought it home from the city morgue.

She needed to go home.

Now.

⸻

The first thing Venus had to do before charging Clarissa Stoneheart's phone was to clean the blood off it. *Somehow*, it felt like she was washing her mom's dead body all over again. A lump of grief formed deep in her throat, swelling. She swallowed hard, but it wouldn't move.

After the device's battery icon hit 5 percent, she turned it on. She waited for the lock screen and typed in her dad's birth year. 1980. When the home screen popped up, anxiety maddened her insides. A hesitant thumb clicked the phone icon. In the call log, an unknown number occupied the top two spots.

Both received on the night of her murder. The last received call was only a few minutes before her mother's death. It was only a minute-long conversation.

Did the caller warn her mom twice, but she refused to heed them?

"Do it," It urged. *"Call."*

As if on autopilot, her thumb made all the necessary clicks for her to make the call. Her pulse skyrocketed as she brought the phone to her ear.

It rang and rang and rang.

But on the last one, someone picked up.

"Hello?"

She recognized that voice, choking on her breath.

Silence.

"Venus," Miss Florence said. "I know it's you, chile."

Venus ended the call quickly.

***

"I've been waiting for you." The old rocker Miss Florence sat in creaked with every rock. Venus halted on the cracked concrete path at the old woman's words. Her grimace of uncertainty turned feral, her every last nerve pulsating with fury. She pounded up the porch steps, a vein along her temple ticking to a harsh beat.

Anger poisoned her voice. "Why did you call my mom twice the night she was murdered?"

Miss Florence nodded approvingly at the question. "To warn her."

"So, you *do* know who killed her," Venus said, quivering. "You've known this whole fucking time."

"That fateful day, Rissa came to me, desperate to have her premonition penned," Miss Florence admitted. "When I got to the second line, she told me to stop. She said there was no need to finish it because she already knew the answer."

"So, that's why you crossed it out in the journal." Though Venus stiffened, her thoughts still raced. "But why call her? You can't stop the inevitable."

"No, not all premonitions are steadfast. Sometimes, they can split at the ends, moving in different directions." Miss Florence's expression grew into one of regret. "I tried to warn Rissa twice to nudge her on the opposite path, but it didn't work because she didn't want it to because taking the other path meant losing you."

Venus sidestepped that painful truth, repeating Nisha's wisdom she'd clung to for weeks to stay afloat: "Fate is beyond our control." She threw her hands up, irritated. "Her death was decided long, long, long before she was born."

A long creak filled the air as Miss Florence rocked way back in her seat. "If fate is beyond our control, *why* don't The Sisters know what to do with you?"

For a moment, Venus froze, then spat out, "I don't know and don't care." A demand slung out her mouth, "Now, tell me who ki—"

"All callings have downsides and limitations," Florence interrupted, holding a palm for Venus to hold back her tongue. "That's why I must write my visions in riddles. Saying it plainly will upset The Sisters. They give me my premonitions. If I please Them, I can see each premonition's plot twists and split ends clearly. They probably ain't too happy with me right now because I've already said too much."

Venus seethed, her body shaking. "Oh, fuck The Sisters!" She barreled across the porch and seized Miss Florence's shoulders, jolting them hard. "Tell me now, dammit!"

"I'm sorry, Venus, but I can't." Miss Florence's mouth sunk into a frown, her voice a deep shade of pity. A hue that colored right over Venus's anger, staining her with sheer devastation.

"Please," she whimpered, her voice on the verge of breaking. Although she fought back her tears, she could only hold them back for so long. Miss Florence softened at the plea but held firm to her decision. Venus's knees buckled under the weight of unbearable silence. She fell to the porch floor.

Karma sat heavy on her head like a crown. This was punishment for all she'd done. Punishment for all the secrets she held and lies she wielded.

Her fists gripped Miss Florence's floral dress, and she buried her face in the old woman's lap. Between sobs, she rasped and gasped, her shoulders trembling.

"I said I can't give a forewarning plainly, but that doesn't mean I won't tell you the rest of that riddle," Miss Florence said, stroking Venus's hair tenderly. "I've held on to it since Rissa died, waiting to tell *you*."

She lifted her head slowly, her voice coarse and broken. "What?"

"Listen carefully, chile." Miss Florence grasped Venus's chin, tilting it up slightly. "For what your seed tilled has levied a cost. If led down a garden path, do not get lost."

Venus's tear-stricken face crinkled in confusion, the riddle turning her tired mind to mush. "I don't understand."

"In time, you will."

CHAPTER
THIRTY-FOUR

Based on the evidence found at the crime scene and the toxicology report, we can confidently conclude the victim overdosed from being poisoned by two love potions. We've identified Baldwin Tillery as one of the culprits. However, the other is unknown.

—Ifrah Yousuf, chief of the Witcher Crime Task Force
Audio excerpt from press debriefing

JULY 26, 2023

VENUS DESERVED AT LEAST ONE HUNDRED SEATS AT THE GALA, BUT she settled for two. Tonight, Uncle Bram was her date, wearing the black suit he had worn to his sister's funeral. As for her, she chose a flowy pink strawberry dress her mom had given to her as a sixteenth-birthday gift. Her rose gold septum nose ring lined with green gems.

No wigs to hide her pink hair.

No shades to hide her bloodshot eyes or dark circles.

Together, they went as themselves, abandoning the masks and costumes they wore for each other.

As her uncle escorted her along the marina's main path, she wasn't fooled by his expression of cool neutrality. His concern and anxiousness came off his burly body in palpable waves that licked at Venus's skin.

He gave her a sidelong glance. "Jay texted me last night. She said she wasn't coming with Malik tonight because being around human politicians—"

"Gives her the hives," she finished, her tone dull. She fully expected her sister would come up with an excuse to not come, but she was too tired to flinch at the sting.

"Tonight's your night, Pinkie," he said. "We'll worry about everything else tomorrow. Unless you want to turn back. Nobody will fault you."

Venus shook her head, stubborn. "No, I want to see this."

Even though all her hard work made whatever she drank or ate taste like blood, she was determined to enjoy herself at this banquet.

They found Levi standing in front of an empty marina slip.

He turned halfway and pulled a hand from his crimson dapper suit to issue a wave. "Good evening."

"Why are *you* here?" Uncle Bram arched an eyebrow.

Levi smiled, dimples tinting his cheeks. "Since Janus opted not to come, Malik invited me instead as his plus-one as a token of thanks for all the work I've done for WASP this summer."

Venus rolled her eyes. "How kind of him."

"Agreed," Levi concurred, nodding enthusiastically. "It's one of the kindest things anyone has ever done for me." He pulled out a modified heart-shaped poker chip from his pocket. It'd been included in the gala invitation's envelope. "But how the heck will this thing get me on the yacht? It didn't come with instructions."

She plucked her own from her chained clutch, rubbing a thumb across an ancient-tongued phrase impressed in gold around the rim. A glass lens at its very core.

Calypso.

"Actually, it *did* come with instructions," Venus said. "Calypso is derived from the Greek word *kalypto*, which means to hide or deceive."

"You've lost me." Levi rubbed his neck, feigning embarrassment.

She cocked her head at the act, wondering if Malik warned him about her—about her calling. She wondered if Levi knew she felt almost every little negative emotion of those near her. Maybe, not. Because if he did, he wouldn't even have bothered to pretend to be something he's not.

Uncle Bram sucked his teeth. "Boy, just do what we do."

Venus brought it to her uncle's left eye like a monocle.

Levi followed suit hesitantly. As magic took hold of his eyes, he squinted and reeled his back, blinking wildly.

Then she peered through the lens herself, a sharp burn infecting her sight, too.

Blurry. Clear. Blurry. Clear.

The once-empty slip now had a tender bobbling gently within it. Uncle Bram climbed into the small boat first. Levi went next, offering his hand out to Venus.

Begrudgingly, she took it.

Once seated, the tender roared as it came to life, piloting out of the slip and toward the Washington Channel's dark lapping waters. Venus pressed a hand against her belly, bearing through the choppiness. At the channel's mouth awaited an obnoxiously glorious megayacht burning brightly against the night. The tender slowed to a halt by the stern's stairs ascending onto the main deck.

Two guards blocked the top of the stairs. For a single moment, she considered the possibility that they'd be turned away until she remembered Presley's demands protected by a blood oath.

The blond guard bowed his head. "Welcome, Miss Stoneheart and company. Thank you for your attendance."

The brunet guard matched his actions, gesturing for them to step onto the main deck.

They made their way to the capacious main salon decorated with blown-up photos of WASP founders and early beginnings. Her heart turned over at seeing her dad and his good deeds.

Weaponize your love.

Lit candelabras and lush flower arrangements of red tulips and pink begonias ran down the middle of the rectangular dining table. *Danger* said one flower. *Caution* said the other.

A fitting choice as the chattering four targeted senators stood in a group, oblivious to the honeyed trap they willingly walked into.

All except Senator Mounsey. He observed from his seat at the table, his demeanor rightfully cautious. His wariness dripped its way down Venus's spine like hot wax.

The night of his party, Matrika said she had other plans for the senator. Chelsea even said he'd be at tonight's gala, but Venus still didn't understand why, especially since he couldn't be poisoned like the others.

His attention met hers, and he tilted his head curiously. Either to place her with a name or to ponder how out of place she and her uncle were.

As Senator Hoage went to drink his wine, he paused midway at their arrival.

He widened his eyes, breaking away from the conversation. "Leviticus?"

"Uncle Ed," Levi acknowledged, cool disdain darkening his face.

Venus's body tensed in shock, breathing out, "What?"

"What a good surprise seeing you here," Hoage said, clapping his nephew's back.

Levi's gaze sharpened. "Is it?"

"Of course," Hoage sighed, admiring Levi's face. "Looking at you is like looking into the eyes of Hellie herself. I miss that old bat dearly." He lifted his half-empty wineglass in remembrance, then drained it in one gulp. "Now, why in the hell are you here?"

He clenched his jaw at his uncle's question.

Venus could taste the bad blood Levi had for his uncle, a metallic flavor scraping over her tongue.

Uncle Bram cleared his throat to get her attention, nudging his chin toward the banquet table. "Maybe we should head to our seats."

"I'll be there in a minute." Her voice was calm, but an undercurrent of strain flowed through her words. "I just need some air."

Venus didn't give him a chance to reply, retreating outside. She walked quickly to the aft deck and gripped the railing, bowing her head. The lukewarm wind rolling off the channel hugged her. She gulped at the fresh air like an antidote to soothe a creeping sense of uncertainty inside her.

Footsteps approached.

Levi's concerned voice followed. "Venus? Are you okay?"

Another emotion of his she couldn't feel.

Another little act.

She turned to face him. "So, you're a Tillery."

"A disowned Tillery," he corrected, coming near slowly. "My mom unknowingly married a witcher a few months before the Great Discovery. When the truth came out about what he was, Grandmother Hellie gave my mom a choice: him or the family. Mom's choice was the wrong one."

Venus frowned. "Why was it the wrong one?"

A humorless laugh shook his shoulders. "Because Dad didn't marry her for love. He wanted her for the Tillery fortune. He abandoned her while she was pregnant with me, and Grandmother Hellie wouldn't take her back, either, not wanting the bloodline to be tainted with witcher blood."

"You were born human, though," she said.

Levi crossed his arms on the railing beside her, gazing out over the channel to DC's lit-up skyline. "By then, my aunts realized their inheritances would be much bigger if they didn't have to split it five ways. They conspired to make sure Mom stayed disowned."

Silence.

"Growing up, we didn't have much," he said, a half smile surfacing on his lips. His wounded sadness slid under her skin like a needle, bleeding a wince from her. "Mom saved every penny she could. Then she got sick and those pennies she slaved over weren't enough to help with her treatments."

Levi straightened up his posture, shifting his empty gaze over to her. His voice held a strange note that raised her tiny hairs on end. "So, I went to the Golden Coin, I paid the fee to look into the Black Book and found the Love Witcher."

Dread and shock coiled around Venus's lungs, squeezing out a shaky breath. She staggered back as the truth hit her hard. Her heels caught on her dress's hem, and she fell on the deck's polished wood floor.

"Between Prospero's fee and paying for a storge potion, it drained every last cent we had. I posed as a waiter at one of Grandmother Hellie's socialite luncheons and poisoned her tea." Levi advanced toward her as she crawled backward to get away from him.

His unadulterated hatred swarmed around her, *sting, sting, stinging* her mercilessly.

Her back hit the aft deck's furniture.

Levi continued on, unperturbed. "Then suddenly, I finally knew what a grandmother's love felt like. She welcomed us back into the family. I convinced her to pay for Mom's treatments, too, and she did it. Everything was going according to plan until," he paused, a flush of hot anger washing over his eyes as he crouched to Venus's level, "you and Baldwin fucked it all up."

He snatched her chin, forcing it upward. "You couldn't have waited until my love potion wore off before you brewed one for Baldwin's thieving ass?"

"I didn't know. If I had, I would've told him n—"

"I don't give a fuck what you would've done," Levi interrupted, his tone menacing. "My mom took the fall for my love potion. The family pitied her, chose not to turn her in to the cops, and played dumb. They thought her dying poor was punishment enough."

Venus hissed as his grip on her chin tightened, his nails digging into her skin. After brewing those last two potions, she wasn't strong enough to fight back.

Still, her deviation seethed, *"Let me out! Let me out!"*

"They also thought Baldwin fled the country, but I know the truth because I tailed him all the way to the nature reserve because I wanted to end him myself. He drove in and he never came back out, but I saw you and Presley leave."

"What do you want, Levi?" Venus bit off each word, spitting them at his face.

His mouth curled slowly into a smile. "I want you to sit at that banquet table and watch what happens next."

"Or else what?" She grimaced in disgust. "You'll turn us in to the cops? Not a smart move considering the culprit responsible for the first love potion is still wanted in the case."

"Or else you'll be the reason Presley Carter dies," he said.

Venus cut him with a glare. "If your cousin was no match for Presley, what makes you think you'll be?"

"Because they've sworn a blood oath to me. That's why. You thought they came back to DC because they were homesick?" He pouted mockingly at the word homesick, batting his lashes. "I'm the only person on this whole fucking planet that knows where my cousin is and who put him there. That's enough incentive to agree to a blood oath."

The old scar on Presley's palm.

She felt the blood drain from her face. "What? Why?"

"Because Malik loves to talk, and, as his intern, I learned quickly of

Presley's value to you and others." Levi bopped her nose with his finger. "Your greed took my mom away. Your greed set my whole life on fire. Now, you're going to go back inside and watch all your hard work go up in flames."

Venus yanked her chin from his hold. "Does Malik know his human ally intern is an awful human being?"

"Are you sure you want to know the answer?" he asked, arching an eyebrow. "There's no going back once you know." He tilted his head, roving his regard along her body. "Or perhaps you already know and just want confirmation."

Loathing seeped from her pores. "Just tell me, dammit."

Standing up, Levi rocked back on his heels, considering his reply. "He didn't until Clarissa told him. The last time I saw her was when she delivered the love potion to me three years ago. When we crossed paths at Epione this summer, she knew I was up to no good."

Venus's heart halted midbeat, ice sliding around it. A cold dread splintered through her body. Miss Florence's voice coated every corner of her troubled mind:

For what your seed tilled has levied a cost.

If led down a garden path, do not get lost.

She brought a trembling hand to her mouth. Her lungs held her breath hostage. She hated riddles, but the answer stared down at her, towering over her, smug and triumphant.

Your seed. Clarissa's dumbass daughter, Venus.

Tilled. Tillery.

Levied. Levi.

A cost. His revenge.

A garden path. Deceive you, beguile you, betray you.

"I told you, Venus," Levi said, his look one of pity. "There's no going back once you know."

Suddenly, Venus felt too tight in her own skin. As if there was only enough room for the truth or her sheer anguish.

She lifted her teary, hateful eyes up to him. "You killed my mother?"

"Only because she wanted to protect you from me by sending you away," Levi said, "and I couldn't have that. If it's any consolation, I felt awful afterward. Nor did I like coercing a comatose man into a blood oath after his projection watched me gun down his ex-wife."

"I'm going to kill you, Levi." Her rage tangled around a whisper. "I swear on Clarissa Stoneheart's grave, I'll fucking kill you."

"I'd like to see you try." Levi backed away, wagging a finger at her. "But until then, you must be on your best behavior."

"*I want his blood,*" It hissed.

You'll get it, she promised in her mind.

As she stepped back into the main salon, it took every ounce of her strength to feign a mask of reserve.

"Venus." Presley sauntered up, wearing a royal blue slim fit suit, gold nails, and a bejeweled mustard-yellow headband. "I was wondering where you were."

Guilt ate her alive, all her bad choices preying on her and those she loved. She wanted to hug Presley tightly and never, ever let go. She wanted to kiss their scarred palm and whisper for forgiveness.

"I was just…" Venus paused, searching for the right word, "…outside." She cleared her throat. "How long have you been here?"

In an effort to stop herself from giving in to *Its* acute urge to kill Levi, she crossed her arms tightly.

"I've been in the galley chatting with the waitstaff, who happen to be

Nisha's familiars," Presley said. "They're more interesting to talk to than snobby senators or my family."

As if on cue, Matrika arrived in a sculpted evening gown the color of love. Her lipstick a perfect shade of velvet red. Her dark hair in a chignon.

Graceful, glowy, goddess-like.

Though magic flowed in Venus's veins, being in the Grand Witcher's presence made her feel unremarkable, plain, human.

Restlessness crawled underneath her skin like a swarm of bugs, but she had to be patient. After tonight, a just punishment was on its way. Matrika would answer to the Grand Coven for all her misdeeds, the judge and jury.

At least, she'd have that.

Levi wouldn't be so lucky. He would only get an executioner for what he'd done.

Matrika ambled over, picking a piece of lint off Presley's attire. "I hope you both will be on your best behavior."

"It depends on how the night goes," they stated coolly, staring at their mother with disinterest.

Upon Nisha's arrival, the tension between the two sisters became palpable.

A guard approached, offering his arm. "Would you like me to escort you to your seat, Your Grandness?"

"Of course," Matrika said, accepting his gesture.

As the two walked off, Nisha approached. She wore a maroon silk saree with a high-neck sleeveless blouse, all covered in shimmery gold embroidery. Her hair fashioned in a rose twisted bun. Red and gold Jhumka earrings adorned her ears.

"Is everything to your liking, Presley?" she asked.

"I can't complain."

"I aim to please," Nisha said, then sliced her attention over to Venus: "As for you—"

Venus interrupted, "Let me guess. Behave?"

Nisha smiled. "Not at all. Enjoy yourself."

"We'll see," Venus said before they parted ways, finding their spots.

The Sharma sisters sat at opposite heads of the table. Presley claimed a spot to the right of their mother. A choice that surprised Venus—and Matrika, for that matter.

Levi sat directly across from her and Uncle Bram. The last empty seat at the table beside him.

She glared at him, and he lobbed her a wink.

"Good evening, guests," the Grand Witcher said. "Thank you for gracing us with your presence at the Labor of Love gala. My sister Nisha and I hope this night will be one to remember for you. Before we begin—"

Malik emerged from thin air, taking up the seat beside his intern. "My apologies for my lateness and the interruption." He tipped his head in gratitude at Presley. "And thank you for the invitation."

They tried on a smile, but the effort never quite reached their eyes.

As the interaction unfolded, Venus wondered whether Malik and Presley knew of each other's blood oaths to Levi. Deep down, she believed so. To ensure his plans went smoothly tonight, Levi would've had to introduce his oathed pawns beforehand.

Venus just wished she knew what watching her "hard work go up in flames" entailed.

"What is the meaning of this, Sharma?" Hothead Harry barked, shooting up. "I only accepted the invitation because it'd be an intimate event."

"Actually, Senator Cavendish. You accepted the invitation after you accepted a bribe of fifty grand," Nisha noted, lifting her water glass for a sip.

Radliff gawked. "You got fifty grand? I only got thirty!"

Nisha shrugged. "He negotiated his fee. You accepted what was offered."

Bickering ensued among the senators sans Mounsey. Thirty grand for Westbay. Hundred grand for Hoage. Everyone's anger rushed through Venus like a stampede, leaving her breathless. Uncle Bram blanketed their hand over hers, his warmth giving comfort.

"What did you get, Winston?" Westbay said, her voice sour.

"Nothing," Mounsey said coolly. "I came as a token of goodwill."

Westbay scoffed, shaking her head. "You're so naive, Winston."

"Why are we here, Sharma?" Cavendish asked, slamming a fist onto the table.

"Oh, you know exactly why. This is all about the Registration Act. But that doesn't explain why they're all here," Senator Hoage noted, pointing a finger at the unwanteds.

Venus, Bram, Malik, Presley, and even his own nephew, Levi.

It hissed, *"Should've let his ass turn into an icicle."*

Malik rubbed his temple, his irritation flaring up on his face.

"Enough!" Presley's command barged through the complaints, thundering through the room. "Every single guest at this table deserves their seat. You doubt their worthiness, but your behavior makes us doubt yours."

Their words left the senators speechless, taming them.

Shaming them.

Levi nodded approvingly. "Bravo."

Venus wanted to grab her knife, crawl across the table, and stab his throat.

"Well said," Senator Mounsey said, giving light applause.

A soft glow of pride glimmered on Matrika's face, then dissipated quickly.

The waitstaff blew in with trays, platters, and drinks, placing each targeted senator's favorite choice of poison before them. A short glass of whiskey for Senator Cavendish, a cosmopolitan for Senator Westbay, a spiked sweet tea for Senator Radliff, and a red wine for Senator Hoage.

All impressed at the efforts to flatter them. To pamper them.

Presley beckoned a redhead waiter with Dutch braids to bend her head, whispering in her ear. She nodded, walking off.

Venus raised her glass boldly. "To the labor of love."

"To the labor of love," everyone chorused, joining the toast.

Well, all except Malik, who instead drank in what happened next.

As Senator Hoage downed his wine, his eyes bulged as he choked, falling over. One by one, they tumbled over like dominoes, gagging on the fruits of Venus's labor. Westbay. Cavendish. Radliff. Hoage.

Writhing, flailing, dry heaving.

A sick satisfaction crawled all over Venus as her potions carved out a spot in their hearts, making room for the love of an idea.

"What the hell is going on?" Mounsey snapped, skewering Matrika with a bewildered pair of blue eyes.

"A revolution, Mounsey," Nisha said. "We wanted you to see it yourself."

Confusion puckered his face. "Why me?"

"Well, we would've poisoned your drink, too, but someone already beat us to the punch," Matrika said. "Your father."

The truth and the storge potion clashed within him, the latter winning. Until the potion wore off, the senator's love and loyalty for his father were stalwart and rose-colored.

All his anger gathered in his tone at the allegation. "What? No. He wouldn't do that."

"Oh, but he did. I was there the night he came into my bar. He wanted you to love him again. So, he hired a brewer of love," Nisha said, her manicured nail giving a casual gesture at Venus. "And if you still don't believe me, the Love Witcher herself can tell you."

He shot a look at her.

"It's true, Senator Mounsey," Venus admitted. "You've got a familial love potion inside you. You'd be dead if you drank the same potion as the other senators."

Levi feigned shock, gasping aloud. "That sounds awful."

A wedge of anger lodged itself in her throat. She tried to swallow around it, but all it did was grow and grow and grow.

Mounsey struggled to make sense of everything as his brain churned with the storge potion. Then denial gave way to an acceptance of Mister Mouse's betrayal.

Because the poison in his veins gave him no other choice.

"That doesn't explain why I'm here," he said.

"Originally, we wanted to bribe you, but you're not like other politicians," Matrika said. "So, we have a different proposal."

Gradually, the commotion on the floor died down to nothing. The other senators reclaimed their seats, their blank stares all at Matrika.

Her words should be your salvation.

That's what the peitho potion's notion said.

And so, the four waited for her command.

"You intend to run in next year's presidential election. We can support your efforts. Anonymously, of course. If you win, you'll have four senators that'll help you establish control over the Senate and"—Matrika took a long sip of her wine, a tactic to make others hang on her every word—"the House too once we've poisoned a few representatives. Together, we can kill anti-witcher bills and undo existing ones."

Venus cut free a laugh at the audacity. "And who's going to brew the love potions for that?"

Matrika answered, "We'd like it to be you."

Uncle Bram's head snapped toward Nisha, slamming his gaze into hers. "The fuck you say. She's outta the Black Book."

His protective anger swathed Venus like a heated blanket. Despite being in the presence of enemies, she felt safe for a moment.

Nisha thrust out a sigh, relaxing in her seat. "Don't you want the world to be a better place for your nieces, Bram?"

"Hell naw," he tossed back. "Not at their expense."

"I'd be a dummy to brew for your trifling asses again," Venus said.

"You'd be a very, very rich dummy," Nisha returned. "Millions would solve a lot of your problems."

"Not when both of you are one too," Venus countered.

Nisha smirked, not believing a single word.

Not long ago, the right number of zeros after a dollar sign would've made Venus pliable.

But a bag wasn't enough anymore.

As if reading her mind, Levi asked, "Do you love your sister enough to do it for her?"

Venus narrowed her eyes toward him. "Don't you *ever* question what I would or wouldn't do for my sister."

Presley came to her defense, their tongue sharp. "Let's leave the kids out of this."

When the redhead waiter Presley spoke to earlier returned, she replaced Matrika's empty glass with a full one. Then left.

Malik cleared his throat, shifting his focus to Senator Mounsey. "If you take Madame Sharma's bargain, WASP will endorse you. We have millions of members across the country. Witcher and human. That's millions of potential voters and donors."

"Oh, how generous of you, Malik," Matrika said flatly, tracing a fingertip around the rim of her wineglass.

"She doesn't trust him," It noted.

Venus trusted his ass even less than before now that she knew he was Levi's pawn. She only wished she knew the rules of the game, so she could check Leviticus Tillery for good.

Contemplation sat heavily on Senator Mounsey's face. "Can they hear any of this?"

They, as in his colleagues.

"No, they're waiting for my orders," Matrika assured him before addressing her new minions, "Senators."

"Yes, Your Grandness?" they chorused.

"Tomorrow, the Registration Act will come to a vote. Each of you will vote no," she instructed. "It must be killed."

"Yes, Your Grandness."

Matrika smiled at their obedience. "Now, you may enjoy your meals."

Just like that, the deed was done. Venus waited to feel something. Pride, relief, bitterness, anything. But she felt absolutely nothing, as if desensitized by her own accomplishments.

How fucked up was that?

Impressed, Mounsey nodded. "Alright, I'll do it."

"Wonderful." Matrika clapped her hands once, delighted. She ordered nearby guards, "Bring the dagger for a blood oath."

Mounsey's mouth fell open, his jaw trembling. "A blood oath? Are my word and honor not enough?"

"Hell naw," Uncle Bram muttered, an invisible hand sopping up the butter chicken sauce with naan for him to take a bite of.

"A blood oath is the only way to ensure you'll follow through on your promise to us, Senator Mounsey," Matrika said, accepting the dagger the guard presented. "But you must have a sliver of willingness in your heart."

An oddness coiled around Venus's bones at the sight of the weapon. Days ago, Venus used it to crack open a shield like an egg to get to Matrika within its center.

She failed to kill the Grand Witcher.

A failure she didn't mind as much now.

Tonight had to happen.

She wouldn't have seen Levi for who he truly was otherwise.

"Or else what?" Mounsey challenged.

Matrika tapped the bloodied dagger's tip on his wristwatch's face. The watch he proudly showed off at his party a few weeks prior. A possession he inherited from his father.

"Then your father will run out of time much sooner than his doctors predicted," she said. "All because of you."

None of tonight would've been possible without monsters.

"Only monsters get things done."

A lesson Venus understood more than ever now as the senator took part in a bloody handshake. A guard spoon-fed him the necessary words, and he regurgitated the oath through gritted teeth. He blacked out from the agony.

Another guard took a potion bottle of frosted glass and uncorked it. Matrika tossed the mint-green concoction into her mouth like a shot of whiskey. Her palm's incision wrenched itself back together and she used her dinner napkin to mop away the blood. A troop of three more guards came in mere seconds after.

"Take Senator Mounsey to a guest room so that he may rest," Nisha commanded her children. "We want to make sure our future president is comfortable."

After they collected the senator and exited, Nisha applauded Venus. "Congratulations, little Stoneheart. None of this would've been possible without you."

"Too much blood was spilled to get here," she said, lobbing another barbed look at an amused Levi.

"Rissa would've *never* cosigned this." Uncle Bram pointed a fork at Venus and all her flaws. "Look at her. That's ya'lls doing."

Matrika heaved a sigh, mildly irritated. "Sacrifices had to be made."

"Sacrifice? That's the last thing I'd call Julius Keller," Venus spat out, a sneer curling her lips. "He's a scapegoat you let me roast."

And now she sat directly across from her mother's murderer.

"He preyed on innocent witchers for sport," Matrika countered. "He deserved his end."

Slow claps drew everyone's attention to Levi.

CHAPTER
THIRTY-FIVE

Has history taught us nothing? Old worlds must be burned for new worlds to rise.

You cannot want a revolution and fear its fire. Everything must burn.

—Malik Jenkins, WASP cofounder

"I MUST SAY YOU SERVED YOUR PURPOSE WONDERFULLY, MATRIKA," Levi said, sliding his gaze between the Sharma sisters. "As did Nisha and—"

Nisha tossed her head back, snorting a laugh. "Is this the part where I say you're welcome? By the way, who the fuck are you?"

"Don't interrupt me again," he ordered.

She tilted her head, raising an eyebrow. "What will you do if I do?"

"We'll have to," Levi said, his tone tightening, "put you in a time-out."

"You and what army?" Nisha's amusement fled her face, anger flashing in her eyes.

An intensifying ache formed behind Venus's brow as both his aggravation and Nisha's anger fought for space in her head. She grimaced, biting her bottom lip.

She wanted them out.

"The one *you* built," he said, gesturing to the familiars scattered around.

Matrika said, "You have *no* control over my sister's children or her."

"You're right." Levi said, slicing his attention to the banquet table's opposite end, "but someone on this yacht does have control over her."

Matrika narrowed her eyes. "How do you know that?"

"Because I told him," Presley replied.

"Why?" Nisha asked.

"Because before you swore a blood oath to them, they pledged to *me*," Levi admitted.

Shock.

An emotion neither Nisha nor Matrika could hide away, wearing it on their faces like second skins. Theirs formed two rocks that sank into the pit of Venus's stomach.

A disappointed frown etched across Levi's lips. "Don't look at me like that, Matrika. You're the *queen* of blood oaths."

"You speak of my wrongdoings, but what of yours?" Matrika hissed. "Or are you trying to pretend you didn't kill Clarissa? She told me everything."

"So, she knew he did it," It said, squirming beneath her skin like a pit of angry serpents, "and still let Keller take the fall."

An achy, sourness brewed in the back of Venus's throat. She grabbed her water and chugged, desperate to wash down the nausea.

"What?" Uncle Bram snapped, his magic dropping his fork.

Levi's shoulders shook from quiet laughter. "Damn, you got me."

Slamming the glass down, she cut her stinging, teary gaze to Presley as their voice echoed through her head.

"Venus, I had no idea. I swear."

Uncle Bram's temper consumed his face, directing it all at Malik. "Did you know about this?"

"Did he know?" Levi repeated, glancing at Malik, who kept his eyes downcast. "Since I've commanded him not to speak of that night, I'll speak for him. He had no choice but to watch."

Like a volcano, Bram trembled, ready to explode, his response bleeding through his clenched teeth. "Why?"

"He wanted her out of the way so he could get to Venus and me," Matrika stated coolly, her expression unreadable. "I had my suspicions, but I didn't think you had it in you."

Levi tsked at that. "That's not the whole story."

An angry bulge in Uncle Bram's jaw twitched. "Then what is?"

"According to Malik, poisoning politicians with love potions isn't anything new," Levi said, enjoying bites of his meal. "WASP tried to kill the Limit-12 Law, but that plan died when Darius did. Clarissa swore off politics altogether after that. With the Registration Act on the table now, I'm the one who encouraged Malik to ask Clarissa to get Venus to brew the peitho potions."

Disappointed. Rejection.

Those two words pealed through Venus, sharp and true. Goosebumps tightened her skin as a realization dawned on her. "You're the one who left that yellow carnation on the doorstep."

A proud grin showed off Levi's teeth. "I thought it'd be a subtle touch she'd appreciate."

"Appreciate?" Venus hissed, wishing she could reach across the table and strangle him with her bare hands. "She hated it!"

Matrika added, "Hated it so much she ran to me to tell me all about it."

"I'm glad you and Nisha were able to bring life to a dead plan. Look how far we've come, but things need to go differently." His magic pointed his fork at Matrika. "See, the problem is I need the senators to vote yes."

Venus reeled her head in shock.

Now, you're going to go back inside and watch all your hard work go up in flames.

Levi wanted the Registration Act to *pass.*

All because of her.

His confession shattered Nisha's cool. "Have you lost your fucking mind?"

"No, I've never been saner in my life." Levi held up his palms in a *hear-me-out* gesture. "I've waited for this for a long time. Isn't that right, Venus?"

In quick response, she showed off her middle finger.

Matrika reached for her wine. "You can't make me do your bidding, Leviticus Tillery. They're *my* senators."

Presley stiffened their gaze at the glass, horror growing in their eyes. Their feelings crowded Venus's chest, leaving her breathless.

Why would they be—?

"Matrika, wait! Don't drink that!" Venus exclaimed. "It's poisoned with a peitho potion to obey Malik and the Grand Coven. But I suspect that was a lie, too." Then she bit out, "Wasn't it, Levi?"

Matrika froze.

Levi clucked his tongue. "Got me again."

"You don't want to remove her from power," she said, her tone matching the hardness of her glower. "Through Malik, you'd have power over her blood. Over her connections. Over her blood oaths."

"Now, you're catching on. Being a disowned Tillery gets you nowhere in DC. Power's the only currency around here that matters." He tapped a finger against his temple, smiling at Venus like a proud friend. "The peitho potion you brewed will ensure I have that once she drinks it. After everything you've done, it's what I deserve. Don't you think, Venus?"

The sight of his pride sickened her.

"I'm not drinking a damn thing," Matrika snapped.

"I can't deny it's admirable, but with enough force, stalwart things can break, and I know your breaking point."

"Do your worst," she spat.

"As you wish, Your Grandness." He bowed his head respectfully, then fixed his eyes on Presley. "You pledged an oath to me. Prove your loyalty. Stab yourself."

So much pain, rage, fear, and more clashed in Venus that she wasn't sure whose was whose. It all maddened her blood, making her veins throb and burn.

A cry stretched to the main salon's every corner as Presley drove the ritualistic dagger Matrika had used earlier into their shoulder. She clasped a hand to her mouth to restrain her own sob.

Presley grunted, their teeth gritting together as they dislodged the blade.

Levi smirked. "Again."

They obliged with an agonizing growl as they pierced their thigh. Tears streamed down their face.

Venus had a terrible need to pummel Levi, the burning urge prowling restlessly around her ribs.

Nisha flinched, and Uncle Bram scowled.

"Levi, stop it!" Venus implored, her palms slamming onto the table.

He considered her desperate appeal briefly, then shook his head. "Naw, I don't think I will." He then instructed Presley to press the knife against the column of their throat, the edge's bite beckoning a blood drop to cascade. "Now, slit you thr—"

Matrika snatched the knife from Presley's grasp, plunging it into her belly. Her guttural scream filled the air as the blade sank in.

Nisha shot to her feet, shouting out a horrified NO!

Between ragged breaths, the Grand Witcher wheezed out, "Senators."

"Yes, Your Grandness?" they chorused emptily.

"You will listen to Venus Stoneheart's every command. You will never obey Leviticus Tillery," she rasped before tipping over, spilling out of her seat.

As her body hit the floor with a heavy thunk, the senators all uttered, "Yes, Your Grandness."

"Mom?" Presley's voice cracked as they dropped to the ground, shaking Matrika's shoulders. "Mom!"

All the others shifted their gazes to Venus.

She wanted to run.

She wanted to scream.

She wanted to cry.

She wanted to hide.

But she couldn't move, Matrika's final words pinning her in place. A tangled knot of shock and Presley's anguish climbed up her throat, threatening to choke her.

You will listen to Venus Stoneheart's every command.

"If you care enough about Presley or Malik at all, you won't try anything stupid," Levi warned her, his tone emptied of emotion. He glanced over to a devastated Nisha and a fuming Bram. "You two as well."

Venus curled her quivering lips in disgust. "How's your plan coming along, Leviticus?"

"Oh, the night's still young." He tilted his head, studying her with increasing interest. "Nisha, call for the guards. First, tell them to protect me at all costs. Then leave this yacht and take her"—he flung a shooing gesture to the floor where Grand Witcher's body lay cradled by sobbing Presley—"with you. If you disobey me, only *you* will be left in the Sharma family tree."

Nisha tensed, her nostrils flaring. She shoved herself upright. A promise bright in her angry, tearful eyes. She swirled on her heels and sauntered to the deck, shouting the command.

Uncle Bram shook his head. "What the hell happened to you, Levi?"

"Your niece."

In the yacht kitchen's walk-in freezer, Venus leaned against a metal shelf stocked with bulk-size bags of various meats, hugging herself tightly against the cold. The guards had taken Uncle Bram's phone, crushing it under a shoe's sole as a precaution. As if he'd call the WCTF for help. It wasn't *just* his distrust or pride that prevented him from calling the cops. Chowing down on tasty-ass food as a plot unfolded to overthrow and undermine the government made him an accessory. But being the uncle of the girl who weaponized her love potions made him protective.

Uncle Bram shrugged off his suit jacket and helped her into it to keep her warm. It draped her body like a trench coat a few sizes too big, its sleeves nearly swallowing her arms whole.

"I'm glad you're here, Uncle Bee," she admitted.

He kissed her temple. "There's no place I'd rather be, Pinkie."

Uncle Bram undid his cuff buttons, rolling his sleeves. "We're outnumbered. I can bulldoze a way through for us, but if you stand behind me, you'll have a target on your back."

The downside of being a squad of two against a militia of many. Venus refused to let Levi Tillery win, even though, like a potion, she brewed him into the monstrosity he was.

"I think I can change that."

"Pinkie, what are you tryna do? You're in no condition to break your vow—"

"Uncle Bram, I need you to trust us on this."

"Us?"

"Us as in me and *It*."

"If you die, I'mma use Ty's Ouija board to cuss you out."

"Sounds like a plan." Venus grinned weakly at that, limping to the door. Her palms pressed against the chilled door. She reached within herself in search of a nugget of energy, hunching over in agony.

Harrowing *deep, deep, deeper* than she'd ever imagined.

She likened it to rummaging around her organs.

She seized her last hope, its hotness like a little ember of dying fire.

Venus sensed a horde of violent intentions beyond the door. "There's eight in the kitchen."

"Their general left them behind. All ripe for the taking," It purred.

Though she had a few scraps of strength left, she'd treat them like a last supper.

"Open the door and gimme cover," she ordered, curling her fingers into fists. Uncle Bram looked at her before taking a deep breath. A plume of smoky milk rushed out of his mouth, filling up the metal box they stood in. His magic flung open the door, a flood of thick haze rushing out, tangling around the guards.

The fight within them called out to her loud and clear, resounding through her bones and plucking her veins like harp strings. She homed in on two vows of harm, shrieking a cry as she wielded *It* to spear through her vow of abnegation.

Pain exploded inside her, cracking her bones from the inside out.

Blood dribbled out of her nostrils and darkness nibbled around the edges of her sight, but she trucked on. She gritted her bloodied teeth and cast unseen hooks to haul her prey into the freezer. Uncle Bram did a nimble side step, pressing his back against a shelf to get the hell out of the way.

She collapsed to her knees as the pair of bodies sailed overhead, slamming into the rear wall.

"You good, Pinkie?" Uncle Bram asked. The desperate concern in his voice let her know he wanted to *move, move, move* to help her up.

As a severe headache chewed on her brain, she clocked the intense orbs of light piercing the veil of smoke. Her heartbeat elevated its tempo.

"Naw, we ain't okay," It said.

She growled, ducking out of the way. "Uncle Bee, incoming!"

Uncle Bram's magic yanked the door closed, blocking the onslaught. Five spherical indents littered the doors, crunching loudly on impact. The box jolted. The smoke thinned to a haze.

As the guards struggled to their feet, not wanting a feast to go to waste, *It* roared: *"Let me out, let me out, let me out!"*

Venus unleashed *It*, coughing up blood-tinged spit.

It poured out of her skin as an entity of eager tentacles and struck the guards, plunging straight into their chests. In her hands, their willpower throbbed warmly like a heart.

Their obedience was in her hands now. Like a black widow, *It* injected *Its* venom and crawled back inside her, *Its* satisfaction splintering through her. She slumped against the wall and slid down to the floor, breathless and exhausted, instructing her brand-new soldiers to rise.

The two obeyed, ready for the next command.

As another assault pummeled the door, Uncle Bram offered her his spare hand. "I gotchu, Pinkie."

He aimed his other at the door, his magic keeping a tight grip on the handle. She grabbed it with her hand, stumbling to her feet. Her knees gave way and she nearly fell, but his magic hooked an invisible arm around her waist, holding her upright.

She broadcasted a command through the bond weaved by *It*: *Fight for me.*

The abused door creaked and groaned as magic from the outside pried them apart, a collective effort breaking through Uncle Bram's hold. *Her* guards conjured spheres of pure electric energy and thrust them forth, betraying their kin.

War ensued.

Blood against blood, blow against blow.

The symphony of violence emboldened *It* and her, flooding strength into her legs and pouring steel into her backbone.

She funneled the excess through the link, feeding her two warriors an edge sharper than a blade.

Within the freezer, Venus felt the tide of struggle shift.

Uncle Bram escorted her to the doorway as the last goon toppled over, a head rolling off his neck and landing on the floor.

Broken bodies tainted the tiles, fruits of loyalty lying among the ruin. Venus's fighters stood among the carnage as a pair of victors.

"We need to move," Uncle Bram said as they stepped over a head of espresso-brown vacant eyes. "This ain't over."

"Far from it," Venus said. "I think this was merely the appetizer."

Anticipation twisted her stomach as they all moved like a pack of four toward the kitchen's double doors. Beyond them, she sensed an army. A torrent of vicious desires blinked on as blips on her internal radar. She lost count after fifty.

"Oh, that'll be fun," It laughed, the rich dark sound rippling through her. Adrenaline quickened her pulse as she *ached* for Levi's head.

Within her, five emotions rallied together.

Rage, fear, pain, shattered hope, and the headiest of all: *enough is enough.*

That sentiment carved into her as they returned to the main salon. She scanned the dining area's landscape and its obstacles.

A quartet versus a legion, but Venus wasn't afraid of the odds.

Enough is enough.

She curled her fists, planting her heels on the floor.

She screamed, barreling ahead like a general leading the charge.

Uncle Bram cracked his knuckles before he barged forward, throwing elbows and knocking faces in.

All at once, the two opposing forces stampeded into a savage clash. Venus reached for her deviation and lashed *It* out like a cat-o'-nine-tails, striking the front line. *It* created new recruits who attacked her foes, thwarting the attempts on her life.

Venus manipulated puppet strings and made a shield of bodies around her. *It* gorged on the fruits of carnage surrounding them, bloating in might and greed. Pain capsized her as her body was too small for *Its* growth spurt.

Her legs gave way.

Like a fish out of water, she gasped on the floor.

"Stop," she choked out.

"Get up, Venus," It snarled, drunk on power. *"We have to fight. We have to survive."*

It contaminated her willpower, and she bowed her spine involuntarily as *It* attempted to get her *up, up, up.*

But she was too weak.

Her mastery of the guards severed like a vein, her control hemorrhaging. They all turned to face her, the dark glaze over their eyes evaporating.

She was a wounded deer destined for death at the feet of wolves.

An invisible cord twined around Venus's ankles, yanking her up and away.

She dropped into Uncle Bram's arms.

"I got you," he assured.

A guard bowled a shock wave at them. Uncle Bram dodged the attack, homing in on the extravagant chandelier. Chains and wires anchoring the ornate fixtures to the ceiling severed, plummeting, crashing, and crushing guards. He used the diversion to escape to a hideaway behind a westward bar counter.

"Stay here," Uncle Bram announced in her mind, leaping over the bar counter to fight on.

"We did our best, right?" It waxed tiredly.

"We did," she whispered.

Silence answered her back.

Venus leaned her head back and closed her lids, a slideshow of bodies haunting her. Her mother's body on a morgue slab. Julius Keller's burning body on a pyre. Malik's comatose body on his hospital bed. Burning bodies. Dancing bodies. Bullet-riddled bodies. Bodies in vulgar positions. Her own dead body on an ER gurney. Matrika's body carried away by guards.

Venus broke out of her mind's prison as her blood-tether wrenched out from her a pained cry. She writhed on the floor, her tiny hairs rising as the atmosphere thickened. Her shaky hands gripped the countertop's lip as she bucked against her agony. She pulled herself up enough to witness a hurricane-like swirl of a doorway forming in the main salon's centermost.

She endured her affliction, tremors rattling through her.

Janus emerged, fresh blood caking her hand.

Patches charged in behind her, his lips pulling back in a snarl.

A man-sized hawk followed right after.

Blood pleases Sister Nature.

"The reinforcements have arrived!" Janus exclaimed, then ducked aside as energy-ball missiles came at her and sailed through her closing doorway. She drew a circle on the ground, bearing a portal underneath an incoming herd of guards' feet. She stuck out her tongue as they all fell through, ferrying through time and space elsewhere, ending in a *splash!*

Patches launched off the ground, attacking a guard's face with claw strikes that left deep gouges.

The hawk barreled forward to pick up a guard, carrying her through a window and taking her to the skies.

"About damn time!" Uncle Bram barked, slugging the nearest guard, his fist shattering the man into a pile of pieces.

A satisfied Janus dusted her bloodied hand on her shorts.

Their uncle bludgeoned his way through, leaving shards and fragments in his wake.

The hawk soared back into the room and grabbed a guard's arms with its claws, smashing through another glass window.

Patches crunched down hard on a throat, creating a fissure that snapped the head off its shoulders.

Brawn and doorways whittled the numbers to none.

The hawk's stark screech filled the air as it swooped down, unfolding into Tyrell's shape.

He landed in a squat, one fist propped on the dining room's ground.

He hacked a gag, Leap flopping out his mouth. "Uh, gross."

Nisha's children laid around them busted into so many pieces. Fruits of loyalty galore.

Venus limped from behind the counter, bracing its edge for support. "I didn't think you wanted anything to do with me."

"Miss Florence prophesized that something would snap us apart like a bone, but only I had the power to thread our blood-tether through loops and holes to bring us back together," Janus confessed, wringing her hands.

That clever crone.

"I was all wrong about Mom's murder, Janus," Venus said, stinging moisture gathering in her eyes.

"I can't say I've completely forgiven you, but—"

Venus shook her head, cutting her sister off. "No, Janus. I'm not talking about that. I mean, Matrika didn't kill Mom. It was—"

Malik appeared at his daughter's side. "What are you going to do? Tell her another lie again?"

"Janus, *don't* listen to him," Venus warned. "He's being told to say that."

"Oh, so now that punk letting your ass talk?" Uncle Bram growled, throwing his hands up. "Janus, listen to your sister."

"Not you too, Uncle Bee." A tear rolled down Janus's cheek.

A cold chain of her sister's disappointment tangled around Venus and spilled chills over her skin.

He patted his chest, hurt cracking his voice. "Why would I lie, Jay?"

Malik glared. "The real question is, why *wouldn't* you? You're just as guilty. You helped keep us apart. In your eyes, I was never good enough for your sister or my daughter. Always in Darius's shadow."

Uncle Bram wagged his head. "We'll talk it out when you ain't that punk's puppet."

"Exactly! Janus, get away from him. Malik's in a blood oath with Levi. He's being forced to say these things." Venus clasped her bloody hands together. "You can't trust him."

"Why should I trust you?" Janus tossed back, glancing to her shoulder as her father rested his hand there. "You've lied, hurt, and done so much worse."

A million thoughts rushed through Venus's head, but a realization bobbled to the surface as her attention homed in on Malik's hand.

To support.

To possess.

His hand.

"The night I visited you in his hospital room after Senator Mounsey's party," Venus said, her nods desperate but encouraging. "You went to hold your dad's hand, and what did you find, Janus?"

"I found..." her sister hesitated, her tone unsure, "...a scar."

Venus showed off her marred palm. "It looks *exactly* like this one, right?"

"Yes, it does." Janus nodded, trailing off. Her eyebrows drew together. She glanced back and forth between Venus and Malik until something clicked in her head. She wrenched her shoulder away from him, stumbling in reverse. "It's true, isn't it?"

"Jay-Jay," Malik began.

"Don't you Jay-Jay me," Janus whispered, her body locking up in quiet rage. "Where is he? Where the fuck is Levi?"

He opened his mouth.

"Not another word, Malik." Levi entered the ruined salon, sighing as if he were inconvenienced. Familiar remains crunched under his soles. He crinkled his nose as he stepped on a fruit of loyalty. "I'll handle this myself."

Presley limped behind him like an obedient servant, but a scowl of animosity twisted their face.

Malik hung his head in relief, no longer compelled to tell more lies.

Patches scampered in front of Venus, rising on his haunches. He hissed, primed to fuck Levi up. The protective hiss ignited a spark of déjà vu within her mind. For a mere moment, she was no longer on a yacht cruising down a dark channel.

Venus was in her wrecked kitchen again, staring at Malik and Levi. She recalled how Patches had hissed at their unwelcome guests. At first, she thought the familiar had inherited her mother's grudge against Malik, but that wasn't it at all, was it? Patches hissed at *Levi* that day. The cat tried to warn her then, and she paid him no heed. He could only have known the depth of Levi's deception if her mom had instructed him to spy on the bastard.

A memory of her mom's voice breezed through her:

Show me everything you saw.

"Where are the senators?" Venus demanded.

"Safe," Levi assured. "Since they can't obey my command to leave the yacht, the guards had to knock them unconscious first. You knew I couldn't leave without you, Venus. So, I'll make a trade." He pulled the ritualistic dagger from his pocket. "I'll sever the blood oaths with Presley and Malik in exchange for a blood oath with you. With Matrika exiting stage left, she took her connections, which crowns *you* as the most powerful witcher in the nation." He smirked. "Congratulations on your promotion."

Presley shook their head, then hunched over, hissing as pain poisoned their body for disagreeing with Levi's plan.

"See? *That*"—Levi gestured to them with the dagger as they collapsed, suffering for disobedience—"won't happen anymore."

Presley stammered out, "D-d-don't, V-v-vee."

"And the Registration Act?" she asked.

"Well," Levi chuckled, wagging his head, "that'll still pass, but giving yourself over to me will soften all the harm you've done. All the lives gone because of *you*. You've been very selfish, Venus. Prove to your loved ones you give a damn about more than yourself."

Silence stained the air as Venus weighed her choices.

All the lives gone because—

An idea sparked to life in her mind, incinerating his words from it.

"Fine." She nodded.

"What? Vee, fuck no!" Tyrell asserted, his body drenched in sweat. He grimaced as his bones shifted underneath his skin, but when Leap croaked, his skeleton behaved.

Janus and Uncle Bram also protested, but she held up her palm, silencing everyone. She tried to remain calm and focused as her family's collective alarm rang in her head like loud-ass bells.

"I've made up my mind," she stated, her eyes never leaving Levi as she staggered over to him. She snatched the dagger from his hand, slitting her palm.

Levi grinned, half pleased and partly pained as he sliced his palm next. Their hands locked together in a grip, their bloody cuts kissing.

"I pledge myself to thee. My loyalty will never flee. Measure my servitude with every heartbeat and breath. To which, this bond will sever by your tongue or upon my..." she paused before the last word, narrowing her eyes. "Release them both now and I'll say the oath's final word."

She reached within herself, rummaging through the weak puddle of her deviation. *It* stirred and whispered the word there as she seized her last crumb of strength.

"Alright, let's do it on the count of three," Levi agreed. "One, two, thr—"

Venus used her other hand to punch him square in the face, relishing the crunch of his nose under her knuckles. He grunted at the impact.

"I didn't kill your mother, Leviticus Tillery," she hissed, her knuckles colliding with his cheek. "Your shitty family *chose* money over her and you. They're the ones you should be mad at, but you chose to fuck with me and mine." Another punch sent him to his knees. "*You* took my mother by your own choice. You say you feel sad afterward? Well, here's *your* choice to show her how much."

"Ty!" Venus yelled, driving her fist into Levi's teeth to keep him occupied. "Remind me again about Spirits and choices!"

"Uh, uh, inanimate objects or a person." The words sprang out of her cousin's mouth in a panicked rush. "The operative word being *or*!"

Venus shouted out:

Spirits, spirits, hear our cry.
We come before you but an ally.
We're grateful for all that you do
And your generosity is what we need of you.
There is a soul that we seek,
Let her come forth.
Let Clarissa Abigail Stoneheart speak.

Silence.

Utter silence.

No croaky whispers.

She *couldn't* even speak. Her heart felt like a fist pounding against the inside of her chest.

Had it been because she changed the spell's last line? Could it have been because she took away the opportunity for the Spirits to speak? Or was she too weak? Or worse, a complete and utter failure?

Disappointment and rejection, once again.

Her sticky, bruised hands fell to her sides, regret weighing heavy on her.

Levi wiped his tongue across his blood-stained teeth, laughing. "You fucked up, Venus Stoneheart. So, you *want* the Registration Act to fail. Fine, but you've condemned Presley and Malik to—"

The words withered as an awful gasp skidded down his throat. His eyes flashed open wide, his hand desperately gripping his collarbone. His sheer horror roiled in Venus like a violent disease as a force lifted him off his knees—off the floor.

Mom.

The unspoken word trembled on her tongue as Levi floated higher, thrashing and shrieking in pain as his body broke itself from the inside out.

Limbs twisted and snapped without warning. Blood gushed from his eyes, nose, and mouth.

His fear and confusion polluted Venus's veins.

Then Levi made a sick gurgling sound. His eyes rolled back to the whites as he fell limp, plummeting. Bits and pieces of familiars crunched under his weight.

His corpse's aura dissipated.

In relief, Presley uncoiled on the floor, their breaths ragged.

Janus raced to her, tackling her into an embrace.

The spirit of Clarissa Stoneheart was gone, but her distinct love permeated the air.

THIRTY-SIX

Wait til y'all see what's up our sleeves next.

—Blanche Radliff, a senator

JULY 27, 2023

HOURS AGO, THE NATION WATCHED THE REGISTRATION ACT DIE IN the Senate, inciting near-equal parts of outrage and ovation. Some humans took to the streets to protest while witchers partied like it was Independence Day. Though all the other anti-witcher laws were rooted in place, the failed bill threatened their standing. A reporter in a Senate corridor asked Westbay what was next on the chopping block. To which she smiled, then answered, *"Nothing's safe."*

The threat wasn't her own, though.

It was Venus's.

Those two words set off tempers like a lit match to a firecracker.

Venus nearly jumped out of her skin at her vanity bench as a firework set off way too close to home. Her teeth worried her bottom lip, an anxious groan bubbling in her throat. She breathed through the ache pulsing in her chest's center, adding to the pain that sloshed around in her marrow every time she dared to move or breathe.

Chelsea was half-right about a long road to recovery. Only wrong about how long was long. Venus suspected she'd had at least two months of daily misery before existing didn't feel like it was more trouble than it was worth.

But she didn't mind, per se.

Neither did *It*.

Pain taught her lessons not even her mom did. Like how to pace herself, listen to every ache and pang instead of ignoring them, and give herself permission to *rest*. She didn't blame her mom for not teaching her those things.

Clarissa Stoneheart only passed on what generations of Stoneheart brewers had passed down to her. The only thing Venus hated most was that her mom didn't know rest until she was laid to rest. Neither did her dad.

Her eyes fell on a Polaroid, tucked in the vanity mirror's frame, of Darius placing a kiss on his laughing pregnant wife's belly.

"Rest'll have to wait," It said.

"Just a little bit longer," Venus concurred, rising from her cushioned bench with a grimace.

She limped to her sister's door, gently rapping her knuckles on the wood. "You ready, Jay?"

Then earlier that day, she sent out a group text message:

billboard @ 8pm.

It was nearly twenty minutes til now with a sixteen-minute walk ahead of them. A trek Venus didn't look forward to. Not when every step made her suffer. A portal could've alleviated her predicament, but after yesterday, she doubted her sister had enough strength to conjure one.

For a sliver of a moment, Venus was in the backseat with her sister and Presley. Uncle Bram at the wheel. Tyrell and Leap in the front passenger seat. Her arm curled around Janus's shoulder as they leaned into each other, her cheek propped on a crown of ombre curls. Presley's hand blanketed her sister's. All their gazes were blank, vacant, empty as they struggled to comprehend what happened back on that megayacht.

Within a blink, she stood in front of her sister's door again, watching it open and her sister emerge from the dark of her room. Janus lingered in the doorway, wearing heavy eyelids, deep circles, and a rumpled fit.

They both regarded each other, the wavelengths of their grief entangling.

Venus opened her weary arms, and Janus didn't hesitate to fall into them.

When their hug broke apart, her sister passed over noise-cancellation headphones. "I enchanted them to filter out fireworks and loud-ass noises, but you'll be able to hear voices just fine. It's the least I could do after you *literally* just saved the country."

"I'll try to save the country more, if it means getting nice presents from you," Venus teased, slipping on the headphones. Exactly as promised, they blocked out all the noise.

Together, they walked hand in hand down the hallway and into the living room. Uncle Bram came into the kitchen through the back door, a levitating foil tray of barbecue tailing him. He fired up the backyard grill shortly after he and Venus sat on the couch, watching the Senate voting session on C-SPAN. Patches kept him company, lounging on a lawn chair.

After everything that went down at the gala, Uncle Bram retired from the Golden Coin this morning, taking an undisclosed retirement package he only described as what he "damn well deserved."

With his teeth clenching a lit cigarillo, he asked, "Y'all headin' out?"

"Yeah, don't eat all the food, Uncle Bee," Venus warned, heading for the front door.

"I'll save y'all a little *something* something," he promised.

Leaving the house, Venus gripped her sister's hand tight at all the fireworks and firecrackers going off. Mister Lionel watched from his window, his red-hot anger seeping through her. Her deviation crunched on the fiery flavor like a piece of cinnamon candy, pleased with the taste.

Children played in front yards. Music and chatter poured from backyards. The scent of good food wafted in the night air. Oldheads sat on porches. Families also paid their respects to the Grand Witcher by lighting white candles on their windowsills and porches.

As far as the public knew, Matrika Sharma died in her sleep last night. A bag as big as the one Nisha offered Epione made the hospital administration very agreeable. But moments after Matrika Sharma took her last breaths, Senator Mounsey's short-lived blood oath to her died, too.

After a car passed them, Venus stepped off the curb and onto the clear street, but Janus didn't budge. Their united hands like an unbreakable tie.

Worry slashed through her. "You good?"

Considering—well—everything, it was such a dumbass question to ask, but sometimes, dumbass questions were chances for others to be *seen, heard, felt.*

"No. Far, far, far from it." Janus blew her cheeks out in frustration, joining Venus in the street. "But we need to do this."

At the meetup spot, Presley and Tyrell waited for them.

All four looked like last night had chewed them up and spat them out.

But they were all alive and that's what mattered.

Venus and Janus let go of each other's hands.

Presley whispered *hey* to her, and she whispered it right back. Their arms curled around her waist, and she propped her cheek against their chest. Their sorrow, regret, and anger beat like three different hearts in their chest.

Matrika.

She sacrificed herself for Presley.

A tiny piece of Venus believed Matrika only wanted what was best for Presley by leaving them behind. She suspected protection was once an early intention, but somewhere down the line, Matrika veered off the main path to take a thornier one.

Using others to shield herself from brambles and briars.

Venus couldn't deny that she and those around her were no different from Matrika in many ways. Or Levi, for that matter.

Love was an awful, messy thing that made you do awful, messy things to *prove* you wanted it.

To prove you deserved it.

Comfort ran underneath the pain streaming through Venus's body like an undercurrent. Her muscles were stiff as fuck, but if Venus could, she would've given herself permission to melt just a little.

Venus wasn't exactly sure what to call *this thing* between her and them, but maybe, it didn't need a name yet. She didn't know what this was, but she needed it like she needed Uncle Bram's and Aunt Keisha's wisdom that steered her straight, Tyrell's and Hakeem's goofiness that made her laugh until her belly hurt, Patches's loyalty that kept her safe, and her sister's love that made her want to stay on this Earth until they were both gray-haired crones.

"Thanks for coming, y'all," Janus said.

"As if we had a choice." Their cousin rolled his tired eyes playfully.

She glanced up at the night sky, thinking. "You're right. Y'all didn't."

"What's this all about, Jay?" Tyrell tipped his head sideways.

She clapped her hands once, gathering everyone's attention. "Let's get down to business." She reached into her hoodie pocket and pulled out a crinkly slip of paper, handing it over.

"Let Our Vision Erase Discrimination," Venus read it, confusion wrinkling her brow. On her skin, her little sister's nervousness was palpable and prickly.

Janus chewed on her bottom lip, nodding. "It stands for LOVED. The grown-ups were right about one thing. We can't wait for politicians to do what's right. We can't stop at just the Registration Act." Her somber cinnamon-brown eyes flitted to Venus. "Thanks to Matrika, you've got four poisoned politicians under your thumb, *plus* Senator Mounsey after we told him we'd honor his deal with her. Matrika and Nisha *wanted* you to brew exclusively for them, but I think we should start a love potion operation together."

"You want to what?" Venus stepped back from the group in a backward stumble.

Janus gestured to Presley. "Well, Pres has the Sharma family's wealth, the Underbelly, and Nisha's legion at their disposal."

She shook her head, sighing. "You *can't* force them to work with Nisha."

"No, I want to," Presley assured. "Aside from her kids, I'm all that she has left. I'm severing her blood oath to me, so we can start fresh. So, we can do things the right way." A pause, then in a strained voice: "For Matrika."

Venus's expression softened.

Tyrell slung an arm over Presley's shoulders, drawing them close in a sideways hug. "Sounds like a good-ass plan."

They both exchanged weak grins.

"Tyrell's got Aunt Key and Leap helping him learn to keep shape," Janus continued, then paused to point to herself. "As for me, Venus'll teach me how to brew when she recovers." Her fingers snapped as she remembered something else. "Oh, and Uncle Bram, too."

Venus drew in a stuttered gasp of shock. "You two would really do that for me? You'd would pledge vows of abnegation for me?"

"I would set this world on fire for you," Janus said, "and Uncle Bram would knock down all of DC for you."

"Today wouldn't have been possible without *you*, Vee, but the fate of this country shouldn't rest solely on your shoulders," Presley said. "With all of us, we'll split the burden. None of us got to have to decide on this ton—"

Tyrell sucked his teeth, interrupting them. "Naw, I already know my answer. Count me the fuck in."

Janus shrugged. "I drafted up the plan. So, it's already got my cosign."

Emotion welled in the back of Venus's throat, tears straining her eyes.

"There's three sides to a revolution. The right side, the wrong side, and the sidelines," It said. *"Which side do you want us on?"*

The fireworks illuminated the darkness above like bursts of graffiti, a warm summer breeze snaked about, and War lived at peace in her bones.

The others gathered into a circle around her, making her the heart of it.

Their heart.

Venus knew all about hearts.

She needed to beat on for everyone's sake and hers.

She heaved a sigh, her lids coming down. "Aw, fuck it."

CHAPTER
THIRTY-SEVEN

For millennia, we've sacrificed the right to be ourselves freely for the sake of human comfort. Are you not tired, kindred? No longer are we in the Dark Ages. Society has evolved past hangings and burnings. Surely, humans will see we're still their spouses, friends, and neighbors. They'll know our magic is a gift, not a weapon. They'll know we want what they want: peace.

—Address of Grand Witcher Serafina Brightwell
at the Winter 1999 Grand Summit

WINSTON MOUNSEY ANNOUNCES
2024 RUN FOR PRESIDENT

BY CANDIS JOYNER AND JILLIAN KUMAGAI, *THE SOCIETAL MIRROR*

August 28, 2023

After months of speculation, Senator Winston Mounsey has officially announced his bid for the 2024 presidential election. The announcement came in a four-minute video released Tuesday. In it, Mounsey states June's fatal WASP-organized street protest and the failed Registration Act recalibrated his campaign's focus on what matters most: a unified nation.

"As our peers live in unity around the world, we're a nation stuck in the Dark Ages," Sen. Mounsey says in the video. "Fear and hatred don't nurture prosperity. They strangle it. We cannot call ourselves the greatest nation if we hold little regard for one another. This nation needs to be on the right side of history or we'll imprison future generations to live in our past. If I'm elected your president, everything I do shall be for our future."

The trending hashtag #forourfuture rippled across social media platforms, generating millions of responses.

It comes as no surprise among the senators who endorsed the bid were Sens. Harry Cavendish of Florida, Edward Hoage of Texas, Martha Westbay of Ohio, and Blanche Radliff of Louisiana. Alongside Mounsey, the squad of four ensured the Registration Act's downfall on the Senate voting floor in mid-July.

If elected as president, he could benefit significantly from this four-way alliance.

Heavy contender Mounsey enters the fight as an Independent without having to seek nomination from a party.

With the recent passing of his father, he claims he has nothing to lose now.

But only time will tell if voters, humans and witchers, will see him as their champion.

GLOSSARY OF TERMS

ANIMA: A witcher's life essence or spirit. Humans define it as a soul.

BASE LIQUID: A magic-less foundational concoction required of all potions.

BINARY-NOTE POTION: A potion that contains two keynotes: a base liquid and a notion. The duration of its influence lasts a maximum of four to six months. The degree of recoil is significant.

BIRTHRIGHT: Six innate powers common to all witchers. In no particular order: telekinesis, manipulation of the natural elements, telepathy, precognition, a secondary sight, and spell casting.

BREWBUG: An illness due to chronic brewing. Symptoms include fatigue, nosebleeds, nausea, coughing or spitting up blood, dizziness, fainting, fevers, heart palpitations, and ocular blood vessel ruptures.

CALLING: A magical ability a witcher develops at the age of thirteen. Some were common or hereditary, and others were rare. There's no definitive list of how many there are.

COVEN: A group of witchers.

DEGREE OF RECOIL: A potion's level of chemical blowback.

DEVIANT: The host of a deviation.

DEVIATION: A contaminated volatile form of a witcher's calling due to severe trauma. In some cases, this mutated magic can temporarily infect witchers and humans alike.

DISCIPLINE: A specific category of potion.

DOMINION: A local network of covens.

ELDER: An honorific reserved only for master brewers.

FAMILIAR: An extraplanar spirit that pledged servitude to a bloodline to earn the physical form of an animal, or in rarer cases, a humanoid form known as an agathion. Very few can switch between both forms.

FEALTY FEAST: The act of harvesting and eating a familiar's essence to fortify vows and replenish magic wells.

GRAND WITCHER: An elected executive head of a dominion. The highest position within the witchery hierarchy.

HIGH WITCHER: An elected leader of a coven. The second highest position within the witchery hierarchy.

LAYER: A subpower of a calling that emerges with a witcher's maturity.

MAGIC WELL: Also known as a well of magic. The capacity of a witcher's magic. It is an internal source of magical strength.

MAKE-DO: An enchanted edible used for temporary fixes.

NOTION: A command or idea conjured by a brewer to influence a drinker.

PLEDGE: A brewer's commitment to their discipline. If broken, a brewer's magic is forfeit as a consequence.

POTION: A brewed concoction that produces magical effects when consumed.

PURIFICATION: An ancient practice that expels dangerous impurities from a witcher's blood and magic by using milk baths as a conduit and fresh flowers as a sacrificial host.

RESTORATION: A ritualistic act of a witcher replenishing their magic well by consuming bewitched herbal teas and/or health potions.

SINGULAR-NOTE POTION: A potion that only contains a base liquid as a keynote and has weak but functional magical influence over the drinker. The duration of its influence lasts a maximum of two weeks. The degree of recoil is low.

TRINARY-NOTE POTION: A potion that contains three keynotes: a base liquid, a notion, and a drop of anima. The duration of its influence lasts a maximum of ten months to one year. The degree of recoil is severe and often fatal.

VOW OF ABNEGATION: The act of a brewer abstaining from their birthright and calling. A time-old tradition practiced for strengthening a potion's potency and increasing a brewer's odds of survival. If broken, the brewer will experience agony as a consequence. Though vows can be reaffirmed, only time (or loopholes) can fortify it.

SPECTRUM OF LOVE

AGAPE

Unconditional love

EROS

Lustful love

LUDUS

Uncommitted love

MANIA

Obsessive love

PEITHO

*Love of ideas,
persuasion*

PHILAUTIA

Self-love

PHILIA

*Friendship love,
platonic love*

STORGE

Familial love

RELIEVE A GRIEVING HEART

(TRINARY-NOTE PHILAUTIA POTION)

This is to be brewed for a Patron seeking relief and peace after loss and heartache. Caution the Patron to not take this forged comfort for granted. The potion only numbs, but heartache still waits for them.

INGREDIENTS (IN THIS EXACT ORDER):

1 possession of the loved one

2 cups of rosewater

2 cups of sweet red wine

¾ cup of St. John's wort

¼ cup of azalea

8 ginseng roots, sliced and peeled

1½ cups of coconut milk

3 teaspoons of poppy seeds

6 almonds, crushed

1 raw honeycomb

METHOD:

Burn the loved one's possession to ash. Add water and ashes to a cauldron over high heat. Bring to a rolling boil. Add in the reminding ingredients in the exact order prescribed.

NOTION:

Let this heartache ebb,
Let the numbness swell.
Untangle from sorrow's web.
In peace you shall dwell.

FORGIVE
AND FORGET
(BINARY-NOTE STORGE POTION)

The potion is to be brewed for a Patron seeking forgiveness from a blood relative wronged by them. The potion erases the Drinker's hurtful memories related to the Patron and instills the need to forgive. Caution the Patron that memories *will* return once the potion's effects wears off. Rifts may widen and worsen as a result. Timing is crucial. Brew on the night of a NEW MOON.

INGREDIENTS:

3 cups of oat milk

7 teaspoons of crushed pearls

5 tablespoons of rum

½ cup of absinthe

1 cup of white tulip petals

3 tablespoons of dried lemon peels

8 cherry pits

1¼ cups of ladybugs in honey

4 sweet basil leaves

1 small yellow onion

METHOD:

In cauldron, bring water to a boil over medium-high heat. Slowly whisk in the oat milk, crushed pearls, rum, and absinthe. Add remaining ingredients in the exact order prescribed. After bottling, leave Potion outside a NEW MOON night to cool.

NOTION:
My wrongdoings, you must forgive.
Separate good times from bad like a sieve.
Cut this tension like a tie
So that we may see eye to eye.

ASKING FOR A FRIEND

(BINARY-NOTE PHILIA POTION)

This potion is to be brewed for a lonely Patron seeking friendship from a colleague or acquaintance. The Drinker will seek out the Patron. Caution the Patron that this friendship lasts a maximum of twelve weeks, but duration varies. For longer-lasting results, pour the potion into a hot beverage intended for the Drinker.

INGREDIENTS:

1 slip of paper with the Patron's phone number

6 alstroemeria petals

1 cup marshmallow and chocolate, melted

3 tsp pea seeds

4 swan eggs

5½ yellow roses

2 tbsp of pink salt

1 cup softened butter

2¼ cups cider

16 sunflower seeds

METHOD:

Put water, cider, butter, swan eggs, and pink salt into a cauldron over medium-low heat and simmer for 6 minutes. Tear or cut the Patron's phone number into pieces, then stir in. Turn heat to medium-high. Place a glass or metal bowl over cauldron's mouth to melt marshmallows and chocolates. Stir mixture to an even consistency, then pour into cauldron. Add remaining ingredients.

NOTION:

You may not know them well,
But a friendship shall ring within you like a bell.
Listen to it well to weave a bond.
Day by day, your heart shall grow fond.

ACKNOWLEDGMENTS

Content Warning: Mention of suicidal ideation (in second paragraph)

This book has been the realest, hardest thing I've ever written. So, it's only fitting I'mma keep it 100 percent real in my acknowledgments, too.

First and foremost, I am grateful to God for giving me the perseverance to write this novel on days when my chronic panic and exhaustion made it hard to exist, and on days when my mental illnesses made it a battle to want to exist. Without Him placing the most amazing, supportive folks in my path and life, this book would not have been possible because I wouldn't be alive.

My sincere gratitude to my parents and grandparents for everything you've overcome and sacrificed to provide me opportunities and a life that shaped me into who I am today. As my biggest cheerleaders, you all always encouraged me to pursue my passions, dreams, and goals. I know we get on each other's nerves, but I love you all down to my marrow and more.

Thank you to my flesh and blood (Florida, Ohio, Michigan, Louisiana, Tennessee, California, errbody, errwhere) for your unwavering love and support throughout my entire writing journey. Your encouragement and belief in me have been a constant source of inspiration. I'm so grateful to be a part of our big family tree.

To Robert: Thanks for all the heartfelt bickering, cuss-outs, and wild adventures. We've been each other's ride-or-dies since college, helping each other dodge actual bullets.

To my sisters-in-teaching, Jones, Reed, and Wilkerson, for taking me under your wings as a first-year teacher and being my rocks for the seven years we taught together.

To my fellow Gemini and friend Emily: You've been there every single step of the way. Thank you for the text messages, the phone calls, the Zooms, the writing sprints, being my study buddy in online courses, and being the ultimate freak in the Excel spreadsheets. You're a precious bitter cinnamon roll too pure for this world.

To my many, many friends I've made in the query trenches, submission hell, and beyond, including but not limited to Megan, Madelyn, Camille, Caro, Aria, Seina, Mire, Matt, Jena, Amanda, Britney, Shauna, Jas, Vianna, Sami, Allegra, Gabi, Elnora, Latrice, Avione, Dane, Tamara, Melody, Déborah, Pine, the Real B Hive, Ashlye, Veena, Destiny, Alechia, Eliah, Tanvi, Ebony Lynn, Megan L., Jen, Jael, Sarah, Jem, TJ, Amber, Cayla, Nina, Gigi, Ashley, Faye, Bea, Cindy, Marlee, Thais ,Mona, Lauren, Erin G., and Erin B.! And so, so, so, so, so many more! Thank you all for all the laughs, tea, and unwavering support. All of you have pushed me to be a better person, a better advocate for myself and others, and a better writer.

Thank you to the 2023 Debuts group and the 2024 Debuts group for years of kindness, support, and wisdom.

To my literary agent, John Cusick: You believed in my evil little pastel book when very few did. The years we've spent together have been a learning experience I'll never forget. Thank you, thank you, thank you for the lessons you've taught me.

To my editor, Annie Berger, for her dedication to this project and for teaching me so much about myself as an author. This journey has been one filled with self-discovery and new discoveries, as well as editorial assistant, Jenny Lopez, for all her insights and support! Without either of you, *Poisons* wouldn't be what it is today.

And thank you to Annette for her kindness, patience, and understanding as my surrogate editor as I worked on my first edit letter while severely ill in late 2021 and early 2022. It really, really meant a lot.

Thank you so much to the very, very talented Michael Machira Mwangi for the gorgeous, breathtaking, heart-stopping front and back cover art. He didn't just understand the assignment. He graduated summa cum laude with a doctorate in snatching breaths away.

Immense gratitude to the brilliant minds of the design team of Sourcebooks for all the thought and detail that went into the book design, inside and out.

I want to thank everyone at Sourcebooks for all their hard work and for welcoming me with wide arms! From the sales team, the marketing and publicity team, the production editorial team, and all the teams and individuals I've hadn't the pleasure of meeting yet: A BIG THANK-YOU! I'm so thankful to be a part of the Sourcebooks family.

And to Alex: Thank you for being my rock. Thank you for your visible and invisible labor to support me and our family. The long, exhausting shifts at the hospital aren't easy. Being a janitor is a thankless job. And when we both come home from a long workday, you work even harder to make my life a little easier, so I can imagine worlds and write books like this one. I see you, my love. I do.

ABOUT THE AUTHOR

Photo by Luca Rodriguez

Bethany Baptiste is a preschool inclusion advocate by day and a young adult SFF novelist by night. If she's not writing an inclusion support plan or a story, she does retail therapy in Florida bookstores and takes scheduled naps with her three chaotic evil dogs. You can visit her at bethanybaptiste.com or @storysorcery on Twitter.

sourcebooks fire

Home of the hottest trends in YA!

Visit us online and
sign up for our newsletter at
FIREreads.com

· ·

Follow
@sourcebooksfire
online